THAT'S ODD. MUST BE RUST.

Sophraea looked closely at the strange streaks marring the usually dull dark gray metal. Ten slender streaks curled around the bars, five on the left side, five on the right.

Handprints.

Sophraea barely breathed, looking at the marks so plainly visible and so clearly the color of dried blood, the marks of hands that had reached through the gate from the graveyard side.

Can't be. They leave us alone. They have always left us alone. The dead don't bother Carvers.

With careful backward steps, Sophraea retreated. Behind her, the bushes swayed, as if someone invisible brushed by them, returning to the center of the City of the Dead.

ED GREENWOOD

PRESENTS

WATERDEEP

FORGOTTEN REALMS

ED GREENWOOD

PRESENTS

WATERDEEP

CITY OF THE DEAD

ROSEMARY JONES

Ed Greenwood Presents Waterdeep

CITY OF THE DEAD

Cover art by: Android Jones
First Printing: June 2009

9 8 7 6 5 4 3 2 1

ISBN: 978-0-7869-5129-1
620- 24026740-001-EN

U.S., CANADA,   EUROPEAN HEADQUARTERS
ASIA, PACIFIC, & LATIN AMERICA   Hasbro UK Ltd
Wizards of the Coast LLC   Caswell Way
P.O. Box 707   Newport, Gwent NP9 0YH
Renton, WA 98057-0707   GREAT BRITAIN
+1-800-324-6496   Save this address for your records.

Visit our web site at www.wizards.com

DEDICATION

Special thanks to Ed Greenwood and Susan Morris for loaning me the keys to Waterdeep and letting me play in the cemetery. A big electronic hug of gratitude to Erik Scott de Bie, James P. Davis, and Steven E. Schend, terrific authors all who shared their wisdom and said such kind words about the characters I sent adventuring earlier in the Realms.

Thanks to Mike, Jacki, and Gayle for listening to the early drafts. And thanks to all the friends of the FORGOTTEN REALMS® who wrote to me about my first crypt: your comments, suggestions, and general insight are always welcome. I promise you that the dog lived a long and happy fictional life.

This one is for Phoebe Matthews because she knows where the story started.

INTRODUCTION

I will never see the City of the Dead the same way again.

Oh, I always knew it was a pleasant (if slightly creepy) park by day, walled off from the rest of the city and left to the birds, the mourners, and those who met in the vast, sprawling cemetery when the sun was high, to picnic and chatter, or romance each other, or just to talk (sometimes friendly gossip, sometimes exciting business deals, and sometimes matters far more sinister).

I knew the City of the Dead very well. I created it, more than forty years ago, seeing it first under a cold, bright moon, silent stone statues staring down at two sinister wizards—one with a skull for a head, and the other having no head inside his cowl except restlessly writhing tentacles. The statues stared without moving, and were ignored. The ghosts of the dead, and a few undead who were floating skeletal hands and heads, moved to the best vantage points to watch the wizards confront each other—and also got ignored. It pleased me, in the very bad fantasy short story I was then writing (at the tender age of eight), to have one wizard entomb the other alive with a spell on the very spot where, the next day, some laughing young noble ladies spread their picnic cloth. Before long, one of them would inadvertently utter a word that would free the entombed wizard so that he rose straight up, in ominous silence, to bulge that cloth, spilling flagons and cheese and grapes in all directions, and sending those ladies shrieking among the tombs . . .

Heh-heh. I knew the City of the Dead, all right.

In my imagination, I can stroll around it (a little bit of Highgate burial ground in London, something of Mount Pleasant in Toronto, and a lot of little touches from other cemeteries in many places all over the world). I knew someone maintained the place (that is, beyond merely carrying off the bodies of those unfortunates who'd died of fright there during the night), but I hadn't really thought more about it.

Until now, when this wonderful book in your hands introduced me to the family who tends the graves of the City of the Dead, plucky young heroine and all, and I *really* got to know the place.

I created Waterdeep, the bustling fantasy city around the City of the Dead, too, and down the decades have brought many a sneering, prancing, strutting, foppish, reelingly drunken, catty, or ruthless noble of the City of Splendors to life. In Realms books I wrote or read, or in DUNGEONS & DRAGONS® games I played in, the nobles of Waterdeep seemed to *demand* the spotlight every chance they got, crowding their ways onstage. I loved them, swaggeringly fashionable warts and all—but I never met one of them who captivated me as thoroughly as Lord Adarbrent, in this book.

Rosemary Jones has created a truly classic character in this lonely old lord, and given us a great heroine and hero team who *aren't* all-competent, a suitably skin-crawling villain, and a great supporting cast, to boot. From the overgrown tombs and crypts to the grand rooms and kitchens of the wealthy, she has brought Waterdeep to life.

Better than that, she has told a wonderful *story*. One I know I will want to read over and over again.

Frankly, you don't have to know anything more about Waterdeep to enjoy this book, though those who do will be delighted at what's in these pages. Pay attention; if ever you should meet a skeletally thin, dark-clad old man with a cane striding among crypts, it's always useful to know how to properly greet him.

Ed Greenwood
January 2009

PROLOGUE

SPRING 1467

On such a day as this, a day of such good weather that people wandered in the streets with no more business on their minds than to dally in the warm sunshine, Waterdeep irritated Lord Dorgar Adarbrent.

He walked muttering through the crowds, pushing the more aggravating pedestrians aside with his cane. He knew his irritation was irrational.

After all, on a fine day, the city presented itself in its greatest glory: the gleaming statues, the marvelous buildings, the crooked streets, the busy harbor, the hustle, and the glamour. But there it was. The vibrant city, the noisy and argumentative city, annoyed him. Yet, for almost all his long life, Lord Adarbrent had loved Waterdeep more than any living thing.

On such a day, Lord Adarbrent's unquiet mind drove him to the quietest place in all of Waterdeep, the City of the Dead. At the Coffinmarch gate, he turned away from the southern end of the cemetery, avoiding the many visitors and public monuments there. Instead he trod the lesser paths leading north, toward the tombs emblazoned with the old names, the noble names, the names of families once known and now long forgotten by all but him.

Soon his own footsteps crunching upon the gravel were the only sounds he heard. Oh, if he concentrated, there were the indistinct whispers that always filled the air in that silent place, but the sun was

1

bright overhead and the shadows were driven into hiding beneath the bushes or in their graves and he had never been afraid of ghosts.

At last he reached the tomb he sought. He unlocked the bronze door. A slight rustle stirred in the dark and a whiff of rose oil, faint as the memory of a dream, issued forth. His mind immediately soothed, Lord Adarbrent descended the mausoleum's steps into the gloomy, peaceful depths.

—W—

The ball sailed over Sophraea's head and landed with a *splat* in the middle of a mud puddle. From her viewpoint as a goalpost, watching her various older brothers and many young male cousins scramble after the ball, five-year-old Sophraea could not tell if the boys had scored a point or incurred a penalty. It did not seem to matter. Everyone was sliding through the puddle, fists flying. The misshapen and much abused leather ball rolled away unheeded, stopped finally by an uncarved headstone.

Above the little girl, the sky shone a cloudless blue, only the thinnest ribbons of white clouds scudding past the crooked gables of Dead End House.

The ringing of hammers against wood, iron, and marble echoed through the yard as Sophraea's father, uncles, and older cousins began their morning's work on the gravestones and coffins commissioned for the recently deceased of Waterdeep's richest families.

Sophraea's mother, grandmother, and aunts had agreed that the first day of Tarsakh was a beautiful day for cleaning. The Carver women were busy turning over carpets, sweeping out dust, and generally scrubbing Dead End House from basement to attic.

Swept out of the door with her brothers and younger cousins, Sophraea sat upon a stack of clothing abandoned by the boys, kicking her legs and wondering what to do. After designating her as a boundary marker in one of their endless ball games, Sophraea's older brothers had told her to "stay put and don't follow us," an instruction she heard so often as the youngest member of a large and mostly male family that she forgot it immediately.

While the boys fought and tussled for the possession of the battered leather ball, Sophraea grew more and more bored with her job as a coat weight. With a shout, her brother Leaplow jumped on her cousin Bentnor, who had just regained his feet after the last wrestling match, and the rest of the boys piled on top.

Realizing that nobody was paying any attention to her, Sophraea slipped off the pile of the boys' coats and wandered to the far end of the courtyard.

The gate to the City of the Dead stood ajar, one of her bigger cousins having just carried a bronze marker through it. One of the black and white Carver cats slid through, intent on its own business in the graveyard. Beyond the gate, Sophraea could see the tangle of spring flowers, tall bushes, and gleaming marble tombs. A buzz of bright wings amid the flowers attracted her eye.

Little Sophraea Carver stepped through the open gate and into Waterdeep's great graveyard. No one saw the tiny girl with the head of black curls disappear into the haunted pathways of the City of the Dead.

Behind her, the shouts and the thuds of the boys at play faded away. As she trotted down the crushed stone path, Sophraea passed beneath the shadow of a marble monument, the statue of a tall woman dressed all in armor weeping into the hand covering her face. Tears trickled through the stone fingers to fall into a simple basin at the woman's feet. Sophraea kneeled and peered into the pool, trying to catch a glimpse of spring tadpoles or her own reflection. But the water was too brown and murky, stained by the remains of winter's dead leaves.

A quick search yielded a long branch, light enough to carry to the basin and long enough to satisfactorily rake the leaves out of the pool. Happy with her work, Sophraea forgot about her brothers and did not even notice when the hands of the statue moved, so the weeping woman now peeped through open fingers at the child laboring by her marble feet.

Despite the bright sun, pale fingers of mist twined around the rooftop of the tomb behind the little girl. The statue raised its head and glared. The fog slipped back to a hole in the ground. Oblivious, Sophraea continued to clear the pond of debris.

Eventually, the long evening shadows crept across the grass to touch the edge of the pool. Leaves stirred in the bushes surrounding the pool, although no breeze ruffled the little girl's dark curls. Sophraea looked up. The sun had sunk low enough to be hidden by the great mausoleum before her.

Having lived all her short life above the workshop where her family created such figures as the marble statue above her and the stone sarcophagus and barrel tombs surrounding her, these monuments to the dead did not worry the little girl. But the shadows growing darker in the corners and the bushes rustling around her made Sophraea think that the time had come to find her way home. Besides, she was hungry and if she didn't get back quickly, the boys would probably snatch more than their fair share of supper.

Setting off on the path as fast as her short legs could trot, Sophraea rounded the corner to face a brick and timber tomb built like a miniature Waterdeep mansion. The tomb's bronze door swung wide open. Stepping carefully through the door was a tall man, who ducked his head a little to avoid knocking off his wide-brimmed hat against the marble lintel. The bronze door gave a mournful squeal as he pulled it shut behind him.

Taking a large iron key from his pocket, the gentleman locked the door with a distinct click. He turned and Sophraea instantly recognized the face as exactly the sort of creature her brothers whispered about in the hallways of Dead End House late at night when they were supposed to be climbing the stairs to their bedchambers.

Beneath the wide-brimmed black hat, the visage presented to the terrified child was a cadaverous mixture of yellow and white, the gentleman's pale skin heavily pockmarked across the nose and cheekbones. His lashes and eyebrows were a mottled gray and the color of his eyes a muddier brown than the pool where she had been playing.

Recently dared by her brother Leaplow to peek in a coffin after the occupant had been tenderly placed there, Sophraea did not hesitate to identify the figure now bending closer to peer at her as a corpse!

"Are you lost, child?" said the corpse in a suitably creaky and cracked voice.

"No," whispered Sophraea, too terrified to either scream or run. Then she repeated something that she had heard a hundred times around the family table but never understood. "I am a Carver. Carvers can't get lost."

"Of course." The corpse nodded in solemn agreement. "But it is close to sunset. Perhaps you should go home now."

Sophraea just stared back, still frozen into place by this unexpected encounter.

"You came through your family's gate. The Dead End gate." Each word that the corpse spoke was carefully enunciated, much in the manner very ancient relatives used to speak to the youngest Carvers. This mixture of not quite a question, not quite a statement was exactly like the type of conversation Sophraea endured during the visits of her grandmother's elderly lady friends. Perhaps the gentleman was not a corpse, she thought, but simply the male equivalent of the wrinkled, white-haired ladies who sat around the kitchen table.

"Did you come through the Dead End gate?" asked the elderly corpse man again. "Do you know your way there?"

Sophraea bobbed her head in tentative agreement.

"I will walk with you. It is time that I returned home."

One pale and age-spotted hand slid into a deep pocket. Slowly he withdrew his closed hand and extended it toward Sophraea.

"Would you like a sweetmeat?" he said.

Sophraea shook her head violently. Seeing the ancient face crease with an odd look of uncertainty, as if he knew he had said something wrong but wasn't sure how to correct himself, she added, "I am not supposed to take sweets from strangers. And it is too close to my dinner time. Mama would scold me."

Stepping into the last full rays of the sun, the elderly gentleman leaned over the child. "You are a good girl."

He patted her awkwardly on the head, like a man more used to hounds or horses than children, and pocketed the sweet.

That close, Sophraea saw the wrinkles and spots on his skin looked exactly like those on the hands of the old ladies who came to eat cake with Myemaw and gossip about how the city was once so much grander. Even the mustiness of the elderly man's coat held the same smell of preserving herbs and old house dust as the ladies' cloaks.

"I thought you were a dead man," Sophraea burst out in her relief and the old gentleman's gray eyebrows rose to his scanty hairline at her pronouncement. "But you're alive! I am sorry, saer."

Removing his wide-brimmed black hat, the old man bowed with exquisite courtesy and stated, "Lord Dorgar Adarbrent, most certainly alive and entirely at your service." A rusty sound came bubbling out of his throat, something halfway between a polite cough and a chuckle, as he replaced his hat.

"Sophraea Carver," said Sophraea, dipping into a brief curtsy as she would to one of her grandmother's friends.

"Now, child, let me walk you home. You should never be in the City of the Dead after dark." The old man scratched his chin as he stared at the child. "Hmmm . . . in fact, even though you are a Carver, you are quite too young to be here alone at any time."

"That is what everyone says. Sophraea, stay here! Sophraea, don't go there!" confided the little girl, turning obediently at the wave of the nobleman's hand and leading him back along the path toward the Dead End gate. "But the boys were kicking their stupid ball. It is so *boring!* All I do is sit! So I left and nobody told me to stop."

Lord Adarbrent gave another rusty chuckle. "Ah, I see that the boys were the ones at fault."

Sophraea skidded to a halt. Although she was five, and growing up in the tail-end of a big family had left her with a large vocabulary, she wanted to make certain that she understood Lord Adarbrent.

"Does that mean the boys are in *trouble?*" she asked carefully.

"I rather suspect that they are." Lord Adarbrent nodded, hooking one finger over his nose to hide a smile.

"Oh, good!" cheered Sophraea. "I want to see that!"

As she drew nearer the gate, Sophraea heard shouts, but in a higher and much different tone than when she had left. Recognizing her mother Reye's cries, Sophraea quickly climbed the steps to the Dead End gate.

"Wait for me, child," cried the old gentleman.

Sophraea paused at the top of the gate stairs. Behind her, Lord Adarbrent peered uncertainly through the twilight gloom.

"Come along," said Sophraea. "I must go in."

At the sound of her voice, his head swung up and he stared directly at her. "Ah," he said with satisfaction, "I see the gate now."

"Are you coming?" Sophraea asked.

"Certainly," the old man said, climbing up the moss-slicked stairs.

At the sound of another shout from her mother, Sophraea turned and ran to the center of the courtyard.

All her brothers and all her younger cousins were lined up before her mother Reye. Her uncles Perspicacity, Sagacious, Vigilant, and

Judicious stood in their workshop doors, attracted by the noise. All had worried lines creasing their big foreheads. Out of the windows hung at least two aunts and Sophraea's grandmother, each adding her shouts to Reye's scolding.

"How could you have lost her!" yelled Reye. "You were supposed to be watching Sophraea!"

"Don't know," muttered Leaplow.

"Wasn't me," added Bentnor.

Lord Adarbrent gave a small cough behind Sophraea. Reye whirled around and, catching sight of her daughter, sped across the courtyard to snatch the child up. "Where have you been?" she said. "Look at your skirt. You're all dirty down the front. Where were you?"

The scolding and questions flew so fast around Sophraea's head that she didn't know when or how to answer. Her father came up to them more slowly. A giant of a man, he looked over his wife's head at Lord Adarbrent and nodded at the old gentleman. "Thank you for bringing our Sophraea back."

The nobleman waved one age-spotted hand in dismissal. "The child knew her own way back. Quite a clever girl, Carver."

With a final bow, Lord Adarbrent crossed the courtyard to the street-side gate and let himself out.

"You've been in the City of the Dead!" shouted Reye. "Oh, you bad, bad boys, to let her go through that gate! She's much too young!" Reye swatted bottoms right and left. The boys fled howling with excuses of "didn't see her!" and "it's not my fault!"

Sophraea's smirk at the rout of her brothers quickly ended as her mother whirled back.

"You bad girl!" cried Reye, swatting Sophraea hard enough to be felt through her petticoats and then hugging her even harder. "You must never go into the City of the Dead alone! It isn't safe! Especially after dark!"

"Sorry, Mama," mumbled Sophraea.

"Now, Reye," said her father. "No harm was done." He squatted down to look Sophraea straight in the eye. "But you must promise never to go through that gate without me or one of your uncles."

"Never?" protested Sophraea, who knew "never" could last as long as a year or more.

"Not until you're a grown girl, pet. The City of the Dead is no place for small children alone. Especially at twilight." Her father hoisted Sophraea up on his shoulder, to give her a ride back to the house. She wrapped her hands around his broad neck and leaned her cheek upon the top of his curly head. "Oh, oh, you're strangling me!" cried her father in mock terror. "What must I do to get rid of this terrible monster!"

Sophraea giggled and kicked her heels upon his shoulder. "Take me home!" she cried.

Despite all the excitement and fussing that followed at supper, Sophraea did not completely forget her father's orders not to venture alone through the Dead End gate, perhaps because Leaplow made his own promise "to wallop her good" if she ever got him in that much trouble again. But like many Carver family rules, it became relaxed and stretched until she routinely trotted up and down the mossy stairs on errands with the rest of the family.

Like her boisterous brothers, Sophraea grew up assuming that any haunts or horrors on the other side of the wall would never harm her. After all, she was a Carver and those buried by the Carvers rarely bothered the family.

And Sophraea's belief in her family's safety never wavered until the winter that the dead decided to use the Carvers' private gate to go dancing through the streets of Waterdeep.

ONE

WINTER 1479

Rain and wind rattled the window, wakeing Sophraea Carver from her troubled dreams. After rolling over twice and punching her lumpy pillows three times, Sophraea sighed and sat up. The last live ember in the bedroom fireplace gave out the faintest red glow. The window shook again as another blast of Waterdeep's wet winter hit it. The rotting month of Uktar certainly was starting with a roar of watery fury.

Sophraea slid out from under her tangled blankets. Barefoot, toes curling when they encountered the cold floorboards, she padded to the window. Leaplow had promised to fix the loose casement many times, but her brother never seemed to make it up the four flights of stairs to her bedroom. Which meant that once again she had to deal with the noise and the draft in the darkest hour of the night. Grumbling a little under her breath, Sophraea grabbed the edge of the casement, meaning to shove the bolt as hard and tight as she could. But a flicker of light caught her eye.

Her bedroom windows faced east, overlooking the City of the Dead rather than the crowded streets of Waterdeep. It was quieter on this side of the house, gravely quiet as the family often joked. From her room at the very top of the house's crooked east turret, right under the roof, Sophraea could see all the northern half of the graveyard from the Deepwinter Vault all the way to the Beacon and Watchway Towers.

This late at night, there should be nothing to see. No lights should be shining in the City of the Dead except the few lamps left burning to mark the main paths and mausoleums, and most of those were in the south end where the grand civic memorials stood, well out of sight of her window. The City Watch would have closed and locked all the public gates at sunset. Sophraea knew no honest citizen would be wandering through the old graveyard and the dishonest ones generally kept away after dark. There were far more profitable and less dangerous targets for thieves to be found amid the bustling nightlife of Waterdeep's best and worst neighborhoods.

But the whirling ball of light appeared again, a wildfire flicker that started in the north end of the cemetery. It leaped and swirled in patterns resembling the pathways leading away from the northern tombs. The light flickered out and then reappeared much closer to the cemetery wall, almost directly under her window.

Fully awake and quivering with curiosity, Sophraea threw open the casement and leaned out of the window. Wind blew her black curls into her eyes. With an impatient shake of her head, she peered down into the back courtyard. Far below, she heard a metallic rattling. Someone or something was trying to enter through the Dead End gate. The strange glow shone directly beneath her but on the graveyard side of the wall.

High above it and invisible in the dark night, Sophraea tried to make out what the light was. Could it be someone holding a lantern? Was there some unusually intrepid thief attempting the family gate?

The clattering at the gate stopped. The wind died down and, for a moment, Sophraea thought she heard another sound, the rise and fall of an eerie wail. Then the light winked out.

Sophraea watched for a few minutes more, but another gust of icy rain convinced her to slam the window closed.

Thoroughly chilled and shivering, Sophraea dived beneath her blankets. She wondered if she should tell her parents about the strange lights around the gate. But it is probably nothing, reasoned Sophraea, nothing at all to worry about. And that odd noise at the end, the noise that sounded so much like a woman sobbing, that was just the wind, Sophraea told herself firmly as she buried her head a little deeper under the pillows.

The next morning, Sophraea woke to the usual sound of big male relatives banging down the stairs of the Dead End House. *Bump, crash, thump,* that would be Leaplow two floors below doing his usual dive down the south staircase toward the kitchen. *Rattle, slam,* shouts, that would be Bentnor and his twin Cadriffle racing along the west staircase to snatch a bite to eat before joining their father in the coffin workshop.

The City of the Dead appeared to be its usual damp tangle of winter bare bushes and trees in the gray light of a cloudy morning. The rain-darkened roofs of the mausoleums showed as black squares amid the shrubbery. Peering from her window, Sophraea could not see anything unusual. The past night's disturbances had left no obvious mark upon the grounds.

One of the family's multitude of black and white cats strolled along the top of the wall separating the City of the Dead from the Carver's courtyard.

As she laced her favorite velvet vest with a new ribbon, Sophraea could not stop thinking about the strange ball of light that had floated through the graveyard.

Later, after arriving at the family kitchen, she received a flurry of instructions from her mother whisking breakfast on and off the table as fast as the men could gobble their bread. A lighter stream of chatter gushed forth from her aunts, also dancing around their large sons and their wives, as they teased the family's newest daughter-in-law, a pretty Henndever girl who was still a new enough bride to blush at the aunts' jokes and her husband's embarrassed shrugs and grins.

But the Henndever bride grinned just as broadly as the rest when her harassed husband finally grabbed her, kissed her soundly to the accompaniment of the aunts' sighs, and clattered down the stairs to work.

Sophraea's sensible father and equally staid uncles were long gone, already busy in their workshops. With her mother obviously distracted by the bustle of beginning the day, she stayed silent about the strange light that she had seen in the graveyard.

Somewhere in Waterdeep, Sophraea mused as the morning wore on, there were battles being fought across rooftops, intrigues being plotted in shadowy taverns, and clandestine assignations being made in perfumed bedrooms. But here, in her courtyard, there was laundry. Basket after basket of laundry filled with the enormous shirts and pants needed to cover a Carver male.

With the rain blown out to sea for the moment, Reye asked her daughter to get the laundry hung. Certainly flapping in the backyard was a better choice than draped over the backs of chairs in front of the kitchen fire or strung along the curved staircase banisters, the usual method of drying indoors during the wettest months.

A whistle sounded behind her as Sophraea struggled to fling the dripping trousers of her brother Runewright over the line. Spinning around, Sophraea saw a tall, thin man come slouching through their public gate that opened onto the alley leading to Zendulth Street.

Dressed in faded tan leathers from head to toe, the young man, and he looked only a year or two older than herself, bore a general air of brownness, the brown of new wood or the fawn of autumn leaves. His hair was a medium brown, his close-trimmed beard was a darker brown, even the long sharp nose and high cheekbones were tanned a travelers' brown. The only spark of color in his face and figure was a pair of extraordinarily bright green eyes shining below dark lashes long enough to be the envy of any girl.

"I was told I could find a stonecarver here," said the thin brown man.

"Monument, marker, gravestone, or statue?"

"Statue, please," he answered with a quick smile. "Do you do all the rest?"

"My uncles build the monuments and do the fine stone ornaments and my cousins engrave markers in bronze or marble. My brothers can cut a coffin to fit you in less than a day, but that's wood and not stone for most folks. My father carves the best statues," Sophraea explained. She pointed out her father's workshop, third door on her left facing into the yard. "You'll find him there."

The young man nodded but seemed rooted to where he was, staying in the courtyard to watch her toss one of Leaplow's shirts over the line.

"And are you a Carver too?" he asked.

Sophraea threw Bentnor's second best tunic on the line before answering. "I'm Sophraea Carver, but I'm no stoneworker if that's what you are asking."

She dived into the basket to pull out another set of wet pants, the left knee sporting a large hole, which meant patching would be needed. If it wasn't patching, it was darning. There was always sewing to do, but never the sort she liked. Since the young man showed no signs of shifting from under her clotheslines, she repeated, "My father is the one you want to see. Third door, where I showed you."

"Actually, I'm quite fond of the view from where I am," he replied with a wink and a grin as the stiff breeze whistling into the yard plastered Sophraea's skirts against her legs and tugged loose her dark curls. "My name is Gustin Bone, in case you were wishing to know."

"Not particularly," Sophraea answered with an ease of practice borne of shopping expeditions into Waterdeep's markets.

As she had grown older, more than one young man unacquainted with the size and sheer numbers of her male relatives had tried to flirt with her. Sophraea never minded the flirting, but it did get tiresome to see her cousins, her brothers, and even the occasional uncle take a young man for "a pleasant walk" around the City of the Dead to explain the family's closeness and their natural concern for the only Carver daughter.

This young man might be as tall as some of her cousins, but he lacked the breadth to go with the height. Thin as a spear and shoulders bent with a scholar's slouch, Sophraea doubted this one would ever speak to her again after even the shortest stroll with Leaplow or Runewright.

Since Gustin Bone's feet seemed stuck to the cobblestones under his boots, Sophraea used a trick that usually caused her male relatives to disappear like smoke up one of Dead End House's crooked chimneys.

"I could use some help," she said, indicating the nearest over-flowing laundry basket. "Perhaps you could hang those shirts."

"I'm not one for physical labor," Gustin Bone stated without moving. "But thank you for the offer."

"Come along then, you might as well bother my father instead of me," Sophraea said, marching over to the door of her father's workshop and rapping on it with a brisk knock. The top half of the door swung open and her father's bushy bearded face peered out. "There's a man here to see you about a statue."

"Weeping goddess or shieldbearer or infant sleeping?" asked Astute Carver, leaning on the lower half of the door.

"Is that all you do?" asked Gustin Bone.

"I can carve anything you want," said Astute. "But those are the most popular for monuments. The first for lost lovers, the second for fallen warriors, and the third. Ah, the third is for the heartbroken parents and always the saddest of the lot to carve."

"I need someone to carve me a hero," said Gustin Bone.

"Any particular one?"

"No, just a stone man of heroic aspect. Taller, bigger, broader than ordinary men, a great paladin like the old stories," said Gustin. "And make him as lifelike as possible."

"Creases in his clothing and those wrinkles that paladins get from squinting at enemies on the distant horizon?" speculated Astute.

"Oh excellent. As real as you can make him!"

"I could even give him pores in his skin. By the time that I'm done, there's more than one who will wonder if he's simply sleeping or waiting to draw his next breath."

"Wonderful," said Gustin reaching across the half door to clap Astute's shoulder. "Absolutely what I need."

Astute straightened up and looked over the young man, a long speculative look that Sophraea had seen him use before.

"What I need," Astute finally replied in the careful drawl of a Waterdeep man who knew the importance of remuneration, "is money to pay for the stone and for my labor."

"Certainly, certainly," said Gustin, producing a thin brown leather pouch from the front of his tunic. He dropped it into Astute's broad palm.

"A trifle light," said Astute.

"A partial payment only, saer," promised Gustin. "The rest will be coming soon. A day or two to make my arrangements."

Then the surprising young man grabbed Sophraea's hand and bowed over it with a smile. "Pleasure, truly a pleasure," he said. Those wickedly long lashes blinked, momentarily hiding his extraordinary green eyes. "I'm sorry that I cannot stay longer."

A little popping sound filled the courtyard. The young man grinned again at Sophraea, bowed elaborately toward her father, and then sprinted for the public gate.

"Fish guts and torn garters!" exclaimed Sophraea. "What was that all about?"

"Language, my girl!" said Astute.

"I didn't say anything bad," protested Sophraea.

Astute shook his bearded head. "Ew, girl, you know how your mother feels about outbursts like that."

"Bad enough that your brothers can't keep polite tongues in their heads," sang Sophraea. "But surely you can act more like a lady."

Astute chuckled at her perfect mimicry of Reye's most recent and constant scold.

Another gust of wind tugged at Sophraea's skirts and remembering the full baskets of laundry, she turned back to the lines. But all the baskets were empty and all the laundry was neatly hung, wafting back and forth as it dried. A pale glow outlined each item, slowly fading away even as Sophraea stared.

Sophraea could feel her mouth hanging open, snapped it shut, and then looked over her shoulder at her father.

"A very surprising young man," observed Astute with a chuckle at his daughter's astonishment. "I think he liked you. Perhaps I should have a little talk with him when he comes back."

"Don't bother," said Sophraea with a firm shake of her head. "But I do have something to tell you."

Putting thoughts of the brown lad firmly out of her head, Sophraea started to tell her father about last night's light in the graveyard, but the heavy clopping of hooves outside the street gate interrupted her. A jingle of harness signaled that a coach had stopped outside their public entrance.

"Ah," sighed Astute, "I forgot that he was coming today. Go get your uncles. He'll want all of us to wait on him."

From the heavy frown that marred Astute's usually mild expression, Sophraea didn't need to ask who to announce to her uncles. Only one man annoyed the family so completely, but was also so rich as to be impossible to turn away. Obviously, Rampage Stunk was about to give the Carvers another set of orders about his mausoleum.

Sophraea sped to each door of her uncles' workshops, banging on them loudly to be heard over the hammering and sawing inside. One by one, her uncles popped their heads out of the doors. An aunt or two appeared at the windows overlooking the courtyard.

"It's Stunk," Sophraea called to them.

"I hope he left his hairy brute of a servant behind," she muttered to herself.

TWO

In Waterdeep, a city that lived and died by gossip, Rampage Stunk somehow discouraged speculation about the size and extent of his fortune. His personal wealth, like his stomach, was known to be much larger than the ordinary man's and that seemed to be the extent of others' knowledge of Rampage Stunk's business.

Sophraea found him an unpleasant man. Something about the way he thrust himself forward, his stiff black hair looking as if it had been dipped in ink and then slicked down with grease, his head always cocked at an angle on his shoulders as if listening for gossip about others. Even the heavy tread of his peculiar swaying walk seemed to state that here was a man who did not mind crushing those beneath him.

Stunk strode into the yard as he had many times before, as if he expected everyone to move out of his way, swinging his arms with his hands curled into meaty fists. With no regard for courtesy, he bulled his way past her waiting uncles and Sophraea's other relatives.

As usual, a retinue of servants trailed after the fat man from the North Ward. Besides being one of the most cutthroat of negotiators, it was said that Stunk also was quicker to take offense than most men, often seeing an insult in the most innocent remark and not at all reluctant to retaliate with force. Certainly, wherever he went, he took a host of unpleasant types with him, all of whom were always ready for a fight.

Stunk stopped in front of Astute Carver, shifting a little from side to side as was his habit. He thrust forward a scroll, the greasy marks of his hands clear on the parchment.

"The pediment was too plain," he said. "I made some changes. It is much better now."

Astute Carver took the scroll from his client with a stifled sigh. Some months before, Stunk had commissioned a large memorial for the remains of his long-dead mother and, as needed, his other family members.

Eventually, Stunk planned to occupy the center sarcophagus, a creation of his own design. Every month or so, he visited the Carvers, adding details to the work. Currently he favored a barrel-design tomb set to one side to hold the bones of "lesser family members" as he called them; two pedestals to hold the urns for the ashes of his mother and, eventually, his still living wife; a colonnade of ornamented pillars surrounding his own resting place; and a number of other stone ornaments scattered about to memorialize his self-claimed attributes and achievements.

It was, in the words of Sophraea's uncle Perspicacity, "quite the most florid and horrid design ever to be visited upon us." Her other uncles Judicious, Vigilant, and Sagacious had all rumbled their agreement.

However, Stunk was willing to pay for his folly, as Astute reminded his brothers, and the family never turned down a good commission.

Work progressed slowly. So far, only certain ornamental pieces such as funerary urns had been completed as Stunk tinkered with his design, but those two pieces alone were large enough to fill one whole room in the basement of Dead End House. Stunk's mother still rested in her original plot in Coinscoffin, the merchants' graveyard, and Stunk seemed more concerned about getting his eventual monument carved to his satisfaction than moving the old lady.

Sophraea suspected Stunk's only motivation for his plans to bury his family near him was to be assured of a crowd of sycophants to surround him in death as they did in life.

Fidgeting on the edge of the crowd of younger Carvers waiting for the business to conclude, Sophraea noticed that Stunk's current retinue contained the glowering brute who was said to be his body-guard, the pale and sneering manservant with the six knives clearly sheathed around his person, the two young red-haired louts with the scarred hands and the flattened noses of dockyard bullies, and the hairy man in the livery of a doorjack who always hung at the back of the group.

The last man had a bestial cast to his face, a mid-day scruff of dark beard and greasy lank curls doing little to hide his generally unpleasant visage. As always, the hairy one turned toward Sophraea and sniffed the air in her direction. His pink tongue darted out and licked his chapped lips. Then he smiled at her.

Sophraea shuddered. There was a man that she would be happy to have her brothers walk through the City of the Dead and drop into the nearest open grave. Maybe even throw a little dirt on top of him.

"They get uglier every tenday, don't they?" whispered Leaplow to his sister. "Where does Stunk find his servants? Wonder if we could beat them in a fair fight?"

Although slightly older than herself, Leaplow often seemed far younger, at least in Sophraea's opinion. Like the rest of her brothers, he had inherited their father's dark curly hair and pleasant grin, but not half of Astute's clever patience. As nearly everyone in the district knew, Leaplow was a notorious scrapper, fond of picking fights for the fun of it. Sometimes Sophraea felt more like Leaplow's keeper than his younger sister, attempting to teach him some good sense.

"Hush," Sophraea said, knowing how her brother always was tempted to do something foolish. Her cousins Bentnor and Cadriffle (who were exactly the same age as Leaplow) also were constantly in scuffles and liked earning extra coin by wrestling and boxing

21

whenever they could find a match (although they had run out of men in the neighborhood willing to challenge them). But the twins could at least keep a cool head in a fight and knew when to run. Not that they'd needed to run after they'd grown to their full size. Leaplow, however, never backed down from any fight. He enjoyed the excitement too much and would keep swinging until someone was unconscious. Then he was just as likely to pick up his opponent, clap him over the shoulders, and buy him a drink.

"I'm sure I could take that hairy one," Leaplow muttered to his sister.

"Shush," she said, firmly treading on his foot closest to her. "You still haven't paid Father for all the damage you did last spring."

That fight, which Leaplow called a "wonderful way to spend a day" and the family called "a disgrace to our good name," had nearly wrecked some of the most important southern monuments in the City of the Dead.

Leaplow chuckled in happy remembrance. "That dusty fellow gave me some exercise. You're right, just one hairy doorjack would not be nearly as much fun. How about I take on those red-haired brothers?"

"The City Watch would not like it," answered Bentnor, leaning over Leaplow's shoulder to size up Stunk's retinue. "They're still a bit cranky about that last mess you started and we had to clean up."

"You'd think they'd be happy we did their work for them, knocking out those thieves," Leaplow answered back. "Still, I felt sorry for the one that ended up with that broken nose. Guess nobody ever told him not to pick a Carver's pocket."

In their neighborhood, the bully boys and other miscreants left the Carvers alone. After all, it was a well-known fact in neighborhoods north of the Coffinmarch gate that anyone foolish enough to punch one Carver had to deal with a dozen extraordinarily stalwart lads punching back. Or, and there were certain members of the thieves' guild who said this was even worse, all the Carver wives laying about with their brooms and pots and pans. The Carver men tended to marry strapping big women, the sort who could drop a man with one kick of a boot or one full swing of a fist.

Only Myemaw Carver, Sophraea's grandmother, and Sophraea were tiny women and at least looked harmless. Except, as Binn the one-eyed butcher's boy often said, "the little ones are even tougher than the big ones in that family!" Binn had never really forgiven Sophraea for clouting him when he tried to sneak a kiss.

But there was something different about Stunk's men and Sophraea was glad that Bentnor had distracted her hotheaded brother. Like Stunk, his men tended to push their way into the center of the crowd. They all had an angry air, as if they liked a fight too, but in a bloodier and more deadly way than Leaplow's constant sparring. Sophraea doubted that Stunk's men would just use fists or feet like her brothers or her cousins. The retinue clustered around the fat man all wore blades or, in the case of one redhead, stout cudgels.

Astute Carver had warned her and her brothers more than once to be careful around Stunk's servants: there had been tales in the streets of the people who crossed Stunk or his retinue being ambushed by "unknown" assailants.

So, "hush and don't cause trouble," Sophraea reminded Leaplow again, reaching up to tug his ear down to her level despite his yelp of protest.

"So are you ready for us to start the foundation?" Astute Carver asked Stunk, the merchant's drawings still rolled up in his fist and ignored.

The fat man rocked back and forth a couple of times before ponderously nodding. "Your work on the urns appeared satisfactory," he said with an odd note in his voice, as if he wished he could find some further fault.

"Then in which part of the Merchants' Rest shall we be building?" asked Astute, using the more polite name for Coinscoffin.

Stunk had no such refinement. "Coinscoffin! As if I would be buried there with all the paltry shopkeepers, miles away from Waterdeep proper."

"But that's the only place with enough room for a plot of this size!"

Astute unrolled the scroll to show two smaller buildings that flanked the semicircle of columns surrounding the main tomb where Stunk's sarcophagus would eventually lie.

"My tomb will be there," said Stunk, pointing across the wall to the City of the Dead to the astonishment of the entire Carver family. "As befits a great man of Waterdeep."

"There's no land left within the cemetery's walls. Every scrap of ground is already claimed." Astute only voiced what the rest of the Carvers had known from childhood on.

"You will build my tomb inside the City of the Dead," said Stunk, gesturing at his manservant. The lanky individual slid forward with another scroll and a sneer. "Tear down the structures as marked and begin building my tomb."

"Tear down?" Astute took this new scroll and unrolled it. His brothers clustered close, each peering over Astute's shoulder, muttering at what they saw. "There are two tombs in the City at this spot. My family has maintained them for generations."

"And now you will take care of something far finer."

"But what about the bodies?" Perspicacity asked, nudging his brother Astute.

Stunk shrugged his shoulders. "Everything is quite legal. And any removals will be handled with the utmost respect by my men."

Astute stared at his brothers and they stared back at him. All five big men looked at Stunk with less than cordial expressions. Sophraea's cousins and brothers began to cluster closer to their fathers. One of Stunk's redheaded bullies unhooked his cudgel from his belt.

"Well?" asked Stunk, no more expression on his face than on a piece of blank granite.

"I need to see the deeds," said Astute finally. "We cannot start such work without the proper papers."

"You shall have them," said Stunk. "And I will have my monument exactly where I have said."

The fat man turned and walked with his rolling gait out of the yard, not bothering with even the slightest gesture toward a courteous farewell.

"What do you make of that?" Leaplow asked his sister. The pair wandered away from the muttering conversations of their older brothers, uncles, and father, toward the little gate in the wall that opened into the City of the Dead.

Sophraea peered through the gate at the tangle of bushes and trees overshadowing the path leading to the northern tombs. Was it the breeze that trembled the branches or was it something else?

"I think it is trouble," she finally said. "How are *they* going to react if we start tearing things down?"

"We're Carvers," said Leaplow with his usual brash confidence. "They don't bother us." Then, obviously remembering his trouble last spring, he added, "Well, not usually. And never Father or the uncles."

"Because we maintain the tombs, not destroy them." As soon as she voiced that thought, Sophraea knew exactly the same idea would have occurred to every member of the family. No wonder her uncles were still in a huddle, tugging at their beards and rumbling their doubts at each other.

Still, the City of the Dead did look quiet. At least the bit that she could see from where she stood. She put her hand on the latch, the old prohibition against wandering through the graveyard alone, even at twilight, certainly no longer applied to her. Even her mother Reye had accepted that the shortcut through the City of the Dead was the fastest route for her daughter to use to certain shops in northern Waterdeep. Sophraea had walked the graveyard paths all summer long with no incident at all.

"That's odd." Leaplow startled his sister by bending around her to peer at the gate, almost bumping his forehead on the twisted iron bars. "Must be rust."

"What?"

"That." Leaplow tapped red marks that showed clearly on curlicues of iron.

Sophraea looked closely at the strange streaks marring the usually dull dark gray metal. Ten slender streaks curled around the bars, five on the left side, five on the right.

Slowly Sophraea put out her own slender hands and twisted her fingers around the bars. When she pulled them away, the marks of her hands remained for a brief moment before fading away. The marks were exactly the same as the red streaks, except reversed.

"Handprints," Sophraea barely breathed, looking at the marks so plainly visible and so clearly the color of dried blood, the marks of hands that had reached through the gate from the graveyard side.

Leaplow shook his head in a fierce gesture of denial. "Can't be. They leave us alone. They have always left us alone. The dead don't bother Carvers."

"Whatever it was," said Sophraea, tracing the pattern on the gate with one slender finger and ignoring Leaplow's protests, "it came from the City of the Dead."

The rattle of branches scraping together startled both brother and sister. The pair leaped back from the gate. A splatter of rain followed the gust of wind.

As usual, a shift in the wind distracted her volatile brother. He shook the rain off his head and his worries out of his brain.

"I'm for supper," said the always hungry Leaplow, heading back to Dead End House with a quick stride.

But Sophraea lingered behind. She put her hand on the gate's latch again, remembering the odd light of the night before. Perhaps she could see something more on the other side. But the shadows shifted in the graveyard and another cold blast of wind hit her face like a warning.

With careful backward steps, Sophraea retreated. Behind her, the bushes swayed, as if someone invisible brushed by them, returning to the center of the City of the Dead.

THREE

Everyone told tales of the great duels and the unfortunate spells that had once filled the City of the Dead and spilled into the streets of Waterdeep. And everyone, most especially her ancient relative Volponia, said to Sophraea that those days were gone. The Blackstaff had tamed the wizards, the City Watch kept the thieves from stealing too much, the guards prevented riffraff adventurers from creating unusual trouble for ordinary citizens, and even the young lords and ladies were said to be a much more staid and responsible nobility than generations past. Although the broadsheets were always full of some tale of wicked mischief among the aristocracy and very entertaining to read too!

"Scandals," Volponia had sniffed one morning, crumpling up an old copy of *The Blue Unicorn* that Sophraea had brought her, "not worth the ink on the paper. Some dressmaker going bankrupt. Some young lords teasing the Watch into chasing them. Huh! In my day, the misdeeds of Waterdeep's famous and infamous rocked the heavens, toppled rulers, and changed the very boundaries of kingdoms."

"Being so much older than the rest of us, dear Aunt Volponia," said Sophraea's grandmother Myemaw with the usual touch of acid in the honey of her voice, "you would remember such things."

"I remember you sashaying through that courtyard below with a berry pie in one hand and a loveknot of ribbons in the other hand, girl," shot back Volponia, with a snap of her elegantly manicured fingers at Sophraea's grandmother. "Back before you married my handsome nephew, back when you were the scandal of the neighborhood."

Sophraea's granny began to giggle. "Oh, and you in your tall boots, Volponia, stamping here and there and shouting like you were still commanding from your quarterdeck. Oh, we were all the scandals then!"

The two old ladies fell to chuckling over the gossip sheets until Volponia yawned and said, "I miss those days. When the mangiest dogs had a real bite behind their bark. Why even the ghosts of Waterdeep were grander creatures than the colored mists that float through the streets now!"

Inspired by this memory, Sophraea hurried upstairs to talk to Volponia about the strange light that she'd seen the night before and the bloody handprints on the family gate. The rest of the Carvers were still in a buzz of argument over Stunk's visit and his proposal to tear down tombs within the City of the Dead, but the old lady would listen to her.

When a firm voice told her to "hurry up and enter," Sophraea slipped around the door into the great room that filled three-quarters of the top floor of the tower.

With three sets of windows facing north, west, and south, even the usual pearly light of a cloudy Waterdeep twilight was sufficient to reveal every knickknack teetering on the dozens of small tables and shelves cluttering up Volponia's boudoir.

Volponia's bed was covered with embroidered silk quilts and had a canopy of tapestry curtains protecting the occupant from stray drafts. The bed also stood closest to the south window. The previous evening, when Sophraea had paid her last good nights to Volponia, the bed had been shaped like a wooden sled, covered with red woolen blankets and azure furs, and been positioned closest to the north window.

How or why Volponia changed her bed quite so literally, nobody knew. The old lady still owned a number of trinkets purloined from faraway places during her days as a pirate captain. Some, like the crystal bell that was always close to hand, kept her well-supplied with the comforts that she craved and made her a very light charge upon the family's resources.

The only demand that Volponia ever made was that the other turret bedroom, the one that shared the same floor with hers, "not be occupied by one of those great galumphing male Carvers. I love my nephews, my grandnephews, and my great-grandnephews, but they all take after my brother. He snored loud enough to wake every soul in Waterdeep and I have enough trouble sleeping without listening to such thunder every night."

So, as the only girl born in two generations and a silent sleeper, Sophraea occupied the other bedroom and received regular doses of Volponia's advice growing up. Also a fair amount of criticism as in "well, why are you standing dithering in the doorway. Step in or step out, but don't make a draft!"

Whisking her skirts around the tippy tables and wobbly china and crystal mementos with the ease of long practice, Sophraea hurried to the bedside and kissed Volponia's parchment dry cheek.

"I came to ask about a glowing light in the graveyard, not to be scolded," she said with mock severity as she plopped down upon the bed. The mattress was very firm, probably stuffed with horsehair, Sophraea guessed.

"A light in the graveyard?" said Volponia, hitching herself higher on her satin-covered feather pillows. "What was it?"

"I don't know," said Sophraea, "but it moved around the City of the Dead, from far to the north along the paths to our gate."

"Well, I can't see the City from my windows. Just a bit of the wall and watchtower. A dark night, last night, and a stormy one. I barely slept with all the rattle of the wind and rain. I'm sure I would have noticed any light if it had moved around the house."

"The rain woke me too. That's why I saw the light. It was definitely inside the City and never passed the gate."

"Perhaps it was the Watch upon patrol."

"No," Sophraea could be just as firm as Volponia. "I've seen the Watch chasing thieves through there before. Lots of torches and shouting, lots of lights. This was just one light, and it seemed to move around on its own."

Volponia frowned. "A haunt?"

"It didn't look like a spirit," replied Sophraea with the sophistication of a seventeen-year-old who had grown up in Waterdeep. "At least not the sort of ghost that you usually see. It was brighter, or moved differently. The things you see on the streets, the mists, they tend to float around. This looked like it went where it intended to go."

"Magic, perhaps?" Volponia speculated with a frown. "But it would take an unusually brave wizard to be casting spells in the City after dark. There are things buried there who don't like disturbances. And I can't see the Blackstaff being all that kind to anyone who meddled with magic inside the graveyard. Perhaps you should tell your father. He can always get a word to the right ear."

"Perhaps," agreed Sophraea, "if I knew what to tell him. It was just one light, and rather small. But there were these handprints on our gate today. Leaplow thought it was rust at first . . ."

"But?" asked the shrewd Volponia.

"I thought they were handprints, dark red-brown handprints, from somebody reaching from the City's side."

"The color of old blood?" Volponia spoke with the relish of a former pirate captain. "Just the sort of trick that ghosts like to play. Or those who mean you to think the dead are making trouble. You should talk to your father; Astute's no fool."

"He's busy. Stunk came today."

"A troublesome man, from all that your grandmother has told me," said Volponia. Although the old lady never left her bed as far as the family knew, she liked to hear the news and Myemaw was her major source of information.

31

"I don't like him," admitted Sophraea.

"If you really want to know what that light was, you should ask a wizard," Volponia stated.

"I don't know any," Sophraea replied. Then she thought of Gustin Bone, but she wasn't sure what he was. Did making all the laundry jump on the line make him a wizard? Maybe he was just an adventurer with some type of magic ring or conjuring piece. Such things were not unknown in Waterdeep.

"There's that old woman down on Coffinmarch, but everyone says she is crazy mad witch," Sophraea added, because she did know where Egetha kept her shop and she had no idea at all where Gustin Bone had come from or where he went.

"That's just your brothers' opinion of Egetha and that's just because she caught them sneaking around her back windows, trying to watch her conjure. But Egetha never did much more than sell beauty charms to old maids and protections for young men with mischief on their minds."

"Really, I didn't know that."

"Exactly how old are you? I keep losing track with your generation."

"Seventeen."

"That's still too young for me to be discussing most of Egetha's stock with you. Go ask your mother if you're curious." Volponia fidgeted in her bed, obviously dismissing the topic to the disappointment of Sophraea's curiosity. But her next words caught the girl's wandering attention.

"The quality of magic may have sadly deteriorated from the days of my youth, as have a great many other things," said Volponia, "but there must still be a place where you can find a decent wizard for hire in Waterdeep."

"I'm sure I don't know where, Auntie," said Sophraea, "and I'm certain that I wouldn't know how to pay one if I did find him."

"When I was still captaining my own ships, you went to Sevenlamps Cut if you wanted a wizard, especially the cheap kind whom nobody would miss if they drowned or were eaten by sea serpents." Volponia sniffed. "If you asked around, you could find someone to hire out on the streets."

"Well, wizards cost money and I don't have that much."

"Promise to pay with a kiss." Volponia actually smirked. "Used to work for me when I was your age."

"I'm not going to kiss some smelly old wizard, you wicked thing!"

"That's the problem with your generation. No imagination." The old lady rooted with one hand under the covers of her bed and pulled out a tarnished brass box, decorated with strips of faded green ribbons. She shook it and listened with a frown to the tinkle of the contents. Twisting one end of the box open, she emptied a single silver ring onto her covers. Handing it to Sophraea, she said, "There's probably half a wish still left in that ring and that might interest the right type of wizard."

"I don't know. A wizard might be more trouble than he's worth," Sophraea answered, still thinking about the twinkle in Gustin Bone's bright green eyes.

Fidgeting with Volponia's gift, she slid it on her middle finger. A plain ring, a little tarnished, with no fancy marks or flashing gems, it looked like one of those trinkets that the foolish bought in the cheaper parts of the Dock Ward. It was hard to believe that it contained any magic at all.

"Maybe I shouldn't worry about the City of the Dead," she said to Volponia. "After all, Leaplow is probably right, the dead don't bother Carvers."

"Especially if Leaplow restrains himself from punching them in the face," chuckled her ancient relative. The tale of Leaplow's misdeeds last spring had risen quickly to the old woman's chamber.

"But if someone is stirring up trouble, shouldn't I find out who?" Sophraea continued to twist the ring on her finger, but she kept looking out of the closest window, wondering if the light would reappear in the City of the Dead that night.

"Well, if you do make up your mind any day soon," Volponia said with a shrewd glance at Sophraea's wrinkled and rather worried forehead, "do let me know. It will give me something to fret over. I have so very few distractions at my age. It may be some time before Leaplow creates another scandal."

Sophraea smiled and slid from the bed. "I'll let you know if I decide to investigate, I promise. Do you want me to bring you anything?"

"No need," said Volponia, reaching for her crystal bell. "I'll ring up whatever I want later. And your grandmother will be along once her supper is done for a little chatter."

"Don't tell too many good stories without me," said Sophraea on her way out the door.

Volponia called her back. "Weren't you going to talk to Lord Adarbrent? About that letter of recommendation?"

Sophraea sighed. "He hasn't been back in almost a full month."

"He will be. He's just as obsessed with his final rest as that Rampage Stunk. So you're going to do it? You're going to take that job with the dressmaker?"

"It's an apprenticeship," said Sophraea for the umpteenth time. "And she won't take just anyone. You have to show that you have a noble sponsor."

"Sounds like a snob," Volponia had expressed this opinion many times too.

"She's considered the very best in the Castle Ward. And what am I to do? Stay here and sew shrouds?"

"Your aunts Catletrho and Tanbornen seem to enjoy it. As do a couple of their sons."

"Not me. I want to work with fine materials."

"Some of the nobility like silk shrouds as much as silk shirts or sheets."

"I want to see my creations on the living!"

"That's harder for a Carver, I'll admit. Although, if your fancy dressmaker puts you to embroidering camisoles and petticoats, you won't see much of those either after they leave the shop. I doubt she'll have you dressing her best customers from the start."

"No, of course not, the apprenticeship is seven years. But her apprentices have established their own shops."

"Still seems a long time to tie yourself to someone who isn't family. And she wants her girls to live in the shop, I hear."

"I'll have a half-day free twice a month. I'll visit."

"Won't be the same," grumbled Volponia, pulling her blankets closer around her thin old body.

"Ah, don't," said Sophraea, dropping to her knees by the bed. She clasped one of Volponia's long, thin hands in her own equally slender fingers. "Everyone has been arguing against this. But you don't know what that shop is like. It's so beautiful, all those piles of velvet, silk, ribbons, lace, and embroidery. And little delicate chairs with gilded legs. None of the ladies ever talk in anything but the most genteel tones. There's no shouting or banging or kicking a stupid ball against the wall of the house at all hours! And nobody who works there smells of anything stronger than soap!"

"Can't say that about the Carver boys." Volponia patted Sophraea's dusky curls. "But we'll all miss you. That's why we fuss so."

"I know," Sophraea said, springing up and hugging Volponia one last time. Every time she thought about leaving Dead End House, Sophraea couldn't help the stupid tears clogging up her eyes and making her sniff. She loved her family but she really could not see spending the rest of her life sewing shrouds. And she certainly wasn't big enough or strong enough to carve monuments or build coffins like some of her sisters-in-law.

Besides, if she lived in Castle Ward, there would be some distance between her and her overly protective relatives. She might even get to flirt with the same man more than once!

>———W———<

Much to Sophraea's surprise, Lord Adarbrent arrived at Dead End House early the next morning. Since they had first crossed paths in the City of the Dead, the elderly nobleman never failed to greet her courteously. More than once, she had heard him refer to her as "a good girl" to her father.

Of course, Sophraea was not sure that Lord Adarbrent actually realized that she was seventeen and fully grown. He still tended to offer her sweetmeats and pat her on the head, just as he had when she was five.

But she had a letter of recommendation all written out for him in her very best hand and only one or two very tiny smudges from being carried around in her apron pocket for days on end. If he would only sign and seal it, she could apply for the dressmaker's apprenticeship in the Castle Ward.

Despite her best efforts, Sophraea could not attract Lord Adarbrent's attention. The old man had hurried across the courtyard with only the barest of bows in her direction to knock on the door of her father's workshop.

"Lord Adarbrent," said Astute Carver with genuine pleasure at the interruption. The two shared a passion for the history of the tombs contained within the walls of the City of the Dead.

Usually during a visit, the conversation would turn from Lord Adarbrent's current plans to the history of the City of the Dead. Lord Adarbrent greatly admired the Carvers' family ledger, which recorded all the details of their work and had often called it an "incomparable history" of the cemetery.

Once the old gentleman had found the design for a curl of seaweed carved by a Carver ancestor on a mausoleum's door. He told Astute and Sophraea where that emblem could be found etched in a certain family's crest. Lord Adarbrent then related how that twist of seaweed was linked to the long forgotten tale of a blue-skinned wife who came from Naramyr and vanished back into the Sea of Fallen Stars after her noble husband's death.

"They were a restless family after that," finished Lord Adarbrent one rainy afternoon as a much younger Sophraea perched wide-eyed and wondering on an overturned urn, listening to his story of the elf wife. "None of them could ever bear to see a ship making ready to leave the harbor, for fear that the lure of the wind and water would be too great for them."

Lord Adarbrent, Astute Carver often declared, was the only man in Waterdeep who knew the great City of the Dead better than the family. And Lord Adarbrent would hem and haw in his usual manner, murmuring "You are too kind. I have learned a great deal since I began my visits here."

That day, however, the elderly nobleman was almost curt in his exchange with Astute.

"I need to look over your ledger," he said far more abruptly than usual.

"Certainly, my lord," said Astute, pulling down the big book bound in black leather and setting it on his worktable. "Can I fetch you a chair?"

"No need," said Lord Adarbrent as he waved him away. The old man leaned heavily on his gold-headed cane, carefully turning the crackling pages of the family's ledger. "He's gone too far . . . that upstart . . . this is a matter of honor."

Astute winked at Sophraea. In Waterdeep, old Lord Adarbrent was often called the Angry Lord for his mutterings as he stalked through the streets. Less kind souls also referred to him as the

Walking Corpse for his dour physique. The Carvers rarely saw that side of his character, but obviously something had touched off the nobleman's well-known fiery temper.

Finally, with a hiss of rage, the old man turned away from the ledger. "Venal cur." He glared out the workshop door as if he could see the person who annoyed him so through the walls and buildings of Waterdeep. "Well, that is what I needed to know."

He scratched his chin, a habitual gesture of contemplation for the old gentleman. "Now. What to do? What to do, indeed!" he muttered to himself.

With an obvious start of recollection, Lord Adarbrent acknowledged Astute Carver. "I am sorry, more sorry than I can say, that I must leave so soon after arriving."

"You are welcome here, my lord, whether for a short visit or a long one."

"Very kind, very kind, I'm sure." The old nobleman hesitated in the workshop doorway, as if trying to decide where to go next.

Given the gentleman's mood, Sophraea wondered if she should wait to ask him for his signature. A kitten wandered out from under her father's workbench, part of the latest litter deposited there by the Carver's striped mouser. The black-and-white furball tangled its tiny claws in her hem and purred. Even as she reached down to disengage the kitten, Sophraea decided she could not put off asking Lord Adarbrent for another day.

The customers' bell clanged. Two men entered through the street-side gate, the long and lanky Gustin Bone and the hairy doorjack of Rampage Stunk. Lord Adarbrent took one look at the latter man and spun sharply on his heel, striding across the yard to the gate leading into the City of the Dead.

"My lord," Sophraea started forward, dropping the kitten back with its littermates and pulling her letter out of her apron pocket. Two of her cousins carried a newly polished coffin out of

Perspicacity's workshop. Sophraea dodged around them.

But she was too slow to catch Lord Adarbrent. He plunged through the gate and charged into the City of the Dead. Sophraea ran down the moss-covered steps leading to the gravel path, intent on catching the old man. But even as she rounded the Deepwinter tomb, she lost sight of Lord Adarbrent.

With a sigh, she stuffed the letter back into her apron pocket and turned back toward home. The next time, she promised herself, she wouldn't hesitate. She'd catch his lordship just as soon as he set foot in the Dead End courtyard and she would get that signature. She just couldn't spend the rest of her life waiting. She needed to make her dreams happen.

Yet, looking back at Dead End House looming over the cemetery's walls, Sophraea felt the usual pang at the thought of leaving home. The long windows glowed a warm yellow, a sign that the aunts were already lighting the lanterns to chase away the late afternoon gloom. She could swear that the wind brought her a sniff of wood smoke and supper cooking from the house's crooked chimney.

As Sophraea retraced her steps, a faint sound caught her attention. A whisper of a noise, not nearly as loud as the rain beginning to patter on the dead leaves littering the pathway or the wind scratching the branches together.

Sophraea stood perfectly still, listening. It faded away even as she concentrated, the sound of a woman sobbing, a very young woman sobbing as if her heart was broken, "lost . . . lost . . . lost."

The crunch of very real feet on the gravel distracted Sophraea. Gustin Bone was hurrying toward her.

"There you are," he said with a smile lighting his bright green eyes. Then, as he took in the Deepwinter tomb behind her, those same eyes widened. "Ah, this isn't your kitchen garden."

"Of course not," said Sophraea, a little impatiently, distracted by trying to tell if the whisper she'd just heard was the usual moan to be expected in the graveyard or something else. "This is the City of the Dead. Why would you think it was our kitchen garden?"

"I saw you go through that little gate in the wall," Gustin continued, "and I thought . . . I mean, the big houses in Cormyr, they have gardens walled off where people grow their herbs and vegetables."

"We have a solarium on the second floor of the house for herbs," Sophraea informed him, still only paying half attention to the young man. "And we buy our vegetables in the market."

Gustin slowly spun in place, taking in the multitude of tombs, the memorial statutes, the ornamental and somber shrubbery, and the urns stuffed with flowers weeping shriveled petals onto the ground below. On the roof of the closest tomb, grotesque carved figures hung over the edge, peering down on the pathway.

"But this is the famous City of the Dead!" he exclaimed. "Aren't all the gates guarded by the Watch? And aren't the gates into it bigger?"

"The public gates are very large and guarded, of course. But this is our gate, the Dead End gate. It's just for the family," said Sophraea marching back toward their gate. "To bring things through. It would be a terrible nuisance if we had to go all the way to the Coffinmarch or Andamaar gates just to take a marker to a grave."

"And what were you bringing here?"

"Nothing. I was trying to catch . . ." Sophraea skidded to a stop and scowled at Gustin. "It's none of your business. What are you doing here?" She emphasized the "you" in the exact same suspicious tone as Myemaw used when saying "And what are you boys planning to do tonight?"

Gustin reacted just like her brothers. He shuffled his feet and mumbled, "Nothing . . . I just saw you and . . ."

"Oh, come on," said Sophraea. "If you want to see my father about your statue, he's in his workshop."

"Of course," said Gustin briskly. "That's why I'm here. To see your father."

Sophraea shut and latched the Dead End gate. "He started your statue this morning," she said, "selecting the stone and roughing out the shape. My brothers Leaplow and Runewright will do the preliminary work under his direction and then he'll add the fine details later. It's a handsome stone he picked. I think you'll like it."

"I do want to see it," said Gustin following her to the workshop. "I have heard that he's very good at his work."

"The best in Waterdeep," said Sophraea with no small pride. "All of the Carvers are. Well, except Leaplow, but he can be good when he thinks about what he is doing. But my father and my uncles are the most skilled. They know how important their craft is. It's the last gift the living give the dead, a box to house the body, a stone to mark their passing, so they make their work beautiful."

"I never thought of it like that. And what do you do?" Gustin Bone asked.

"I'm not in the business. I'm going to be the first Carver to leave Dead End House and become a dressmaker."

"Gifts that the living give the living." The young man dodged around a stone cherub with a broken wing waiting for repair and a stack of lumber seasoning for spring coffins. A Carver cat curled atop the lumber gave him an inscrutable look as he passed by.

Sophraea giggled as she pushed open the door of her father's workshop. "I guess you could call it that."

Inside Astute Carver and her uncle Perspicacity were pouring over some long scrolls. Rampage Stunk's scruffy knave was still there, leaning insolently against Astute's workbench and cleaning his nails with a long thin dagger. Sophraea could clearly see the stiff black hairs sprouting on the back of the man's dirty knuckles.

"We should have Myemaw look it over too," said Perspicacity, "but I think it is legal."

"I am afraid that you are right," agreed Astute. "But who would have thought that a family could sell off their deeds like that?"

"It's property," said Perspicacity. "Just like a house or any land, I suppose. And it's not like this one was close to them or would even remember who was lodged inside. The seller is a fourth cousin on the distaff side, I think. I'd have to look at the ledger to be sure."

"Well, they do say Waterdeep is changing and changing fast. But who would have thought . . ." Astute noticed his daughter and the young man close behind her. "I am sorry, saer, but I am just finishing some business here. Give us a moment more."

"No rush, no rush at all." Gustin bowed slightly in the direction of all the men in the workshop. Stunk's servant ignored him but Perspicacity gave the younger man a friendly nod. Gustin turned away to examine Astute's chisels and mallets, all neatly hanging from rows of hooks set into the rough plaster walls.

"Tell your master that we will begin the work as soon as the materials arrive," Astute instructed the servant.

"He will be displeased by any delays," growled the man.

"He would dislike hasty work done with shoddy materials even less," replied the unruffled Astute. "Stunk only wants the finest, and that takes time, as any good craftsman knows."

The servant shrugged one shoulder. "Very well, I will give him your message." He stowed his dagger in his shirt. Passing by the Carver's open ledger, he paused to read a page.

"That's a curious book," he said, flicking over the pages much more quickly than Lord Adarbrent. "A lot of old names. My master likes old histories. He might pay you something for this."

"It is not for sale," Astute said with great finality and, turning his back on the hirsute doorjack, began to chat with Gustin about the stone that he had selected for the young man's statue. Perspicacity joined the two men in their discussion.

Only Sophraea noticed the servant tug sharply at a page in the ledger, digging in his yellow fingernails.

"Stop that!" she cried, attracting everyone's attention. "You will rip it!"

The hairy man backed away from the book, his hand snaking toward the dagger in his shirt as the two big Carver men advanced upon him. Behind them, Gustin's eyes glowed like twin emeralds.

"Leave me alone," whined the servant. "I didn't do anything."

Astute snapped the covers of the ledger closed and put the book away on a high shelf. "Go on. Your business is done here."

The servant hurried to the door, barking in a whisper to Sophraea as he passed her, "Meddling girl, you'll be sorry."

FOUR

If she had been asleep, the sound of sobbing would have woken her. As it was, Sophraea was already awake, staring at the ceiling of her room and thinking of what she would say to Lord Adarbrent. She was sure that he would sign the letter, but what if he said no? And what if the dressmaker didn't think the Walking Corpse was quite the right type of reference? Of her own ability to do the job, Sophraea had no doubts. She was as gifted with a needle as her father was with a chisel and awl. And there was always good work available for a girl who was a clever seamstress, given the enduring passion of the Waterdeep nobility for the latest cut of the sleeve or the newest style of embroidery to decorate the collar, and the equally lasting obsession of the richest merchants to dress their own families in the style of the oldest blood of Waterdeep. But, ever since she'd seen those gilded chair legs, she'd really had her heart set upon working in that shop in the Castle Ward.

Still, nobody would believe that Lord Adarbrent knew anything about fashion of the current year, much less the past fifty years. His full coats and wide-brimmed hats matched the styles of her grandmother's youth. But he was definitely a lord and a well-known lord, given his constant muttering perambulations throughout all of Waterdeep.

Preoccupied with her plans, Sophraea first thought that the faint sobbing sound filling her room was just the moaning of the wind outside. But as it rose in intensity, and then faded away, only to come back again, the girl realized that something more than the wind cried in the City of the Dead.

With a strong feeling that she had done this before, Sophraea pushed back her blankets, slid out of bed, and padded across the cold floor to the window. Having latched the window tight earlier, she now had to wrestle with the bolt. Shoving hard against the casement, she finally banged it open and thrust the window wide. The wind caught it and slammed it hard against the outside wall to the ominous sound of cracking glass.

Sophraea decided she'd blame all damage on the storm. Leaning all the way out of her bedroom window, she could see the same strange light swirling along the boundary wall that separated the courtyard of Dead End House from the City of the Dead. The ball of light seemed to hesitate and then stop in one spot. In the dark, Sophraea wasn't sure but she thought that it might be a little farther along the path to the Deepwinter tomb and not quite at the family gate.

The light continued to bob in one place and then suddenly flashed brighter. Leaning so far out the window that she was forced to grab the edge of the window frame to keep her balance, Sophraea peered into the rain and the wind. She thought she saw another light, more yellow and dimmer than the first one, and this light was on the Dead End House side of the wall.

The sound of a woman sobbing faded away or maybe it was only the wind still murmuring in the gables. But Sophraea heard something else, a scraping sound, like an iron file on a steel lock, coming from the courtyard.

"Thieves!" she exclaimed. Thieves were trying to steal into the workshops. It had been years since anyone had been so foolish, but there was always some idiot adventurer attracted by tales of the stockpiles of materials that the Carvers kept in their workshops.

Not even pausing to grab her slippers, Sophraea flew down the stairs, banging on the doors at every landing, screaming at the top of her lungs, "Up the house! Thieves! Thieves!"

Behind her, the rumble of regular snoring was replaced by snorts and grunts and deep bass cries of "Waaa . . . What?" and, from her aunts and mother, "Get up! Get up! Roll over so I can get out of bed, man!"

Tripping over one of her brother's mallets left in the hallway, Sophraea hopped on one foot for a moment, waiting for the throbbing of her stubbed toe to subside. On the ground level, she paused at the door leading into the courtyard. Behind her, but still a couple of floors above her head, she heard the thump of big bare feet hitting the floorboards and more shouts of "Aarrgh, that's cold!"

She eased open the door. The wind blew the rain from the outside to the inside, splattering across her cold toes and making her think longingly of her warm fur slippers five flights of winding stairs above her.

In the yard, a dark shape was crouched over the lock on the door of Astute's workshop. A lantern sat on the cobblestones next to him, creating a small pool of amber light in the middle of the dark courtyard.

Seeing it was only one man, Sophraea grabbed the abandoned mallet and snuck across the courtyard. The thief was trying to pick the lock open with an iron file, obviously unfamiliar with the complexity of the locks built by Uncle Judicious to foil tomb robbers and other adventurers. Of course, the workshop lock was only an early model, but it still would take more dexterity and skill than displayed by the man worrying it with a bent file. The thief sniffed and licked his lips, a small growl escaping from his throat as the file slipped out of the lock.

Sophraea raised the mallet high and brought it down with a smash on the man's head.

Being considerably shorter than the thief, Sophraea's aim was a little off and she just caught him between the neck and shoulder. The man gave out a tremendous howl. Another pair of masked bravadoes appeared in the courtyard, sliding in the public gate from where they had been keeping watch. The customer bell started to clang but one of the men reached high and ripped it out of the wall. Suddenly faced with three very large and masked bullies, Sophraea let out a screech of her own.

She was answered from inside the house by a dozen deep yells as the Carver men poured out the door in various states of nightwear and semi-dress. More than a few swore and skipped as their bare feet hit the slick cold cobblestones.

What ensued was hardly a fair fight. It was a dirty, sprawling, brawling kind of battle with lots of yelping and thumping and a couple of cries from younger Carvers of "It's me! Your brother! Get off, you idiot!"

Another masked man rushed in from the street-side gate. He dodged the Carver cousins and didn't seem inclined to fight. Instead, he grabbed at the arms of his comrades. "Come on, let's go!" he bleated. "He'll kill us if we get caught by the Watch."

Somewhere in the charging back and forth, the lantern got kicked over and then extinguished with a howl from Leaplow as he trod with bare feet across the burning wick.

Sophraea was carried out of the center of the fray, still kicking and screaming, by her uncle Sagacious. He dropped her on the front doorstep with a strong admonition, "Stay here, poppet, before one of us hits you by mistake."

Then Sagacious and his wife Catletrho rushed back into the fight. She wielded a broom, he swung his fists, and the bullies fled howling before them.

Later, the women claimed that the brooms had won the day, chasing the bullies out of the courtyard and down the street.

It was the boots, added the men, that let the bandits get away.

Almost all the Carvers had extremely bruised toes from where the bullies had stomped down on their bare feet and made their escape. Leaplow also had a fine burn on his instep which Myemaw later insisted on smearing with butter and binding with a big white bandage, much to his embarrassment.

But at the height of the fight, the family raced down the street in pursuit of the thieves, leaving Sophraea and Myemaw forgotten on the front doorstep.

"Huh," said Sophraea, who was still clutching Leaplow's old mallet. "I could have fought them off."

"Yes," answered Myemaw in her practical way, "but why bother when you've got so many tall relatives who are having so much fun."

Sophraea's grandmother stood in the doorway throughout the fight, well-wrapped in a warm woolen robe. She had lit a candle in the hallway so the open door was clearly visible if the family needed to retreat. Obviously prepared for anything, Myemaw carried her knitting bag looped over her arm, with the extra long steel needles sticking out of the top. Even more deadly than the needles was the black ball of yarn that Volponia had given Myemaw years ago. At Myemaw's command, the yarn ball could entangle a dozen rambunctious adolescents, or any robber, and drop them trussed to the ground.

As was the family's emergency plan, Myemaw guarded the door throughout the fight, ready to use the yarn and needles on any intruder who dared to invade the house.

"But they always set me out of the way," grumbled Sophraea.

"Only because they love you and because Reye yelled so much every time your brothers brought you home with a black eye or some other interesting scrape."

"Piffle," sighed Sophraea. "It's just because I am short. They all think I'm as fragile as Volponia's china ornaments. If I was taller, then I could be in fights and Mother would not fuss."

Myemaw did not argue. She just handed Sophraea her extra

slippers. "Brought them with me," said the old lady. "Figured that you would have forgotten to wear any."

With a grateful hug, Sophraea slipped the warm sheepskin slippers over her cold feet.

There were still yells and other noise on the other side of the wall bordering the street, but no one was left in the dark and silent courtyard.

"I'm going up to the kitchen," said Myemaw, apparently satisfied that Dead End House was no longer in immediate danger of invasion. "Everyone will be too excited to go to sleep when they get back. So I might as well stir up the soup pot and see if we have any wine to heat."

"I'll help you in a moment. But I want to check the graveyard gate and make sure it's latched and locked."

The old lady fetched a candle from the hall table and lit the wick from her own candle. She handed it to Sophraea. "Go on, but take that mallet with you too."

"Thank you for trusting me out on my own," her granddaughter replied.

With a smile wickedly reminiscent of her friend Volponia, Myemaw said, "I was always the shortest one until you came along, and it took a few years before those big Carvers learned exactly how well I could take care of myself and my family. You'll do just fine on your own. I've never doubted that. But don't do anything too rash. We only need one Leaplow in this family."

Sticking the mallet through the belt on her nightrobe, Sophraea sheltered the flickering flame of the candle with her curled palm as she stepped into the night wind.

As she walked to the graveyard gate, a memory niggled at her mind. There had been something familiar about the first thief, something about the way he sniffed the air. "He acted like that hairy doorjack of Stunk's," Sophraea said to herself.

But why the servants of such a rich man would bother stealing from a tradesman workshop, especially one filled with fine materials bought by their master, was a puzzle that Sophraea couldn't solve.

She found the graveside gate still locked. Peering through the bars, Sophraea could see no marks upon the mossy steps or the path revealed in the candlelight. The rain had stopped and the wind died down a little. Beyond her own small circle of light, the moon revealed a swirling white mist that clung to the bare black branches and blurred the edges of the tombs.

As she stared, Sophraea could make out pale shapes in the fog. But everyone saw shapes in the mist in Waterdeep. They were harmless mirages, nothing to worry about.

Except, one shape was a bit more solid than the others: a man carrying a lamp, that's what it looked like. A man in a broad-brimmed old-fashioned hat and long coat carrying a hooded lamp that only cast a dim light. A man leaning on a cane and looking directly at her.

Sophraea blew out the candle with a quick breath and drew back into the shadow of the wall.

The man lingered for a moment more, then walked away from the gate, following the path that led around the Deepwinter tomb and farther north into the City of the Dead. Another pale figure, glowing slightly around the edges, drifted through the fog and followed his dark shape away from the Dead End gate.

Sophraea put her hand on the latch, ready to unlock the gate and follow. But a strange chill touched her. Suddenly, she felt that it would be a very bad idea to go into the graveyard alone. She started to shrug off the foreboding when she remembered some of Leaplow's past misadventures. Those that the Carvers buried rarely bothered the family. Sometimes they even gave out a friendly warning or two, and only Leaplow was rash enough to ignore such signs.

As certain as she was that her brother would have bounded

down the steps with a shout and wildly waving fists, Sophraea knew someone or something was telling her to stay out of the City of the Dead. Dangerous magic was brewing on the other side of the wall, old shadows were stirring, and even a Carver should tread warily after dark in the graveyard.

"Find a wizard," Volponia had advised her. The old pirate knew what she was talking about, Sophraea decided. There was trouble simmering within the walls of the City of the Dead, magical trouble that would take more than a mallet and a pack of unruly relatives to quell.

FIVE

Sophraea was still mulling over the previous evening's events when her mother Reye thrust a shopping basket into her hands.

"With that midnight supper last night," said Reye, "we have nothing left in the house for tonight. See what you can find in the market. Take Leaplow if you need some help."

"I'd rather go by myself," said Sophraea, thinking she might cut down to Coffinmarch and call on Egetha. The woman wasn't the right type of wizard, at least according to Volponia, but she must know other magic-users in Waterdeep.

Reye started to protest, then shook her head. "I keep forgetting how old you are. You're right. It would probably be easier shopping without Leaplow. But keep . . ."

"My money hidden and don't talk to strangers!" Sophraea grinned at her mother.

"Go on, go on." Reye flapped her hands at her only daughter. "I obviously can't teach you anything."

Sophraea just laughed, pulling her second best cloak off the peg by the door. Outside a low dark sky threatened an eventual downpour. However, even though the chimney tops were lost in the clouds, the rain held off as Sophraea walked quickly to the market.

Once there, she found barrel after barrel filled with slightly soggy root vegetables. Winter storms kept the more distant traders away and the selection coming from nearby farms was the usual boring winter fare.

While bargaining with one vendor who at least had some greens that were supposed to be green, Sophraea heard a familiar voice behind her.

"I haven't the full price yet," said the lilting accents of Gustin Bone. "But give me just a little time and I can pay for the room all winter."

Peeking around a pile of dried fruits, Sophraea saw Gustin deep in conversation with the neighborhood silversmith.

"I get a good price for that room most seasons," said the man who was as round and heavy as one of his bowls. "Seeing as it opens onto the alley and there are no stairs."

"Certainly, you should charge more for such a prize," agreed Gustin, smoothing back his well-trimmed beard. "And I will be happy to pay once I get my little exhibition open."

"A spell-petrified hero," said the silversmith. "Can't say that I have ever heard of such a thing."

"Shh, shh." Gustin laid his finger to his lips with exaggerated caution. "Don't want the citizenry of Waterdeep to hear too much before we are ready."

"We?"

"Well, I'm thinking a small portion of the viewing fee should belong to you by rights; it being your room and all. Of course, in return, you might agree to a smaller deposit on the room. A little less now, as it were, for much more later."

The silversmith smiled that smile so often seen upon the streets of Waterdeep, the one that says "I know you're trying to get the best of me, but I'm sure that I can get the best of you."

Gustin returned the silversmith's smile with one equally as bland.

"Well, it's hard to rent a room in winter," said the silversmith finally. "And people will pay to see the oddest things, just for entertainment."

"I tell you, the ladies will weep with sympathy for such a brave paladin turned to stone in his prime," Gustin said. "And the gentlemen will pay to let them in to take a look. Especially when the gentlemen can comfort them afterward."

"Very well, I'll take what you have now and a portion of the fee later."

"Quite the best business decision that you've ever made."

In perfect accord, the two men nodded at each other, spat into their hands (at which Sophraea rolled her eyes in disgust), and shook upon the bargain.

His business successfully concluded, the satisfied Gustin went whistling past the outraged Sophraea. She swung her basket in front of him, knocking him hard in the stomach.

"Oof!" Gustin stopped abruptly. "Sophraea Carver. I didn't see you there. Do you need help carrying that basket home?"

His voice was still as cheerful as ever, but his face fell when Sophraea began to scold.

"You're a cheat!" she said to him. "My father is carving you that stone man. It was never any living hero. Spell-petrified paladin, I don't think so!"

Gustin dragged the sputtering Sophraea into a nearby alley.

"Hush," he said. "You don't understand."

"I understand very well," returned Sophraea. "You're just another adventurer trying to cheat a little coin out of our pockets. The ladies will weep . . . Well, they should if they waste their money on your foolishness."

"My foolishness is very harmless entertainment," retorted Gustin. "And they will come, especially after my hero walks through the market here, seeking to return to his family home."

"It's the silversmith's spare room!"

"I'll say that his family lived there many generations ago and he has spent all these long years seeking his way home, one last tiny spark of a living soul trapped inside the stone, driving him to his final resting place."

"Oh, that's terrible! Who is going to believe that?"

"Well, the citizens of Marsember, Arabel, and Daerlun, for a start," huffed Gustin. "It's how I make my living. Displaying the rare artifacts of a more magical time, before the Spellplague swept through the world. A tragic petrified hero always packs them in, especially after I get the chapbook printed telling about his great deeds and battles. A simple piece that can be bought on the way in or the way out."

"But my father is carving the statue now. How can you have done this in Marsember and those other places?"

"Different statue, obviously," said Gustin with exaggerated patience. "But the wagon tipped over on the way here, the statue broke, and pieces were never as interesting as a whole body. I have to say, what your father is doing is much more lifelike than my last hero."

"I still think it's a terrible cheat. And why would anyone pay to see such a thing?"

"It's the marching through the streets that usually does it, I tell you. I know you have more of a history here of walking statues, but in Cormyr, most folks are impressed with that kind of magic." He grinned at her, his humor obviously restored. His green eyes twinkled, inviting her to share the joke with him.

Flabbergasted by his unrepentant attitude, Sophraea just fumed for a moment. Then she spun on her heel. "I'm going to tell my father," she said as she started out of the alley.

"No, wait." Gustin grabbed at her arm and pulled her back.

"Hey, let her go!" Binn, the one-eyed butcher's boy, skidded into the alley, aiming a wild punch at Gustin. The young man ducked. Binn threw his delivery aside to go after him.

Sophraea screeched as a greasy, bloody package splattered against her. She shoved the disgusting thing away, yelling at Binn, "Don't. I can take care of myself."

The butcher's boy was too caught up in his heroics to pay any attention to the maiden that he thought he was rescuing. He swung another punch at Gustin, who being a good head and shoulders taller than the lad, just leaned out of the way.

Sophraea pinched Binn's arm, hard, to make him listen.

"Ouch!" The boy rubbed the bruise on his upper arm. "That hurt, Sophraea."

"Serves you right for not listening to the lady." Gustin had retreated strategically behind Sophraea only to let out his own yelp when her elbow poked back into him.

"Both of you just stop it," she stated firmly. "Binn, it was very nice of you to defend me. But I need to talk to this man. Alone."

"You're sure you don't want me to fetch some of your brothers?" asked Binn, staring with malice at Gustin.

"No!" said Gustin and Sophraea together.

Binn picked up his package of meat, dusted it off with one casual slap against his leg, and left.

"I'm not sure that I'd eat anything that came from that butcher," mused Gustin.

"We don't," said Sophraea. "We get our meat two streets over."

"That's a relief."

"Not that you'll be eating any of it," said Sophraea firmly.

"I'm not invited to supper?" Gustin grinned at her. "Even after I defended you from that homicidal butcher's boy?"

"You didn't defend me. I defended you."

"Well, I was just getting ready to . . ."

"And I'm still going to tell my father about the trick that you're planning with that statue. He's a very honest man and I'm sure that he won't approve."

"Please don't do that." Gustin looked quite crestfallen. "He might stop working on it."

"But you can't expect us to help you trick people out of their money," said Sophraea stepping out of the alley and back into the bustle of the market.

"It's not easy being a wizard these days," Gustin pleaded as he followed her out of the market. "There's just not as much money in magic as there used to be! I need that statue."

Sophraea paused in her angry march down the street. She gave Gustin a straight stare, ignoring the people pushing around them. "Are you a good wizard?" she asked.

"Better than some, worse than others." Gustin paused, a suspicious look dampening his grin. "Why do you ask?"

"I could use a wizard," answered Sophraea with a rather nasty smile.

SIX

Gustin Bone absolutely refused to go into the City of the Dead at night.

"I am not suicidal," he told Sophraea, "and, even in the hinterlands, the tales of the strange haunts occupying Waterdeep's largest graveyard are well-known."

"Nonsense. It's not like that anymore," Sophraea said, with more confidence than she felt. After all, something strange was stirring in the graveyard and, even though she was a Carver, she'd rather not be stumbling around the tombs in the dark. "But we can go in daylight if you prefer."

Not wishing to explain her mild blackmail of the wizard to her family, Sophraea arranged to meet Gustin two days later at the Coffinmarch gate, the largest and most public of all the gates into the City of the Dead. She arrived well before he ambled into view. Nobody paid any attention to the short girl impatiently tapping her toe against the cobblestone.

Sophraea fidgeted in place, fussing with the linen cloth covering the contents of her shopping basket. As always, they were out of something needed at Dead End House. That day, it was dried fruit for a sweet loaf that Reye wanted to bake. Sophraea had stopped at the fruit seller's shop, certain that the old lady's careful measuring and weighing of the contents would make her late.

Instead, she was on time and the wizard was missing.

Gustin strolled casually up the street, waving a cheerful greeting at her.

"You're here bright and eager and early to go ghost hunting," he said.

"Shh!" said Sophraea. "I don't want to give my business to the entire street. And, besides, I don't know that it was a ghost."

"Oh it has to be a ghost," replied Gustin, walking beside her to the gate. "Everyone visits the City of the Dead to see the ghosts, hunt for treasure in the tombs, and marvel at the monuments."

"Hunt for treasure! Where did you get such an odd idea?"

"It isn't true?" Gustin reached into his tunic and withdrew a small battered book. "I'm sure it says something in here about treasure in tombs . . ."

"Anyone caught looting in the graveyard would be severely punished by the City Watch," Sophraea said firmly.

"But if they weren't caught?"

Alarmed by this line of questions, Sophraea stopped in the middle of the walk, ignoring the exclamation of a fat dwarf who nearly trod on her heels. The dwarf sidestepped into the gutter and splashed past them. Sophraea shook her head severely at Gustin. "Don't even think about stealing from a tomb. There are other guardians besides the Watch!"

Gustin shrugged and then grinned at her. "I never liked stealing. It too often proves less rewarding than you'd think. Every time you take something, odds are that you'll end up cursed, pursued, or just plain unlucky."

"I thought you were a wizard, not a thief," said Sophraea, wondering if she should go strolling through the City of the Dead with this outrageous young man.

"Absolutely, I'm a wizard. But magic is not the most lucrative of careers, at least not for me. I like to eat every day, several times a day if I can," said the tall and very thin Gustin Bone.

"So you tell lies about stone statues?"

"I give people an entertaining story and if they choose to give me coin in return, I'm happy to have it. Nobody is hurt by the exchange and I can pay for my meals."

A true child of Waterdeep, Sophraea couldn't argue too much with Gustin's desire for gold in his purse. Fortunes rose and fell all around them, as certain as the waves in the harbor, and many in Waterdeep did not hesitate to do real harm to others in their pursuit of wealth. In comparison, Gustin Bone's threat to the citizens' purses was rather mild.

The usual winter drizzle limited the number of people wanting to explore the pathways inside the City of the Dead. Even the members of the Watch on guard had retreated as far under the wall's overhang as they could and still remain at their posts. All of them were well-wrapped in their cloaks against the cold.

"There are better places to take your girl," said the tallest one with a wink at Gustin.

"Drier," mumbled the shorter fellow trying to huddle deeper into his cloak.

"I wouldn't give much for a man who took me walking in such a gloomy place," added the woman, who looked at Sophraea with sympathy.

With an indignant sputter, Sophraea started to explain that she wasn't out walking with the wizard, at least not in the romantic sense of the word. Gustin just tucked her arm through his, smiled sweetly at all three Watch members, and said, "Well, I thought about a stroll through the Sea Ward, but you know the ladies. Some of them find monuments quite moving."

"I never said any such . . ." But Gustin dragged her quickly away from the Watch.

"Do you want them trailing after us?"

"No, of course not."

"Then smile at them all and come along."

After a turn in the path hid them from the Watch, Sophraea

reclaimed her hand. Tucking it firmly through the handle of her shopping basket, she said, "We need to go north. I saw the light first there. Somewhere near the old noble tombs."

"Old nobles?"

"The families who were buried inside the walls. Only the oldest nobility kept their monuments on the grounds. The rest were moved long ago, and anyone who dies now, unless they belong to one of the old noble families, is buried in the newer sites."

"I thought there was only one graveyard in Waterdeep."

"Within the walls, yes. But we use the portals to go to the others like Coinscoffin or the Hall of Heroes. A lot of the richer, older families have small markers, a statue or a plaque, for their private portals to their own gravesites."

"I'm sorry," said Gustin, "but did you say portals?"

"Certainly."

"Real portals, little pools of magic that move you from one place to another?"

"Of course, how else would they manage it?"

"It really is a city of wonders," whistled Gustin. "The guidebook didn't lie."

"Don't they have portals to move bodies wherever you come from?" Like most who were born in Waterdeep, Sophraea had never thought much about how others lived outside the city. Although, if she did think about it, she would be forced to express a certain conviction that they didn't live half as well organized as those fortunate enough to dwell in Waterdeep.

"I've heard talk, everybody has heard stories about portals, of course, but people don't just use them for . . . well . . . for everyday business."

Sophraea pondered this for less than a moment. "But what would you use them for?"

"Descending into demon realms, visiting the gods in their

palaces, that sort of thing. Not carting coffins to their final resting place."

"Why would you want to go to a demon realm?" She couldn't see the sense in that. Demons were supposed to be unfriendly creatures with unpleasant habits.

"I didn't say that I did."

"Well, the City of the Dead's portals go to very specific places," said Sophraea resolutely. "It's all down in the family's ledger. I can show you if you want."

They rounded another monument, one carved with a frieze of flowers with tightly furled petals. Sophraea paused to trace the stone petals with one hand. "That's one of Fidelity's carvings," she said to Gustin. "He was my great-grandfather. A flower still in bud meant a youth had died, one fully in bloom indicated a mature person."

"And for the really elderly, did he do a bare twig?"

Sophraea giggled and shook her head. "No, a sprig of evergreen, usually, or one of the herbs that grant long life."

"And do all the carvings have a message?"

"Most do. But the meanings change with the generations. That's why we keep the ledger, so we remember why a family asked for a particular decoration and who carved it. And you should avoid tombs like that." She pointed out a grave marker that was set flush into the ground. Above it, a cage of iron was mounted, with the bars sinking into the earth.

"Why?"

"It's a dead safe," explained Sophraea. "Judicious came up with the design. It keeps the restless ones from leaving their graves and roaming through the City."

"Do corpses walk much around here?" Gustin glanced over his shoulder. They were the only ones on the path, surrounded completely by monuments.

"Not as much as they used to. But a particularly unquiet grave sometimes needs something extra like that. Most of the dead safes aren't within these walls, but out at the other graveyards."

As they walked on, the pathways became more overgrown. While not derelict, the tombs were obviously smaller and less visibly kept up than the more important public monuments in the southern part of the City of the Dead.

When Sophraea made a turn to the left, she told Gustin, "This should cut through to the place where I first saw the light."

When Gustin questioned Sophraea about her sense of direction, she realized that he didn't know about the family talent.

"All the Carvers can just do that," she finally said, "those of us born into the family always know where we are in the City of the Dead. Some of the aunts and sister-in-laws seem to have the talent rub off on them too. Perhaps it comes from working here all the time."

"But you don't work in the family business. You're a dressmaker or will be soon."

"Odd, isn't it? Maybe it is because I was born a Carver. Anyway, we just can't get lost inside the City of the Dead," she told him.

Skirting around a large and rather foreboding marble tomb, the roof overhung with grim gargoyles carved from dark red granite, they came upon a memorial statue of a woman in full armor, weeping into her hands. Sophraea stared into the little basin of clear water at the statue's feet. An old memory stirred. "I know this place," she said.

The long-legged wizard twisted around. "I swear that bush over there moved," he said.

"Don't be ridiculous."

"No, it moved, it changed position."

"What?"

Gustin cocked his head to one side. "Interesting. See, it was all bunched up there. Now it's longer, with a pointy bit at the very end over there. Sophraea?"

"Hmm?" She knew, in that strange way that she'd always known exactly where she was in the City of the Dead, that they were too far south of the place where she had first seen the light. That was more north and west of their present location, near that small tomb where she first met Lord Adarbrent. "Brick and mortar," said Sophraea out loud, fixing the location in her mind. "With a bronze door."

"Sophraea," Gustin sounded much more insistent. "Do you see shapes in bushes?"

"What are you talking about?

"Shapes in bushes, like you see shapes in clouds?"

"I don't know. Sometimes you see faces in the shrubbery here, shadows of things that have gone. Ignore it."

"No, I mean that bush really looks like a tail, a big long twitching tail and that bit . . . that round big bit . . . that looks like a hind leg ending in a large clawed foot."

Sophraea glanced over her shoulder at the dark green hedge surrounding a round memorial, a simple pillar polished and carved to look like a storm-blasted tree. The hedge obscured the carving, but Sophraea pushed aside the leaves to look at details, she could see the stone cut in the shape of bark and broken branches protruding from the trunk.

"This is really old, probably one of Fidelity's, for somebody famous, I just don't remember the name," she said to Gustin, circling the hedge to find an opening. When she came to an open place, she crossed the winter-browned lawn to examine the stone tree more closely. A druid, she thought, the family used to carve tombstones like this for druids but there weren't many inside the graveyard walls.

"Sophraea, I think the bush is moving again," said Gustin.

"It's just a hedge, they used to plant hedges like this around certain gravesites, mostly to keep people from getting too close," said Sophraea, moving closer to take a better look. Moss covered a metal plaque set halfway up the trunk of the stone tree.

"I swear that bit looks like a snout, a dragon's snout," said Gustin.

"Where?"

"That bit hanging over your head."

Sophraea looked up. The wizard was right. The long leafy branches overhanging her head looked amazingly like a long nose. Whiffs of mist clung to the branches, giving the impression of smoke curling up from a dragon's nostrils. Smooth, curved thorns resembled fangs. The longer she stared, the more teeth seemed to appear, rather as if a large mouth was opening wide above her head.

"Sophraea!" Gustin yelled. The wizard rushed forward, only to be swatted aside by the twiggy spikes of the creature's tail.

Sophraea leaped away from the hedge as the giant jaw snapped closed above her. As she stumbled backward, a leafy paw sprang out and caught the edge of her cloak. She tripped and fell. The shrubbery pounced on her like a large cat on a very small mouse.

SEVEN

Sophraea squirmed under the leafy paw holding her effortlessly down. The pressure was firm on her back but not painful. She pushed her hands into the muddy ground and shoved back. Twigs and branches curled around her, flipping her over effortlessly.

Sophraea blinked at the long and definitely draconic face looming above her. "Let me up!" she commanded.

The creature curled up its long neck and twisted its head to one side. Large and leafy ears waggled back and forth. Sophraea found herself staring into a bright red berry eye.

"Go on," she said in as firm a voice as possible when sprawled on the ground and pinned down by a bush. "Get off me!" The eye blinked but the paw did not shift and she was held fast by the creature. "Please!" The nostrils twitched and the head dropped. Long slender vines sprouting on either side of its mouth tickled under her chin.

"Oh, how perfectly ridiculous," said Sophraea, recognizing this gesture as something similar to the way that the baker's dog begged to have its ears scratched.

"You're a very nice bush, a good shrub," she said. "Now, get off of me!"

The creature rustled its leaves in a pleased manner but kept Sophraea pinned to the ground.

Out of the corner of her eye, Sophraea saw Gustin stalking forward. Something burned between the loosely closed fingers of his hand. His eyes were blazing emeralds under his long black lashes.

"Don't set it on fire!" Sophraea yelled. She hated to think of this beautiful if inconvenient creature being destroyed.

"This should just sting a little," Gustin said, neatly leaping over another sweep of the long spiky tail. "But cover your face."

"No!" cried Sophraea.

"Stop!" the shout reverberated through the clearing. "Leave the guardian alone."

"Not if it keeps holding her," responded Gustin, lifting his arm to throw his spell.

"Stop! At once!" A tiny green-skinned man sprang forward, stabbing at Gustin's knee with a long thorn that he wielded like a sword. Although he only came up to the wizard's waist, this diminutive fighter obviously had no fear of the bigger man. He lunged again, attempting to stab Gustin.

The wizard yelled and jumped to one side, narrowly avoiding a skewered knee. Sophraea swatted her basket at the nose of the creature holding her down. "Bad bush!" she scolded, no longer willing to coax it. Gustin was under attack and needed her help.

The leafy head swung up. Sophraea's basket missed it and flew through the air to hit the little man in the back.

"Ouch!" he cried, tumbling to the ground. He dropped his sword, which Gustin scooped up and held high above the little man's head.

"By the vine and twisted bramble, I hate big people!" cried the small but ferocious warrior, kicking out at Gustin's ankles.

"Let her go!" Gustin dodged this way and that, trying to fend off the little man while Sophraea yelled encouragement from where she was trapped.

"Only if you promise not to hurt the guardian," huffed the little man.

"Absolutely. Certainly. Just let her go."

The little man whistled three notes in a descending trill, more like a birdsong than any language, and the leafy paw lifted from Sophraea.

With a sigh of relief, the girl scrambled up, grabbing her basket and shaking the worst of the mud off her skirt. Around her, she could feel that heavy silence that meant somebody or more likely several souls were listening hard. The usual almost unnoticeable whispers were gone.

"Give him back his sword," she gestured at Gustin. "Quickly." Out of the corner of her eye, Sophraea noted that the stone hand of the warrior woman had shifted slightly, so she was no longer weeping but peeping at the small group assembled before her.

"I beg your pardon? And have this mite hamstring me?"

"I am a guardian of the tomb," declared the little man.

"You heard him, they are guardians." She turned to the small warrior. Now that she wasn't lying under a bush, she could see that he was clothed from head to toe in dark green leaves, overlapping each other in the same manner as a warrior might wear armor. Brambles curled around his wrists and waist as further protection. With his green skin and dark brown hair, he blended perfectly into the shrubbery around them.

"I apologize, I should have known better than to go so close to that monument. Have you been guarding it long?" Sophraea asked.

"You're a Carver, aren't you?" The little man retrieved his thorn sword from Gustin. He made quite a flourish as he sheathed it by his side. "One of Fidelity's?"

"Great-granddaughter."

"Really. Fidelity was the last one that I spoke to, but that has been more than a few seasons. So Fidelity's great-granddaughter? A short one like you. Who'd have thought it?" The little man pointed a thumb at Gustin. "And who's the long shanks? He's too skinny to be a Carver and your line never ran to magic."

"I've either been insulted or complimented," observed Gustin.

"His name is Gustin Bone. And yours?" asked Sophraea, ignoring the wizard.

"Briarsting."

Sophraea walked up to the leafy creature that had retreated to curl around the monument. "It's a topiary dragon," she told Gustin, gently stroking the quivering long branches that served as the creature's whiskers. "I thought these were all destroyed long ago."

"This one is the last," admitted Briarsting. "We used be a full Honor Garden, a complete thirteen of petals, thorns, and topiary beasts. But now there's just this old boy and myself."

"Do you know what he is talking about?" Gustin asked Sophraea.

"Some tombs, important ones, have guardians. This one must have been very special, a memorial garden filled with more than just the usual shrubbery."

"She was a great hero," said Briarsting, looking at the stone tree that once marked the center of the Honor Garden. "And died in the defense of Waterdeep. But she was a druid too, and it was thought a living memorial was more fitting than an ordinary tomb. So we came, and the elves set such magic here as to give us both a task and good living."

"I'm sorry that we disturbed you," said Sophraea. "I didn't think that there was a topiary beast left in the City of the Dead."

The little man seemed mollified and even inclined to chat. "We don't have any visitors these days," he said. "Just the odd person wandering by and looking for something else."

"Have you seen any wizards here lately?" Sophraea was almost certain that the lights that she'd seen in the City of the Dead were signs of magic, although she couldn't imagine why a wizard would want to venture into the graveyard after dark. The dead tended to punish those who cast spells near their graves. And the Blackstaff took an even dimmer view of unauthorized magic in a place so prone to peril.

"Haven't seen any wizards where they shouldn't be. Other than him." The thorn pointed rather rudely at Gustin, who made a face back at the little man.

Sophraea settled herself comfortably on a memorial bench set near the topiary dragon. She rummaged through her basket, pulling out a little of the dried fruits to share with both Briarsting and Gustin. "I've been seeing a light in the City of the Dead, usually in the middle of the night. Perhaps it's the dragon or another guardian."

"It's not us," Briarsting said. "He doesn't glow in the dark and I don't light fires near him. Too many dry leaves this time of year." The dragon sat back on its haunches and waggled its ears as if it knew they were talking about it.

"How about ghosts?" asked Gustin.

"They don't usually glow that brightly," started Sophraea only to be interrupted by Briarsting.

"It might be one of the more substantial dead," said the thorn. "Two tombs were opened recently. The remains were removed to other parts of the graveyard. And the dead can take offense at such actions. Especially if the removal is being done by amateurs."

"Amateurs?" Sophraea asked. "If a family requests a removal, it's usually us or one of the other funerary families."

"Why would anyone move coffins and urns?" asked Gustin, pinching a little more of the dried fruits and nuts out of Sophraea's basket.

"To make room," said Sophraea, with the certainty of one raised in the funeral business. "The old tombs are all full. Sometimes, when a new family member dies, somebody has to be . . . well . . . shifted to another location."

"First come, first removed. Last come, last interred," joked Gustin.

"It's not something that is done lightly!" Sophraea said. "You wouldn't believe the arguments that some families get into about who should go and who should stay. And if the dead decide to get involved in the decision, then it can be a real quarrel."

"The dead do that?" Gustin paused, a handful of fruit halfway to his mouth, and looked over his shoulder at the seemingly peaceful tombs.

"Sometimes, the dead want to travel," Briarsting informed him. "Sometimes they don't. But I don't think it was anything like that. With those kinds of removals, the difficult kinds, you get Carvers, for one thing, supervising the opening and the closing. And I didn't see any of your lot around."

"No, we haven't done anything like that for ages," Sophraea began.

"Didn't a Carver open up something in the south end last spring?" asked Briarsting.

"Leaplow," sighed Sophraea. "That was not official. And that's been all properly sealed since." Then she remembered the fat Rampage Stunk. "There's a client now who'd like a couple of tombs opened, but nobody has started any work yet."

"Didn't think I'd seen your lot around here. Where there's Carvers, there's always a nice funeral afterward, with the new resident being laid to rest and all, everything done just right," concluded the thorn, snatching the last of the fruit out of the basket before Gustin could get to it.

Sophraea resigned herself to stopping at the fruit seller's place on the way home.

"Still, there have been workmen nearby," Briarsting said, settling back on the bench. "Amateurs. Clearing out a tomb, like I said."

"Which tombs were opened?" Sophraea asked.

"Markarl and Vesham."

"Those certainly are Carver-built tombs. Old ones too. Both are down in the ledger. A bit north and east of our gate,"

Sophraea said. "That would be close to where I saw that light the first time."

"They're working there right now," said Briarsting.

"Then we should go take a look," Sophraea said to Gustin. "I don't understand why Father or one of my uncles hasn't reported this to the Watch. They know it's not safe to trespass here. There're laws for a reason. And only Carvers should work on Carver tombs."

The bronze door on the Markarl tomb was locked tight but the Vesham tomb stood wide open.

Two burly men wrestled a marble urn through the door with grunts and some groans. The piece was heavy and the wide curling handles had to be angled precisely to fit through the door.

"Smash it into pieces," grumbled one man. "That would make it easier to clean out!"

Sophraea started forward to stop such vandalism, but the topiary dragon caught her skirt on its thorny teeth and dragged her behind the evergreen hedge that marked the boundary of the plot nearest to Mairgrave.

"What are you doing?" she scolded the bushy beast.

"Shh," said Briarsting, laying one green finger against his lips. "It's the City Watch."

Gustin, who was almost bent double to hide behind the low hedge, added, "The little man says that the Watch has been coming by on regular patrols and they know all about those tombs being open."

"Well, they can't approve of this," Sophraea stated firmly. She popped up to peer over the branches at a trio of sturdy men in armor rounding the corner. Two were tall and rather young, but the third was an older man with a huge salt-and-pepper mustache clearly visible beneath his helmet. She waited for outcries and the scuffle that usually occurred when thieves clashed with Waterdeep's defenders.

Instead, to her surprise, one of the men hauling on the urn simply said, "Oh, you're back. Give us a hand then. It's heavy."

"Shift it yourself," replied the mustached Watchman with a frown. "We're not here to help you. We're only here to make sure that you do not take more than you are allowed. And that you take proper care of what you remove."

"Like we want an enormous stone vase full of old ashes." With another grunt and shove, the workmen finally freed the urn from where it was caught in the doorframe. They staggered onto the path and set it down with a thump.

"Careful," warned one of the younger Watchmen. "Any damage will earn you a fine. That's been explained to your employer."

"Not even a nick," replied the insolent worker.

"That can't be right," said Sophraea, practically up on tiptoe to see clearly over the hedge, despite the combined tug on her skirts from the skulking Gustin and Briarsting.

The youngest Watchman saw her bobbing up and down behind the hedge, trying to pull free her skirt from her companions. "You, girl, what are you doing there?" he challenged her.

With a last firm jerk to set herself loose, Sophraea stood straight. "I'm Sophraea Carver," she said. "I was just showing my friend some of the tombs my family worked on." She grabbed Gustin's collar and hauled him upright beside her.

"Amazing detail, even on the feet of that memorial bench," the wizard added smoothly, even as he twisted out of her grip. Sophraea stepped out from behind the hedge in front of the Watch.

"I didn't know Carvers came so small and cute," said the youngest man, ignoring Gustin following her.

"She's Leaplow's sister," hissed another guard to his companion. "The one that Kair tried to flirt with."

The impending grin on the first guard's face faded and his look grew decidedly blank. "Oh, well, then, we wouldn't want to delay you on your business," he said to Sophraea. "Give our best to your brothers."

"And your cousins," added the second young man. "To say nothing of your uncles."

"Do I know any of you?" Sophraea asked the Watchmen.

"No, but you let our friend Kair carry your basket home from the market," said the older one with a large bushy mustache.

Sophraea had a vague memory of a nice Watchman who once walked her home, only to be met at the door by Leaplow and Runewright. They'd probably shown him a shortcut through the City of the Dead, she decided with a sigh.

"Do you know my brothers?" she asked, just to be sure.

"We've had a few wrestling matches with Leaplow," answered the youngest Watchman, rubbing his neck at the memory, "and those twins who go around with him."

"Bentnor and Cadriffle," Sophraea supplied. "They're my cousins."

"That's them," the youngest one confirmed with a wince of remembered pain.

"Cleaned up a few taverns behind your brothers and your cousins too," added the leader of the group.

"Can't mistake a place that the Carvers have passed through," chimed in the third.

"Ah," Sophraea said. "You do know my family."

"So he's a friend of yours?" asked the youngest Watchman, finally nodding at Gustin.

"I'm new to Waterdeep," Gustin said, flourishing the small book that he removed from his tunic's upper pocket. "Sophraea very kindly offered to show me some of the antiquities of this graveyard. I'm very interested in antiquities, being in possession of a very fine but unusual statue . . ."

His story trailed off after a sharp poke from Sophraea.

"Well, isn't he the brave one," whispered one Watchman to his companion. "At least they won't have to take him far to do a walk through the graveyard."

"I'm sorry?" said Gustin.

"Ignore them," said Sophraea, not wanting to go any further into that discussion.

"Hoi!" yelled one of the forgotten workmen. "You lot coming with us or staying here to chitchat with the skirt?"

The oldest Watchman turned and directed a stern frown at the men waiting for them. "Get on with your business. We'll be right behind you."

"Should they be doing that?" asked Sophraea, watching the workmen stagger away with the memorial urn.

"They have permission," said the oldest Watchman. He gave a curt order to the younger men who seemed to be inclined to stay and chat with Gustin about the girl that was standing next to him and her ridiculously large number of male relatives. The two younger watchmen gave Gustin sympathetic punches on the shoulder as they bid him farewell.

"But should they be doing that?" Sophraea repeated to their retreating backs. A chill breeze touched her cheek. Her sense of direction in the City of the Dead seemed to swell and expand, almost as if she could see the whole City from above. In that odd vision, the pools of shadow that marked the doorways into ancient tombs seemed blacker than ever before. There was a disapproving stillness, an echo of emptiness that muffled her hearing. And something more, a cold and growing anger that was spreading through the City, a fury barely contained, that burned like ice laid across her fast beating heart.

"Sophraea!" Gustin shook her shoulder lightly. "Sophraea, what's wrong?"

With a start, the girl came back to herself. "I don't know," she told him. "But it doesn't feel right here. It feels strange. Spooky."

"It is a graveyard," the young wizard pointed out. "It's the famous City of the Dead. Isn't it supposed to be haunted?"

"But it's never felt like that to me! Not to any Carver."

"Felt like what?"

"Threatening."

But she couldn't explain it better and finally gave up trying. Instead she led Gustin to the open doorway of the Vesham tomb. Inside, the niches, where the urns and caskets should have been displayed, were swept clean.

Outside, clear tracks in the mud showed the workmen had visited both tombs repeatedly. Equally solid bootprints on the edges of the main path bore witness to the City Watch's careful observation of the work.

But it took Sophraea two more circuits of the plot, trailed by the curious Gustin, to realize where she truly was.

"This is where Rampage Stunk plans to build his monument," said Sophraea slowly, staring at the two small tombs sitting close together.

"How do you know?" asked Gustin.

She pointed at the marker stakes surrounding both of the little tombs. "That's the shape of his colonnade. He's been talking about it forever with my father."

Gustin murmured some words that Sophraea didn't understand and sprinkled a little powder on the ground between the two tombs. The ground fizzled and sparked wherever the powder had landed.

"Somebody has been letting off spells close by," stated the wizard.

"Can you tell what they were doing?"

He shook his head. "My ritual just shows magic happened here. It might be something that happened a long time ago or just yesterday. And I can't tell what type of spell it was."

Further examination of the earth around the tombs showed some disturbance, odd bumps in the lawn nearest the little brick-and-mortar tomb.

"But I can make some guesses," said Gustin after getting on his hands and knees in the wet dirt. "This looks like something happened underneath here."

"Underneath?" Sophraea stared at the ground between her boots. In her head, she was paging through the family ledger, trying to remember what tunnels would run under this section of the City of the Dead.

"A magical explosion?" speculated the lanky wizard. He stood up and beat the mud off his knees. "The ground was definitely pushed up from below."

"Rodents? Lizards?" Briarsting ventured. "Anything can be digging down there."

"No," said Sophraea, turning about to take a hard look at the close packed tombs on every side. "Not here. Spells would have been laid down when these tombs were built to keep out any vermin."

"Well, then," said Gustin, "that's the magic that my spell detected."

"No," Sophraea said with a shiver, remembering the icy anger she felt near the empty tomb, "I think you were right the first time. Something is happening. Something new. Something underground."

With one final pat on the topiary dragon's nose, Sophraea and Gustin took their leave of Briarsting. The thorn promised to come to the Dead End gate if he heard or saw any more unusual activity in the City.

"It will be good to be on patrol again," the little man said to Sophraea. "It gets a bit lonely out here in the winter with only the Walking Corpse wandering through on occasion."

"Lord Adarbrent?" asked Sophraea, remembering the last time

that the old nobleman disappeared down the pathways in the City of the Dead.

"He's got family close by," said Briarsting. "Big mausoleum, the Adarbrents have."

"Green marble, iron door, two memorial urns in the shape of sailing ships flanking the entrance, and the name picked out in gold leaf above, " said Sophraea, without even thinking.

"Bit unnerving how the Carvers all do that," remarked Briarsting to Gustin. The wizard nodded.

"Lord Adarbrent has been visiting us for years," said Sophraea. "He and my father discuss it all the time. One of the urns cracked during a heavy freeze and we replaced it. Lord Adarbrent wanted it to match the broken one exactly. He wants everything to always look exactly as it did."

"Not a man fond of change?" ventured Gustin as they walked away.

"No," said Sophraea, with a last wave to Briarsting and the topiary dragon. "He's very famous for his resistance to change. Lord Adarbrent is always marching around the city and muttering at people about the history and the importance of this bit of Waterdeep or that bit. Or telling them that there are forces out to change Waterdeep all together."

"Sounds like an absolute terror."

"Oh no," argued Sophraea. "He's always been very kind to me. When he notices that I'm there. Just, well, changes upset him."

As they walked along the path toward the Coffinmarch gate, Gustin kept up a steady stream of chatter, asking Sophraea about the nobles of Waterdeep. She barely heard him, she was so lost in her thoughts. Could someone really be rash enough to raise the dead with magic? For that was what she was sure she had felt. Not the usual comfortable wandering of one or two ambulatory spirits. No, this was something darker, angrier, rousing even those dead who wanted to be left alone.

But she didn't know exactly what was going on. She wanted to talk to her family but she did not know what to tell them. That she stood in the middle of the City of the Dead at the start of winter and felt cold? They'd pat her on the head and probably buy her a warmer cloak. Oh, and her mother would remind her to take one of her bigger brothers with her when she went walking through the graveyard at twilight.

She needed to know more. She needed to understand what she had felt so she could explain it properly. And, if it was magic, she needed a wizard to help her.

"So, if we want to tell what was really going on, we need to go under the tombs," mused Sophraea out loud.

"I'm not going to start digging up the ground here. Who knows what spooks that would raise!" responded Gustin with an exaggerated wave of his hands.

"There were other ways to get under the City of the Dead," countered Sophraea, "but we'll have to go through the house. There's no help for it. I will have to introduce you to my family."

"But I've already met your father and your uncle and at least a couple of other Carvers . . ." said Gustin as Sophraea steered him back toward the Coffinsmarch gate.

"That's not quite the same as being approved by my mother, and my aunts, and my grandmother," replied Sophraea, "but I can't take you through the house without somebody seeing you. We need to think of a good explanation of why you were visiting me other than courting."

Gustin's mouth dropped open. "Courting!"

"It's the first thing that they will assume," said the exasperated Sophraea. "I know. I'll say that I found out that you were a language teacher and I need to brush up on my . . . noble Cormyr . . . to get the job in the dressmaker's shop."

"But I don't know any noble language of Cormyr," protested Gustin. "I'm not even sure there is one."

"Just don't tell my family that!" said Sophraea.

"And just think of all the grief that you've been giving me about my statue," huffed Gustin, trotting alongside the girl. "At least I'm not telling fibs to my family!"

"No, you just tell them to the entire city at large!" she retorted. Sophraea blushed a little, because she really didn't approve of telling falsehoods, but anything was better than her mother, her aunts, and her grandmother making assumptions about a young man visiting her. And, what would be more painful for Gustin, telling those assumptions to the Carver men.

Sophraea convinced herself that this one small lie was just a strategy necessary to get to the bottom of the strange doings in the City of the Dead.

Still arguing, Sophraea and Gustin left the City of the Dead, completely missing the tall, thin, and very elderly man standing in the shadowed doorway of a green marble mausoleum.

Once they were gone, Lord Adarbrent walked quickly to the Mairgrave tomb. He unlocked the bronze door and addressed the pale ghost standing inside.

"It will be well," he promised in his slow and formal manner. "They know nothing about our revenge and they may even prove useful."

CHAPTER EIGHT

"I t's waterfowl stew again," said Reye, stirring the pot. "And there's more than enough in the pot for a guest."

When Sophraea pulled Gustin into the kitchen and stammered out her explanation of tutelage in exchange for the occasional meal, Reye only asked, "Does this mean you'll stay at Dead End House for a little longer?"

"Until the lessons are done," Sophraea hedged.

"That's good," her mother replied and Sophraea squirmed. Reye had said less about her plan to leave Dead End House than any other member of her family. But that was Reye. Unlike the rest of the family, she tended to keep her opinions to herself.

Sometimes Sophraea wondered if the whole family wasn't so set against her leaving to become a dressmaker, she might have reconsidered working in the Castle Ward. But she'd announced her decision on too many occasions to change her mind now. At least nobody was raising a fuss about Gustin.

Leaplow leaned over the stewpot to take a sniff. "Like everything else in Waterdeep, it's more a promise of fowl than anything else," her brother said, ducking a swat of Reye's spoon.

"Take a seat and wait your turn," scolded his mother.

"Tip what's left of the roast fowl into the soup, boil it until the bones float free, and then add vegetables and keep adding vegetables and water all winter," said Gustin, following Leaplow to peer in the pot. "As well as whatever herbs are handy and salt to taste."

At Sophraea's look of surprise, the wizard smiled. "We used to do it the same way where I grew up. We got our birds off the river or in the woods. Funny to smell it here though. I thought the food in Waterdeep would be more exotic."

"You think we all dine on dragon soup and roast cockatrice?" chuckled Myemaw as her hands flashed above the vegetables, sorting them out, chopping down with her sharp little knife, and then tipping the whole collection into the stewpot.

"In this guidebook that I have, one that was written here," began Gustin.

"You should never believe anything printed in Waterdeep." Sophraea's grandmother tapped her palm with the flat of the knife. "Most authors will tell incredibly outrageous lies to get you to part with your coin. Cut your gold out of your purse faster than any member of the thieves' guild."

Gustin sat on the nearest stool, thrusting his long legs under the broad table. Soup, bread, and assorted pickled vegetables were passed in heaping bowls up and down the line of Carvers.

"Outrageous or not, there are wonderful stories in my guide-book," he said to Myemaw. "I found it when I was small, in a stack of old paper that my uncle intended to use in the outhouse. Every chance I could get, I'd read that book. I just knew that Waterdeep was the city for me."

"Oh dear boy," chuckled Myemaw filling his bowl to almost overflowing, "the whole world thinks that."

Most of the men kept their noses in their meal, eating steadily, but Sophraea's uncle Judicious chatted with the latest addition to their dinner table.

"Been in Waterdeep long?" the older man asked Gustin.

The wizard shook his head and snagged the heel of a loaf off a nearby plate to crumble into his soup. "Just long enough to find lodgings and start a couple of small business ventures."

"I swear the city has more strangers in it than native-born," Judicious continued. "It's why I never felt the need to travel. Everyone always comes here. If I want to see all the world's folks, I just stroll down to the harbor."

"Actually, he never traveled because he could never carry away all those tools in his workshop," said Myemaw. "And Judicious would never leave any of his tools behind."

"I have the best locks and locksmith tools in Waterdeep," explained Judicious. "More than one of my designs for the mausoleums has been adopted by others for the finer villas and mansions in the North Ward."

"If you get him started on locks," warned Sophraea as she passed Gustin another plate of bread, "you'll be here until breakfast."

Gustin emptied the second plate as quickly as he had the first. "If the food is always as good as this, I'd be very content."

But, finally, even the wizard had to declare himself full.

"We should start our lessons," said Sophraea, piling up Gustin's soup bowl and bread plate to hand to her cousin Bentnor for washing. Bentnor passed it off to Cadriffle, who turned to pass it off to someone else, only to find the rest of the men already had slid out of the room. With an exasperated sigh, he headed for the tub of soapy water waiting in the corner of the kitchen.

"The smallest parlor should be empty," said Reye.

"That's a good idea," said Sophraea, not looking directly at her mother. "We'll go there."

Sophraea immediately pulled Gustin toward the back of the house. She pushed open one door and showed him the small, neat parlor that was almost never used in the winter. The family preferred the big common room off the kitchen during the coldest months, she explained to Gustin, as the heat from the two kitchen chimneys kept that room nicely warm. "As does having a dozen Carvers stuffed in there at any given time," she added.

"I've noticed your family tends to the large size," he replied.

"All except me and Myemaw," agreed Sophraea, crossing the

parlor to pull open the not-very-secret door built to look like a fireplace cupboard. A stack of candles sat on the table at the top of the twisty dark staircase leading down. Looking up at the wizard, Sophraea asked, "Can you keep track of time in your head?"

"Fairly well," replied Gustin.

"We can't be gone forever," warned Sophraea, lighting a candle and shoving it into a holder. "But there's always a lot of chatter and chores after a big meal. We should have time to get under the tomb if we hurry."

><==W==<

"So where does this stair go?" asked Gustin, following close behind Sophraea. Shadows cast by her candle flickered upon the wall beside him. Within two turns of the stair, a glance back over his shoulder showed the door to the neat little parlor was lost to view.

"To the lowest basement," she replied. "Step carefully, sometimes things get loose down here."

"Things?" said Gustin.

"You know, corpses that aren't quite settled in their coffins yet. Unusually large reptiles slipping in from the sewers," said Sophraea as she drew back the bolt of a door bound with three bands of iron. It swung open silently on well-oiled hinges. The air from the lower depths smelled drier than many dungeons that he had been in, but still had that tang that let him know they were heading underground.

"But the boys did a cleaning down here a few days ago," Sophraea continued, "all the way down the stairs to the bottom basement. Myemaw insisted."

"Did they find anything?" asked Gustin, trying to sound as nonchalant as her. One thing he had figured out on his first day in Waterdeep was to never show any surprise or astonishment to its citizens. Even though every step down the most ordinary street made him tighten his jaw muscles just to keep his mouth from dropping open at the sights and sounds of the city.

Look at their earlier walk through the City of the Dead. A functioning topiary spell, a casual conversation with a thorn about the possibility of the dead moving around on their own, and the sure signs of some major ritual or curse surrounding those two tombs. That was just in the north end of the graveyard, the area that his guidebook said was quiet and of little interest to travelers.

And look at the girl tripping down the stairs so lightly in front of him. None of what they had encountered had surprised her. Perhaps startled or more likely annoyed, especially when she landed under that topiary dragon's paw. But she'd remained completely calm in that Waterdhavian way that made him feel like he was twelve again and had just rolled off a farm wagon with hay still stuck to his hair.

"Mostly they cleaned out some rodent nests," she answered his question. "And a couple of lizards. But nothing too nasty."

Gustin reached into his tunic, tapping for a reassuring moment his guidebook to Waterdeep. But he didn't need the large spells and rituals hidden there. It was just a gloomy staircase leading into a basement stacked with coffins and corpses. Perhaps a few rodents or a lizard. Nothing to bother a well-traveled young wizard like himself. Sophraea wasn't the only one on this staircase who could exhibit an unruffled attitude.

A scrabbling of claws sounded overhead. A glance toward the ceiling revealed a flick of a scaled tail before whatever it was disappeared back into shadows.

"See," said Sophraea. "Just a lizard or two. You get them down at this level. They help keep down the bugs."

"I don't mind bugs," he said, shaking his wand out of his sleeve. He tapped one end against the back of his left hand and a small white flame sprang up. At least that allowed him to see his feet as they followed Sophraea round another bend in the stairs.

She stopped to unbolt another thick wooden door. "Last one between the stairs and the basement proper," Sophraea said.

"I keep forgetting this is so heavy," she added, pulling the massive door toward her. Gustin reached easily over her head and grabbed the door's edge to shove it open with his free hand.

They emerged in a dark cellar room, lit only by one guttering candle on a table near the door. Two men sat at the table, making loud slurping noises as they finished the last drops of something dished out of the iron kettle resting between them. Even in the dim light, neither could be mistaken for fully human. One had tentacles instead of hair and the other had scales instead of skin.

The big man with tentacles writhing around his head pushed back his chair, rising quickly as soon as he spotted them in the doorway. The smaller man, who resembled a two-legged fish, pursed open his mouth as he turned in his chair toward the girl, revealing a double-row of sharp pointy teeth.

The tentacled man hurried forward, his arms opened wide, a dripping fork in one hand.

Gustin grabbed the girl in front of him and, ignoring Sophraea's squeak of protest, pulled her behind him. He joggled her hand, causing her to drop her candle. The little flame winked out, leaving the basement full of shadows, the only light the single candle burning on the table.

The stranger's tentacles fanned out around his head, whipping back and forth like a snake about to strike. The one with two rows of teeth sprang out of his chair to follow his companion.

Gustin's hand flew up and the flame flared at the end of his wand.

Sophraea latched onto his wrist, shoving down his hand. "Wait," she cried as she had in the graveyard when she wanted to protect the topiary dragon.

He began to pull away but Sophraea shifted her grip, pushing at his wand to direct the flaming tip away from the man advancing toward them.

"Don't . . . be careful . . ." Gustin warned the girl.

Trying to take the wand out of Sophraea's grasp without hurting her, Gustin lost his own grip on it. In fact, as had happened once or twice before, he was sure that the cursed thing twisted deliberately under his fingers. With its usual spite, the wand spun out of his hand. Swearing under his breath, Gustin made a flailing grab for it. The flame detached itself from the end of the rod, rolled itself into a ball of sparks, and whizzed out of reach.

Sophraea squeaked as the ball of sparks sped past her nose. The strange little ball ricocheted off the wall, and bounced back over his head. He waved his arms wildly, trying to deflect it away from his hair, trying to call up a shield between them and the out-of-control ball of sparks as quickly as he could. The spluttering ball of light flew upward, colliding with the ceiling.

With a sharp crack, a chunk of plaster broke loose and fell from above, hitting him squarely on the top of his head.

His knees buckled and he fell back onto the sputtering Sophraea. Just like a farm boy falling off the barn roof, he thought a little incoherently as he tumbled into the girl that he had hoped to impress with his quick wits and magic.

There wasn't much of her but what there was cushioned parts of him nicely as they both landed on the hard cold stone floor. Still, she wasn't very long and Gustin cracked his chin on the top of her head and, then, the back of his head on the stones below them.

After one more breathless squeak underneath him, Sophraea

balled her hand into a tight little fist and punched his closest ear.

"Ouch," Gustin groaned. The girl might be tiny but she could hit hard.

"Get off me!" Sophraea cried.

And the big man with tentacles for hair lunged at Gustin.

NINE

For the second time that day, Sophraea found herself pinned to the ground by a large body. Gustin was a dead weight that wasn't actually dead. As a Carver, she knew the difference.

"Sophraea, Sophraea, are you all right?" She looked up into the concerned faces of the gravediggers Feeler and Fish. She hadn't expected them to be in the basement. Usually they went out after dinner for a drink in the Warrens.

Feeler grabbed Gustin's shoulder and rolled him off Sophraea. Fish reached down a scaled hand to help her to her feet. After a quick "thank you" to Fish, she bent over Gustin. He struggled to sit upright with his head between his knees. Muffled groans emitted from him with greater drama than she felt was necessary. After all, he'd hit her on the top of the head when he fell and she could feel that lump forming. And she had not punched him that hard. When she tipped his head back, he blinked at her, looking somewhat cross-eyed.

Squatting down beside them, Feeler patted Gustin's arms and legs. His tentacles waved around his head, a sure sign that the big man was a bit upset by all the magic that had been whirling through the basement. To Sophraea, however, he spoke in his usual mild deep tones, "Nothing broken. Perhaps a bruise or two in the morning. He'll be fine."

Relieved but unwilling to show it, Sophraea asked Gustin sharply, "What was all that about?"

"Why did you grab me?" he countered. "Don't ever do that again! That's dangerous!"

"You were attacking my friends."

"I was just trying to give you some light. You dropped the candle."

"What sort of light makes a hole in the ceiling!"

Gustin shook the plaster dust out of his brown curls, wincing a little at the movement. "It's a wand with several uses, that's what it is. But you can't break my concentration or I lose my grip on it."

"What kind of wizard are you?" she demanded.

"Fairly good, by all standards," replied Gustin evenly as he crawled around on his hands and knees, patting the floor in front of him. With a grunt of satisfaction, he located his lost wand, tucking it back up his sleeve. "But this little item isn't all that reliable. It likes to slip out of its user's hand."

"Then why do you have it?" Sophraea asked as she climbed to her feet.

"Payment for a job. Never take magic items from another wizard. The cheap ones always cheat by giving you trash," said the young wizard with casual condemnation of his profession. "That's why I prefer to make my money in other ways."

Aware of Feeler and Fish listening carefully to every word that Gustin was babbling, she stopped him before he could say more about his schemes and introduced the two gravediggers to him.

"So," said Gustin with a cheerful grin, as if he had not just knocked a hole in their ceiling, "you live down here?"

"People don't bother us here. It's quiet," said Feeler while Fish nodded and lit another candle. Fish rarely spoke in front of strangers, Sophraea knew, because of the odd lisp created by his two rows of teeth and split tongue.

"I am sorry about interrupting your supper," said Sophraea.

"Not to worry," said Feeler, "you're welcome any time."

"We just need to use your door," she explained.

"Your parents know you're going into the tunnels?"

Sophraea gave the type of a shrug that might be taken for a "yes" in dim light. Feeler appeared skeptical and Fish pursed his mouth in a disapproving frown.

"I'll watch out for her, saer," said Gustin.

To Sophraea's frustration, Feeler looked straight over her head at the wizard. "You wouldn't want to know how deep we could bury the body that harmed this child," he said.

"No, saer," said Gustin sincerely. "I'm sure I wouldn't."

"I am perfectly capable of taking care of myself," asserted Sophraea. Really, just because the gravediggers had given her rides on their shovels when she was a baby, that didn't mean that she couldn't protect herself now. "It's not like I haven't been in the tunnels before!"

"With a pack of your brothers and cousins," said Feeler. "Not alone. That's different."

"He is a wizard. With a wand," Sophraea pointed out because she had a feeling that would impress them more than her usual argument that she was fully grown and quite able to navigate the tunnels on her own. "And we're only going a short way. I just want to show him something and then we'll come right back."

With a heavy sigh, Feeler agreed. "But take our lantern with you. Candles blow out too easily."

"But there're lights in the tunnels." Sophraea picked up the lantern even as she protested.

"But that's magic," Feeler said. "And, as your young man pointed out, some magical items are not always reliable. I know you won't get lost, but there're things out there that you don't want to meet in total darkness. What if you stumble across those sewyrms everybody keeps seeing down here?"

Sophraea started to tell the gravediggers that Gustin wasn't her young man, but realized that would plunge her into even more lengthy explanations. Instead, she nipped quickly out of the door that Fish opened, promising that she and Gustin would return shortly and keep a sharp eye out for reptiles and other threats.

Gustin lingered in the doorway.

"Sewyrms?" Gustin said to Feeler.

The man held his two hands far apart, indicating the size from nose to tail tip. "Big ones," he replied. "Some say that there's even a great albino sewyrm, down in the darkest, deepest sewers, living off the garbage. That it's grown so big that it can't even move through the tunnels anymore."

Sophraea snorted. "That's just story! Albino seawrym in the sewers of Waterdeep. Like nobody has ever heard that one before!"

"Well," the wizard began. "I don't think that I've . . ."

She grabbed Gustin's sleeve and tugged him through the door.

"We're just going a little way," she said over his shoulder to Feeler. "Just beneath the graveyard. It will be dry as dust and twice as safe as above ground."

"Come back quickly," the gravedigger prompted.

"We will," Sophraea promised.

The door shut firmly behind them. Sophraea nodded in approval as she heard the latch click down. It would never do to leave Dead End House defenseless on the lowest level, a lesson drilled into her as soon as she started to beg her mother to be allowed to accompany her brothers through the tunnels leading from the basement to the upper streets of Waterdeep. And, although she would never admit it out loud, it was a little comforting to know that Feeler and Fish would wait by the door until they returned.

She gave a quick glance up to the dark outline of the door's watcher. One stony wing was folded halfway across its horned head and its bearded chin was tucked firmly into its shoulder.

"That has to be the ugliest statue that I've ever seen," remarked Gustin, holding the lantern a little higher to cast a light into the niche above the Dead End door.

Sophraea looked upon the ugly creature with affection. She could just make out the slightly notched left ear. Bentnor had jumped up on a bet with Leaplow to pat the watcher's paw. And, of course, once Bentnor did that, Cadriffle had to get high enough to tweak its nose. And once the twins had done that, Leaplow had to best them by twisting the left ear a bit askew. No wonder it kept its wing extended over its head after that!

She opened her mouth to explain the watcher to Gustin and then shook her head at her own foolishness. Such knowledge should only be shared with members of the family and the others who dwelled at Dead End House. No matter how friendly Gustin was, he could not be considered family.

"Come on," she said instead. "We don't have much time."

"So where exactly are we?" Gustin asked as Sophraea hurried down a short dark passageway.

"Into the old sewer tunnels, heading directly under the City of the Dead," she said. She paused for a moment, waiting for the special tug that signaled she was passing under the walls of the City of the Dead. "This is an access tunnel used mostly by the cellarers' and plumbers' guild. If you go the other way, it turns south toward Coffinmarch."

She went a few steps farther in and immediately knew exactly where they were.

"Good, there's the Deepwinter tomb," she glanced up but nothing could be seen in the lamplight except the dull masonry holding the earth above them. It was all instinct that guided her, but she was certain that they were directly below the big mausoleum.

If she closed her eyes, the tunnels around them disappeared. She could picture herself standing on the gravel path twisting through the rain-soaked shrubbery around the tomb's north corner.

"We'll need to turn at the next branching of the tunnels to

reach the spot that we want," she told Gustin, opening her eyes and looking up at the wizard.

"Are your eyes blue?" he asked her.

Surprised, Sophraea shook her head. "No, brown, like the rest of my family. Why do you ask?"

Gustin tilted his head to one side, staring at her. "It's gone now. But, just for a moment, there was this flash of blue."

"Trick of the light," Sophraea guessed, heading into the tunnel that led them past the Deepwinter tomb and deeper under the City of the Dead. "Everything always looks a bit strange down here."

"You use these tunnels much?" Gustin moved easily at her side, his long legs easily covering twice the ground as her shorter, quicker steps.

"We all do. Feeler and Fish the most, because it's the quickest way in and out of the graveyard, and many of the portals that they use are below ground these days. The rest of us use the tunnel to Coffinmarch for a shortcut if it's raining too hard to go by the upper streets. Lots of families have entrances in their basements that lead to these tunnels."

She didn't try to explain to him how she felt like she was walking in two places at the same time, one Sophraea in the City of the Dead above them, the other Sophraea in the tunnels below. It was a slightly disconnected, somewhat floaty feeling, but not altogether unpleasant.

As they rounded another turn, passing by a shadowed doorway, Gustin remarked, "I'm surprised they don't get more unwelcome visitors in their basements. This looks like the perfect arrangement for housebreakers."

"The underground doors are well guarded by stout locks and magic. Besides, we're under the graveyard here. That door just leads into the old Narfuth crypt. There's nothing there worth anything."

"Magical protections on the doors, really? I didn't feel anything in your basement."

"That's because you entered from above, as a friend of the family. The Doorwatcher would have known that and let you alone. Although"—a gleam of amused speculation lit Sophraea's dark eyes—"I suppose that could be why your spell rebounded so spectacularly on you."

"Can't wait to meet this Doorwatcher," said Gustin, but he sounded more intrigued than aggrieved.

"You already have," Sophraea started but then they rounded another corner. Huddled around a couple of torches, shadowy figures blocked the way. Gustin pulled Sophraea into an alcove and shuttered the lantern, leaving them in darkness.

"Best wait until they pass," Gustin whispered in Sophraea's ear, tickling her dark curls with his breath.

"Probably just some neighbors heading home from a party. The City of the Dead's gates would be locked by now and they are using these tunnels instead." But her explanation sounded weak to Sophraea. Most folks avoided going anywhere near the graveyard after nightfall, even underground. Something about how the group scurried together, hands clutching their dagger or sword hilts, and the constant glances back over their shoulders did not suggest a late evening party of revelers.

"I thought that halfling said that she would lead us to treasures," whined a slender man clad in black silk from head to heel. He passed close enough to where Sophraea and Gustin hid that they could hear the whisper of his trousers.

"Who would have thought her hands would be so cold," answered his female companion, a well-rigged fighter bristling with knives, sword, and even a short shield. Another tall man stalked at her side, well-armored and with a hint of orc in his scowling features.

The fourth man, more drably dressed than the others, stopped and stared back into the darkness. He looked straight at the alcove where Sophraea pressed back against Gustin. She held her breath. Gustin's hand tightened on her shoulder.

Then the swarthy bravo shrugged and turned to follow his companions, saying as he left that section of the tunnel, "Well, if there are not treasures to be had tonight, I'm for hot wine and a warm bed. Let's go."

The sounds of this odd quartet died away, leaving the tunnel empty and silent behind them.

Gustin eased out of the alcove, keeping a hand on Sophraea's shoulder to hold her back. He listened for a few cautious minutes and then unshuttered the lantern.

"So this is basically a highway for thieves as well as honest folk," he observed.

"I don't suppose the officials like it," said Sophraea with a shrug, "but you see worse on the streets above. Besides, thieves don't bother people like us." She made the last statement with more ferocity than veracity, but they were so close to the tomb that she couldn't bear to turn back. Something was pulling her, something like that odd sense of direction that she had within the City of the Dead, but stronger.

She knew she would find an answer just about . . . there.

Sophraea stopped so abruptly that Gustin nearly ran her over, flinging out one long arm to catch himself against the tunnel wall.

"What is it?" he said.

"The Markarl tomb," she said, "or just outside of it." With that queer double vision that had haunted her through the tunnels, she saw the little brick-and-mortar tomb that stood directly above them. But the always locked bronze door? Was it a little ajar?

"So now what?" Gustin raised the lantern, casting a wider circle of light. At the very edge of the yellow glow something glittered.

Sophraea darted forward, finding a tarnished gold shoe. She picked it up, holding it high so Gustin could also see it clearly in the lamplight.

It was very small and obviously made for a lady. Fashioned in a style popular long ago, the shoe's brocade fabric was badly frayed along the edges and the thin vellum soles decayed.

"Where do you think it came from?" she said out loud.

"A corpse," muttered Gustin.

She clutched the little shoe in one hand, reaching out her other hand to touch the walls. Solid stone met her hand, dewed with the usual dampness encountered in that part of the tunnels.

Sophraea continued poking around the edges of the muddy passageway, which smelled more like sewer than crypt, not that it was easy to tell the difference.

"I don't think there would be a body this deep," she said. "This is a storm drain, only full in worst rains, but they'd never risk a body washing out from here. That's why the tombs and portals are above. The water is supposed to drain down and then out."

"So somebody dropped it passing through. Or the water did carry it here? And, by the way, how hard was it raining today?" Gustin peered at the dank walls, as if expecting water to suddenly come pouring in.

"Not that hard." Sophraea shook her head at a newcomer's lack of knowledge of Waterdeep's precipitation. "Something like that would take a true downpour. Not that mizzle we're getting right now."

The passageway seemed even more shadowed and dank. A cold and clammy feeling settled with a shudder upon her bare hands and face. As they retraced their steps to Dead End House, Sophraea felt compelled to look back over her shoulder. The tunnel remained empty behind them.

She glanced at the wizard beside her. He seemed completely unconcerned by the shadows flickering along the walls that made her start and stare. Of course, he was a wizard, one of those adventurers who had roamed everywhere from what little he had told her. Sewer tunnels under a graveyard wouldn't bother him. And, she thought, raising her chin and holding her head a little higher, she wasn't worried either. He needn't think just because she was younger, and shorter, and had never been outside the walls of Waterdeep, that a few thieves passing them in the tunnels or some oddly shaped shadows swirling across the ceiling above them would frighten her.

Then she heard the soft exhalation, like a woman trying to muffle a cry.

"Do you hear something?" Sophraea whispered to Gustin, resisting the impulse to clutch at his arm.

"My teeth chattering," he answered back. "It's freezing cold all of a sudden."

The damp cold of the tunnels intensified. Sophraea felt like one of the Carver cats on the days that the wind blew from the north. Something was making her skin prickle and she fought an urge to whip around and stare again into the shadows. In the same odd double vision that let her see where they were in relationship to the City of the Dead, she thought she could see something following them out of the passages. At the very edge of her hearing, she heard something like the soft light footsteps of a woman. Sophraea was sure of it.

"Stop," she hissed at Gustin, tugging at the edge of his sleeve.

"Not here," he hissed back as they reached the intersection with three tunnels, the shortest passage leading to the Dead End door. "There's somebody ahead of us."

She heard a sob.

"No," Sophraea insisted, "there's somebody behind us."

They were directly below the Dead End gate. In her double vision, Sophraea could see the iron bars shake. The sound of a woman sobbing echoed in her head, somewhere above, somewhere behind. Her sense of direction gone dizzy, Sophraea tugged again at Gustin's sleeve.

"We need to stop."

"Not yet," said Gustin, grabbing Sophraea's hand and dragging her toward the Dead End door.

From the middle tunnel entrance burst the plainly dressed bravo who they had seen earlier. His sword was drawn. His expression was unpleasant.

"Stop!" cried the thief, unconsciously echoing Sophraea.

"Not likely!" yelled back Gustin, pulling Sophraea along at a clip of long legs that left her shorter strides nearly flying off the ground.

Over his shoulder, Gustin muttered a string of foreign words. Their pursuer faltered. Then with a growl like a wounded dragon, he pressed after them.

"That one never works on the run," gasped Gustin. "I've really got to stop trying it in situations like this."

"Are . . . you . . . often . . ." Sophraea panted.

"Yes. That's why I can talk and run. Keep going!"

They sprinted to the door, the burly fighter barreling behind them.

Sophraea and Gustin crashed into the door. Sophraea beat out the Carver's secret knock in rapid haste with her small fists, still clutching the old shoe.

"Hurry, hurry, hurry!" she whispered.

She could see their pursuer in her mind; imagine the slash of his sword's blade.

His outstretched hand brushed her shoulder.

Gustin swung around, his clenched fist crashing into the thief's face. That didn't stop their attacker. He fell back with a snarl, then lunged toward them, his sword slashing. Sophraea ducked, throwing herself against Gustin to knock him out of the way. As they fell sideways, the sword's blade hit the door at the height where her head had been.

She was sprawled against Gustin with her arms outspread. He tried to free his hands, caught between them. She struggled to get off him so he could use his wand.

Sophraea pushed her hand into Gustin's chest for leverage, then swung backward with her arm extended. She tried to close her fingers tightly around the lantern's handle, felt the jolt as it hit the thief. The lantern clattered to the floor.

This time the thief shrieked in pain. He wiped blood from his face and lunged toward her.

Sophraea screamed. Feeler and Fish flung open the door and Gustin tumbled inside the room. She fell toward their outstretched arms, almost reached them.

Seeing a tall man with writhing tentacles for hair and another with a double row of shark teeth, the thief hesitated. Then he saw the glitter of the gold shoe in Sophraea's out-flung hand.

The thief lunged at Sophraea, grasping her wrist and pulling her to him. Gustin, just as firmly anchored on the other wrist, pulled her toward the open door.

Feeling like the battered ball in one of her brothers' games, Sophraea let out a shriek higher than any since earliest childhood, when Myemaw had said "That child is small but she has champion lungs!"

All the men winced. Sophraea took advantage of the thief's momentary distraction to stamp hard on his instep with one pointed heel. He gasped and for a moment, froze with shock. Sophraea twisted around, turning as much as possible with the two men still hanging onto her wrists. A second kick, with her equally sturdy and pointed boot toe, caught the thief on the side of the knee, where his armor didn't cover the side of the tender joint.

The man let out a yell, much as Leaplow once did when a younger Sophraea had shown him the maneuver taught her by Cadriffle.

Dropping Sophraea's wrist, Gustin secured a firmer hold on her waist and lifted her away from the thief, even as the frustrated and furious man swung down his sword.

Feeler came flying out of the door to tackle the thief. The blade missed Gustin's head by a breath as he ducked and rolled away, but the pommel clipped his crown.

Sophraea and Gustin rolled together into the center of the basement.

The thief fought free of Feeler's grasp and sprinted away.

Once again sitting in a tangle of the wizard's long limbs on the basement floor, Sophraea found herself being examined in a concerned way by Feeler and Fish.

"Are you all right?" asked Feeler.

"Fine, fine," said Sophraea as she started to scramble to her feet, but stopped when Gustin swayed against her. She dropped the shoe that she had clutched so tightly throughout the chase to steady the young man.

"He hit my head," said the wizard in a blurry tone. Blood trickled down from the brown curls. "It hurts," he confided to her.

"Oh no," said Sophraea, recognizing these symptoms all too clearly from various mishaps in the Carver household. She waved one hand in front of Gustin's glazed expression. "How many fingers do you see?"

"Pretty ones," replied Gustin and promptly passed out on the cold floor of the gravediggers' room.

TEN

The first thing upon waking any morning, Gustin always noticed the smell of his room. Long before he cracked his eyes open or stretched one hand out from under the covers to grope for his boots (he kept them under his pillow in a cheap tavern or under the bed if the door had a good lock), the scent of his current resting place would worm into his nose.

In Cormyr, his room stank like a stable, more specifically like the part of a stable usually carted away in the early morning. Not surprising as that room overlooked a large pile used for fertilizing the inn's vegetable garden.

In Waterdeep, his room on Sevenlamps Cut always reeked of fried fish, which was odd as the tavern owner never fried anything, as far he knew. That man preferred to boil his stews until everything was pale, mushy, and tasteless.

On the road from Cormyr to Waterdeep, when Gustin could find a room and didn't have to sleep outdoors in the back of the carter's wagon (which always smelled damp and just a bit moldy under the canvas), his various rooms had smelled of unwashed travelers.

But this room in Dead End House! Ah, he took another deep sniff even as he snuggled under the feather quilt. This room smelled wonderful. Clean linen on the bed, beeswax polish on the chair by the door and the table set under the window, and, oh truly fantastic, the whiff of something baking straying up from the kitchen. This room smelled exactly the way that he always thought a room should smell in the morning.

Gustin Bone sat up quickly so he could get a better sniff of whatever his first meal of the day would be. His head swam and he clamped his mouth shut to hold back a moan. He tenderly probed the three expert stitches that Reye Carver had sewn in his scalp the night before.

His memory of the previous night was confused.

Going up the stairs out of the basement remained a bit of a headachy blur, his clearest recollection being a too close, upside down view of Feeler's tentacles after the big gravedigger had slung him over his shoulder.

In the kitchen, there'd been lots of chatter. Lots and lots, so he had let his eyes slide out of focus and slumped in the chair where Feeler had dropped him, waiting for the noise to subside. At some point, he heard Sophraea babbling on about how she just opened the basement door a crack to show Gustin the tunnels and this horrible man had tried to break in.

He had heard men's voices outshouting the women's protests.

"We'll get the rat, twist his scrawny neck!"

"Leaplow, I don't like that language in my kitchen."

"Sorry, Mother. All right, come on, we'll catch him and then decide."

"I know what you'll decide. And you know he'll have an army of his friends down there by now," answered Reye Carver.

"So we'll clear them out!"

"And start a war in the tunnels? I think not!" That had been Myemaw, Sophraea's tiny grandmother, the one that made him laugh at supper with her descriptions of what people actually ate in Waterdeep.

"So what do you want us to do?" Leaplow shouted and the floorboards reverberated under his feet as he danced up and down. Like his sister, Leaplow always seemed to be moving fast, impatient for the next step. Only, he went *thud, thud, thud* across the floor rather than the distinct *tap, tap, tap* of Sophraea darting away to get him a towel in cold water.

Gustin distinctly remembered hearing their mother Reye sigh and then say in a weary tone, "I would like all of you out of my kitchen. If you have nothing else to do, go sweep up the courtyard."

"At night? You want us to sweep at night?" Leaplow and his cousins exclaimed together in a way that made the pots rattle on the shelves.

"Just make yourself useful somewhere else!" Myemaw scolded.

Sophraea had draped the cold towel across his head and water had dripped into his ear and down the back of his neck. He'd drooped a bit lower in the chair so she'd lean over him and shield him from all the noise that several truly enormous Carvers in the kitchen were creating.

And then another male voice had said, "Come on, boys," and it sounded to Gustin like an army of boots tromping out of the room.

Unfortunately, he had recognized Leaplow's voice saying, "I think I'd better stay here. I want to know why he was in the basement with my sister."

Gustin slumped into the position of a remarkably harmless fellow. He really hadn't felt up to facing an angry brother.

But it had seemed a pretty unlikely tale that Sophraea told to Leaplow, something silly about wanting to show him the foundation stones laid by the first Carver. As if he'd leave a warm parlor to go looking at a foundation! And he'd been about to say so when Sophraea's soft little hand was clamped tightly over his lips and she had whispered in his ear, "Just moan and don't say anything. We'll get out of this faster."

Then Reye and Myemaw replaced the cold towel with cloths soaked in hot water and a very sharp needle, and moaning was an incredibly simple thing to do.

After all that, when Myemaw had slipped a nice cup of a hot spicy drink into his hand that eased the sting on the top of his scalp,

Leaplow said, "What are we going to do with him? Leave him in the chair all night?"

And Sophraea had protested and said something nice about him being so brave (which was true, he now realized, recalling the fight with the thief, even though she hadn't spoken any other word of truth in the kitchen that night).

Then Reye Carver said in her quiet voice, "He deserves a room of his own tonight so he can rest. We will give him Fitlor's, he certainly doesn't need it anymore."

While wondering vaguely what had happened to Fitlor and why he wouldn't want such a splendid room, Gustin pulled the covers a little higher around his shoulders and prepared to enjoy a short snooze before finding something to eat.

Just as he started to settle back into the warm and comfortable bed, a horrible thought occurred to him. This room was perfect. It smelled perfect. It felt perfect. It was exactly what he had been seeking ever since he ran away from the dull little farm smelling of despair and ruin where he had grown up. And it was only his on a temporary basis.

Once the Carvers figured out that Sophraea had fibbed, one of her enormous brothers or cousins or uncles was going to kick him out of this room, right back into the streets of Waterdeep, where he would wake up every morning smelling fried fish but only finding watery boiled vegetables to eat.

After a few anxious moments, Gustin's usual optimism overrode his black mood. It might be days and days before the Carvers decided to drop him into the gutter. Until that time, this room, this soft bed, this magnificent clean linen, were all his to enjoy. With a sigh of contentment not unlike a cat's purr, the wizard slid under the feather quilt and buried his nose in the pillow. He would sleep just a little longer and then sample whatever was baking in the kitchen for breakfast.

>——w——<

Sophraea slid the bedroom door open a crack. The wizard wasn't snoring, at least not in way the Carvers snored, more a satisfied snuffle coming from somewhere under the blankets. All she could see of him was a few brown curls sprouting out of the top of the huddle of covers.

Relieved that he was apparently fine, she dropped Bentnor's second best shirt and Leaplow's only decent pair of pants on the chair by the door. And, since both her cousin and her brother were a good deal wider than the slender Gustin, she added a spare belt to the pile.

Upstairs, she rapped on Volponia's door.

"I'm awake," came the spirited reply. "What else can an old lady be in earliest hours of the morning?"

Sophraea noted the bedstead was woven from wicker and a high canopy of gauze with brilliant silver spangles swayed above Volponia's head. Rain lashed against the windows but the bedroom smelled of warm spices and the sharp tang of citrus blossoms.

"Tired of winter already?" asked Sophraea as she curled up on the overstuffed silk cushion of the bed big enough for four or five more people.

"I'm tired of all seasons," said Volponia, warming her hands around a steaming stone cup carved so fine and thin that the pale winter light glowed through it. "But never tired of your stories. I heard there was another rumpus last night, a thief actually tried the basement door all by himself?"

Sophraea gave a half shrug and the true story to her oldest living relation. "We were down in the tunnels, and the thief came after us. He grabbed me, I kicked him."

"Caught him where it hurt?"

"Side of the knee. I could see he was wearing an armored codpiece."

"That's my girl, always look for the spot they've forgotten to protect." The old pirate captain chuckled as she sipped her morning brew.

"Gustin, he's the wizard that I mentioned finding, pulled me away."

"Men, they always look out for each other."

"No, no, he was trying to help. And he got clipped on the head so Mother and Myemaw sewed up the wound and put him to bed in Fitlor's old room."

"Well, it's not like Fitlor's going to need it any time soon."

"Absolutely. And Gustin seems all right. Which is a relief. Because I didn't mean anyone to get hurt. I just wanted to find out what's going on in the graveyard."

"And did you find anything?" Volponia asked when Sophraea's breathless explanation had wound down.

"Just this." Sophraea pulled the little gold brocade shoe out of her apron pocket and dropped it in Volponia's lap.

"A lady's dancing shoe," said Volponia, turning it over with her long fingers. "Obviously not new."

"Gustin thought it was off a corpse."

"Quite possibly. It was something of the fashion once if a noble maid died young to dress her in a ball gown and her best dancing shoes for burial."

"Truly?"

"During the dark era," said Volponia, referring to those long and bitter years after magic changed and the world rearranged itself in a manner not altogether unexpected. "I suspect it was a way to wish her brighter and happier times after death."

"So somebody was disturbing the corpses near the Markarl tomb," guessed Sophraea. "Or," and this was a more troubling thought, "the dead are starting to walk."

"If they are, then trouble is coming," Volponia told her. "The

City of the Dead had been quiet for a long time, the Blackstaff and the Watchful Order did their best to make the wards strong along the wall, but when I was very young, the ghosts used to get out and cause some real harm. And sometimes the more intact corpses walked and other trouble too."

"Ghosts appear everywhere in Waterdeep and spirit mists too," Sophraea pointed out.

"I'm not talking about those feeble shadow shows and their prophetic nonsense. That's just leftover magic from the Spellplague," said Volponia and then sketched the symbol in the air that the very elderly tended to make to ward off another coming of that terrible blight. "The old ghosts of Waterdeep were different. They were much stronger and much more terrible. When the dead walked, they were substantial," she said in an echo of the warning that Sophraea had heard earlier from the thorn, Briarsting.

"But why disturb us?" Sophraea said. "Why try our gate? We've always been respectful of the City and its residents."

"The Dead End gate, the Carvers' own special entrance into the graveyard," Volponia mused, handing the shoe back to Sophraea. "Well, that's the answer to the question, isn't it?"

"I don't understand."

"All the gates into the City of the Dead are well-guarded by the City Watch and well-warded by the Blackstaff. Aren't they?" the old pirate asked Sophraea.

"Of course, I was just through the Coffinmarch gate myself. Three members of the City Watch and the wards very clear to see."

"Where's the Watch below your window then? Where's the ward on the Dead End gate?" the old lady tapped one lacquered silver nail against her cup's rim.

"But our gate isn't a public gate. No one uses it except the family."

"Exactly. Nice respectable family, the Carvers. Make the coffins, carve the headstones, arrange for the graves to be dug, and polish up the tombs when needed. So if they go and carve themselves their own private gate into the City of the Dead, what's the worry?"

"Are you saying our gate isn't protected?"

"Well, that gate was here, just a part of the yard and house, for as long as I can remember," said Volponia. "Just one of those odd bits of Waterdeep that most people don't even know about and, more disturbing for us, that somebody or something has remembered. If I wanted to go out of the City of the Dead and I wasn't allowed out, I wouldn't march up to one of those public gates. I'd go here. To the tradesman's gate with no wards or City Watch."

"I tried to tell them downstairs," said a worried Sophraea, "but they just all say that the dead don't bother us."

"Some of the men have heads as thick as the stone they carve!" Volponia stated firmly. "No, the Carvers always are too comfortable with the City of the Dead. Since they haven't had any real trouble in a generation or two, they've largely forgotten about the precautions they should take."

Volponia peered into her cup, as if she could see the past and the future swirling together in the steam. For all Sophraea knew, perhaps the old pirate could. Unexpectedly her ancient relative asked, "Did you ever get that letter from Lord Adarbrent?"

"No," Sophraea admitted, quite astonished to realize that she'd literally forgotten about the letter still sitting in the other pocket of her apron. But she had been so busy, with topiary dragons and chases through tunnels, that securing a dressmaker's apprenticeship seemed . . . well . . . not exactly important, she compromised to herself.

Downright dull, whispered back an inner Sophraea to her dismay.

"Waterdeep is getting a bit like the Carvers," said Volponia, "a little too complacent about the City of the Dead. Lord Adarbrent is old enough to remember what real trouble can be, never mind his constant muttering. He sees more and understands more than most people think."

"Are you sure?"

Volponia nodded briskly and made a shooing motion with her hands. "Go to the Walking Corpse," she said, "because there is nobody in all of Waterdeep with a better understanding of the dead. All his family and friends perished long ago."

Downstairs, Sophraea ran into Gustin, who was sliding out of the kitchen, munching a roll dripping with honey.

"Well met!" he said upon spying Sophraea tripping down the stairs. "Your grandmother suggested I go watch your father work on my statue."

Eyeing the roll, Sophraea returned, "Probably because she wanted some food left in the kitchen for lunch."

"O, unkind maiden," said Gustin, thumping his heart with the hand holding the roll and leaving a spot of honey on Leaplow's second best shirt. He licked a finger and rubbed it out. "I'm sure that she was just trying to add to my education."

"I hope you didn't add to hers and tell her what you're planning to do with that statue."

"I really don't understand why you think your family wouldn't approve. Nice petrified hero stumping through the streets of Waterdeep, searching for his long lost love. It's just the sort of story most folk find very touching." He grinned at her, his green eyes sparkling under his long black lashes.

"Right after which, you empty their purses." All right, he had a nice smile, she was willing to admit that to herself. But that didn't mean she was going to let him twist her around. She'd grown up at the tail end of a pack of mischief makers, Leaplow being as big a flirt as he was a fighter, and she knew the breed when she saw it.

"Your family doesn't work for free and the animation of stone requires some costly ingredients," said the young wizard with too much personal charm for her peace of mind continuing his argument. "And this is one way to make magic pay. Which is what a wizard is supposed to do."

"I'm not sure the Watchful Order sees it quite that way."

"Organized labor, governmental types. They do tend to look down on us poor freelancers."

Years of being teased by older brothers made Sophraea doubt Gustin's sincerity. "Do you even believe half of the nonsense you spout?" she asked him.

The wizard smiled broadly at her and popped the last of the roll into his mouth. "Half of it, certainly, at least half the time. Of course, depends on who is paying for the beer. I'm just as happy to argue the other side too. Magic must be carefully regulated, spells only taught by the best master to the best pupil, that's the only way to regain the trust of the populace after the Spellplague, and so on and so forth."

"So is that what you truly believe?" she asked.

Gustin gave a long rolling shrug of his shoulders. "I believe that there are wizards happy to point fingers at those marked by the Spellplague and mutter about how they wouldn't be caught dead working with them. And others who envy those powers so much that they seek the same down dangerous paths. Some look for new forms of magic in faraway places and some stay forever in the same place trying to recreate spells that their grandfathers cast and nothing else. The world has changed, everyone agrees on that, but none of the wizards that I've met can agree on how to live with those changes or without them. So I try not to worry about such things. I've taken my learning where I could and used my magic as best I could. And that's good enough for me."

Blinking a little at this sensible speech from the irrepressible Gustin, Sophraea hung her apron on a peg by the door. She removed the golden shoe from its pocket and dropped it into her wicker basket.

"Where are you going?" asked Gustin.

"To see Lord Adarbrent," she replied, taking her rain cape off another hook and swinging it around her shoulders. "I want to ask him about this shoe."

"You know," said Gustin, casually borrowing another rain cape from the hall pegs. "I don't think I have ever seen the inside of a Waterdhavian nobleman's house." The cape was Bentnor's and fell in great dark blue folds around the wizard. "I'll be happy to escort you."

"I don't recall asking for an escort."

"Well, I could go watch your father at his carving. But I might start chatting to him about where I was last night, out in the tunnels, under the City of the Dead."

"That might be more painful for you than me," pointed out Sophraea, trying to keep her expression calm. No one in the family would ever harm her, and all would fly to her defense against any outsider, but the discussion of her behavior would go on for days! And her mother would look disappointed, and her father would sigh, and she would want to sink into the floorboards.

What was worse, they'd all think that she'd done it to flirt with this wizard and nobody would listen when she'd try to explain about the dead wandering inside the graveyard or in the tunnels below.

"Still, you have to admire my fearless honesty in the face of great personal danger," Gustin continued to tease. "Especially considering the stories that those Watchmen wanted to tell me about your brothers."

"Oh, come along then!" She exclaimed and walked into the yard, only to halt at the sight of Rampage Stunk's hairy doorjack standing there. The man sniffed at her and licked his tongue across his large yellow teeth.

"Ugh," said Sophraea, waiting for the man to move out of her way.

"I've orders from the master for your father," the servant said to her.

"He's in his workshop," she said, suddenly glad of the tall form of Gustin Bone behind her.

The servant's eyes flicked over the wizard. His nose wrinkled and his upper lip pulled back from his teeth as he snarled, "Magic-user."

"Oh, whenever I can," Gustin replied with a wave of his hand. The silver wand popped out of his sleeve and sent sparks flying into the air. "I could probably provide you with a nice little charm to keep the hair off your back and the fleas away if you'd like."

The man growled, "I am a servant of Rampage Stunk, the greatest man in all of Waterdeep."

"Well, that's a bit of a stretch," whispered Sophraea to Gustin. "He's rich but he's not that well known."

The servant twitched his head to look straight at her. "He will be, little miss, he will be. And your family should be very grateful for his patronage. And grateful to his servants too! After all, my master and my master's friends are planning many new tombs in the fancy graveyard there. And if the Carvers don't want the work, somebody else will," he gloated.

"There isn't room inside the City of the Dead for that many new tombs," protested Sophraea, thinking if the noble dead were disturbed already by the changes in the Markarl and Vesham tombs, more changes were sure to bring disaster.

"There will be room," boasted the servant. "My master will make sure of that."

ELEVEN

The fact that a nobleman of Lord Adarbrent's stature lived on a street called Manycats Alley caused Gustin to snicker.

"It's a very grand neighborhood," explained Sophraea. "Only the finest families of Waterdeep have mansions here." The mansions along Manycats had been remodeled in the newest style, with the old gatehouses and courtyards now completely enclosed, so anyone entering from the front would not be plagued by Waterdeep's perpetual rain. Stairs with beautifully wrought iron rails ran up from the street's pavement to a gleaming polished door that had replaced the old and more open gate of a century ago.

Sophraea climbed the eight steps leading to Lord Adarbrent's great door.

"You'd think they'd give this street a better name," snorted Gustin as Sophraea swung the bronze knocker shaped like a ship's anchor.

"Like what?" she countered.

"Rich Dogs Avenue, Highbred Cats Boulevard," suggested Gustin.

She giggled and then glared at him. "Don't. This is serious."

The creaking door of Lord Adarbrent's mansion opened. A pale old servant in the livery of Waterdeep's past listened politely to Sophraea's request.

"Follow me," he said finally.

The servant led them, very slowly, through the enclosed courtyard past a long dry fountain. Another two steps led into the mansion's great hall, with its cold marble floors and long bare benches where petitioners would have once waited for the lord of the house. A broad staircase disappeared into the gloom of the upper rooms. No candles burned despite the lack of light from the narrow windows facing the courtyard. The fireplace grates, one at each end of the hall, were swept clean and bare.

A few faded maritime flags hung limply on the walls. The formerly bright colors muted by time into pale reminders of the family's once great shipping interests.

"I think it was warmer in the tunnels," muttered Gustin.

"Shh," said Sophraea.

The servant opened a small black door near the back of the hall, motioning them forward. The little waiting chamber was just as cold and gloomy as the great hall, but it at least had a few ancient chairs rather than bare benches. This was obviously where the better class of petitioners would have waited for the former Lord Adarbrents.

After wrestling with the stubborn silk draperies covering the long windows of the room, the servant pulled back the curtains to allow a narrow view of the damp winter garden outside. No fire burned in this grate either, only a trace of cold ash lay scattered across the hearthstones.

Once the servant left to inform Lord Adarbrent of their presence, Gustin sprang up from the rickety chair where he had been seated by the servant. He took a quick turn around the room, examining the smoky dark portraits of former Adarbrents decorating the walls. One portrait bore a mottled brass plaque engraved with the family's founding patriarch "Royus." The grim fellow in the painting looked as if he'd just swallowed something extremely bitter.

"I don't think Time just stopped here. I think Time curled up behind the wainscoting and died," Gustin said, staring up at that particular long-dead member of the Adarbrent family.

"Hush," said Sophraea, still sitting very straight on her

uncomfortable chair because she didn't know what else to do. "Someone will hear you."

However, she had to acknowledge that there was a peculiar smell permeating the mansion, a sharp tang just under the usual old house smells of damp, cold, and dust. Perhaps Lord Adarbrent needed a cat, a good mouser like the ones who lived in the Carver workshops. She could always bring him a kitten.

The thought of the Walking Corpse of Waterdeep with a kitten caused Sophraea to giggle. Gustin turned away from rearranging the seashells lined up on the mantelpiece and asked, "Care to share the joke?"

Sophraea shook her head, hiccupping a little as she tried to regain control, and then relented, saying, "I was just thinking that I could give Lord Adarbrent a kitten."

"One of that fluffy black-and-white set living under your father's workbench?"

"Yes, can you just imagine a kitten here?"

"Not very well," admitted Gustin with chuckle. "Those drapes would be in shreds on the floor by morning."

"But it does seem appropriate," said Sophraea, giving away to laughter, "for a nobleman who lives . . ."

"On Manycats Alley," Gustin guffawed.

The stately clatter of boot heels across the bare marble floor of the hallway outside interrupted their laughter. Lord Adarbrent appeared, dressed very much as he always did for walking the streets of Waterdeep, the long rusty black coat with its oversized pockets hanging past his knees. Only his broad-brimmed hat and slender black cane were missing.

The old nobleman blinked a few times at their presence in his waiting room.

Blushing and hoping very much that he had not heard their joking, Sophraea rose from her chair and curtsied.

"Dear child," Lord Adarbrent addressed her as he usually did in her father's yard. He bowed deeply. Upon spotting Gustin standing by the mantelpiece, he bowed again. Gustin hastily replaced the seashell that he had been fiddling with and bowed in return.

"Visitors. How . . . unus . . . ah . . . how pleasant," Lord Adarbrent faltered, rubbing his chin in a gesture of puzzled contemplation.

Sophraea wondered when the old gentleman had last entertained guests in his house. Given the condition of the room and his own state of surprise, she guessed it may have been a few years. Actually, given the state of the debilitated curtains, a few decades might be an even better guess, she thought.

"Lord Adarbrent," she said, speaking quickly to fill up the awkward silence, "this is the wizard Gustin Bone. He very kindly escorted me here today as I wanted to ask you—" She stopped, uncertain how to say "we found a shoe, we think it came off a corpse, do you think the deceased nobility are roaming in the City of the Dead?"

Luckily, Lord Adarbrent seemed to have overlooked her incomplete sentence and was bowing again to Gustin. "So nice," he said in his careful style, "to meet a young man with the manners to know that a young woman should not go unescorted and unprotected through the streets of Waterdeep."

Sophraea was about to point out that a great many ladies and women of other classes walked abroad alone and were perfectly capable of protecting themselves. Except she realized that Lord Adarbrent meant it as a compliment to the wizard and there was no point in distressing the old gentleman.

"My lord," she said instead. "We recently noticed some disturbances in the City of the Dead."

"And underneath it," added Gustin.

"And, knowing of your great interest in the history of the place, were wondering if you could make some suggestion about this?" she asked, withdrawing the little golden shoe from her wicker basket. "We found it near the Markarl tomb."

"Almost directly under it," added Gustin again, despite Sophraea's frown at him. She really didn't want to start explaining how they had been in the tunnels the previous evening. Especially as she was sure that Lord Adarbrent, who didn't believe ladies should go unescorted through the public streets, would not approve of her traipsing underground in the sewers.

Lord Adarbrent was very gentle in his handling of the shoe, turning it over with a sigh. "Such a pretty thing," he said, "I remember when I was young, all the ladies wore such finery to the great balls."

Since neither Sophraea nor Gustin could imagine Lord Adarbrent as a young man, they made no comment.

"My lord, I'm very worried about the disturbances in the City," said Sophraea. "Rampage Stunk has ordered two tombs removed for the building of his own monument. And I think . . . well, I think that the dead are upset. It is possible that the dead are walking. I would go to the Watch or to the Watchful Order, only I really don't know who to speak to." And, she added silently, I really don't want to explain that my family built an unprotected gate into the City of the Dead several generations ago that everyone has overlooked and that may pose a great danger to Waterdeep.

"There is no reason to involve the City Watch or the Order," said Lord Adarbrent. "Rampage Stunk's activities"—he paused and smacked his lips as if trying to clear a bad taste out of his mouth— "Stunk's plans are known and approved, by the highest authorities, as I have been repeatedly told."

Looking at the deep and angry lines on the aged nobleman's face, Sophraea fancied whoever had told Lord Adarbrent had had an unpleasant task.

"Stunk holds the deeds to those tombs, sold quite legally to him by the last foolish remnants of two once great and very noble families," Lord Adarbrent concluded with a scowl. "If he chooses to make other arrangements with that property, it is well within his rights as a citizen of Waterdeep. Or so it was explained to me." The last sentence ended on a note perilously close to a snarl.

The old man patted Sophraea's hand where it rested upon the handle of her wicker basket. "It was very good of you to come to me, dear child, but your father and his brothers already made the same inquiries once they realized where Stunk meant to build his tomb."

"Oh," said Sophraea, quite dismayed by this revelation. "I didn't know."

"But, do the dead of Waterdeep respect the same laws, my lord?" asked Gustin. "We certainly saw some signs of magic around those tombs the other day."

Turning to the wizard, Lord Adarbrent said, "I think you are somewhat new to our city?"

"I arrived a short time ago."

"Ah, well, you will learn. Waterdeep is a very old city, with magic sunk into its foundation stones. I doubt there is anywhere that you could walk in this city and not see some mark of a past spell or incantation."

Lord Adarbrent handed the little tarnished shoe back to Sophraea and she tucked it back into the basket without a thought.

"Thank you for the visit," he said, showing them out of the room. The servant waited at the already open door leading to the courtyard, making it clear that the visit was at an end.

Sophraea curtsied, Gustin bowed, and Lord Adarbrent waved off these gestures of respect with a murmured, "No need. Such nice manners, always a pleasure."

As a further courtesy, the old nobleman escorted them across the courtyard, tutting under his breath at the state of his fountain and muttering something about meaning to have the dwarves take a look at it.

Outside the great door, standing on the stairs leading to the pavement, they saw a group of men clearing the furniture out of a fine but rather dilapidated house a little farther down the street.

"Rampage Stunk," Lord Adarbrent growled in much stronger tones than he had used inside. "The dowager isn't dead more than five days and he's already bought the house from her heirs. He will sell it for a fine profit to one of his fancy friends and I'll have more jackanapes pretending to be noblemen living on my street. No manners, no breeding, no sense of tradition . . ."

Startled, Sophraea saw the old man's hands clench into fists and then deliberately relax.

"Ah well," muttered Lord Adarbrent, lifting his hand to his nose to hide his expression from them. "It is his right, as a citizen of Waterdeep. Good day to you."

The great door swung shut behind him with a definite slam.

"Well," Sophraea said to Gustin, "I can see now why some people call him the Angry Lord."

"Actually, I thought he would be more upset by your news," mused Gustin. "I thought a lord of the city would worry that the dead were leaving their graves to haunt the streets. In Cormyr, there would be war wizards stalking about and reporting to the king if such a thing happened."

"Lord Adarbrent is right, this is Waterdeep. Odd things happen all the time," explained Sophraea, hooking her arm through Gustin's in a friendly fashion. "Look, I think it's going to rain. Let's go back to the Andamaar gate and cut through the City of the Dead. It will be faster that way."

"You just don't like walking down streets where living people are wandering," teased Gustin.

"It's not that," said Sophraea. "But on the way here, you kept stopping and staring at everything and asking me if this is where that battle was fought or where this wizard made his stand."

"Aren't you interested in the history of your city?"

"Not nearly as much as I am in getting home before it pours," she tugged Gustin down Manycats Alley, past the spot where Stunk's servants were loading boxes and bags into a big dray wagon.

"I'm sorry you didn't get the answers you wanted," Gustin said.

"I'm just fussed, I guess. That's one of Myemaw's expressions," Sophraea told him. "After all, spirits appear quite frequently in the City of the Dead, and elsewhere too. And they are mostly harmless. Maybe I shouldn't worry."

"Oh," said Gustin, smiling down at her, "you strike me as the sensible sort. You don't worry without cause. Something odd has been going on around those tombs. And in the tunnel last night, something frightened those thieves, long before that one decided to attack us."

Peculiarly pleased by being called a sensible sort, Sophraea started to reply when they were interrupted by a shout.

"Well, if it isn't the little rude bit from Carver's yard," Stunk's hairy doorjack strode across the street toward them. His shout brought the other Stunk servants sidling around the dray wagon and into the center of Manycats Alley. The two red-haired louts with their cudgels laughed to see Sophraea pull Gustin back from the hairy doorjack's advance.

Gustin shook off Sophraea's hand. "I did tell you that I was a wizard, didn't I?" he asked the big man bearing down on them.

"Like I'm afraid of some street charlatan," the servant replied.

A twist of his arm and his wand appeared in Gustin's left hand. Beneath his long lashes, his green eyes sparkled. "Didn't ask if you were afraid," he crowed, grinning. "Just wanted to make sure you understood what kind of fight you were getting."

Looking at the growing semicircle of Stunk's men surrounding them, Sophraea took a firm grip on her wicker basket. "You should let us pass," she said as calmly as she could. "You know my family. You don't want to start a fight with the Carvers."

"Carvers, what are Carvers?" said one of the redheads. "Bunch of fancy gravediggers."

"We're Stunk's men," said the other. "Nobody crosses us. Nobody hits us with buckets and brooms."

"When did we?" started Sophraea.

One of Stunk's men slapped the other on the back of the head and said, "Shut up you fool."

"It was you!" shouted Sophraea. "You were the ones breaking into our workshops! Thieves!"

"Shut her up!" yelled the thin nervous servant who always lurked in the back of the group. "Stunk will kill us if he hears about this!"

"Great balls of flame," muttered Gustin as he swung his wand above his head. "Why can't I do enormous balls of fire when I need them!"

Nevertheless, his spell *zing*ed through the air. Half the men shouted and dropped the makeshift weapons they were carrying, lifting their hands to their mouths as if their fingers stung.

Unfortunately, the other half still retained their weapons and charged the wizard. Gustin whipped off Bentnor's oversized cape and enveloped the closest man rushing at him, tripping the bully onto the street.

Sophraea screamed loudly and swung the wicker basket underhand with deadly accuracy at one of the louts intent on hitting Gustin. Not protected by an armored codpiece, this lout went down with a sharp cry of pain.

But more came on, and Sophraea found herself lifted bodily from the street even as Gustin fell with a shout beneath two men struggling to keep the long-armed wizard from casting another spell.

Hairy hands locked around Sophraea's waist and tossed her into the outstretched hands of another sour-smelling creature. With her feet off the pavement, she kicked wildly. She felt her shoes connect with solid flesh and heard the howls of rage.

Another shout sounded from farther up the street. Sophraea screamed again for help. The doorjack grabbed her, trying to stifle her cries.

"Curs! On my very doorstep! You dare!" Lord Adarbrent exclaimed, charging down the steps of his mansion into the street, swinging his long black cane with deadly precision.

The redheaded bully lifting a cudgel to brain Gustin gave a cry of pain as the black cane smacked across the back of his hands. He dropped the cudgel, right onto Gustin's shoulder, and beat a hasty retreat.

Seeing who it was who attacked them, the other servants scrambled to the wagon. They climbed up on it, crying out "it's that old lord, best go, Stunk is going to kill us!"

Lord Adarbrent raced after them, moving more swiftly than a man half his age, slashing right and left with the cane. Each blow fell with wicked accuracy, causing great cries of pain.

The thin nervous servant grasped the reins and clicked to the horses. Another slash on the hindquarters of the lead horse and a fierce yell from Lord Adarbrent caused the startled cob to lift its neck with a bugling cry and begin an awkward gallop. The wagon rocked and rolled down the street, bits of baggage dropping off in its hasty departure.

Too stunned to move by the swift turn of events, the hairy doorjack still grasped the kicking, shrieking Sophraea. She flung her head backward, knocking his chin up and causing him to bite his tongue.

"Yow!" he cried. "You witch! I'll break your neck."

Turning sharply on his heel, Lord Adarbrent pulled the wood sheath of his sword cane off and revealed the long, sharp, and deadly steel blade. He pressed the point against the hairy doorjack's throat.

"You will release the lady, gently," He commanded. "Or I skewer you like the dog you are."

Other shouts could be heard from the entrance of Manycats Alley and the pounding run of many armored men.

"Quickly," said Lord Adarbrent. The ancient nobleman's eyes burned with a bright fierce light and anger flushed his wrinkled cheeks. But his hand was steady and the steel blade never quavered a hairsbreadth from the hairy doorjack's pulsing vein. "Or I let the City Watch take your corpse from my doorstep."

With a growl, the hairy man dropped Sophraea, not too gently, back on the cobblestones. She pinwheeled her arms to maintain her balance and managed to clip him on the side of his head with her basket.

With a yelp of pain, the hirsute doorjack turned and loped off, following the lurching wagon and his fellow servants racing down the street.

Gustin struggled to his feet, rubbing one shoulder. "Ah, well," he said in his usual cheerful tones, "at least they didn't hit me over the head."

He wiped the smears of mud and blood on his hands against the back of his tunic. Sophraea tutted at this, pulling a clean handkerchief out of her pocket. With years of practice from cleaning up Leaplow, she dabbed at the scrapes on Gustin's face and hands.

A trio of burly Watchmen thumped up to them.

"Saers," one commanded. "Lay down your weapons."

He seemed a bit disconcerted to find only the ancient and very well-known Lord Adarbrent leaning negligently upon his cane, a small young woman with ruffled curls clutching a wicker basket, and a tall, thin young man picking up a large rain cape.

"We heard an affray," began the one Watchman in stentorian accents.

"Nothing of importance," said Lord Adarbrent, looking down his nose.

"Actually," began Sophraea, ready to report Stunk's servants to the City Watch. Lord Adarbrent turned and gave her a stern look.

"Nothing of importance," he repeated to the City Watch. "I am simply bidding good-bye to these two young friends, who will now go straight home."

"If you say so, my lord," said an older Watchman, who gave one of those shrugs that said so clearly "We know you are lying and you know we know, but what can you do in Waterdeep?"

"I appreciate, as always, the City Watch's discretion," Lord Adarbrent bowed and retreated up the steps to his door, which swung quickly open at his approach. It closed just as definitely behind him.

"High adventure and dark dearlings, just like the book promised," chuckled Gustin as he slipped his wand back into his sleeve. He tucked his hand around Sophraea's elbow and guided her away from the Watch. The three men stood stiff and silent, watching the wizard and the girl walk away. "Even a duel in an open street with a nobleman and timely intervention by the City Watch."

"High adventure? That was just a street brawl. My brothers spent most of their youth with my cousins in just such fights. Leaplow still battles with everyone he can find," said Sophraea, momentarily distracted from her wrathful muttering about impolite things that should have happened to Stunk's men. She considered telling her brothers and cousins. Declaring war on Stunk's men had considerable appeal—Leaplow would love it! She bit back the thought. If she did such a thing, she would never hear the end of it from her mother.

"And dark what? What was that word you used?" she continued as the wizard's earlier statement finally sank into her mind.

"Dearlings," replied the lanky wizard. "Isn't that the local term for a sweetheart?"

"Of course not. I have never heard such a thing in my life. Where did you hear it?" Sophraea snapped, still cranky that she couldn't have all of Stunk's servants locked up in some dungeon deep beneath the castle or pounded in the head by some of the younger Carver males.

"I read it. In my guidebook to Waterdeep. See!" exclaimed Gustin reaching inside his tunic and pulling out a small book. The cover was stained leather, sloppily stitched onto the pages, obviously replacing a much older cover that had been torn off and lost long ago. A crude map of Waterdeep, printed in faded inks of brown, green, and blue, unfolded from the back.

"This must be older than Volponia," said Sophraea, taking the book from him and frowning at the creased and crumpled page. "This map is all wrong. This street, for example, doesn't run into this alley. There's a building there. A big storehouse."

"What's a storehouse or two?" Gustin asked as he retrieved his book, folded the map correctly so it lay flat inside the back cover, and gently turned the pages to the beginning. "There are wonderful descriptions in here. Essays on all sorts of marvels. And see, right here at the beginning, it promises 'high adventure and dark dearlings' to any who come to Waterdeep."

Sophraea stopped in the middle of the pavement to lean over Gustin's arm and read the line that his long finger traced for her. "I'm sure that was a mistake. Some printer's error," she said, shaking her head. "There's no such thing as dark dearlings."

"Oh, I don't know," said Gustin with a funny little smile. Sophraea peered up at him, wondering what made him grin so. Rain began to splatter in larger and larger drops on the cobblestones.

"Here, you'll get all wet," the wizard said, reaching out to pull up the hood of her cloak and cover up her black curls. "Dark dearlings . . . Yes, it still seems very accurate to me."

TWELVE

In Sophraea's troubled dreams that night, a lady walked. She was a very young lady, very pale, and her face was hard to see beneath the high-piled curls and fine lace hood she wore.

The lady's dress was spangled with brilliants, and her little feet glittered in gold brocade shoes. She danced through the paths of the City of the Dead, hurrying as if to a great ball. And behind her, in long lines, they came. The noblest of the dead, the revenants of the great families of Waterdeep, all dressed in the richest robes and most elegant costumes of the centuries.

In crimson lace and sapphire wool, in tawny leather and gilded armor, they came. Rows upon rows of the noble dead followed the dancing lady out of the City of the Dead and into the sleeping streets of Waterdeep.

A terrible crack, like the breaking of a bell, woke Sophraea from the nightmare.

After lighting a candle and pulling on a pair of slippers, she ran down the staircase in her nightgown. She was certain that the noise was real, although she grimly hoped that the rest of the dream was just nonsense stirred up by her worries.

Around her, the rest of the house slept in its usual rumble of snores and grunts.

She reached the courtyard door and pulled aside the locks. Drawing a deep breath to give herself courage, she twisted the handle.

"Sophraea?" the whisper came from behind her.

She spun around, one hand hard against her thumping heart.

A tall thin shadow slid down the staircase. "Sophraea?" whispered Gustin. "Is that you?"

With a cry of relief and annoyance, Sophraea fell upon the wizard. "What are you doing here?" she whispered.

"I heard this noise, something breaking. It woke me up," he said. Then, almost reluctantly, he admitted, "It's more than that. Sort of a feeling that I get. When I let off a spell or someone lets off one near me. This was really strong and unpleasant. Then I heard you go running past."

"How did you know it was me?"

"Your brothers do not run that lightly down the stairs."

"True."

She danced impatiently from slippered foot to slippered foot. Gustin was right, there was a tingle in the air, a disturbance that was more than winter drafts and bad dreams. It was like being in the City of the Dead, she decided, and knowing that there was a grave open just behind you. One wrong step could tumble you backward into the embrace of the dead.

"Why are you here?" Gustin whispered, interrupting her troubled thoughts.

"I heard something too," she admitted. "And I dreamed the dead were walking past the Deepwinter tomb toward our gate."

"Oh," breathed Gustin, looking dismayed.

"It was probably just a dream."

"I sincerely hope so," said the wizard.

"I'm going outside," said Sophraea, drawing herself as tall as she could, "to see what is there."

"Do you really think that is a good idea?"

"Probably not, but I don't think I have any choice."

Taking a deep if slightly unsteady breath, Gustin nodded and said, "I'm coming with you."

"You know," said Sophraea, patting his arm to reassure him and herself, "I do think that you are very brave wizard."

"Right now," said Gustin, unlatching the door and opening it for her, "I agree with you."

The courtyard was completely empty. Nothing stirred in the shadows, not even one of the Carver's many cats.

"There's nothing there," Gustin stated the obvious.

"Is that a good thing or a bad thing?"

"I'm not sure. I've never had any dealings with the dead," said the wizard. "You're the expert there."

"I'm a Carver and I am not afraid," said Sophraea with greater bravado than truth, advancing into the courtyard, the candle held high in one trembling hand. "The dead don't bother us. We take care of them. They leave us alone."

"I'm a friend of a Carver, I don't want to bother the dead, I absolutely want to be left alone by the dead," Gustin stated as he followed her. Then he whispered to Sophraea, "Do you think that will do any good?"

With a cry of dismay, Sophraea stopped short of the Dead End gate. The iron bars were shattered in half, the pieces of the gate now hanging open from the lock and hinges.

"Something did come through here," she said. Then she started down the mossy steps into the City of the Dead.

"Wait," said Gustin, grabbing the back of her fluttering nightrobe and pulling her into the courtyard. "Where do you think you are going?"

"Maybe I can find Briarsting," she said. "He could rouse the guardians within the City of the Dead. Maybe they can bring the ghosts back before anyone finds out. Our family is going to be in such trouble if anyone finds out they came through here!"

"Sophraea, it is quite literally the dead of night," Gustin argued. "We have no idea what went through here or what is still stirring on that side of the wall. You cannot go into the graveyard in your nightrobe!"

Then the wizard let out a low moan.

"What is it?" Sophraea said, struggling to pull free from his grasp.

"This is your nightrobe, isn't it?" he moaned again, still clutching a handful of her skirt. "What you sleep in?"

"Of course," she said, finally tugging the sturdy confection of quilted silk and lace out of his hands. "What else would I be wearing?"

"Well, I got dressed," pointed out Gustin, taking Sophraea by the shoulders and steering her firmly back to the open doorway of Dead End House. "Of course, that's because I don't have . . . No, I am not having this discussion with you and I am not being found with you in your nightrobe."

"You're not in my nightrobe," Sophraea said, thoroughly confused by the conversation. "I am."

"Don't make it sound worse," said the young man, shoving her up the stairs and into the house. He was slightly hindered by the fact that he was trying to keep his eyes directed at a point somewhere above her head.

"Gustin, what are you talking about?" she exclaimed. "We have to do something about the noise we both heard."

"Sophraea," said the wizard firmly. "There is absolutely nothing we can do until morning. Not safely. In the morning, we can look for Briarsting and see what can be done. But now, for my sake, please, please go to bed, before one of your very large male relatives wakes up and catches me with you in your nightrobe."

"You know," she said mounting the stairs, secretly relieved that she wasn't in the middle of the City of the Dead, "you're not as brave as I thought you were."

"I am willing to face any number of the dead," whispered Gustin as he slid back into his room, "before I face your father, or your brothers, or your equally terrifying large uncles and cousins. Or, what's probably worse, Myemaw and her carving knife." He shut his door with a decisive click.

Sophraea stood there, tapping her foot against a floorboard, wondering if she should take just one more look at the shattered gate.

Gustin's door popped open again. "Besides, you do not want to encounter ghosts at night," he whispered, "not when they are at their strongest. Go to bed, Sophraea." His door clicked shut again.

Not completely ignoring the wizard's advice, Sophraea stayed within the walls of Dead End House, just creeping through the lower rooms, looking out the windows facing the City of the Dead to see if she could see anything.

Outside, the fitful moonlight revealed nothing. Eventually the clouds totally hid the moon, so outside was complete blackness. All she could see was the pale reflection of her own face peering into the darkened glass.

After one last restless circuit through the lower floors, checking to see that doors and windows were tightly bolted, Sophraea acknowledged she was exhausted. She went back to the main staircase.

At the bottom of the stair, Sophraea spotted her wicker basket, the one that she took to Lord Adarbrent's house. With a murmur of annoyance, she recalled the letter of recommendation lying completely forgotten at the bottom.

"I never gave it to him," she scolded herself. "Well, we had some distractions," she forgave herself a second later.

Pulling aside the cloth covering, she rooted for the letter. It crackled under her fingers. But something else was missing.

"The shoe!" exclaimed Sophraea. The brocade shoe, she was sure that Lord Adarbrent had handed it back to her. Yes, he had given it to her and she'd tucked it right down in the basket. Had it fallen out in the fight with Stunk's servants?

No, she was just as certain that she had checked the basket as they'd hurried back to Dead End House. And she remembered tucking the shoe a little deeper under the linen napkin she used to keep the contents dry. She hadn't wanted the Watchmen on the Andamaar gate to ask her about it.

After they'd gone through the Andamaar gate, they hadn't stopped, because it was dusk and Gustin kept making remarks about not wanting to be stuck in the City of the Dead after dark. As if she could miss a turn or not get them to the Dead End gate in record time!

Perhaps the shoe had rolled out after she dropped the basket in the corner by the stair. There'd been the usual scuffling crowd of Carvers all trooping into the house at the same time, intent on finding a hot supper. Bentnor, Cadriffle, and Leaplow had even started some nonsense with Gustin, shoving back and forth, about who had the right to go up the staircase first.

She hadn't been paying much attention then, just trying to get her cloak hung up and ignoring a sister-in-law's impertinent questions about "how are those language lessons going? Isn't it odd that you need to do so much studying while walking around the city with the young man?"

Sophraea lifted her candle high, hoping to see the glitter of the tarnished brocade. For some reason, she was certain that it was important the shoe be found.

Farther down the hallway, she glimpsed something shining against the dark wood of the floor. In the light of her candle, Sophraea saw very clear footprints, the footprints of a lady dancing in circles. The footprints glowed with an eerie light and then disappeared.

Behind her, Sophraea heard soft footsteps. She whirled around, but there was nobody there. The candle shook in her hand, sending the shadows quivering across the paneled walls.

A distinct chill nipped her cheeks and Sophraea remembered Gustin's warning about ghosts being strongest at night.

She felt something brush her shoulder. Her candle blew out! Shivering in the dark hallway, she smelled a blend of melted candle wax and the thin drift of smoke from the wick. There was something else too. She stood very still, her breath shallow while she tried to recognize it. Yes, there was another scent, a mix of old brocade and the faint scent of rose oil.

Sophraea sprinted up the stairs, leaped into bed, and very firmly pulled the covers over her head.

Yet, even with her ears muffled under the pillow, she could still hear the dancing steps of the dead and their dreadful laughter as they made their way to a ball.

THIRTEEN

A ball was underway at Rampage Stunk's home, a very splendid party full of wonderful music, extraordinary food, and exceptional wines.

The fat man smiled to see so many rich guests under his roof, especially since he had hundreds of schemes to lighten their purses and make his own heavier.

Along the edges of the ball, there were a number of the shabbier nobles of Waterdeep, the kind with long lineages and very little coin. Rampage was glad to see them there too. They may not have wealth but they did have property, either houses in Waterdeep, or estates in the country, or even neglected family tombs in the City of the Dead.

Rampage knew that ready coin would part these nobles from their old family holdings. Most would not even guess at the true value of what they were selling. That made the fat man smile even more and even tap his feet in time to the sprightly tune being played by the very expensive band he had hired.

The fat man did not dance, although he could see his tall and elegant wife passing easily through the figures, nodding to her noble kin as she completed each movement. Well, that was why he married her, to draw even the most snobbish of the lords and ladies to his table and his influence. Family ties still bound this city together, and he would use any rope to twist a ladder for his own rise to power in Waterdeep.

More platters of steaming delicacies were circulated among the guests and taken to the gamesters playing for fortunes in the long tables clustered at one end of the ballroom.

"By the gods' bounty," cried one excited gourmet. "Isn't that roast cockatrice?"

All the best for his guests, Rampage Stunk believed, as he intended to take the very best from them. He grabbed a succulent bit from a tray passing him by and popped it into his mouth with a greasy chuckle.

At the very edge of the room stood Lord Adarbrent. As always, the old nobleman was dressed in black from head to toe and leaning on his slender dark cane, a deep scowl of disapproval drawing angry lines in his ravaged face.

Rampage Stunk smiled and nodded at him too, calling, "Good evening, my lord!"

That gentleman's scowl deepened, but his nod was civil enough. That was the man's weakness, Stunk thought, noble to the core and never rude in someone else's house.

Stunk knew his servants had been foolish enough to be caught in a fight outside Adarbrent's manor and he had whipped the instigators soundly for it. The old man hated him. It wouldn't do to give the Walking Corpse any more reasons to complain.

Not that anyone paid attention to Lord Adarbrent's complaints. Rampage Stunk had poured enough gold into the right hands to stop any ears that might be willing to listen to the Angry Lord's diatribes.

He was helped, of course, by all the recent events in the city. There was a certain amount of chaos among the Watchful Order. Not that they were to be ignored or trifled with, but the whole wizardly organization was a bit consumed with internal affairs. And the City Watch and the guards had their own problems to deal with, including some quite obvious threats to Waterdeep's safety and future security.

In such momentous times, Rampage Stunk found, very few cared about the occasional changes of property between the old nobility, now considerably diminished in wealth, and the rising merchant class, so nicely endowed with spare coin from the flourishing trade flowing through Waterdeep's streets.

Nobody cared in fact but one very cranky nobleman, who wandered the streets of Waterdeep, raging against the deals struck by Rampage Stunk. And nobody listened, really listened, to the rantings of Lord Dorgar Adarbrent. The fat man laughed and signaled for another glass of wine.

Rampage Stunk knew Lord Adarbrent had accepted his invitation simply to see who supported Stunk and who was likely to sell their family heritage to him. Very good, let the old man realize exactly how powerful Rampage Stunk had become. There was nothing that he could do.

Somewhere on the dance floor, a woman shrieked. Unlike the shouts and shrieks earlier in the night, this was a very shrill cry, one tinged with fear.

Stunk frowned, turning ponderously in his place to spot the cause of that cry. He hated to see his guests disturbed from the pursuits that would eventually benefit him. Stunk peered into the crowd, looking for a troublemaker. Was it one of the younger blades? Some of the half-elves had disturbing ideas of proper behavior at times.

Another cry, this from a man by the lower tone, and just as startled. Then another, and another.

"Look, the windows!" shouted someone from the dance floor.

Stunk swung his clumsy body around, knocking a wine glass from someone's hand.

Behind him a voice said, "Oh dear, I am so sorry," and so he knew he had bumped into someone of no significance. Without bothering to check, he clumped toward the windows.

All along one side of his magnificent ballroom, Rampage Stunk had installed great windows that ran from floor to ceiling. Earlier in the evening, they had let in the dying sunlight, sparking fire in the long mirrors that ran the opposite length of the room.

In summer months, of course, they could be pushed open, to allow the dancing to continue onto the long terraces of his garden. In winter, once the darkness set in, his marvelous windows served as second mirrors, dimly reflecting back the glowing candles and the shimmering costumes of his guests.

But now, the windows no longer mirrored the guests within the room. Instead, each window glowed with a pale pearly light, revealing another party that danced upon the terraces outside.

A grim company swirled behind the glass, corpses dressed in the finest fashions of Waterdeep, the fashions of yesterday, the fashions of one hundred years before, and the fashions of much earlier times. Slowly they pirouetted, mimicking the movements of the guests within.

Stunk squinted through the dark glass. With considerable effort, he kept his smile on his fat face.

"A bit of entertainment," he said in a loud voice.

His wife appeared in front of him, tall, elegant, dressed in a gown that he was sure had cost him a fortune.

She looked annoyed, but then, she always did. In a voice lowered so that only he could hear it, she murmured, "In very poor taste. Did you arrange this?"

Stunk ignored her and reached out a hand to stop one of his men who was hurrying by carrying a tray of wine glasses. "It is only the usual ghosts. Nothing new. Make that clear to our guests," he told the man.

Waving another servant to his side, he whispered, "Send a few of the men outside with lanterns. See if you can scare them off."

The servant's eyes widened but then he nodded and said, "We will try, saer."

"Try?" Stunk growled. "Succeed, man, or find employment elsewhere."

The ghosts outside continued to dance. The men dressed in disintegrating satin coats and breeches and high-heeled pumps bowed to their ghastly partners. The women dipped and curtsied, holding out their wide skirts of fading brocade trimmed in tattered lace. Beneath once elegant white wigs or confections of molting feathers, strands of hair drooped across their foreheads. They floated closer to the glass, mouths open in dark smiles, and their faces appeared to be nothing but shadows and empty eye sockets.

The guests within the ballroom came to a stuttering, murmuring, fearful halt before this show. With elaborate bows and curtsies, the dreadful guests outside ended their own dance. With languid elegance, they turned to face the ones within and raised their arms, shaking back silk and lace to reveal hands of rotting flesh or polished bone.

The ghosts took a deliberate step forward. All together, they knocked against the glass. Skeletal fingers curled into claws and scratched the windows while others beat against the panes. The sound resembled hail bouncing off the glass.

"It's only a spirit mist," faltered one young lady to her escort. "There's nothing to those."

"They look a bit more rotted than the usual spirits," he muttered back.

"They look a great deal more solid too," answered a friend, taking a quick gulp of his wine.

A glass shattered somewhere in the room, dropped by a nerveless hand, and all the guests jumped and then tittered at their fright.

"It's just the usual ghosts," someone said, prodded by one of Rampage's servants whispering hasty instructions from his master. "Nothing to worry about."

A woman seated at the gaming tables shrieked again. "That's not any ghost. That's my grandmother! Fanquar, Fanquar"—she shook the sleepy husband at her side—"do you think she knows I sold her favorite necklace to pay my dress bills?"

"Wouldn't be surprised," Fanquar muttered as he slid deeper in his chair. "You practically ransacked the old lady's jewel box before the corpse was cold."

The corpses outside stopped their knocking. Now they pressed close against the glass, so ghastly faces could be clearly seen beneath the wigs and wide hats. They turned their heads from side to side as if seeking someone within the ballroom.

The guests inside drew back a collective pace.

"That does look like my uncle," said one spendthrift young lord to another. "The one that wanted his art collection preserved for the glory of Waterdeep."

"Didn't you sell those statues to buy a new horse?" asked his friend.

"Well, yes." The young noble shifted uneasily from one foot to the other. "But I'm thinking perhaps I should give the tapestries to my cousin Lady Alshiraina. She has been wanting to do a public display for the children of Waterdeep, so they can learn their noble history. That might lessen the old boy's frown."

A wavering face flattened its nose against the pane, empty eye sockets turned toward the young noble. The face neither smiled nor frowned. It seemed to be waiting for something and in no hurry. The lack of expression was terrifying.

Glancing at the shadowed figure now stolidly planted on the other side of the fragile window glass, the young man's friend gulped and blurted, "Give away the tapestries. An excellent idea. Perhaps we should leave to plan it right now."

"Close the curtains, close the curtains," Rampage Stunk bellowed at his servants. He snapped his fingers at the musicians, who sat open-mouthed and staring among their instruments. "Play, play loudly, or you'll collect no fee tonight!"

The heavy velvet drapes hid the ghastly party outside the windows. The music rippled through the ballroom. A few guests, those most deeply in debt to Rampage Stunk, took to the dance floor again, prodded there by his servants.

But the rest of the uneasy crowd remained huddled against the mirrors, as far away from the windows as possible.

Behind the drapes, a rattling of panes could be heard. A shaking of the casements. Even the ominous cracking of glass.

With whispers and murmurs, the guests began to flee for the tall doors leading out of the ballroom.

Stunk stepped in front of one retreating couple. "Leaving so early? The evening has hardly begun."

"Such a lovely party," the woman murmured, looking toward the door.

"I did want a word with you," Stunk said to the husband. The man was deeply in his debt and Stunk was sure the guest would not dare leave against Stunk's wishes.

The woman caught her husband's elbow. He looked at her and then at Stunk, and for a moment at the covered windows. With a bow and a face stiff with fear, he said, "I am at your service at any other time, saer. However, at the moment, my wife is feeling a bit faint and I really must take her home."

Within moments, the room emptied. Soon there was no one left but Rampage Stunk, his pale wife standing alone by the banquet table, and his servants.

Stunk's wife turned to face him and mouthed, "I told you that such entertainment was in poor taste."

"Do you think I invited them? Are you quite mad, my lady?"

As Rampage Stunk began to rage, he realized one other guest remained within the room. At the far end, nearest the doors, stood Lord Adarbrent, rubbing his chin in a satisfied manner.

The old man plucked a full wine glass from a forgotten tray. With a deliberate smile, he toasted Rampage Stunk and drained it dry.

"An excellent party," the elderly nobleman said and, with a final deep bow to Stunk's wife, Lord Adarbrent left.

Letting out a howl of fury, Stunk swept the glasses off a nearby table, shattering them upon the floor. His servants fled. His lady wife with a disapproving shake of her head silently glided away.

"I don't know how he did it. I don't know who helped him," shrieked Stunk, stamping his feet like a small child who has had a favorite toy snatched away. "But I will find out. And they will pay! They will pay in blood!"

FOURTEEN

Leaplow Carver rolled his way home, just a little foggy from having had more than one drink. But a man needed to celebrate and soothe a heated constitution. And that bout with the big sailor who thought he was the best wrestler on land or sea had certainly left Leaplow sweating. Still and all, it had gone well. Leaplow had never been to sea, but he could safely say that he was the best wrestler within the walls of Waterdeep.

He rubbed his eye and winced. It would be black and swollen by morning. He should remember to ask Myemaw for some cold meat to cool it when he got home. Glancing at the yellow moon riding low in the sky, he considered his grandmother's temper if he roused her out of bed because he'd acquired another black eye. Better to wait for morning, he decided.

People suddenly filled the silent street. A great crowd of revelers appeared, spinning all around him. The men and women were richly dressed and obviously returning from some masquerade in the northern part of the city. For some wore skeleton heads over their faces, bone gleaming under their broad-brimmed hats or finely trimmed wigs.

One pretty young lady grabbed at Leaplow's hand. He started at the coldness of her touch. She must have been outside for a long time, he thought. But she smiled at him sweetly and tugged him into the dance.

Leaplow went with a kick of his heels and a happy shout. Because if there was anything he loved as much as fighting, it was dancing with a pretty girl.

Round and round the street they whirled, and the rest of the nobles jigged and bobbed with them.

The cobblestones rang under the pounding of Leaplow's hob-nailed boots, but the lady on his arm glided silently beside him. She drifted and spun, light as thistledown in the moonlight, and Leaplow chortled at her grace.

The dance swung up the street and then swirled through the alleys and the broad avenues.

Finally they reached a place that Leaplow recognized. A bell jangled over his head as they entered through the public gate into Dead End's courtyard. The house's windows were all dark, a sure sign that the entire family was sleeping.

"Shh, shh," Leaplow tried to shush the party without realizing that he was the only one making any noise.

The pretty lady patted his shoulder and waved good-bye. Leaplow blinked and stumbled to halt, waving after her. But she faded through the gate leading into the City of the Dead and her party faded with her.

Leaplow slid down until he was sitting on the cobblestones of the courtyard. He found a lump of granite to pillow his aching head. With an enormous yawn, he began to settle back for a nap.

"How nice of them to bring me home," was his last thought before he fell asleep.

And it wasn't until morning, after his cousin Cadriffle woke him with a pail of cold water, that he noticed the iron gate leading into the City of the Dead was hanging wide open, the lock broken, leaving Dead End House unprotected and vulnerable to excursions from the graveyard side.

>———W———<

Sophraea sat beside her bedroom window, watching the night sky change from black to pale gray. For the past five mornings, the family had gone into the courtyard to find the Dead End gate shattered by the roaming dead.

At least now, nobody in the family doubted that real trouble stirred in the graveyard. But, at the same time, none of the Carvers could quite agree on what to do, except to keep quiet about the gate and try to fix the problem themselves. Especially since the broadsheets started publishing the threats of Rampage Stunk against any and all involved in the dead's persistent attempts to invade his mansion.

Late the previous day, Uncle Perspicacity did what he had done on the preceding nights. He built up the fire in the forge until the heat reached the temperature he needed. And then, sweating and weary, he worked steadily pounding away the damage to the gate and strengthening the bars with added bands of metal.

While he worked, the other uncles stood around and argued with the aunts about what to do next. Some, like Judicious, thought the addition of chains and padlocks would be enough to keep the ghosts from breaking through. Others, like her aunt Catletrho, argued for more drastic steps, like bricking closed the opening. But the majority of the family was not quite ready to give up the entrance to the City of the Dead that was so handy for their work.

With their hands wrapped in rags to protect them from the still cooling metal, Leaplow, Bentnor, and Cadriffle had picked up the reforged gate, carried it back, and fastened it in place. Then Uncle Judicious added his locks and chains, checking everything more than once.

Sophraea kept watch at the window throughout the night. As had happened on previous nights, she heard the gate shatter. Remembering the exhaustion etching lines on the faces of her family, she decided not to wake anyone. Instead, she'd go down to the courtyard first and see how badly the gate was damaged.

If the gate was destroyed, she would not hesitate. She would go into the City of the Dead and see if she could find out how or why the dead were so persistently marching through Waterdeep to the house of Rampage Stunk.

For the past five days, she had argued with Gustin, certain the answers lay beyond the wall and inside the graveyard, answers that could only be found after the dead had left their tombs for their nightly revelry. And for five nights, the wizard had stubbornly refused to venture into the City of the Dead after sunset.

But all his spells and investigations during the daylight hours had yielded no answers. With dawn so close, Sophraea decided, venturing into the City of the Dead should be safe enough. And, she thought, this time she would go alone.

Her mother would not approve. Her father would shake his head against it. Leaplow would say that she was too small to do anything. Not that Leaplow was any tower of sense or rational action! In fact, if she said anything about her suspicions that the trouble started at the Markarl tomb, the rest of her brothers, sisters-in-law, cousins, uncles, and aunts would add their contradicting opinions, just as they had for the past five days.

Sophraea sighed. No matter what she did, her family would have a dozen arguments against it and so worrying about what they would say was no reason to hesitate. She grabbed her shoes and pulled a cape over her sturdy winter gown.

Her bedroom candle was nearly burned down to a stub, but there was enough left to light her way down the stairs.

She moved carefully, carrying her shoes past Volponia's door. The old lady was a light sleeper and as troubled as the rest of the family by recent events.

Sophraea avoided the centers of the treads where they were most likely to creak, tiptoeing on the firmer edges. The loud steady snores of the Carver males overrode any sound made by her soft footsteps.

Once down to the main level of the house, she made a quick

detour through the kitchen. The banked-up fire left the room unnaturally cold and silent. In less than an hour, the Carvers would be up and the fire roaring, breakfast baking, the day starting properly. A Carver cat slid around the door and stared at her for a moment, waiting to see if she would produce any food, then slipped from the room on its own mysterious errand.

Prompted by the rumblings of her own empty stomach, Sophraea grabbed her shopping basket and stocked it with seedcakes from the pottery jar. After all, there was no reason to starve while wandering through a graveyard just before dawn, she reasoned. But another part of her overactive imagination scolded her for the delay, telling her that she was a coward, afraid of what she would find past the shattered gate.

Another bit of her brain whispered temptingly that perhaps the gate was still intact and there was nothing to be seen.

Sophraea shook her head to silence all the arguing voices and left the kitchen to continue down the stairs.

When she reached the outer door, she set her candlestick on the floor and worked at the latch with both hands. Once the door was open, she leaned out and listened.

A low wind rustled the branches. Otherwise there was no sound. She picked up the guttering candle, stepped outside, then eased the door closed.

She crossed the cobbles until she reached the gate. Stopping to listen, she turned and looked up and down the yard. Not so much as a shadow moved. Sophraea raised her candle and stifled a scream of frustration and fear.

It had happened again! Where the latch should be, there was a huge gaping hole. Small bits of broken metal littered the ground. The bars were bent or broken, hanging crookedly from the cracked hinges.

She slowly pushed open the broken bits of the gate. Perspicacity had done his usual excellent job with the repairs. The hinges didn't creak.

When the opening was wide enough, she slipped through, determined to find answers. Perhaps someone living had passed this way during the night, someone who was controlling the ghosts, driving them into Waterdeep. Bending over to hold her candle near the ground, she searched for footprints. Once before she had seen the tiny marks of dancing shoes. This time all she found were scuffs where the moss-slick stairs led down to the rain-darkened gravel paths.

She heard a distant sound of laughter, thin, high-pitched, or was it sobbing? She strained to tell where the noise was coming from. As usual her sense of the graveyard expanded until she knew exactly where she stood in relation to the Dead End gate, the tombs, and the paths running throughout the City of the Dead. All the public gates were locked tight and she sensed additional members of the Watch stood outside each one, looking in, wondering as she did which members of the noble dead roamed abroad.

The branches overhead shook with a rattle of leaves. Sophraea gasped, startled out of her trance, then muttered, "Look at me, panicking at a breeze."

The breeze turned into a quick gust and blew out her candle.

She stood absolutely still, not blinking, not breathing. And then she heard footsteps, very quiet ones, barely crunching on the gravel of the path, and knew that someone was sneaking up on her. Moving silently, she pulled the snuffed candle out, dropped it into the basket hooked over her elbow, and tightened her fist around the top of the metal holder. It was a heavy candlestick with a wide base.

As the footsteps moved nearer, she raised her arm above her head.

She could sense him now, a presence behind her, something breathing, not a ghost.

As she felt rather than saw him reach toward her, she swung around. A hand grabbed her other arm and she bent forward to retain her balance, then kept swinging. The candlestick collided with solid flesh.

And a familiar howl sounded in her ear.

"Gustin?" Sophraea whispered.

The wizard staggered away from her. He gasped and doubled up, his arms wrapped around his waist.

"Gustin, what are you doing here?"

"Getting my ribs broken," he rasped.

"Why did you sneak up on me? Oh dear, I'd better take you back to the house and wake Myemaw. She can bind them up."

She heard him catch his breath. His voice shook but he managed to say, "No, I am quite all right, Sophraea."

"But what are you doing out here?" she asked.

"Following you. Someone is using dangerous magic to stir up the dead. You shouldn't be out here at night by yourself. It's not safe. I thought we agreed that we would only come here in broad daylight."

"But we haven't found anything so far in broad daylight, and it's not really night, it's practically morning," she argued, "and I heard the gate shatter last night. And, just now, I heard something else. Oh, there it is again!"

From the distance she heard thin screeches of laughter and the sound seemed to be coming closer.

"Come on, we shouldn't stand out in plain sight," she said and led him deeper into the City of the Dead until they reached the Honor Garden. When she saw the stone tree trunk, she pulled Gustin behind it.

"Who are we hiding from?" Gustin whispered.

"If I knew that, I might not be hiding," she whispered back. "Gustin, when did you follow me here? I didn't see you in the yard."

"I heard you open the outer door," he said. "There I was, nice and warm in a clean bed, then one of your mad cats came dashing through the room, leaped right in the center of my stomach and, once I was awake, ran off."

Sophraea almost chuckled. "You should latch your door."

"I think your cats can walk through walls," muttered Gustin. "But being awake, I decided to get up and go looking for something to eat. I was in the kitchen when I heard the door open. And I thought, who would be fool enough to go out before it was light?"

Suddenly, the odd laughter grew nearer, a loud mingling of moans and insane giggles. She could hear shuffling, as though a small army approached. Clutching her candlestick, Sophraea leaned out to squint into the dim pre-dawn light. At first all she saw was empty path.

Then they came floating, twisting, dancing by, feet occasionally touching the ground, ghostly hands beating out a rhythm, heads swaying to some music that Sophraea could not hear.

They were dressed in flounces and tatters and spiderweb trimmings, faded velvet and dulled silk. Some had faces of shadows and starlight. Others were worn down to bones gleaming white under the waning moon. They moved in a swirl of cold air that smelled vaguely of mold and perfume and death.

Sophraea pressed back against Gustin. If they saw her, those ghastly remnants of the dead, what would they do? She was torn between fear and pity. She dreaded the thought of being dragged along in their company. But more, she felt so sorry for them, wandering like that, unable to rest quietly in their graves.

Night gave way to the first weak rays of sunlight. The damp clean smell of wet grass replaced the faint scent of decay.

Leaning close to Gustin, she breathed with relief, "Dawn."

They both watched and kept silent, not daring to say more,

hardly daring to breathe, until they saw the last of the dead revelers disappear into the morning shadows.

"You can come out now," a clear voice said.

FIFTEEN

The wizard jumped, so startled by the disembodied voice behind them that he bumped into Sophraea and almost knocked her over. Her own heart raced and she was hard pressed not to scream.

"It's early for you to be here," said their unseen companion.

A shifting of green shadows tugged at Sophraea's extra sense of the graveyard surrounding them.

"Briarsting, is that you?" Sophraea demanded, looking around. "Where are you?"

Leaves rustled in a hedge behind them. In the shadows, the topiary dragon blended with other more motionless shrubbery. The thorn gestured from under the shelter of the topiary dragons' belly. "The dead will be back in their mausoleums, tombs, coffins, and graves in a moment."

"You could have told us you were there," she complained, the beat of her heart settling into a less panicked rhythm.

After patting the leafy dragon's neck, Sophraea and Gustin slid out from behind the stone tree trunk and around the bristly beast. Above them, the sky turned dull gray as the early morning sunlight tried to penetrate the cloud cover. The main gate would be open to Waterdeep's Watch. Patrols would go through the pathways to see what disturbances had occurred in the night. Soon the City of the Dead would also be open to the public, if the City Watch decided it was safe.

"When did it start last night?" Sophraea questioned Briarsting.

The little man scratched his nose and then shrugged. "Just after moonrise. I was dozing but the shrubbery here woke me."

The topiary dragon waggled its ears at them.

"Straight down the paths and through our gate?" She thought she knew the answer but she had to ask.

Briarsting nodded. "Just as before."

"And then off to haunt Rampage Stunk." Sophraea sighed. More threats and sensation stories were sure to appear in every broadsheet in Waterdeep. The previous day's *Blue Unicorn* had been bad enough. She still had it in her basket because she couldn't bear to show it to her family and worry them even more.

"Was the same ghost leading them?" Sophraea asked the thorn.

"The dancing lady? Yes, I saw her clearly." Briarsting had been their spy in the cemetery at night, as worried as they were about the constant disturbances, and more than willing to give what information he had. But the thorn and his shrubbery friend could do nothing to stop the constant escape of the dead from their tombs.

"I saw your father too," he added.

"My father? When was that?"

"Last night. From sunset until almost midnight, sitting on the ground with his back against the gate."

That made no sense to Sophraea. Surely he was mistaken. She had seen her father in the house last evening, going over plans for a strengthened gate with her uncles. "Are you sure it was my father?" she asked.

The thorn turned a brighter green from annoyance.

"I haven't seen him in many a year, but I must tell you, young miss. He hasn't changed a bit. Looks exactly the same as he did thirty years ago," he declared. "I know Astute Carver when I see him."

"He's gone gray," she said, frowning. But Briarsting seemed so sure, she didn't want to upset him. "Probably the dark. If you saw him in daylight, you'd know he's aged."

"I have excellent eyesight," Briarsting huffed.

Muttering about missed breakfasts and curses, Gustin stalked along the paths toward the two small tombs still flagged for destruction by Rampage Stunk. The Carvers had halted work on the site four days ago and sent word to the furious Stunk that nothing could be done until the dead were resting quietly. The merchant had sent numerous messages but Astute and his brothers remained firm. Even necessary burials and other funeral rites were being carried out as quickly as possible these days, the coffins being almost hurried through the City of the Dead to the waiting portals and their final resting place.

"Has he had any luck in figuring this out?" Briarsting asked Sophraea, climbing up on a marble memorial bench to watch Gustin pace muttering around the Markarl tomb.

"Not really," admitted Sophraea, digging a seedcake out of her basket and handing it to the always-hungry thorn.

"Not at all," confessed Gustin even more honestly as he saw food appearing from the basket and joined them on the bench. "I never studied necromancy. And that's about all that's truly certain. Someone has loosed a magnificent necromantic curse against Rampage Stunk."

The wizard nipped a seedcake out of the basket. Hooking the edge of one foot on the bench, he wrapped his long arms around his knee, rocking back and forth. "Wish I knew how they did it. But I'd bet all my nonexistent wealth that the spell started here. Something about the aura of this spot."

"Don't feel too bad," Sophraea said. "Even the Watchful Order couldn't find the cause."

After the first night of the wandering dead, some senior wizards from the Order arrived in the City of the Dead to check the wards on the walls and public gates.

When the attacks continued, the Blackstaff issued a proclamation saying that Waterdeep and its citizens were quite safe. Since the City of the Dead's gates and walls were quite obviously sealed and no breaches in the defenses found, the so-called "noble dead" just as obviously did not come from there.

On top of that magnificent reasoning, the Blackstaff's proclamation continued that the "contained disturbance" bore the earmarks of a trade dispute between rival merchants, aided by renegade wizards. Those wizards would be found and punished accordingly, the proclamation concluded.

"So, all the corpses in velvet showing up on Stunk's doorstep are just illusions," quipped Gustin. He pulled another seedcake and a copy of the *Blue Unicorn* from the day before out of Sophraea's basket. He shook his head over the headlines. "At least according to this story, the haunting of Stunk's mansion is all illusions and other reports around Waterdeep were created by a hysterical population. The writer concludes by telling his readers to not believe everything they see is real."

"I wonder if he would still advise calm if he saw that parade that passed the gate today," she said.

"Quite possibly not," he agreed.

"I hear they found a hand swinging from Stunk's doorknocker yesterday morning," added Sophraea with a sigh. "Hard to see how they can say that's an illusion or a figment of the public's imagination."

"Actually," said Briarsting, rooting in her basket for another seedcake before Gustin ate them all, "that's Lady Mellania's hand. She's always a bit absentminded and asked if you would be so kind as to bring it back for her."

"Why am I supposed to bring it back?" Sophraea said indignantly. "I didn't tell her to leave it there."

"She just thought, since she would be passing by your house, you could leave it on the doorstep or somewhere close to your gate."

"I can't even think of a polite reply to that request!"

"I wouldn't worry about it." Briarsting stretched out his legs on the bench and munched happily. "Told you that she's a forgetful old thing. She won't remember she asked by tomorrow night."

"How convenient," muttered Sophraea.

"It is," agreed the little green-skinned man without irony. "And best that the rest of them don't start thinking of requests. They're enjoying these outings to Stunk's mansion quite a bit, you know. In fact, if you'll pardon me saying so, I haven't seen the north end of the cemetery quite so lively in a century or more."

Sophraea shuddered while Gustin smoothed his beard to hide a smile.

"Still," said the wizard, willing to turn the subject to Sophraea's relief. "If the Blackstaff doesn't think that the dead are coming from here, then you needn't worry so much. After all, that means nobody is looking at your family's gate."

"What the Blackstaff says publicly," said Sophraea, amazed at Gustin's innocence, "and what the Blackstaff thinks are two very different things. Didn't they have politics in Cormyr?"

Gustin shrugged and retorted, "Probably, but I never paid any attention."

"Well," Sophraea continued, "nobody is having the City Watch patrol through here quite so vigorously every day looking for pickpockets. Somebody, somebody very important, does think the dead walking through the streets come from here. They just don't know how the deceased nobility are getting out. And once they figure it is through our gate . . ."

Sophraea didn't know what type of trouble such a discovery would bring, but from the suddenly gloomy expressions of her companions, she suspected they had no cheerful expectations either. Even the topiary dragon looked a little wilted as it hung over her shoulder, begging for a whisker pull.

"It's odd," Gustin observed, "that the Watchmen haven't found your gate yet? After all, they just need to walk the cemetery wall until they come to it."

"They've probably passed it a dozen times or more," replied Briarsting, "and never knew. They're not Carvers, are they?"

"What are you talking about?" said Sophraea. "You don't have to be a Carver to see the gate."

"You have to be a Carver to find it," insisted the thorn. "Or at least to show it to someone else. After all, the Carvers built it for Carver business, not for anything else."

"You're talking about us as if we have magic," said Sophraea. "We're just tradesmen. We have our craft, building monuments and so on, but we're no wizards."

"Your family is part of Waterdeep, aren't you?" persisted Briarsting. "I met your ancestors first when my Honor Garden was laid out. It was a Carver who chipped out the bark on that stone trunk yonder. Another Carver who clipped the hedge into a dragon."

"But not a Carver who animated it," stated Sophraea.

"No," Briarsting agreed. "That was done by the druids and the elves when they came to finish the memorial."

"But the Carvers were there when it happened," Gustin guessed.

The green-skinned man nodded. "This city does things to the ones who live here longest. Even to the ones who are buried here."

"How long has your family lived in Waterdeep?" Gustin asked Sophraea. "Were they here during the Spellplague?"

She shrugged. "We've always been here. Certainly since there was a City of the Dead. It's in the ledger. Stonehands Carver helped build the first wall around the graveyard. He built Dead End House out of bits and pieces left over from that job. At least that's where the foundation stones came from. And when they built the wall higher and stronger, the family worked on that too."

"And built the house higher with leftover stone and wood," Gustin did not look surprised after Sophraea gave a slow nod.

"Magic soaks into the stones," he mused. "But does it go into the bones? That's an interesting idea. Especially if you had the Spellplague in the house."

"What?"

"It's something that Lord Adarbrent said. Magic has soaked into the very foundation stones of Waterdeep. How could it not? The city has been here for so long, through so much. The City of the Dead must have been touched by hundreds of spells. Thousands perhaps. So why wouldn't the graveyard magic soak into a family, especially a family touched by the Spellplague?"

"The boy is brighter than he looks," Briarsting commented.

Gustin waved the thorn's mocking away, stating, "It makes sense."

"The Spellplague never touched my family," said Sophraea. "Not the way that you're thinking. There were more foreign dead to be buried in the time that followed, that's all in our ledger, but we were spared."

"There were none who left and came back during the later years? None who showed the scars?"

"No," Sophraea started emphatically, and then she hesitated. "Well, Volponia. She came back from a voyage, very ill, and settled into her room. But that was long before I was born. Long before my parents even married."

"Does she have any scars? Blue marks?" Gustin asked.

"How I would know? She's my great-great aunt," said Sophraea. "She has always been there, wrapped up in her bed, quite covered from head to toe. Besides, nobody in the family has any magic. You've met them all except Volponia. They're not magic-users, spellscarred or otherwise."

"Not consciously. But you do have talents, very specific talents connected to the City of the Dead, like always knowing where you are inside the graveyard. And your eyes do glow blue, especially when you are inside the graveyard walls. I've seen it."

"Some people learn magic, some people are magic, doesn't necessarily take a plague," Briarsting observed. "Look at elves, look at dwarves. Look at my people. There are some who say that we weren't always green." He glanced down at his dark emerald hands. "Although it's hard to imagine being pink. Such an odd and useless color for skin."

"Exactly, and better put than my ramblings. Magic soaks into people, changes them, makes certain things happen," the wizard said. "So, even before the Spellplague, when Carvers needed a gate, they built a gate, and it only worked for them. Makes sense, at least in a place like Waterdeep."

"But you have gone in and out the gate," argued Sophraea. "And you're not family."

"But I was with you the first time that I went through the gate," recalled Gustin. "At least, I was following you pretty closely. I didn't even realize we'd gone through the wall until I was well within the City of the Dead. And I've always been with you or just behind you every time that we've used that gate."

"And he's living in Dead End House," pointed out Briarsting. "Which makes Gustin as much a part of the house as that pack of cats you harbor. I've never noticed any of your slinky black mousers having any trouble slipping through the gate bars."

"Cats can always go where they like," Sophraea said. Then she thought of another argument. "Lord Adarbrent uses our gate," she pointed out.

"Often?"

"Well, no, he usually enters through the public gate. But I've seen him leave through the Dead End gate, going into the cemetery, more than once," she said.

"What did you say about the basement door?" Gustin continued. "There's no problem going out from Dead End House. The door's guardian knows you're a friend of the house. Maybe the gate works the same way. If you're a friend of the house or have permission of the family, you can see it. More importantly, you can use it, at least to leave Dead End House."

Sophraea sprang off the bench and took to pacing herself, unconsciously following the trail beaten in the wet grass by Gustin's earlier perambulations around the Markarl tomb.

"So if you have to be a Carver? Or invited by a Carver? Then how do the noble dead know where to go? We certainly didn't ask them to use our gate to go gallivanting through Waterdeep." Her skirts swished through the wet grass, rocking in angry time to her agitated movements.

"Maybe the same rules don't apply to the dead?" suggested Briarsting. When the other two shook their heads at him, he added, "I just live with them. I don't necessarily understand them."

"No," said Gustin, "I think Sophraea is right. It took a Carver to lead the dead through. Maybe it only needed to be done symbolically because the dead can see more clearly than the living, at least where magic is concerned. That sounds like a ritual, something anyone with the right spellbooks could construct. Once that's done, the gate could be opened by the dead whenever they needed it or as the spellcaster commanded."

"So you think one of the family is under a spell? That one of my relatives walked into the City of the Dead and led a parade of noble dead out? Do you think that's what Leaplow did?" Sophraea mused, remembering how they had discovered her brother in the courtyard.

"No, your brother just ended up with the dead on that first night by accident," said Gustin, who had questioned Sophraea's brother as closely as he dared. Leaplow still tended to react badly to realization that the prettiest girl that he'd ever danced with spent her daylight hours in a grave. "And Leaplow was never in the City of the Dead that day. He's very adamant that he worked at Dead End House all day carving my statue, left through the public gate to go drinking, and came back to Dead End House through the same gate."

How would Rampage Stunk react to such a suggestion that a Carver had started the curse, Sophraea wondered. She shuddered. The fat man's threats against anyone who had helped bring about his current haunting grew more grisly every day according to the *Unicorn*.

"So who do you think opened the gate and suggested these ghosts and wandering corpses use our courtyard as their shortcut to Rampage Stunk?" Sophraea asked.

"It doesn't have to be quite that literal." Gustin chewed his lower lip, having run out of seedcakes. "As I said before, it was probably a symbolic action, something that the person might not even been aware of. That's how many curses are done, by tricking people into helping the caster. Symbols carry a lot of weight in such rituals. A token that symbolizes permission for the dead to enter."

"So you are saying someone, probably a Carver, carried something through the gate that unlocked it for the dead," Briarsting said. "Makes sense. I've seen a lot of odd mementos used as keys for various tombs around here. A hair ribbon, a dried flower, a twist of wire."

"The shoe!" exclaimed Gustin and Sophraea together.

"What shoe?" asked Briarsting.

"The one we found in the tunnels. A little gold brocade shoe. Volponia said that it had probably been buried with someone," Sophraea explained. "But that doesn't work. I took it through the basement door. And nothing happened that night."

"Wrong door," said Gustin automatically. "The ritual needed the gate."

"What?"

"And my old master said that I never paid attention to my lessons." Gustin looked almost smug. He rapped his knuckles smartly against the bench. "The shoe and the gate were linked together in a ritual. So, until you carried it from the City of the Dead through your family's gate, the dead couldn't follow. That makes sense. At least from a wizard's point of view."

"But I didn't," she began and then stopped. "Oh. On the way home from Lord Adarbrent's house, after the fight. We cut back through the Andamaar gate and along the inside of the wall to go home through our gate. Because I said it would be faster."

Sophraea sank onto the bench in despair. The topiary dragon dropped its whiskery nose into her lap. She patted the brittle late autumn leaves gently, appreciating the dragon's gesture of support, but there really was no comfort. She had done this to her family, placed them directly in the middle of a feud between the noble dead and Rampage Stunk.

She had put them all in mortal danger.

SIXTEEN

Gustin kept patting her shoulder. Briarsting offered her a thin papery leaf and advised "Blow hard."

As for the topiary dragon, it collapsed in a sympathetic heap of quivering foliage at her feet.

Sophraea did not know what they were all so upset about. As she informed them repeatedly, she was not crying. She was not.

"I am going to solve this," she stated for the third time, pleased that she managed the entire sentence without her voice breaking, cracking, or doing any of the other distressing modulations that had plagued the first two pronouncements.

"Well, of course," said Gustin just as briskly with one more pat. "And we are going to help you."

"Absolutely," said Briarsting, still tucking the leaf into her hand. "But what should we do next?"

"End the curse," said Sophraea with a decisive nod. "Obviously. If the dead stop haunting Stunk, then Stunk will stop hunting for revenge. At least, I hope so." She turned abruptly on the bench and poked Gustin in the chest. "You're the wizard. How do I end this spell?"

Looking as serious as she had ever seen him, Gustin said, "I've been thinking about that. I've been thinking about it ever since this began. I don't meddle with the dead. I have nothing in my very limited spellbook that even comes close."

From a distance that sounded deep within the cemetery, Sophraea heard a thin cry. She glanced at the other two. Neither made any sign of hearing what she heard.

"But you do have a spellbook? You understand magic," she continued. Wizards, her tone implied, should be prepared for anything, even a graveyard full of restless corpses intent on bringing trouble to her family's doorstep.

Gustin reached into his tunic and withdrew the guidebook to Waterdeep that he'd shown Sophraea earlier. Once again he carefully unfolded the crudely printed map bound into the back, laying it flat on the bench between them. He tapped one corner of the map and the streets and buildings swirled together in a rainbow of colors, then faded away to show line after line of tiny writing.

There it was again, a scream that strangled away. Neither Briarsting nor Gustin seemed to notice it. A soft nudge against her shoulder made Sophraea start and clamp her mouth closed to keep from gasping. She felt soft leaves brush her neck.

When she turned her head, her eyes looked straight into one of the dragon's red berry eyes. It was wide open. The greenery of his brow drew into a deep wrinkle of worry. So she wasn't imagining the cry. The topiary dragon heard it too.

"All my spells," Gustin said, still looking down at his book. "All learned in bits and pieces, here and there. Animation of stone. That ritual is especially mine, but how is that going to help? Some defensive spells, which are not nearly as powerful as a good offensive spell. A few illusions, which work well. One spell that lets me run away from danger very fast. I'd be happy to use any of these in your service. But I don't see how it solves your problem."

Sophraea didn't see either. Round and round her finger, she twisted the ring that Volponia had given her. "There's a half a wish in this," she finally said, pulling the ring off and handing it to Gustin. "Could that stop this curse?"

"Half a wish?" He echoed, juggling the ring in the palm of his hand. "I doubt it. Wishes are magic based on hope. A half-hearted hope, like a half a wish, probably isn't enough to trump a good solid hate-filled curse. And the one thing that I can tell about this curse: whoever unleashed it really hates Rampage Stunk."

He gave the little silver ring back to Sophraea. She slid it on her finger with a sigh. It didn't seem right that a curse, one not even directed at her family, could create such havoc. But all Waterdeep knew that Stunk was seeking whoever had loosed the curse against him. No one had ever accused the fat man of being fair-minded. He was sure to blame the Carvers and even if they could drive off his bullies or appeal to the City Watch for protection, it would mean days or even tendays of disruption. And Stunk well might hire his own wizards. Dead End House had its protections, but Sophraea still worried about how much the family could withstand before somebody was seriously hurt.

The sound of booted feet crunching heavily down the gravel path propelled Gustin and Sophraea off the bench.

"Is it the Watch?" Sophraea asked as Briarsting leaped to the shoulder of the grieving stone woman overlooking the pool. From there, he hopped to the roof of a mausoleum.

"No," the green-skinned man called down. "It's a dwarf!"

The deep orange of the stout dwarf's waterproof hat and cloak marked him as a member of the cellarers' and plumbers' guild. In one hand he clutched a rake for clearing storm drains.

Sophraea started to murmur a polite greeting. The dwarf stared at her blankly.

"Do I know you, young lady?" he said slowly. "Forgive me my haste but I have urgent business at the Plinth. There will be a jump tonight."

Gustin stepped aside to let him pass. Sophraea watched the dwarf march steadily away from them. There was something odd about the sturdy hammerpipe, the faintest twinge of that same sense that always told her where she was in the City of the Dead.

If she narrowed her eyes and stared really hard at the dwarf, she could see the shadow of a much taller figure marching steadily away from them.

"I thought the Plinth was destroyed," remarked Gustin.

With a start, Sophraea broke her concentration on the dwarf. "Oh, yes, the Spellplague took down the Plinth." The dwarf had disappeared around a corner of the path. "But the dead don't always know current history."

"That was a dwarf. Not a corpse."

"That was a possessed hammerpipe," she corrected him. "There's no reason a member of the guild would be aboveground looking for a long-lost temple."

"Are you sure?"

"Come on, I want to see where he came from." Sophraea headed north on the path, following the clear footprints of the dwarf. She stopped at a leaf-clogged grate and the puddle stretching across the path. "I don't know any hammerpipe who would pass by something like that. No, some ghost has grabbed him."

"Shouldn't we do something?"

"You know exorcism spells?"

Gustin admitted he did not.

"They'll catch him at one of the gates," Sophraea said to soothe both Gustin and her conscience. "Or the City Watch will pick him up on their patrol. It will give them something to do."

Another turn of the path showed an open storm grate and a pile of tools lying next to it, obviously where the dwarf had been working. Sophraea took a hard look at the tomb nearest the grate and the family name carved deeply into the granite.

"One of the Lathkule," she said. "That explains it. A restless family and notorious possessors. This ritual has stirred up too many of the dead."

A gnome's head suddenly popped up from the open sewer line.

Like the dwarf, he was dressed in the orange of the cellarers' and plumbers' guild.

"Here! You, young person," shouted the gnome. "Have you seen my friend? We've found the problem down here."

Sophraea blinked in surprise at seeing this ordinary worker in the middle of the City of the Dead. "I think your friend went down that path," she pointed in the direction that the dwarf had taken.

The gnome scrambled the rest of the way out of the hole, then leaned back to call down. "Firebeard has gone off again. Can you get the clog up by yourselves?"

More muffled shouting could be heard from the hole.

The gnome cast a grimy eye over Sophraea and her companion. He tossed the end of a rope to Gustin Bone. "Haul on this, will you, tall guy?" he said. "Faster we get this cleared, the faster we can get out of here."

With a good-natured shrug, Gustin began pulling on the rope. Slowly, like an exhausted fish being hauled into a boat, a bundle of cloth and bones emerged from the hole. The richly dressed skeleton was followed by a contingent of gnomes and dwarves, all dressed in dark orange. One of the gnomes wore the additional trappings that marked her as a cleric of considerable rank.

"Don't call it a clog," scolded the cleric. "That's not respectful."

"Caused a back-up all the way to Wall Way, didn't it?" said the first gnome in unrepentant tones. "That's a clog in my book. But we got it back here. Now what do you want to do?"

"We need to settle these bones," said the cleric. The skeleton stirred in its muddy finery. With a shake of her head, the cleric reached into her pocket for a vial of glowing liquid. With a murmured prayer, she shook the holy water over the skeleton, which collapsed back on the ground.

Sophraea leaned over the bones to take a closer look. The heavily embroidered robes wrapped around the skeleton incorporated a number of heraldic devices that she recognized as decorating the nearby Irlingstar monument. Another deceased member of an ancient Waterdeep family had been wandering, she realized. Once the body had no doubt been bathed with perfumed water and wrapped with herbs tucked under his burial robes. Now his funeral clothes smelled of the sewers.

"It was kind of you to bring the bones back here," she told the collected members of the guild.

"It's the guild's rules," explained the cleric. "If something washes out of the City of the Dead, it has to be replaced properly. Anything else would cause serious problems. But we don't usually get them trying to dig their way out through a feeder line."

"How far from here did you find these bones?" Sophraea asked.

"Almost to the wall. Most of the lines directly under the wall are small or gated. This one had gotten stuck in one of the smaller tubes, just south and east of the Andamaar gate."

That would put the skeleton on a direct underground path to the Dead End gate, Sophraea thought but didn't bother to explain to the cleric. Instead she pointed out the Irlingstar site. "If you can get him laid down there," she said, "I'll send my uncle Judicious to put a dead safe over the grave. That should keep these bones from wandering again."

"You're a Carver," observed the gnome leader of the group. Sophraea nodded. "Good. Save us a trip and take a message to Astute that we're seeing more disturbances down below. Nothing as big as this, but we're getting more dirt falls from the City above into the lines."

"I'll let my father know. The City Watch is looking for the cause," she added.

The gnome leader snorted. "Like that group of soldiers

understand anything about dirt and digging. Tell your father to send along that Feeler and Fish. I think a couple of graves on the far north are starting to collapse. They'll know what to do. I'd shore them up myself, but you know how it is. Guild rules. We're only supposed to work on the sewer lines."

"Who should they ask for at guild headquarters?"

"Tollemar, that's me, or Firebeard. We're in charge of the City of the Dead's sewers," said the gnome.

The cleric directed the other sewer workers on the digging and placing of the still slightly twitching skeleton in the Irlingstar grave.

"That should hold," she told Sophraea and Gustin after a long blessing over the bones. "But this one has been tough to settle. I had to use almost a full bottle of holy water to keep those bones quiet during the trip back here."

"We appreciate your help," Sophraea answered. "I'd suggest being out of the City before dark. Things have been . . ." She trailed off, not sure how to describe the constant march of the corpses and haunts out of the Dead End House's gate.

"Don't worry," answered Tollemar instead. "I'm not letting any of my people in or under the City after nightfall. Guild rules."

"Probably for the best," Sophraea agreed.

"Now, where did you see Firebeard?"

Sophraea pointed out the right path to follow the missing dwarf. The guild members carefully closed up the grate leading into the sewers, double-checked the lock, and then shouldering their tools, they marched after their missing friend.

Once the members of the cellarers' and plumbers' guild were out of sight, Briarsting and the topiary dragon emerged from behind the tomb where they had been eavesdropping on the exchange.

"If the dead are going into the sewers," said the thorn, "that's bad."

"I know," Sophraea said. "It means all the protections are crumbling."

"What protections?" asked Gustin.

"When they first dug the sewer lines under the City, the Blackstaff laid certain protections against the dead using those tunnels to escape. You still do get things down there, but usually not straight from a grave."

"But the wall continues to hold," observed Briarsting. "You heard the gnomes. That skeleton didn't get completely free."

"But for how long?" fretted Sophraea. "And what if they are trying to use the lower ways into Dead End House?"

Gustin shook his head. "I think the gate is still the only exit that the ritual allows them to use. After all, that skeleton got stuck. It didn't get out."

"That's not a lot of comfort. We need to settle the dead permanently and completely."

"There are great wizards in Waterdeep," said Briarsting slowly. "Ones who can command the dead."

"I'm not going to the Blackstaff," said Sophraea. "Nor to any of the wizards in the Watchful Order. It would be too many explanations and the family is sure to get into trouble about the gate."

"We can hire someone less legitimate," suggested Gustin.

"And how do we pay? I have a silver ring with half a wish," said Sophraea. "I don't think that's going to be enough for the type of magic we need."

The topiary dragon waggled its ears and scratched at the earth with one forepaw.

"There are treasures still in this graveyard," Briarsting translated. "We could borrow a few gems."

"That's not a bad idea," said Gustin.

"No," said Sophraea firmly. "I'm a Carver. And the one thing that we never do is steal from the dead. It leads to trouble. It always does. What do you think happened to Fitlor?"

"I was going to ask you about that," Gustin began. "Didn't he used to sleep in my room?"

"He was a distant cousin," Sophraea emphasized. "And he took something that he shouldn't have, something he found when he was helping Leaplow repair a tomb."

"And then?"

"He went through a portal and never came back."

"Maybe he's just traveling," Gustin suggested hopefully.

"We'd like to think so. But we can't take things from the dead. It never goes well. Look what damage I've done just by removing that shoe!"

"Then why don't you bring it back?" suggested Briarsting. The two humans stared at him and the thorn shrugged. "Look, it's just logic. If taking it out caused the problem, maybe putting it back where you found it will quiet down the dead."

"That's brilliant!" said Gustin, shaking the little man's hand so vigorously that the thorn's feet bounced off the ground. "I should have thought of that. After all, I am the wizard. He's right. If we could get back what started the spell, we should be able to cast some type of basic reversal. I know a ritual that might work like that in a pinch."

"But I don't have the shoe. It disappeared from the house, the night that the dead started walking," Sophraea protested.

"Hmm," Gustin tugged his beard, a green flash burning bright under his long lashes. "Bet I know where it is. But you won't like it."

"Where?"

"Stunk's mansion."

"Oh, no."

"Makes sense. From a wizard's point of view. It's the token, the object that draws the dead through your gate. And keeps drawing them back to one specific place, Stunk's mansion. If it was still at your house, they'd be knocking on the Dead End door all night."

"So we have to go to Stunk's and ask politely to search his house for a shoe that was taken from the City of the Dead?" Sophraea asked.

Gustin nodded. "We could do it."

"How? His servants will recognize us immediately. Stunk knows me. And once he sees me, he'll assume that the Carvers are involved. Which means he will try to cut my family into tiny pieces." She heaved an enormous sigh. "All right, I'll go to the Watchful Order. Perhaps they will know some way to end this."

"No, no," Gustin said excitedly. "We don't need those wizards. I'll tell Stunk that I'm a ghost banisher from Cormyr, able to perform miraculous exorcisms. You can be my assistant. Nobody will stop us from removing a cursed item from his house. And when we do, the noble dead will stop bothering him. Stunk will be happy." Gustin grinned. "He might even pay us. And then I could pay your father for my statue. This could work!"

"But the minute we set foot on his doorstep, his servants will recognize us!"

Gustin pulled out his disguised spellbook. "Illusions! What do you want to be? Redhead, blonde? Halfling? Elf?" He unfolded the map from the back of the guidebook and began muttering, tracing blue and brown lines that transformed from Waterdeep's familiar streets and buildings into spiky symbols and rounded letters. The air began to sparkle around his wildly waving brown curls.

As the magic engulfed him, Gustin started to look much older than usual, balding on top, bushier beard on his chin, and burly. Only his eyes remained his normal bright green.

"You make a charming elf," he said as his hair slowly faded from brown to gray.

Sophraea blinked. The same sparkling light swirled around her.

She reached up her hands to touch the tops of her ears. Both ears felt as rounded as ever.

"They look pointed to me," said Briarsting, realizing what she was doing. "That's a good disguise. Your face is completely different. Moon elf, I'd say. You even look taller."

She stared down at herself, saw a colorful skirt hem and elegant shoes beneath the edge of a brilliantly embroidered cloak.

"So, are you ready to call on Stunk?" said the seemingly elderly and heavily built wizard.

Sophraea shook her head at the visual change in Gustin's appearance. It was a good disguise. Yet, to her ear, the excited optimistic lilt in his voice revealed clearly that the man standing before her was Gustin Bone. Well, perhaps Stunk's servants wouldn't notice that. She resolved not to talk much when they were in Stunk's house. His servants had encountered her far more often than the wizard.

"Let's take the Mhalsyymber gate," Sophraea suggested, setting off briskly, as if to outrace her second and third thoughts about Gustin's hasty plans.

"Hey," said Gustin, for once forced to quicken his own steps to keep up with her, "do we know where Stunk lives?"

"Of course." She shook her head at the newcomer to Waterdeep. "He bought three mansions in the North Ward, leveled them, and built his own mansion on Brahir Street. It's supposed to be one of the largest private houses in all of Waterdeep. It took them almost a year to build it to his satisfaction."

Heading to the Mhalsyymber gate, Sophraea could not remember a time when the City of the Dead felt so strange. The usual whispers and rustles were gone. All around her, the still hush felt like it was extending to the very edges of the graveyard, probing the wall that still protected Waterdeep from those within the cemetery.

The topiary dragon glided smoothly beside them. Just before they came into sight of the gate, Briarsting halted the leafy guardian.

"He can't pass the wall," said the thorn. "But I can come with you if you need an extra sword."

Sophraea shook her head. "No, it will probably cause less comment if it is Gustin and me. But can you take a message to my family? Just don't let them know that I'm going to Stunk's." The last thing she needed was Leaplow or Bentnor and Cadriffle or her uncles to decide that she needed rescuing and to storm Stunk's mansion.

"Do you think that wise?" asked the thorn.

"Better than Leaplow roaring after us," she said.

"Ah, well," Briarsting admitted, "he's not the coolest of heads."

"Let my father know what the gnomes said," Sophraea instructed him. "About disturbances below. And that Feeler and Fish should be looking for unstable graves."

Then she had a second thought and added, "And if you see my mother, tell her that that you passed me on the way and I said I was going to the shops."

Before she returned home, she would think of a better explanation. But she hoped that Reye wouldn't be in the courtyard and Briarsting would only speak to her father. It was always easier to explain things later to Astute. Reye was far more skeptical of her excuses.

With a bird whistle, Briarsting sprang onto the neck of the topiary dragon, waved at Sophraea, and turned the beast back toward Dead End House. She watched them leave with a worried frown, wondering how badly things would go that night when the haunts started marching through the Dead End gate.

Gustin reached out and gave her shoulder a friendly squeeze. "It's still morning and early morning at that," he said. "We have plenty of time to get to Stunk's house and find that shoe. We could stop this curse before supper."

"I hope so," said Sophraea, but she lacked the wizard's confidence. A strange sense of anticipation shivered through her bones as they walked toward the gate leading out of the City of the Dead. She knew the restless dead were all around them, waiting for nightfall in their crypts, tombs, and graves.

If they didn't find a way to stop the curse, Sophraea realized, than tonight's parade of the noble dead would be even larger and more dangerous than before.

SEVENTEEN

The streets of Waterdeep's North Ward were almost as deserted as the pathways of the City of the Dead. Except for a few servants hustling around, well-wrapped in wool cloaks against the cold afternoon wind, Sophraea and Gustin saw almost nobody on their journey to Brahir Street.

"Do you think that the hauntings are keeping everyone inside?" Sophraea worried as they marched along. The closer they came to Stunk's mansion, the more empty the streets. Not even a broadsheet seller was abroad, screaming about the latest scandals.

A splat of rain mixed with sleet hit the back of Gustin's neck and slid under his collar. "I think they're just all staying inside to enjoy hot fires, warm ale, and toasted sausages," he said with a shiver. "That's what I'd do if I was rich."

"Mulled wine," Sophraea suggested, pulling her hood even tighter around her ears. Illusion or no illusion, the tips of her ears were now burning with cold. "And spiced dark cakes. That's what Myemaw always makes on days like this."

"I continue to be impressed by your grandmother's grasp of proper nourishment for the occasion," said Gustin. "I would gladly give up warm ale for mulled wine and dark cakes. But I rather think your uncles and your brothers and your large male cousins would be with me on insisting that toasted sausages should be included in the feast."

"And cheese melted across bread crusts. That's their favorite in winter."

Gustin sighed with satisfaction. "Another excellent choice. Do you think Stunk will serve us refreshments?"

"I'm just hoping we don't end up being somebody's snack," Sophraea remarked.

They heard shouting from somewhere ahead of them. Voices rose, a mixture of noise and curses, the anger clear in the tones. For a moment Sophraea felt relief. At least there is some life out on these streets, she thought.

A large figure dashed from one dark alley opening to another, dodging out of sight. Concealed inside the usual long coat and cap, it could be anyone, but it certainly looked tall and broad enough to be a Carver.

"Something's happening," she said.

"Go carefully," Gustin answered.

More crashes came from nowhere, like mallets pounding on stone. Heavy running steps, boots dashing over cobblestones, more shouts, and then the noise rose with a pattern of bangs that sounded like large children running past a fence dragging a board against the metal posts.

At guarded gates up and down the road, armed men ran out into the street. They stared and turned and yelled questions to each other.

Yet, the street ahead was clear. Guards glanced about, something almost fearful in the poses of these big men well-armored against any threat. No one lingered outside, each hustling back to their posts.

"Here," said Gustin, plucking a broken half brick off the street. He slipped it into the basket that Sophraea carried. He grabbed another and added it to the first. "Take these. You should be prepared."

"What do I need those for? The basket's heavy," she protested.

"You never know when a half brick is going to come in handy," said Gustin, rooting around to see if there were any more on the street. He did find a couple of more broken shards of yellow brick, obviously fallen off some builder's cart, and slipped those to Sophraea's basket as well.

A couple of gnomes, carrying tool bags, hurried past them. One wagged his eyebrows at the other. "Visitors to Waterdeep," he said to his friend. "They really do believe the streets are paved with gold."

"Come on," said the other. "Let's get back to Warrens."

"Don't you think that Stunk's guards will be suspicious of a basket full of bricks?" said Sophraea as the gnomes rushed out of sight.

"First of all, it doesn't look like a basket," said Gustin. He pulled back to look down at Sophraea. "More like a very small velvet lady's purse or amulet tied to your wrist. Secondly, I doubt they'll look that close. If they do, we have bigger problems than what you're carrying and we might need those bricks to help us escape."

Sophraea glanced down at her arm and blinked. She hadn't looked at the basket before. It was just there, as heavy on her arm as it always was when she went out. But when she looked down, all she saw was a cutwork velvet reticule dangling from two slender satin ribbons.

"But it still feels like a wicker basket," said Sophraea.

"And you still feel like Sophraea under that illusion," said Gustin, giving her shoulders a quick squeeze. "That's why we don't want anyone touching us. What they see and what they would feel won't match."

"Well, I don't want any of Stunk's servants laying hands on me," said Sophraea with a shudder, thinking of the hairy doorjack who kept coming to Dead End House.

The streets were quiet again; the only sound the heavy rain beating against the pavement and the rush of water through the gutters. Yet Sophraea could not shake her sense of unease as they hurried past the silent mansions. The dead passed this way each night, she thought, and that's why all the houses seem so barricaded now. There's fear behind those locked gates and curtained windows. No one wants to look out and see what is passing by.

"There really should be more people around," she said, voicing her concerns out loud.

"It's the rain," said Gustin, repeating his earlier assurance.

"No," she said. "It's something more." For the street felt to her exactly like one of the paths through the City of the Dead. She knew exactly where the noble dead congregated each night. She could feel it more clearly than the cold rain soaking her cloak.

"Stunk's house," she said to Gustin, pointing without error at the mansion that she had never visited before.

Unlike Lord Adarbrent's enclosed courtyard and entrance directly onto his street, Stunk's mansion was set back behind a high wall.

The massive gate of gilded iron was firmly closed, even though it was still daylight. Through its thick bars, Sophraea could see a large courtyard filled with well-armored house guards. Rather than lounging around or even cleaning weapons as they might be assigned at some less paranoid merchant's house, these guards were obviously on duty, standing at set intervals and staring sternly into space.

A brick gatehouse bulged out of one side of the high stone wall surrounding Stunk's estate. A bell rope hung down from a tiny slit opening in the wall. Above it was a shuttered window.

"Shall we ring?" Gustin strode up to the rope.

"You're sure that they won't recognize us?" she queried. She still felt like Sophraea. No matter what Gustin said, she wondered if a close examination would quickly reveal her true features.

The wizard pointed at a large puddle forming along one side of the wall. "Look," he commanded.

Sophraea peered down into the murky waters. The dim reflection looked nothing like her. Instead, she saw a slender moon elf, as pale as she was naturally dark, with elegant and distinctly inhuman features, dressed in the finery of a lady of Waterdeep. Nothing at all like black-haired little Sophraea Carver of Dead End House clothed in her second-best winter skirt and carrying a wicker basket full of broken bricks.

Drawing a deep breath to steady her nerves, Sophraea nodded at Gustin. "Pull that rope."

The wizard tugged and a jangle of brass bells sounded behind the shuttered window. A few moments later, the window popped open. A familiar and unpleasant face came into view. Stunk's hairy doorjack peered down at them. With a sniff and snarl, he said, "What do you want?"

"An audience with your master," replied Gustin while Sophraea stayed down wind behind him. "I am a ghost banisher of great renown in Cormyr and other states far to the east. I hear that Rampage Stunk has need of my services."

"That's not for me to say," said the hirsute servant.

"But can you take a message to your master and tell him that Philious Fornasta awaits his pleasure," Gustin flipped a thin coin through the gatehouse window. The doorjack caught it with a quick snap of his hand.

"I'll take your name to the house," the doorjack said and slammed the gatehouse window shut.

"What do we do now?" whispered Sophraea to Gustin.

"Wait," the wizard replied.

They huddled in the lee of the wall, partially sheltered from the chill wind and sleeting rain. A man ran past them and banged on the gate. He held a cloth to his head. Blood seeped out from under his lowered hat brim and ran down his rain soaked face, then dripped from his chin to his coat. If he saw them, he chose to ignore them, which was just as well. Sophraea didn't like the looks of him at all. He seemed familiar and at the same time, she couldn't place him.

"I hope that doorjack hurries or we'll wash away from here," Gustin said, shifting so he blocked the worst of the wind. She pressed gratefully against the warmth of his back.

He spoke in whispers too low for the stranger's ears. Sophraea realized that Gustin, like herself, didn't like the man's appearance.

"I'd rather have someone other than that doorjack leading us to the house," she said. "He's been in and out of Dead End House more than a dozen times on errands for Stunk. He's sure to recognize us if anyone does."

"Not a chance," said Gustin. "These illusions are good for a day or more as long as . . ."

"As long as what?"

"We don't trip over any wards or guardians that dispel magic."

"Would Stunk have something like that?"

"We won't know until we trip over it. But if we do, I've got a spell ready to help us run away!"

Sophraea sighed. This plan to enter Stunk's mansion in disguise felt more and more dangerous. But she really couldn't see another way around their problems. If Gustin was right, and the shoe was hidden in Stunk's mansion, then they had to retrieve it today and end this curse. But she couldn't help the nagging feeling that she'd forgotten some important fact, something that she shouldn't have overlooked.

The massive gilded iron gate began to swing open. The well-oiled hinges gave out no sound. A tall guard beckoned at Sophraea and Gustin.

"You wish to see Rampage Stunk," he said.

The other man rumbled a few words at the guard and pushed past him and hurried around to the side of the house. The guard ignored him.

"We are offering our services in ridding the house of ghosts, haunts, and walking corpses," replied Gustin smoothly.

The guard crooked his head, gesturing them through the gate. Three more men stood close behind him. All were heavily armed and Sophraea noticed none took their hands off their sword hilts.

With that escort, they passed through the outer and inner courtyards, all filled with even more armored guards, eventually climbing the shallow steps to the main entrance of Stunk's mansion.

Inside the vast hall, they were seated side-by-side on a long, bare, and very hard bench. Two of the guards remained to watch them while two others followed a well-dressed servant to a closed door. More knocking and whispered instructions ensued. The first two guards disappeared through the door while Sophraea and Gustin waited.

The guards left with them moved down the hall, stationing themselves at the base of the stairs so they had a clear view of the front and back entrances. Stunk's bodyguards exhibited no more interest in the pair left sitting together on the cold marble bench.

"Didn't you say that Stunk just built this house?" Gustin whispered to Sophraea.

"Less than three years ago," she whispered back, understanding the wizard's raised eyebrows and look of comical confusion.

To give himself an air of ancient ancestry, Stunk had stuffed every nook and cranny of his long entry hall with relics of Waterdeep's past. Ancient stone statues, suits of armor, portraits of pale ladies and supercilious lords, enormous tapestries, shields painted with heraldic devices, and other monuments to Stunk's wealth could be seen everywhere.

Above them hung not one but three greatglories, the extravagant chandeliers burning brightly with candles set amid their crystal drops, despite the murky daylight streaming through Stunk's tall windows at either end of the long hall. The staircase leading out of the hall to the upper rooms was twice the size of the one in Lord Adarbrent's house. Every step was covered with a rich woven carpet.

"I think there're bits of gold in the floor tiles," said Gustin, staring down at puddles formed from his dripping boots. He sounded slightly awed.

"Look at the gleam of that carpet on the stair. More than half the weave is silk," whispered back Sophraea. "And those tapestries. They're ancient."

Like Lord Ardabrent's house, this entrance hallway was cold. But it was not the cold of ancient neglect and decay. Rather it was the chill of ostentatious display, a place meant to impress rather than welcome any guest.

Sophraea shivered in her damp cloak. "How long should we wait?" she whispered to Gustin. "How long will your spell hold?"

"Shh," he said, "they're coming back."

Two guards reappeared in the hallway and indicated that Gustin and Sophraea should proceed through the black door. As they followed, Sophraea heard running boots again. She felt Gustin's hand on her back and didn't turn completely but lowered her head and glanced to the side. Three men in rough clothes and heavy boots rushed out of the back of the hall and out the front entrance.

The guards led Gustin and Sophraea into another massive room, decorated with even more rare artwork. Stationed not so discreetly around the room were more guards.

Rampage Stunk was ensconced in a thronelike chair, near as possible to a roaring fire in a vast cavern of a fireplace. The fat man watched their approach with his head cocked to one side and a narrowing of his cold black eyes. His face was bright red and sweating under hair so black and stiff that Sophraea wondered if the corpulent merchant wore a wig.

A pair of gigantic slavering guard dogs with brass-studded collars and enormous teeth crouched at Stunk's feet. The dogs growled as Gustin and Sophraea advanced closer to the merchant.

Sophraea was ready to retreat, but Gustin's spine straightened in front of her and he flashed an enormous smile.

"My lord, my lady," he said, bowing both to Stunk and to the thin woman seated in the shadow of a screen that shielded her face from the direct heat of the fireplace. "I have come to perform miracles and wonders, the banishing of ill luck, the turning of curses, the expulsion of ghosts, and any other infestation that may mar your fair home."

Gustin Bone's voice flowed up and down, a singsong accent quite unlike his usual cheerful tones and, to Sophraea's ears, quite unrecognizable as the optimistic wizard who frequented the Carver's courtyard. Gustin also refrained from waving his arms around as he usually did. Instead, he kept his hands crossed over the illusionary paunch of his belly.

Rampage Stunk also crossed his arms, but held them higher up, a barricade resting against his broad chest. The glare of his expression did not change throughout Gustin's long recital of his experiences in Cormyr as a banisher of ghosts. Once or twice his eyebrows twitched up in a patent gesture of disbelief but no other expression crossed his broad and frighteningly blank face.

Finally, Gustin's speech fluttered into silence in the face of Stunk's stony regard.

"You sound more like a charlatan than a wizard," pronounced Stunk in his deep and ponderous tones. "I've had some of Waterdeep's finest in this house over the past three days. Why should I take a mountebank damp out of the gutter?"

"If the finest in Waterdeep were unable to solve your problems," proposed Gustin boldly as the nearest guard dog sniffed his boots and licked its fangs, "perhaps the best of Cormyr is the solution. And, truly, you'll find no other wizard like me in Waterdeep." The second dog joined its fellow, making rumbling sounds deep in its throat. Gustin ignored both dogs, never letting his gaze drop from Stunk's face.

A faint smile twitched Stunk's lips. His own eyes dropped momentarily to the dogs creeping on their haunches closer to Gustin.

From her seat in the shadows, Stunk's thin and aristocratic wife spoke up.

"Those others did nothing for us. Hire this man. If he succeeds, pay him. If he fails, send him away," the lady said in her high nasal voice. "I am sick of seeing corpses at my window every evening and having revenants of long dead relatives appearing outside in the courtyard each night."

"But none of the dead have actually entered the house?" Sophraea spoke up, too curious to stay silent any longer.

"Not yet," admitted the lady, "the protections on our home are formidable. My husband paid for the very best. But none of our guests can enter nor can we leave after dark without encountering the dead outside. And certain incidents"—she emphasized the last word heavily while looking at her husband—"have increased. Flowers wither as soon as they are brought inside, fruit decays in the dish, and wine turns bitter in the glass."

"There are ghosts who can play such tricks," Sophraea told the lady.

"I am not pleased by such antics," she replied.

"That's a strong spell if they have such an influence just standing outside," Gustin said.

"We are searching the city for the wizard who brought about this curse," responded Stunk, snapping his fingers to bring the guard dogs back to heel at the foot of his chair. "I will find him and I will break him. And the one who I know is behind him!"

"You have been hunting for days," said Stunk's wife, "and if you do not do something soon about this haunting, I will have to abandon my air of noble calm and succumb to strong hysterics. And then who will host your endless dinners?"

Stunk growled, "Very well." Gustin started to speak but Stunk raised one hand, palm turned toward the wizard. "Don't talk. Don't interrupt. I'll tell you exactly what I expect. You will have only this one afternoon to make your examination of the house and set up what protections that you deem wise. If the dead return tonight, I will consider you a failure and you would be wise to avoid me in the future. If my lady is undisturbed tonight, you may collect your payment from her in the morning since she desires your services."

Stunk's wife simply pursed her lips at the beginning of her husband's rude but succinct summation, but did not speak until her husband was done. She then added: "I am not a merchant. I do not haggle like one. If I have a quiet night, you may present whatever bill you please to my servants. My word on it that you will be paid promptly."

Gustin bowed over his folded hands as the lady rose from her chair. "I am more than satisfied with the bargain."

Stunk's lady wife tucked her skirts tight against her legs, sweeping neatly around her husband to exit via a smaller, red lacquer door set in the far corner of the room. Trailing after her was a previously unnoticed retinue of three maidservants carrying various workbaskets and other household items. The three had been seated as far away as possible from the fireplace and Stunk in his great chair. They all rose in unison from the shadowy corner where they sat when the lady of the mansion passed in front of them. The last one out the red lacquer door closed it behind her with a definite disapproving swish of her skirt and a sharp snap of the latch.

Stunk watched his wife and her maids go with the slightest of sneers on his heavy face. Then he turned back to the pair in front of them.

"You have your instructions. Do not waste my time," he said ponderously, dropping one hand down to pinch the back of a guard dog's neck. The beast snarled under Stunk's heavy hand, black lips pulling back to reveal pointed yellow fangs.

Gustin and Sophraea retreated with haste through the black door leading to the great hallway.

Once outside the heavy door and out of earshot of Stunk and his guards, Sophraea turned to Gustin. "You were wonderful," she said. "I couldn't have stayed so calm. Not with him staring like that!"

"Calm," moaned Gustin as he sank into an uncomfortable but obviously antique stone chair. "I am terrified. All I wanted to do in Waterdeep was see the sights, enjoy a small adventure or two, and make a little coin, not gain an enemy like that evil fat man!"

EIGHTEEN

Once out of sight of Stunk, Sophraea felt her natural courage return, but she had no desire to linger in the merchant's mansion.

"Since we only have today," she said to Gustin, "the practical solution is to go in opposite directions. I'll look downstairs and you go upstairs. That way we can search the place twice as quickly. And then leave."

Although the greatglories still burned brightly overhead, the light dimmed in the great hallway as black storm clouds darkened the sky outside.

"We should really go before the storm gets worse," she added. "We do not want to be on the streets in the dark."

Gustin raised his head from his hands. "What is it? What are you feeling?"

Puzzled, Sophraea stared at him.

"I caught it again. Just now. Same as the tunnels," he said. "And in the City of the Dead."

"What?"

"Your eyes. Just the quickest flash of blue. What are you feeling, Sophraea?"

"The dead," she admitted. "The City of the Dead. But I don't know why. It's never happened outside the cemetery walls before. But it's like I can see a straight path running from here directly back to our gate and into the City of the Dead."

"The curse laid on Stunk," said Gustin. "We are right, you know, it made a path for the dead to follow here. Made a path that they have to follow. The shoe has to be here."

"Then we had better find it," said Sophraea, settling her basket more firmly over her arm. "You go up"—she pointed at the great staircase leading out of the hall—"and I'll go down."

Halfway up the main staircase, Gustin turned around and called over the banister, "Why do I feel like this was a bad idea?"

"Piffle," said Sophraea, trying to convince herself that the shivers running through her body were caused by her wet cloak, "it's still broad daylight and this is the well-guarded house of a wealthy man. What could hurt us here?"

The rumble of thunder shook the house. A crack of lighting illuminated the windows for a brief moment causing the statues and the suits of armor to cast strange and twisted shadows across the floor tiles.

"You don't think that was a sign from the gods?" asked Gustin.

"Go on, hurry up," said Sophraea, "I'll meet you back here."

She set off toward the back of the hall, certain that she would find the traditional "servants' stair" there. One guard, standing stiffly at attention, marked the top of the stairs.

A guard on the servants' staircase, thought Sophraea. That shows an unusual amount of distrust on Stunk's part. She was glad that she didn't work for the fat man.

Downstairs, Sophraea found the cook, a friendly soul who obviously ruled the kitchen, and the various female servants clustered around the warm fire were the usual bevy of Waterdeep gossips. All were perfectly willing to chat with a nice young elf who offered to help them to peel the vegetables for the evening meal.

"Although, dearie, I have to say," the cook remarked, "I didn't think your kind was quite so domestic. Why you ply that little knife so quick and clever that I'd have taken you for one of Waterdeep's own."

Sophraea shrugged and turned the conversation to odd spaces

under the house, the sort of place that she thought the shoe might be hidden.

"Well, there're some rooms below," answered the friendly cook. "Although why you'd want to go poking around in that muck, I don't understand."

"The wizard." Sophraea paused. She couldn't remember the name that Gustin had given the door guards. "My master, the wizard," she recovered and stumbled through an explanation, "is creating a great protection spell." She rummaged in the basket hooked as always over her arm. "I need to take certain charms to the lowest levels of the house."

All she really had was a basket full of bricks. But she waved it around, trusting that Gustin's illusion held and the servants would just see a moon elf gesturing with a velvet bag that could hold magical charms.

None of the women surrounding the table looked at all interested. The laundress folding clean napkins just nodded and said, "That's nice but the ghosts haven't bothered us. They rattle the upper windows something fierce, and some of the servants upstairs have had a hard time, but they don't seem to care about those of us working down here."

Well, they wouldn't, thought Sophraea, but did not voice it out loud. After all, the dead haunting Stunk were all the most noble revenants of Waterdeep's past. In life, they had probably paid no attention at all to kitchen maids, laundresses, and cooks. It was unlikely that they should change their attitudes in the afterlife, she thought.

"Door to the lower rooms is over there," said the cook, gesturing to a little door set by the corner of the chimney. "Watch yourself on the stairs. They are steep. Take a candle with you, for those rooms are dark as well as mighty dank."

Picking up a tallow candle in a tin holder as the cook indicated,

Sophraea lit the wick from a taper. She then proceeded down the dismal stairs leading to Stunk's lowest basement.

The stairs were steep, each step twice the height of a normal stair. Hooking her basket on the crook of her elbow, she held up the candleholder with that hand and pressed her other hand against the stone wall. There was nothing like a railing. One step at a time, she inched her way down. She felt as if the least misstep could leave her a broken heap on the floor below.

Once she reached the bottom, Sophraea discovered that a rich man's basement could be just as full of cluttered jumble as anyone else's. At the very base of the stairs, someone had stacked a few crates and some broken bits of chairs. Cobwebs lightly festooned the pile.

But farther into the cavernous room carved under the warm kitchen, empty barrels and discarded pallets leaned together like drunken orcs. Something squeaked when Sophraea's pale candlelight fell upon it. A skinny tail whipped around a cracked wooden tub and disappeared under a pile of boards.

Sophraea frowned. Stunk could easily afford rat catchers. Undaunted, she pressed forward, resolutely ignoring the scrabbling sound of small claws burrowing away from her. Her steps sounded hollow as she crossed the wooden floor and, with some dismay, she realized that there must be another chamber under this one. Some Waterdeep mansions might have as many as three or four underground floors, dug down into the city's own deep layers.

Where the brocade shoe might be found, she had no idea. However, the night that the phantom lady had danced across the floor of Dead End House, she remembered a pale trail of glowing footprints had been left behind. Perhaps a similar sign of ghostly invasion could be found here.

Raising the candle high above her head, Sophraea peered into the far dark corners of the room. Off to one side, she thought she saw something glint, the faintest twinkle of gold.

Sophraea rushed across the room. A large stack of lumber was heaped against the wall. Between the cobwebbed sticks and broken slats from old crates, she could make out the glimmer of something gold. Setting down her basket and candle, she began pulling the wood aside.

Behind her, a heavy tread sounded on the stair leading up to the kitchen. "Well met!" cried a man. "What are you doing there?"

She froze. Had he come by the women in the kitchen? Had they told on her? No, he must have seen her go into the kitchen. When he followed and found her gone, he'd guessed she was in the basement. But why follow her at all?

Heavy boots banged down the steep staircase, and then she saw who it was.

Stunk's hairy doorjack stood at the bottom of the steps. His eyes widened and he threw his head back to take a large sniff of air. "You're that wizard's elf girl," he said.

Sophraea bobbed a quick curtsy. He stood directly in her path, no way around him if she wanted to flee back up the stairs. "I'm here with the wizard," she agreed pleasantly while bending down to take a firm grip on the basket's handle. "Setting protections for the house."

"You're poking and prying," answered the servant moving toward her. "Stunk wouldn't like that. He doesn't like elves much, either."

He was a good bit taller than she was and heavy with muscle along his shoulders and barrel chest.

"Stunk knows I'm here," she said, sidestepping a bit so the candle wasn't directly behind her. No need to be any clearer a target than she was.

The doorjack stalked forward, head outthrust. Even in the dim candlelight, Sophraea could see how his bristly beard extended down his neck to disappear under his collar. Little tufts of coarse black hair even sprouted from his ears.

"I see a moon elf," growled the doorjack. "But I smell something else. Something human. Something young. Something scared."

"I am not scared!" Sophraea exclaimed, backing into the shadows. She raised up the basket, which was reassuringly heavy with the broken bricks inside.

The doorjack chuckled. "What are you going to do with the poof of velvet?" he snarled. "Tickle me to death, elf-not-elf girl?"

For a moment, Sophraea was confused. Then she realized no matter what he smelled, the hairy man could only see Gustin's illusion. She clutched the basket more tightly, ready to swing it.

"Come here!" snapped the doorjack and he lunged, one hairy hand outstretched. Sophraea leaped away but the man's black nails caught the edge of her cloak and pulled her back.

"Let go. My master is working for Stunk," she said. And then, remembering the quiet power of Stunk's wife in the hall, she added, "I have Lady Ruellyn's approval and protection!"

The doorjack ignored her protests.

"I know that scent," he muttered, hauling her closer and closer, like a wriggling fish hooked on a line.

She tried to swing the basket, but her cloak entangled her arm and she was off balance. Her feet slipped on the dusty floor as he dragged her toward him.

The basket barely grazed his ribs. He gave a grunt and a yank.

Sophraea twisted around, trying to get more solid footing, but the doorjack was stronger than her. She couldn't pull away. He stretched out one hand and fastened on her arm, pulling so violently that she stumbled. The rough floor scraped her open hands when she tried to catch herself.

The doorjack continued to pull at her, trying to force her down upon the floor. Sophraea twisted, let the loose cape slip around her shoulders, and scrambled to her feet. He held on. The collar cut against her throat. Furious, Sophraea spun toward him and lashed out with one foot. He dodged her kick but the cape slid between his fingers. She was able to back up another step away from him.

"I'll get you!" he growled. He shifted, trying to get a better grip. She pulled one arm free and plunged her hand into the basket. Her fingers clamped around a half brick. Hauling it out, she thrust the brick with all her might at the man's hairy face. It crushed his long nose with a loud snap. The doorjack let go with a wild howl.

Sophraea dropped to the floor and rolled away. Once clear of the villainous servant, she sprang to her feet. She knew he was much stronger, but so were her brothers. Through the years she had learned that her small size let her dodge more quickly than a large man. As long as she could stay out of his grasp, she had a chance. Her best defense was to stay beyond his reach.

He staggered back and forth, both hands clapped over the center of his face, blood flowing in a glittering ribbon down his chin. "You broke it," he burbled through the mess. "You're mine!"

While he was distracted, she raced past him and jumped up to the second stair. He heard her. His head snapped up and he struggled to stand, his knees bent, one hand over his face and the other braced on the floor. For a terrible moment they both were motionless, staring at each other. She thought about running up the stairs, but they were steep, double height, impossible for her to do anything other than climb carefully. Knowing that, she hesitated, two steps up, facing him, unwilling to turn her back on him and chance the stairs.

That was a mistake, she realized a moment later, as he sprang forward, leaping more like an animal than a man, covering the distance twice as fast as she expected.

Terrified, she stumbled backward up a step. In her head, she heard Leaplow's advice, "Whatever you do, don't let a man pin you. Hit him, keep hitting him, don't quit!"

She swung the basket high and brought it down like a club on the top of the doorjack's head. His feet slid on the tread and he landed on the floor at the bottom of the steps. From where she stood on the stairs, for once in her life, she was taller than her opponent. She took advantage of that fact. Sophraea thumped the heavy basket against his skull again and again.

With a yelp, the doorjack smashed into the floor of the basement. He didn't move.

For a long moment, Sophraea just stood there, breathing heavily, her fingers clutched tightly around the basket's handle. He still didn't move.

She edged back down the stairs, crept forward and tentatively put out a hand to see if he was dead or alive. The doorjack groaned and she jumped. But he didn't open his eyes, just whimpered a little and curled upon his side.

Sophraea circled cautiously around the unconscious man. She returned to the candle. With many glances back over her shoulder, she reached into the pile of lumber.

But the glint of gold was nothing more than the edge of a broken picture frame. The shoe was not there.

The doorjack groaned again. A quick search of the debris turned up several stout cords that had once been used to tie up sacks of flour. Sophraea lashed the man's hands and feet together, using the best knots her brothers had taught her. All she needed was a little time to find Gustin and get out of this house. With some regret for the destruction of a favorite garment, she tore the muslin flounce off her petticoat and gagged the doorjack.

Sophraea hurried back to the stairs. She looked up. The door at the top was firmly closed. She listened for a minute or two, but could hear nothing of the activity in the kitchen. With luck, nobody had heard her skirmish in the basement.

She shook out her skirts, gathered up her basket, and started up the stairs, only to turn around and go back down.

She scooped the half brick off the floor and dropped it into the basket. Gustin was right after all. You never knew when a good solid brick might come in handy.

Then Sophraea fled up the staircase to the warm kitchen above.

The cook, the laundress, and the other maids were still gathered around the table, gossiping amid a growing pile of peeled vegetables and folded linen.

"Did you finish your job, dearie?" asked the plump cook.

"Oh yes," answered Sophraea, edging around the table toward the stairs leading to the upper rooms.

"Thought I saw that Furkin go down the stairs to help you," said the cook, continuing to peel with quick strokes of her knife and not looking up.

Sophraea froze in place.

"Good thing you didn't stay down there with him," the cook continued. "He's not a nice man."

The other women were also intent on their work, none of them looking up but all nodding in agreement with the cook.

"He was quite polite to me," Sophraea lied, coming closer to the table. "In fact, he offered to stay down there and keep the rats away from our charms."

The cook raised one eyebrow at this statement. "Well, that was kind of him," she said with no inflection in her voice. "We'll just leave him alone then, down in the basement, to keep the rats away."

The other women chuckled and nodded.

"Go on," said the cook, shoving a chair toward her with one foot.

"Catch your breath before you go back upstairs. You're panting so hard they're sure to ask questions. A suspicious lot, those guards of Stunk's."

Sophraea collapsed into a chair and picked up a knife. She pulled a bowl toward herself and began to chop vegetables with the rest of them. "You are kind," she said to the table at large.

The plump cook shrugged. "Some of the master's men are better than others. And some deserve a lesson or two."

"But won't you get into trouble? If Furkin stays in the basement too long?" Sophraea asked. These women had been nothing but nice to her and she didn't want to bring trouble down on their heads.

One thin and elderly maid shook her head. "Stunk rules his men with a hard hand. But we serve his lady wife and answer to her."

"And she dislikes Furkin as much as any of us," piped up the pot girl from her corner by the sink, a mere child of thirteen with her hands sunk into the soapy bucket of dirty dishes. She earned several stern looks from the other women. Abashed, the pot girl went back to her scrubbing.

"So you think your wizard can chase the ghosts away?" asked the laundress, rising above that brief incident.

"We've promised Lady Ruellyn to do the best we can," Sophraea answered. Then, looking around the table at the honest faces of the women gathered there, she decided to tell the truth. "It would help if we could find a certain shoe. A gold brocade dancing slipper, very old-fashioned in style."

The women waved away any knowledge of dancing slippers. "Now," said one thin maid, "Lady Ruellyn has dozens of slippers, but none of gold brocade that I remember."

"My old mistress used to have little dancing shoes with a painted heel, but hers were silver lace and not gold brocade," said another one. "She kept them in a box, with sprigs of herbs stuffed down in the toes to keep them fresh. She never wore them. But my old girl showed me the shoes once and said that they were her first dancing slippers and she meant to be buried in them. Poor thing, I'm sure the family forgot after she passed away."

The rest of the women murmured an agreement and slipped into discussions of past employers. Sophraea soon realized that all of the women had worked for noble families elsewhere in Waterdeep until their elderly employers had fallen upon hard times.

Each woman told tales of how their elderly and aristocratic employers had eventually sold the family homes to Stunk, after the fat man had bought everything else of value from them.

"He makes the old ones loans," whispered one maid whose own hair was more gray than black. "And tells them that they can pay him back bit by bit. But it's never enough some how, and they start selling off pieces of furniture to make the payment, and then the paintings off the walls, and then the jewels that their granny's granny got for her wedding ever so long ago. And, quicker than you think, there's just nothing left to pay Stunk. And then he comes by, all smiles and flattery, telling them not to worry, he'll take the whole property off their hands, they won't have to worry about paying us servants anymore, and he'll set them up some place nice to live out their last days."

"Nice!" interjected the cook, who had moved over to the fire to stir a cauldron puffing out a spicy smoke. She pulled her dripping spoon out of the pot and waved it with little regard for the sugary splatters she sprayed across the hearthstone. "He put my old lady in one bitty little room down by the docks. It was horrid and dark and damp. If Lord Adarbrent hadn't brought her some nice pieces from his own house and a good wool blanket for the winter, she would have been ever so miserable."

Just about to leave the table to look for Gustin, Sophraea picked up the peeling knife instead and innocently asked, "Lord Adarbrent?"

"They may call him the Walking Corpse," said the cook, "but he proved himself a kind friend to my mistress."

"And to mine," answered the gray-haired maid.

"He tried to talk my lord out of taking Stunk's loans," declared the laundress, shifting her basket to avoid the cook's wildly waving spoon and stains on her clean tablecloths. "Would that he had listened to him, I wouldn't be working here."

"But there's no denying that Lord Adarbrent has a terrible temper," added the cook as she stalked back to the table. "Why my old lady told me that he nearly horsewhipped a man to death once. When Lord Adarbrent was young, the nobles of Waterdeep were a different breed. Why just look at a man wrong in those days, and he'd be challenging you quicker than you could blink. *I see you, saer, let us duel, saer,* that's what all the young blades would say when they went on the promenade. And people feared Adarbrents in those days. At least that's what my old lady said!"

"I thought Lord Adarbrent was all alone and had no family," said Sophraea.

"Well, they've all been gone for a long time," the cook responded. "But they caused some stir more than fifty years ago, during one of the bad times."

Sophraea looked up at this.

"Of course, I was just a baby then," the cook went on. "But so much change was happening inside the city's walls and outside in the world. The dark arts attracted certain nobles, especially those who had suffered great losses. Oh, most ladies played at séances at their parties, but there were some who took it a bit further than that. There were some who raised ghosts. The sort that had secret rooms, at the top of the tower or down in the basement, with vats of this and glass tubes of that, and nasty smells seeping out to drive the housekeeper crazy."

Outside, the thunder died away, leaving only the heavy splatter of rain against the high small windows of the kitchen. More rain hissed down the chimney and made the fire smoke. The cook snapped an order at the pot girl, who obediently left her bucket and rattled the damper and plied the poker until the smoke settled.

Then the pot girl crept closer to the table. The laundress slid a stool across the floor to her. Perched on top, the child wrapped her arms around her knees and shivered with delight as the older women began to swap tales of hauntings in old Waterdeep. With an absentminded gesture, the cook handed the pot girl a biscuit to nibble while the stories continued.

While their tales of dark deeds in the City of the Dead rarely matched what Sophraea knew to be the truth (one or two exaggerations nearly caused her to giggle), each mentioned more than once the fashion for ghosts that plagued Waterdeep's finer homes for a brief time long ago.

"So the Adarbrents called forth spirits?" Sophraea finally asked.

"Not the current Lord Adarbrent," said the cook with stout loyalty to the man who had rescued her old mistress. "But he had a cousin who frightened my old lady when she was girl. A truly nasty witch, if you know what I mean. She died from some ritual gone wrong and the family sealed up her rooms the very day that they buried her."

Sophraea remembered the sour, cold smell of Lord Adarbrent's house. Perhaps something was dead behind the old noble's wainscoting, something more sinister than a mouse, and something that needed a stronger cure than the gift of a kitten.

Suddenly the tales of haunting were interrupted by a very live bumping noise below their feet. A crash, like a stack of lumber knocked over by a man rolling around, could be distinctly heard.

"Old chimney flue," explained the cook. "Carries sound up from the basement. Sounds like Furkin is having some trouble with those rats."

"Oh," said Sophraea, jumping up from the table and starting toward the stairs. "Perhaps I'd better go find my wizard now."

"Good idea, dearie," the cook agreed. "Furkin might be in a bit of temper later on."

"When he gets loose," giggled the pot girl and was immediately shushed by the other women.

With hurried thanks, Sophraea headed upstairs. As she left, she heard the cook remark, "Well, that's a nice polite and helpful girl for you. Look at all the vegetables that she's peeled and chopped. Of course, if anyone asks, we haven't seen her for ages, have we?"

NINETEEN

Upstairs in Stunk's mansion, Gustin made a great show of pacing back and forth, muttering the occasional odd phrase. He knew that true magic was much more than empty gestures, but, from his experience, the servants expected this kind of act.

Stunk's valet, a portly bald man given to wringing his hands and muttering "please don't touch that," met Gustin at the top of the stairs leading to his master's private apartment. The young man supposed that the valet was watching to see that he wouldn't steal anything. Two more of Stunk's bodyguards stood stiffly on either side of the lacquered door leading into their master's bedchamber.

When one thin male servant turned the corner of the hallway and yelped to see a wizard down on his knees drawing cryptic symbols on the carpet with a piece of charcoal, Gustin gained the general impression that the whole household's nerves were badly overset.

He continued with his search, carefully lifting up curtains and peering under tables. The upper hallways were just as cluttered with bric-a-brac and expensive ornaments as the lower rooms. The brocade shoe could be almost anywhere and nearly invisible among all the other trophies that Stunk had displayed. Not for the first time, Gustin wished he had a spell that could reveal a desired object. That would be much more useful than many of the odd bits that his old teacher made him memorize!

As he advanced down a hallway toward the door leading to Stunk's chambers, Gustin noticed a silk cloth covered one enormous picture frame in an alcove just outside Stunk's rooms.

ROSEMARY JONES

When he started to twitch the covering aside, the valet moaned and said "Oh do not! I wish the master would just have it destroyed."

The revealed painting showed the wealthy fat man and his aristocratic lady, expensively dressed in the finest materials and jewels, but the faces above the lace collars were the faces of corpses, rotting away.

"Unusual choice for a portrait," said Gustin, quickly letting the cloth fall back over the portrait. "I'm surprised the artist dared to paint him that way."

"It wasn't always like that," said the valet.

"Did it start to change when the haunting began?"

"Oh no, it's been changing for much longer than that, getting worse every day."

"An early warning, one that wasn't heeded," Gustin speculated.

"The master won't have it removed," the valet moaned. "He only covered it after my lady objected to seeing it every time she came up the stairs. My master said that he won't be frightened by such tricks. He was keeping it to feed to whoever was doing this, scrap by canvas scrap until the jokester chokes. At least that was what the master said."

"After my interview with him, I would say that Rampage Stunk has very little sense of humor," Gustin remarked.

The valet shuddered slightly and responded, "Please don't say anything about the master to me." He gave a quick glance over his shoulder to the two guards stationed nearby.

"No, no, of course not," Gustin had no wish to get Stunk's servant into trouble. "I only meant that I was quite impressed by your master's gravity in the face of adversity."

The last was pitched loud enough for the guards to hear and the plump valet gave Gustin a grateful smile. "Secundus Marplate," said the man, bowing slightly and indicating his round person.

"Philious Fornasta," said Gustin Bone, who'd always been fond of this particular persona. Philious had had numerous dubious adventures among the war wizards of Cormyr but, Gustin felt, always exchanged the social pleasantries with exceptional panache.

"Have you been with Stunk long?" asked Gustin as he continued to examine the hall. He rather doubted that the shoe would turn up here or even downstairs where Sophraea was searching. If the curse was directed at Stunk, than the object tied to the curse probably had been placed in the man's personal apartment to draw the dead to him. Which was one of the reasons that he had not objected to Sophraea searching in the basements below. She would be perfectly safe there and unlikely to run into any of Stunk's more dangerous servants.

"I came here following the master's marriage to Lady Ruellyn," explained Marplate as he trailed after Gustin.

"If she's a lady, wouldn't he be a lord?" Gustin asked casually as he opened the doors of a small cupboard. Inside it, he found brushes, a small fire shovel, and a bucket for carrying out ashes, but no shoe.

"Lady Ruellyn carries her own title by right of birth to a very noble family. They have a mansion in Castle Ward," Marplate said. "I can say no more." And then he proceeded to follow Gustin, gossiping as the wizard sniffed around for the missing brocade shoe.

In the valet's guarded opinion, Stunk was waiting to buy just the right title for himself, one that would increase his influence in Waterdeep. "As close to a mask as he can get," Marplate explained and then looked as if he'd regretted suggesting his master was angling for a position of power in Waterdeep.

"So, you can become a noble here if you have enough money?" queried Gustin.

"You would be shocked at what you can buy in Waterdeep," said Marplate quite sincerely.

"Not after living here for a very short time," replied Gustin cheerfully as he walked up to the guards flanking the door into Stunk's chambers.

"I have your master's permission to set my protections throughout the house," he told the guards, who looked doubtful. "Of course, I can always tell your master that I could not enter his rooms and therefore they are unprotected, a consequence of your actions."

The two guards stepped quickly aside. Gustin swept through the lacquered door, gesturing to Marplate to accompany him.

In the suite of rooms that Marplate called "the master's apartment," Gustin found a dressing chamber filled with racks of luxurious clothing and shelves of shoes, but no dancing slipper. A bathing chamber, a small study, and an even smaller library, filled primarily with ledgers for Stunk's various enterprises, also lacked any evidence of the haunting except the candles burning in every room, necessary because of the tightly drawn curtains concealing each window that they passed.

"There're always *things* looking in at night," Marplate said as he checked the curtains, making sure the fabric overlapped at the edges, completely shrouding the room from anyone or anything looking in.

A huge bed dominated the center of the last room, swathed in draperies that allowed the occupant to protect himself from the slightest draft. Gigantic feather pillows filled the top of the bed.

Set neatly to one side was a food safe, a neat contraption of wood and perforated tin made to keep certain types of pastries fresh. Gustin had seen such pieces in bakeries and even the larger kitchens of noble houses in Cormyr. But he'd never seen one in a bedroom.

"The master does a great deal of work in this room," said the valet, obviously feeling the need to explain. "He often needs sustenance in the middle of the night."

"You must spend all your time sweeping crumbs out of the sheets," Gustin said, flipping back the covers to peer under the bed. No shoe. He straightened back up, thinking hard. He was sure that the shoe had to be in the house and, most logically, near Stunk or in a room that Stunk occupied a good deal of the time. Of course, it could be downstairs, perhaps even in the room where Stunk held his audiences. The thought of going back there and searching under the fat man's cold gaze made Gustin shudder.

"There is a maid to change the linen every day." Marplate straightened the covers that Gustin had rumpled. "The master is most particular about such things."

The wizard wandered to the far end of the room where a small table held a number of papers and a few personal items on a tray, like a comb and a bottle of men's hair pomade. Gustin picked up the latter, pulling out the glass stopper to confirm that it was the thick, inky liquid sold in numerous Waterdeep shops with assurances that it would give even the oldest and grayest of gentlemen the luxurious locks of a young man. With a very slight smile at this evidence of Stunk's vanity, Gustin replaced the bottle on the silver tray.

Beneath the inlaid table, he spotted a slip of paper crumbled upon the floor, as if somebody had hurled it there in anger. He glanced back at Marplate. The valet was still fussing with the covers of Stunk's bed, making sure the corners were absolutely straight. Gustin snatched up the note, glanced quickly at the signature, and tucked it in his tunic. He would read it later, someplace where nobody was watching.

"Are you done, saer?" asked Marplate, twitching slightly when he saw Gustin so close to his master's table.

"Almost, almost," Gustin said, circling the room once more. He noticed every time he crossed near the heavily draped windows, the valet flinched. He put one hand upon the crimson velvet curtains to draw them open.

"Oh, there's nothing out there," Marplate said with a nervous start.

"Perhaps I should look for myself." Gustin twitched the curtains open to reveal long glass windows that opened onto a small wrought iron balcony with a planter filled with dead plants. Other than that, there was, as the other man had said, nothing there.

Behind him, Gustin heard the valet give a relieved sigh.

Ah, thought Gustin, this is where the ghosts must appear each night. Throwing his hands into the air and letting his head fall backward until he was staring at the brightly painted ceiling, Gustin cried, "I sense the presence of the dead!"

Marplate let out a startled shriek at Gustin's antics and then clapped both his hands to his mouth.

Gustin slowly rolled his head forward until he was staring at his boots. "Each night, they come here, testing the fortifications of this house. Here they gather, looking in, attempting to reach the master of this place."

The valet let out a strangled whimper.

"They rattle the windows, they shake the handle." Gustin lowered his arms bit by bit and then tested the latch of the windows, rattling it slightly.

Marplate moaned behind him, "Every night, it gets worse. And he won't move out of this room. He always has me open the curtains so he can stare at them. He glowers at the dead and then mutters about how he's going to kill whoever is doing this. And he makes me stay in the room so they all know what I look like too!"

Gustin turned until he faced the man, raising one arm gradually to point at him. The valet quivered. Gustin tried not to smile. The deliberate gesture, the deepening of the voice, it worked every time, he thought. Everyone always thought that the worst magic came on the end of a grand gesture.

He drew in a deep breath and stated, "You are also cursed." Then added in a lighter tone, "But if you give me the key for this window's lock, I may be able to save you."

With trembling hands, Marplate withdrew a ring of keys from his tunic. He handed them quickly to Gustin.

"It's the littlest key," the valet said. "He makes me go out there every morning and see if they have left anything behind."

"Do they?" Gustin thrust the key into the lock and turned it. With a distinct *click*, the window swung open. Gustin walked out on the balcony. It was completely bare as he had seen through the glass, except for the one pottery planter and the dead plants on their withered brown stalks.

"The plants are always dead," answered Marplate, staying well inside the bedroom. "I had the gardener replace them each morning. But today, the master said to just leave it."

"Nothing else?" Gustin asked.

"Well, the first day"—the plump man squirmed a little and pulled out a handkerchief to dab at his bald head—"I found a shoe."

Gustin whirled around to look at him. "A gold dancing slipper, brocade and fashioned in antique style?"

Marplate nodded. "It looked exactly as you described, saer."

"Fantastic! What did you do with it?"

The startled valet pointed at the oblong planter sitting on the balcony. "I had the gardener bury it there. I did not think it would be lucky to bring it into the house."

Gustin rushed back to the planter, grabbing the plants by their woody stems and pulling them up. Dirt and dead leaves went flying as he flipped the plants out of his way.

"Did Stunk know you buried a shoe here?" Gustin plunged his hands into the wet earth. He dug like a frantic dog into the dirt.

"No," Marplate's voice sunk to a frightened whisper. "He would have wanted it displayed, like the painting in the hall. He keeps saying that he is not afraid of this curse. But I know a fetish when I see one."

"Really?" Under his questing fingers, Gustin finally felt the rough texture of the brocade slipper. He pulled it out from the planter. Stained with dirt, the little shoe looked ghastly, a proper grave good. "How did you know that there was a curse tied to this?"

Marplate straightened himself with a sniff of superiority. "I was born in Waterdeep. Such things are not unknown here."

"Yes, I'm beginning to see that." Gustin stuffed the shoe into his belt. "Interesting city, interesting citizens, I must say. But why didn't you have one of the other wizards marching through here earlier remove it?"

The valet blinked in surprise. "None of them ever came upstairs. None of them ever spoke to me. They just stayed downstairs and cast spells of protection around the doors and gates."

"Which must have helped," Gustin said, as much to himself as to Marplate, "as the dead never got this past the threshold. Or maybe it needed someone living to carry it into the house."

The valet gave a worried glance at the shoe now dangling from the wizard's belt.

"Not to worry," Gustin said with an airy toss of Marplate's keys back to the man. "I'm taking this to where it belongs and that should end this curse."

"I certainly hope so," said the valet, carefully stepping onto the balcony to replace the dead plants in the pottery planter.

Gustin hurried out of the room and headed down the main staircase to find Sophraea. A crackle of paper around the middle of his chest reminded him that he still had the note lodged in his tunic. A turn of the stair revealed a niche with an antique statue. At least Gustin hoped it was antique and Stunk did not prefer his statues of naked women to be missing an arm and a head. Ducking behind the headless woman put Gustin out of sight of the guards at the top of the staircase.

He withdrew the note from his tunic and read: "Saer: If you had any honor, which I have good leave to doubt, you would meet me as a man should, in an appointed hour and place. But send your bully boys against me one more time or threaten my home by any word or gesture, and I will horsewhip you as a cur should be chastised."

As he had noticed in Stunk's bedchamber, the note bore the seal and the slashing signature of Lord Dorgar Adarbrent.

Hurrying down the stairs, Gustin met Sophraea as she was hurrying up. As usual, she looked intent, as if the worries of Waterdeep settled on her slim shoulders. In Gustin's opinion, she worried far too much these days. Things had a way of working out. After all, they'd gotten into Stunk's house, the illusion spell was still holding (a bit to his surprise but he didn't intend to tell her that), and they may very well be able to settle the dead by sunset.

"I found the shoe," Gustin told Sophraea as soon as she'd reached the landing halfway up the main staircase. "And I know who set the dead after Stunk."

"It's Lord Adarbrent," Sophraea said as Gustin pronounced the same conclusion at the same time.

"How do you know that?" Gustin asked even as he handed the note over to Sophraea to examine.

"Servants' gossip downstairs," she said, barely glancing at the note before handing it back to him. "Adarbrent has been championing the nobles after Stunk's cheated them out of their possessions. I'm certain that Stunk's plans to tear down parts of the City of the Dead made him even madder. So he used his cousin's spellbooks to unleash the dead against Stunk."

"Oh," said Gustin, a little disappointed that she hadn't been more interested in the note and scarcely looked at the shoe when he indicated it dangling from his belt. It's that being born in Waterdeep, he thought, it just makes them all so hard to impress. Especially a girl like Sophraea.

She tugged at his sleeve. "We need to leave now," she said, starting back down the stairs. "Hurry up."

"So now Adarbrent is slinging around spells," Gustin complained as they went toward the front hall. Sophraea set an even quicker pace than usual and he had to stretch his long legs to keep level with her. "And Stunk's valet knows a fetish when he sees one. Here I thought magic was a rare and unusual talent. An ordinary wizard doesn't measure up to much in Waterdeep."

"Maybe Adarbrent hired a real wizard to read the spells out for him," Sophraea soothed even as she sped across the hall. "However he did it, it worked. But really, we need to leave now. I had a little trouble downstairs."

Ignoring her last statement, Gustin pulled the brocade shoe from his belt. "I found it." Maybe she hadn't noticed it before. He was expecting just a bit more congratulations from her.

"Wonderful," said Sophraea, urging him across the hall with many nervous glances at the guards still stationed at the top of the stairs and near the doors.

"But can we lock the dead back into the graveyard if we return the shoe?" Gustin mused and then answered his own question. "I'm sure this anchored the whole curse to Stunk's house. If the valet had done what was expected, and carried the thing into the mansion, the dead would have been inside the walls days ago."

Two sets of guards were advancing upon them, one pair from the rear of the hall, the other pair from their posts at the great door leading into the courtyard. Sophraea glanced at them and hissed at Gustin, "Whatever the magical reasoning, we should talk about this later!"

Outside thunder rumbled and the sky looked even darker. Gustin began to catch Sophraea's panicky mood. Perhaps it was time for a rapid departure. But when the guards reached them, he said calmly enough, "We have set the protections that Lady Ruellyn requested. We will return tomorrow to collect our fee."

The men stared at him. Behind him, Gustin heard Sophraea gulp, as if she were about to say something and then swallowed it.

Stunk's guards marched to the great door leading to the outer courtyard. One pulled it open as two more arranged themselves in front of the wizard and his companion.

"They will escort you to the gate," said the most senior bodyguard. "Return in the morning for your payment."

Gustin nodded and followed the men out the door. "Keep your eyes on their backs," he whispered to Sophraea. "Don't glance around. That just makes you look nervous or afraid."

"I wouldn't want to look nervous," Sophraea agreed very softly, flipping up the hood of her cloak so it concealed most of her face. "Especially after I left Stunk's doorjack tied up in the basement."

"What?" Gustin almost tripped to a halt.

"Keep moving." Sophraea prodded him. "I don't want to explain here."

The guards swung open the gilded iron gates. Gustin and Sophraea slipped through them. Rain began to pour down, but the pair hurried away from Stunk's mansion, never glancing back until they reached the corner of the street.

Then Gustin risked one look over his shoulder. Oblivious to the rain, Rampage Stunk had joined the cluster of guards at his gate. The fat man just stood there, watching them leave. Another guard came running up to the group, obviously bursting with news.

Gustin pulled Sophraea around the corner of the street, shielding both of them from the stony blank stare of Rampage Stunk.

With some urgency, Gustin asked her, "What is the fastest way back to Dead End House?"

TWENTY

Cutting through the City of the Dead was probably the quickest route to Dead End House, Sophraea reasoned, as she led Gustin back to the Mhalsyymber gate.

She briefly considered going west to the High Road and taking that as far as Andamaar, but that meant twisting back through the little streets to Dead End House. Somehow, she didn't feel as safe on the open streets. That strange emptiness in the North Ward, the eerie silence that felt more like midnight than the late afternoon, still persisted.

For the first time in her life, Sophraea missed the usual clamorous crowds, the hustle and bustle of normal life in Waterdeep. She'd never complain again about Waterdeep's crowded streets, she decided, or about having to slow her steps because of some group dawdling in front of her or having to sidestep some knot of gallants posturing to their peers.

Right now, she had an itch between her shoulder blades, like something was tracking them. Only, whenever she risked a peek around the edge of her hood, she saw nothing but wet pavement and the black shadows that marked the entrances to the littler alleys. And she'd almost missed a turn already, nearly taking the Golden Serpent instead of Mhalsyymber's Way.

With some relief, she pulled Gustin through the public gate into the City of the Dead, acknowledging with a brief nod the Watch standing there. The two older men barely glanced at her. They were huddled together, whispering and staring into the graveyard.

"They are locking all the gates early tonight," one of the guards said.

"We will exit at Coffinmarch," she said. The Watch still did not know about the Dead End gate.

"Hurry," said young man. "The Watchful Order will be here soon."

"New wards?" guessed Gustin, speaking for the first time.

The young man shook his head. "They never tell us anything. Just lock up and lock up tight. But they are expecting trouble, everyone is expecting trouble with the dead tonight."

Sophraea nodded, "We will hurry."

Then they were past the Watch and down the paths that she knew so well.

Inside the City of the Dead's walls, she didn't have to think about which turn or what direction. She just knew the right route.

But it was quiet in the graveyard too, that waiting stillness that she'd felt so strongly earlier that morning.

"Are you sure it is safe?" Gustin asked as if the wizard could read her nervous thoughts.

"Of course, it's still daylight," she answered with far more conviction than she felt. The rain had stopped but the heavy clouds overhead made it as dim as twilight. Every silent tomb that they passed, she looked at twice to make sure that the doors were shut and nothing stirred in the darkness within.

"It's just that you are glowing again," Gustin said.

"What?"

"Not a lot, just a little," he assured. He put one hand on her shoulder, making her stop, and tipped up her head so he could stare into her eyes. Sophraea blinked at seeing his own bright green eyes so close.

"No, it's gone now. It's like the tiniest of blue flames, right in the center of your eyes," he said. "Are you sure that you don't have a blue mark anywhere on you?"

Sophraea remembered her birthmark; everyone in the family had one, at least in her generation and her father's generation according to Myemaw. She started to tell Gustin and then thought better of it, given where her mark was located. It wasn't as if she could show him!

"Come on," she said. "We need to get home."

The pebbles in the path were slick under her feet and she slowed her pace slightly. Something rustled in the bushes to their left. Sophraea looked hopefully for the twitch of a topiary dragon's tail, but there was no sign of the bushy beast or the friendly Briarsting.

To distract herself, Sophraea began to question Gustin on what to do next to quiet the noble dead of Waterdeep.

"Replace the shoe where we found it in the underground tunnels," said Gustin. "I'm certain that it anchors whatever ritual curse was used."

"So if we just put it back, then the dead won't walk?"

Gustin gave one of his long rippling shrugs that started at his shoulders and ran all the way down to his hands turning palm up. "It might not be that simple," he said. "There may be a countercharm or other spell that's needed. I wish I could see the spellbook that he used."

"Perhaps we should go to Lord Adarbrent today and ask him for the book," Sophraea mused.

"You think just knocking on his door and asking politely will get him to end this feud with Stunk?"

Sophraea pushed her hood back so she could see the wizard clearly. "Actually," she said slowly, "he might. If nothing else, Lord Adarbrent is a man of honor. I doubt he meant to involve our family quite so deeply in this war with Stunk. He's always been a good patron and a friend to my father."

"Do you really think a nobleman would care that much about what happens to a tradesman's family? I've seen aristocrats before," Gustin replied, "and none of the breed have ever struck me as having much regard for the lower orders."

"But Lord Adarbrent doesn't see us like that. He doesn't see anyone like that," she continued, remembering the old man with his tentative offer of sweets to a lost child and, later, his long stories told over the family ledger. "He sees us all as a part of Waterdeep. We keep this city's traditions alive."

At Gustin's slight smile at her choice of words, Sophraea shook her head. "No, this place, the City of the Dead, is important to Lord Adarbrent and so we're important because we keep it as it has always been kept. We built the first wall around it, we carve the tombs, and, he knows, as long as we are here, the City will have someone caring for it who loves it as much as he does."

"You talk as if he's fallen in love with a graveyard," said Gustin.

"No, he's in love with Waterdeep. He always has been," said Sophraea with revelation. "Waterdeep is Lord Adarbrent's one great passion. And, for Waterdeep's sake, I think I can get him to give up that spellbook. Maybe we shouldn't be going to Dead End House now. Maybe we should go to Lord Adarbrent immediately."

As she turned to go toward one of the public gates, a flash of gray fur caught her eye. Unsure of what she'd seen, Sophraea slowed down, turning in place. Now she could clearly see a giant gray paw sliding out from behind a black marble urn. A tip of furry ear was visible through the urn's curved handles and a twitch of the bushy tail could be seen near the base.

She clutched the basket's handle with both hands and took a deep breath. It couldn't have been a wolf. There weren't any wolves in the City of the Dead. Ghosts, ghouls, haunts, walking corpses, undead, and restless dead, all those dangers she had been warned about since she was a small child. Those were ordinary threats, like thieves in the marketplace. If you were careful and wise, and avoided certain parts of the graveyard after dark, you could spend your whole life traipsing back and forth quite safely through the City of the Dead. Her family did it every day.

Even outsiders, strangers to Waterdeep like Gustin, could wander the paths in the daylight hours with no fear of attack.

But nobody had ever warned her about wolves. Such a creature didn't belong in the City of the Dead. She couldn't have seen a wolf.

Drawing a deep breath, Sophraea concentrating on using that peculiar sense that let her see throughout the City of the Dead. And, there, right behind a memorial urn, she distinctly perceived something with four large paws, an even bushier tail, and, oh dear, numerous sharp teeth!

Before she could warn Gustin, Sophraea caught a glint of metal behind the wolf. A very large man in a helmet crouched behind a gravestone that wasn't quite large enough to hide him fully.

In her vision, the wolf dashed around the urn and dived under a nearby hedge separating one family's plot from another's.

"Gustin!"

The wizard halted beside her, seemingly unaware of her concern. With a shake of her head, Sophraea tried to see the graveyard as Gustin would see it. Dripping hedges close to the path, a few tombs, no sign of life at all. Their pursuers were still too far away and too well hidden for Gustin to see them. Of course, that must mean that their pursuers couldn't see them either. At least she hoped that was true. Then she remembered that wolves tracked by scent.

Trying to keep her voice calm, Sophraea asked Gustin, "Do you have any spells against wolves?"

"Nothing particular," he answered. "Why?"

"How about men in armor?"

"I have that one I used during the street fight that makes weapons slippery." Gustin looked over his shoulder. "What do you see?"

"Don't turn," she said as she started quickly down the path.

Her odd double vision settled more firmly over her. In one sense, she was still firmly anchored to the Sophraea scrambling down the gravel path in the graveyard. But another Sophraea seemed to be floating high above the tombs. That disembodied Sophraea clearly saw the slinking gray wolf tracking them along the wet path and, to her dismay, more than the one armored man behind it. There was an entire group of Stunk's bullyblades tagging along behind the beast.

"They followed us," she warned Gustin. "Stunk's men."

The wizard quickened his pace and didn't look back.

"How many?" he asked as a crackle of white lighting sparked off the tips of his fingers. He kept his hand low and close to his chest so their pursuers could not see.

"Half a dozen, not more. One is a wolf." Sophraea stumbled along, her double vision causing her to feel slightly dizzy. For one wobbly moment, she felt as if she trod on the bronze roof of a nearby mausoleum as well as by Gustin's side.

"To my right or to my left?" Gustin asked.

"What?" Now one Sophraea jogged around a corner while the other, the floating Sophraea, danced unseen above the head of the gray wolf. The beast snarled below her phantom toes, snapping left and right at the empty air, the hair clearly rising on the back of its bristly neck. The creature couldn't see her phantom above it, she decided, but somehow it knew she was there.

One of the armored fighters yelled at the wolf, his mouth moving silently as apparently her expanded senses didn't extend to hearing. But from the man's angry gestures, Sophraea could tell that he was urging the group on.

"Stunk's men. Are they on my right or my left? Can you tell?" Gustin asked again.

She blinked. Before her, two tall evergreens marked the entrance of a grotto. Her other sight showed the same trees rising behind a long colonnade memorializing the fallen heroes of a long-forgotten war. Stunk's men used the marble columns to hide their approach, but they were almost level with the two people hurrying toward the evergreen grove. With a start, Sophraea realized that she was seeing herself and Gustin.

"On your right, on your right!" she cried and pointed to the columns.

Gustin whirled and flung the spell over Sophraea's head. It cracked through the air, a whip of raw energy. Someone yelled. A red-haired goon leaped up from his hiding place, shouted to see the wizard staring directly at him, and dived back behind a column.

"Stone, stone," Gustin muttered, his eyes burning emerald bright. "Those columns are all stone, yes?"

"Pure marble," Sophraea agreed. That particular memorial had been built by her great-great-grandfather and had been more recently polished and repaired by her uncles. It was supposed to be one of the greatest examples of that period's monuments. Uncle Sagacious, in particular, often took his sons there to show them what "fine carving truly meant."

"Get behind me." Gustin pushed at her. "If one moves, the rest should fall. But get clear."

"What are you talking about?" She shifted down the path. With all her attention centered on the wizard, Sophraea suddenly realized that she could no longer see through phantom eyes. Her sense of where Stunk's men were hiding disappeared.

Gustin pulled out his guidebook to Waterdeep and opened it to the center. Once more the ordinary words and woodblock illustrations began to melt into new and stranger shapes as the young wizard held the book high in one hand. With his free hand, Gustin traced corresponding symbols in the air.

Sophraea saw the nearest column wobble and then sway on its base.

"Jump, jump," commanded Gustin, both his hands now waving up and down.

The column began to rise and then abruptly fall, a weird hopping motion that went higher and higher. Each time it fell back with a shuddering crash against its base.

The third time, a huge crack in the base appeared. The column smashed back in place and then toppled to one side, striking the column next to it. That struck its neighbor and so on, until the entire colonnade hurtled to the ground, encircling Stunk's surprised men in a high wall of rubble.

Sophraea stared, speechless with shock. The marble columns, what had Gustin done to them? What would her uncles say?

A pair of gray ears and enormous paws popped over the top of the debris. Gustin sent another ball of magical energy *zing*ing past. With a yelp, the wolf dropped back behind the barricade.

And Sophraea realized that all her uncles would say is, "He saved our Sophraea's life. Well done!"

"We better run, that last spell was more show than damage," Gustin said.

"Come on," she said. "We need to get to the Dead End gate!"

With a last whip of energy back at Stunk's men to discourage them, Gustin followed Sophraea as she twisted off the main public path and raced down the little used way to the maze known as the Thief's Knot.

Shouts and a wolf's howl sounded behind them.

Nobody ever visited the maze, Sophraea reasoned in her head. Most of the maps of the City of the Dead didn't even show it. She could slow down their pursuers there and take the back path to Dead End House.

And once they were through the Dead End gate, they would

be safe. Stunk's men wouldn't be able to find it or use it to exit the City of the Dead.

They pounded down the path. Sophraea concentrated hard on only seeing the ground in front of her feet. She could hear the wolf's panting and the pursuit of their enemies quite clearly behind her.

TWENTY-ONE

Through complicated twists and turns, Sophraea raced into the memorial maze planted in the City of the Dead to honor a particularly wily leader of the thieves' guild.

The tall hedges closed around Gustin and Sophraea. With a quick hop, she sidestepped a revolving stone meant to trip up the unwary. She yanked Gustin out of the way of a branch that whipped by their faces.

"Look out," Sophraea pushed the wizard back before he could trip a set of bells cleverly concealed behind a small piece of garden statuary with a pointy hat, which was noted in the Carver's ledger as an exact copy of the Master Thief's most revered opponent. Time and weather had softened the famed thiefcatcher's stern features and left the stone gnome with almost an expression of amusement.

Gustin's bright eyes widened as he sidestepped the alarm. Sophraea realized that his earlier illusion of disguise was fraying. His eyes were clearly green and he seemed thinner. She wondered if she continued to look like a moon elf or if she had reverted to Sophraea Carver. Glancing down at her basket, still weighted with the bits of broken brick, she saw that it seemed to waver between velvet ribbons and wicker handle on her arm. The sight made her almost as dizzy as her double vision earlier.

"Where are we?" Gustin stuck close to Sophraea, matching her almost step for step as they followed the curving briar hedge. His quick walking pace was the same as her running stride.

"The Thief's Knot," she answered. "We used to come here as children on hot days. It's always shady here. Leaplow and the twins loved jumping out at the rest of us and trying to make me scream."

Another twist of the path took them by the perpetual flame, burning to light the way of any thief lost in the eternal night.

Then they passed under the arch carved with copies of every piece of jewelry that the Master Thief had ever stolen. The decorative gems had long ago been looted by his mourners, but the stonework still marked the entrance to the center of the maze. The center was perfectly round and felt hushed. Even the wind couldn't penetrate the tall hedges. Once Sophraea had rather liked the silence and even come here to escape the noises of the household and workshops.

"Now!" someone shouted and broke the peace.

She and Gustin froze, staring wildly at each other. Someone else was in the maze, quite close, and whoever it was sounded angry.

"Try it now! Come on, you coward, get up, there's no one here to help you!"

Gustin started to push her behind him.

Sophraea sighed. "Don't bother," she said, "I know that voice!"

Then she shouted, "Leaplow!"

Marching between the hedgerows of the maze, she turned a corner and stopped.

Her youngest brother stood with his feet apart, straddling a lump of twisted coat and cap. A thin trickle of blood ran from his nostril and the flesh around one eye was turning purple. When he saw her, he lowered his clenched fists, grinned and said, "And who would you be, little elf girl?"

His victim rose on one elbow, looked up through streams of blood that covered his face. He looked terrible but at least he was alive.

"Are you going to kill that man?" she demanded.

Leaplow shook his head. "Of course not. We are settling a wager. As soon as he pays me, I will help him back to the Coffinmarch gate."

The soft hair, the wide shoulders, the familiar grin, oh dear, no wonder Briarsting thought he saw Sophraea's father, still a young man, in the City of the Dead the night before.

"Have you been patrolling the graveyard?" she demanded.

"Moon elf, do I know you?" Leaplow said.

"Why were you roaming the City of the Dead at night?" she insisted.

Leaplow scratched his head. She could see the bruises on his knuckles. "Last night, after the dead passed through our gate, I heard a noise. So I went into the graveyard. I thought I could catch whoever was stirring things up. And then there was this girl, I know she's dead, but she's a fine dancer and I thought if I saw her again . . ."

"Into the City of the Dead at night!" Sophraea exclaimed and flung up her hands, interrupting Leaplow. Didn't her stupid brother know how dangerous that was! Well, of course, she'd gone following the dead into the graveyard at dawn. But that was different and Leaplow didn't need to know about that anyway.

"This afternoon, I caught this one with his companions, trying to climb over the graveyard wall into our courtyard," Leaplow went on. "And I chased him all the way to Stunk's house and then I chased him all the way back here. Well, a few of my brothers and my cousins were with me, and a few more of Stunk's men were with him."

The fighting in the streets in the North Ward, thought Sophraea.

"I should have known it was you!" she said out loud.

Not hearing her, Leaplow continued, "So we had a small scuffle, not much of a fight at all, the others ran away and my cousins ran after them. This one ducked into the City of the Dead to hide and I caught him and dragged him here, because the Watch never patrols in here. And he started blustering and making threats, so I told him that if he could win in a fair fight against me, I'd show him how to get out of this maze for free. And if he lost, he could pay me properly to lead him home. Besides, he works for Stunk. Anyone who works for Stunk is in need of a beating."

"Oh, Leaplow, there's no point talking sense to you." Turning to the wizard, Sophraea said, "Come on, we need to get out of here."

Behind her, her confused brother said, "If you weren't a moon elf, I'd swear you were my sister. She is always saying things like that."

Remembering that he was her brother, and no matter how annoyed she felt she did not want him harmed, she said, "There's a wolf outside the maze. You should stay here for a bit until it leaves."

She thought about urging him to come with them. But Leaplow's most likely reaction to a number of armed men running after them would be to turn and fight. Better he remained hidden while she led Stunk's men away from the maze.

"Can't remember ever hearing a wolf here before. I wonder how you wrestle one," Leaplow said, dropping heavily down to sit upon his fallen opponent. The beaten man grunted under his weight.

"I'd rather you didn't," said Sophraea. Then, with an idea born of desperation, she patted Gustin on the chest. The wizard had been watching their whole exchange with an expression torn between amusement and bewilderment. "It's his fight," she said to her brother. "You wouldn't want to spoil his fun."

Leaplow blinked sleepily at the wizard. "You look familiar too. Do I know you?"

"Not at the moment," said the wizard with some relief.

Leaplow shrugged. "Oh well, I am a bit tired." He yawned and settled more heavily upon his opponent. "I have been up all night. I'll keep this one quiet until they're gone. Then I can collect my payment and go home."

On the other side of the thick briar hedge, they heard a sniff and a scratch. The wolf had found them, probably smelled the blood on

Leaplow. Branches shook as the beast tried to claw his way through. A surprised howl came from the wolf as it encountered the thorns hidden behind the evergreens and the shaking stopped.

With a wave to the brother who had no idea who she was, Sophraea grabbed the wizard's hand and hurried back toward the center.

"The wolf can never make it through the thorns," she said. "Even if they find a way in, they'll be sure to get themselves in a tangle. It's nothing but traps in the outer ring."

"What about your brother?"

"They'll never see him, unless he wants them too," Sophraea said. "He knows all the twists and turns of the maze. He'll be safe enough—I hope!"

"And how do we get out?" asked Gustin.

"There's a secret way, of course, just as any good thief would discover. Straight out from the center." Sophraea slowed so she could count her steps past the perpetual flame toward the round stone circle that marked the center of the maze. At the edge of the circle, she turned sharply left and walked straight into the thorn hedge.

Gustin recoiled behind her, then started forward to see if she was hurt.

"Sophraea, where are you?" he called.

She popped her head out of the hedge. "Come on, it's only an illusion here. But be careful, it's not a very wide path." She held out her hand to the wizard, who took it with a smile.

Edging sideways through the briars, Sophraea whispered to her companion, "This will put us close to the Deepwinter tomb. And then it's just a short run from there to our gate. With luck, it will take them some time to figure out that we're not in the maze and start following us again."

They slid out of the hedge and back to a normal path. Two more turns revealed the Deepwinter monument. Just past one black corner, Sophraea could see the high wall surrounding the City of the Dead. They were almost home.

She ducked around the high flowering bush that marked the Carver's gate. The moss-covered steps were still there. But now rather than an iron gate at the top, the steps led to a smooth stone wall, perfectly matching the rest of the high barrier separating Sophraea and Gustin from the courtyard of Dead End House.

"Where's the gate?" they said together.

"Another illusion?" added Gustin.

Sophraea ran up the stairs and felt along the wall. "No, it is real." The mortar under her fingers felt slightly sticky. "When they found the gate broken this morning, they must have decided to wall it up."

A frustrated baying sounded behind them. Stunk's bully boys and pet wolf must have discovered their prey had escaped the maze.

Sophraea ran agitated hands across the stones blocking the Dead End gate. The work was perfect, of course, only the best as usual from her family. And it perfectly blocked their safe exit from the City of the Dead! Her family had trapped her within the graveyard.

TWENTY-TWO

W here now?" said Gustin.

"Coffinmarch. That's the closest public gate."

Frustrated, Sophraea almost pounded against the stones confronting her. The mortar was still tacky. If she screamed, her family might hear. The men could easily tear this block down again with their pickaxes and hammers.

But, and Sophraea stilled at the thought, that would open the gate again for the walking corpses and other noble haunts. Better to keep them out of Waterdeep. She still knew the City of the Dead better than any of Stunk's bullies. With luck, they could elude their pursuers.

Once through the Coffinmarch gate and deep in their own neighborhood, there were always friends who would shelter them or send word to her family.

Her mind made up, Sophraea started down the steps, only to halt at a second howl.

"I think that was closer," said Gustin.

Sophraea nodded. "What spells do you have left?" she asked the wizard.

"The one that lets me run very fast. I can stretch it to cover both of us," he said. "But it doesn't last long."

"Let's get closer to the Coffinmarch gate," Sophraea replied.

"How much time do you think we have left?" Gustin asked, looking up at the gray clouds above them.

From the paler shades of gray toward the west, Sophraea judged it was still late afternoon. "The gates should be open for awhile longer."

"If we can get them to chase us past the City Watch at the gate, we'll be moving too fast for the Watch to catch and they'll run . . ." Gustin mused.

"Right into a fight," enthused Sophraea. "Or the Watchful Order. They should be arriving soon. But what about the wards on the gates? Will that interfere with your spell?"

"Let's hope not," said the wizard, setting out with long strides to follow Sophraea as she led them away from the Dead End House's blocked gate.

As they passed round a small round tomb carved from a pale violet stone and inlaid with silver, a door creaked open. Two shadowy figures stepped out.

Gustin raised his arm, ready to fight, but dropped his hand as he recognized the two men halted in the doorway of the tomb. One had a head full of tentacles. The other's amphibious face was scaled and his mouth open and closed with surprise, revealing a double row of teeth. The two gravediggers seemed as startled as Gustin was, but gave out no yell of greeting to echo his own.

Sophraea let out a glad cry upon recognizing her friends, "Feeler! Fish!"

The two gravediggers had started to turn back into the tomb but stopped at her shout.

"Who are you?" said Feeler, his tentacles waving in agitation around his long pale face.

"Sophraea," the puzzled girl replied.

"You're still mostly moon elf," Gustin said. With a snap of his fingers, the illusion melted away from the pair.

Feeler and Fish blinked together at the sudden transformation.

"Sophraea, we've been looking for you!" said Feeler, hurrying to her. "Your mother was afraid you'd try to come back to Dead End House from the graveyard side."

"We did, but the gate's blocked."

"Yes, the family decided to brick it closed this morning after they saw the damage there," said Feeler. "Then, about halfway through the work, a thorn popped his head over the wall and said he'd seen you in the City of the Dead."

Gustin scanned the darkening sky. A distant howl made him start and remind Sophraea, "We should get moving."

"We need to get out of here," said Sophraea to Feeler. "Stunk's men are following us."

"Stunk! Some messenger came from him earlier, demanding that your father give up the family ledger. Astute sent him right back to Stunk with some hard words, but the fellow made all sorts of threats."

Feeler continued, "Then Leaplow caught some of his men trying to climb over the graveyard wall and a pack of your brothers and cousins went after them."

"We saw Leaplow, he's safe enough in the Thief's Knot," Sophraea told them.

The shouts and sounds of armored men echoed behind them.

Feeler turned back to the open tomb door. "We'd do better underground. We can lose them in the tunnels."

"Go through a tomb?" Gustin asked.

"With the gate closed, I think we should."

Sophraea and Gustin followed Feeler. The round tomb's floor was mostly circular staircase, leading down under the earth. A few glowing lights provided a dim illumination.

"Who is buried here?" whispered Gustin.

"It feels empty," said Sophraea.

Above them, Fish pulled the door firmly shut with a *clang* and then rattled down the stairs behind him, his shovels and other tools clicking in their shoulder straps.

"Nobody's in here. Belongs to a family buried outside," said Feeler. He took the lead down the stairs. "There's a portal at the bottom and a door into the long tunnels running toward the wall."

"Maybe we could take the portal," said Sophraea as they reached the tiny room at the bottom of the stairs. A polished dais of amber marked the magical exit.

Feeler shook his head. Fish nodded in agreement.

"Why not?" asked the confused Sophraea.

"Only one way out and one way back. There's a wolf with them, right?"

"Yes, big gray thing," said Gustin.

"Lycanthrope," said Feeler with conviction.

"A werewolf?" Sophraea suddenly thought she knew who it was.

"That doorjack, the one with the all-body beard," said Gustin echoing her thoughts.

"Stunk's been employing some strange ones," said the man with tentacles and no irony. "There's been talk in some of the taverns where we go."

Fish nodded and grinned to reveal his double row of sharp pointy teeth.

"We had a couple of offers," Feeler added. "High pay too. But we told them we were loyal to the Carvers."

Fish pulled up the heavy wooden door on the other side of the little room. Just outside it, one of the gravedigger's lanterns swung from an iron hook. Fish fetched it down and lighted it with his tinder.

"If we go this way, we may lose them," Feeler said, gesturing them through the door.

"Or lead them back to Dead End House," Sophraea protested. "I know the basement door is guarded, but will it be strong enough to resist a full assault?"

"There's another portal along here," said Feeler, hurrying them down the long tunnel. "It comes and goes with the tide."

Fish made a gulping sound, a glugging deep in his throat.

"Tide's on the turn," said Feeler. "We should be able to slide past, but if Stunk's bullies follow, they won't like it."

"They'll be sucked in?" said Gustin with a lively tone of interest.

"It's not real obvious," said Feeler. "When it comes up, it just looks like a mud puddle stretching across the tunnel floor."

Sophraea stared uneasily at the damp mud under her feet. "Are we close to it?"

"Almost there." Feeler stopped and signaled Fish to go forward. "If the tide is in, better that he steps into it than us. He can breathe underwater."

"Where does this portal go?" asked Sophraea, who disliked Stunk's guards intensely but didn't necessarily want to murder them.

"Most turn up outside the city walls, on the beach," said Feeler. "I've known some halflings to jump in to escape the City Watch, but they say it isn't pleasant, you're usually up to your knees in muck and seaweed from the drop. And there's been talk that one or two landed far out in the water and had to swim in."

Sophraea took a deep breath. "I can swim if I have to."

"I haven't ever been through a portal," Gustin murmured. His eyes were wide and shining in the lantern's light. He stirred the mud with his foot. "It's just the sort of adventure that the guidebook promised that you'd find in Waterdeep."

"There are pleasanter portals," Sophraea told him. "And I'd rather not end up in the bay."

"We have a little time," Feeler assured her. Fish had cleared the perilous part of the passage and waved them forward down the long tunnel, signaling that it was still safe. Sophraea could barely see his lantern bobbing far ahead of them.

As they ran toward the scaly gravedigger, the ground began to hum and shiver under their feet. The wet earth sucked at their feet, as if reluctant to let them proceed. The air reeked with the smell of salt water.

"Faster," said Feeler, stretching out his legs. "Tide's coming in."

Gustin snapped off some rattling words, grabbing at Sophraea with one hand and Feeler with the other. Their magical speed created a breeze that made Sophraea's skirts and curls stream out behind her.

She heard a loud shout and then a howl echoed down the passageway.

"Stunk's bullies are in the tunnel!" she warned the others.

As abruptly as it began, Gustin's burst of speed ran out. Sophraea felt the power drop off immediately. Suddenly her feet seemed incredibly slow, as if she struggled through glue. Each step took enormous effort. Each time she lifted a foot, she heard the mud beneath her soles give a popping sound.

"Come on, come on," Feeler cried, lunging toward Fish.

The other gravedigger stretched out his arms, ready to snatch them to safety.

With a leap, Gustin cleared the steps leading up to the solid rock floor. He hauled on Sophraea's arm and Fish caught her other hand. She felt her toes touch mud, sticky and thick, holding her back. Fish and Gustin yanked. Pain shot through her shoulder joints. And then between them, the two swung her to safety.

Sophraea sank to her knees with a gasp.

Behind them, the tunnel began to glow with aquamarine phosphorescence. Stunk's startled men could be clearly seen. Already the floor beneath their feet was shining wet and the tang of rotting seaweed filled the tunnel.

The mud stirred and then parted, and something huge and white and scaled swam momentarily both across the floor and in the floor. Then the salty scent of the open sea filled the air.

Stunk's men tried to turn and run, but the mud caught them. The air shimmered around them. With an awful *gloop,* fighter after fighter was sucked down into the open portal.

The surface rippled with their passing and then was smooth and still, gleaming wetly under the luminescent glow of the tunnel walls.

Only the werewolf escaped being pulled under. Faster than the armored men, the beast raced through the tunnel and launched himself into the air at Sophraea.

From where she knelt on the solid stone step, still gasping for breath, Sophraea saw a mouthful of huge teeth bearing down on her. The gigantic paws reached for her. Behind her, she heard Gustin and the others shout. Light flashed on the outstretched claws.

Her heart pounded. Her breath stuck in her throat. She sat back on her heels and tried to stand but her legs felt too numb. She'd never make it, never get to her feet in time to run. Her damp fingers dug into the wicker handle of her basket. For an endless moment, she stared, horrified. And then she reacted.

With her own yell bouncing off the walls, Sophraea swung the basket loaded with bricks. It smacked into the terrible beast's nose.

The werewolf tumbled back onto the quicksand floor of the tunnel.

Another *gloop* and he was gone.

Absolutely breathless, Sophraea turned to face her friends. They stared back with an expression akin to awe or maybe it was surprise.

"The women of Waterdeep are amazing," Gustin finally said with great conviction.

"Let's go back under the Markarl tomb," she panted.

"What?" asked Gustin as he caught her hand, holding it in a hard clasp as if he was afraid she'd fall back into the portal shining brilliantly blue behind her. "I thought you wanted to get home. I think we should go back to Dead End House. You'll be safer there."

"We've got to end this," Sophraea argued, but she made no move to pull her hand free. There was something reassuring about Gustin's warm fingers curled around hers. "We must put the shoe back where it belongs. Once we get the dead settled, maybe Stunk will listen to reason. Or we can get Lord Adarbrent to help. But we can't keep running and fighting."

She didn't add that carrying a basketful of bricks was slowing her down and wearing her out. Those bricks had saved her too often to complain about them.

With a reluctant nod, Gustin helped her to her feet and they started running again in the direction that she indicated. Feeler and Fish trailed after them.

"I think it would be safer to go back to the house," Gustin said. "We could fetch some of your brothers or cousins."

They could, and then she could watch Stunk's guards or the noble dead attack her family. Look at what had happened already! The less family members involved, the better, she decided.

"No," said Sophraea out loud. "I started this curse by carrying off the shoe and I'm going to end it."

><del>W</del><

At Rampage Stunk's mansion, the angry fat man questioned a battered and bruised doorjack. The man nursed a bloody and broken nose, but managed to tell Stunk about how he'd been tricked into following the girl and the wizard underneath the City of the Dead.

"It was a trap," he mumbled through his hands clamped over his hairy face. "We got down in a tunnel and then it filled with mud and sucked me in. I thought I'd drown, couldn't breathe, couldn't see. Though I was almost dead, I managed to fight my way back up to the surface and I wasn't in the tunnel anymore. I was in the harbor staring back at Waterdeep."

"So you lost them!" said Stunk.

"But I recognized her," growled Furkin in his mostly human form. "I thought she didn't smell like any moon elf. She's the stonecutter's daughter. The one we saw outside Lord Adarbrent's mansion."

"Sophraea Carver," sputtered Stunk, who had an excellent memory for names. "Gather the guards. We're going to Dead End House. I have had enough of the Carvers and their alliance with that old man!"

TWENTY-THREE

Underneath the City of the Dead, Sophraea's odd sense of place and direction surfaced again. With unerring steps, she led them to the exact spot where she had first found the brocade shoe.

Replacing the shoe in the center of the passage, she backed away from it.

Gustin frowned as he studied the battered focus of the ritual that had stirred up the noble dead of Waterdeep.

"Well," said Sophraea, "now what?"

"That's just it," the wizard replied. "I don't feel anything here. It's not like it was when we were above ground. I could feel magic there."

"And here?" the exhausted girl asked him. The events of the day had finally worn her down. She wanted to collapse in a corner, perhaps sleep for a few days, or maybe just go back to Dead End House and let her mother and Myemaw fuss over her. Outrunning Stunk's men, battling the werewolf, and even trekking so far through the cold and dark tunnels made her sympathize with Gustin's oft-spoken desire to sit in the kitchen next to Myemaw's soup pot.

Nearby, Feeler and Fish waited patiently to escort them back home.

But first Gustin had to reverse the ritual and send the dead back to their graves.

Sophraea asked again, "What now?"

Gustin shrugged. His face reflected the same frustration that she felt. "There's nothing here," he said.

"But we found the shoe here," Sophraea protested.

"We did," he agreed, "but this is not where the curse began. I wish I could explain it better. It's just what I feel—like the way that you know where we are right now."

"We have to do something," Sophraea said.

Gustin nodded, "I'll try a reversal. But, without a specific starting point, I don't know if this will work."

His eyes gleamed under his long lashes as he pulled out his guidebook and his wand. His motions were quick and efficient, none of the large gestures he normally made. A flickering red light gradually outlined his lanky frame. Even Sophraea could feel the crackle of magic in the air as Gustin opened his book and raised his wand above his head.

An agitated Feeler backed farther away from the wizard, his long tentacles sticking straight out from his head as if electrified by the energy of the wizard. Fish gawped at them, his split tongue flickering over his double row of shark teeth. Each lick of his tongue sent a shower of sparks dancing out of his open mouth.

The red light brightened around the wizard. For a brief moment, it appeared as if Gustin Bone was on fire. Then, just as quickly, the light winked out, extinguishing not only the spell but also other sources of illumination. The usual pale glow of the tunnel walls disappeared and even the gravediggers' sturdy lantern flared and then went out, leaving them all blinking in total blackness.

Out of the darkness came Gustin's voice. "That's the first time that ever happened!" he exclaimed.

Sophraea put out both her hands and stumbled toward Gustin, going in the direction of his voice. Each step was terrifying as she walked blindly forward. She lost all sense of where she was, how far away the walls of the tunnel were, or even whether the floor was slanting up or down. Dizzy in the darkness, Sophraea groped with slow steps toward where she hoped to find the wizard.

"Gustin!" she called.

"Here!" he answered but she couldn't tell if he was directly in front of her or just a little to her right.

"My tinder won't work," called Feeler.

"Gustin, what did you *do?*" Sophraea said with feeling.

"Extinguishment," the reply came.

She was certain now that he was standing a little to her right and adjusted her creeping course accordingly.

"I didn't think that ritual would be quite so complete," complained the wizard. "I've put out everything it seems."

"For how far?" asked Sophraea. "Maybe we could back down the tunnel until we reach an area with light."

"I don't know how far," admitted Gustin. "Maybe it is just this section. Or maybe it has spread. It felt like it was spreading at the end."

"Spreading!" She had visions of Waterdeep plunged into deep twilight and more terrible night as every source of light went out. A ritual like that would throw the city into chaos. And what would the Blackstaff do to the wizard who had cast it? Gustin would be lucky if they let him out of the dungeons in time to celebrate his first century.

"You've got to stop it," she urged him.

"I'm trying," came the slightly testy sounding voice of the wizard, now definitely closer to her right hand. Sophraea snatched at the sound of his voice and grabbed a handful of cloth. She heard a muffled, "*Hmph,* let go of my shirt, you're pulling it against my throat, I'm choking!"

Ignoring Gustin's complaints, she threw both arms around the wizard, anchoring herself in the disorientating darkness with a hard hug to his ribs. The wicker basket swinging from her arm banged against his back.

Gustin coughed and sputtered, "I appreciate the sentiment." A

239

few quick pats landed on her head. "But I have to free my arms. I need to use them."

"Just don't move away from me," Sophraea commanded. "If this doesn't work, we need to find Feeler and Fish and lead them out of here."

"We're close to you," Feeler called, a slithering noise undercutting his words. It sounded as if the tunnel was being crisscrossed by snakes sliding over each other. Sophraea sincerely hoped it was just Feeler's odd tentacles waving on top of his head.

A moment later, the gravedigger confirmed her deduction. "I can feel your body heat with my tentacles," he said. "If you stay still, I should be able to come to you."

"Urgh," said Sophraea, trying not to think about Feeler's waving tentacles honing in upon her warm-blooded body.

"Just let me try this before anyone else grabs me," Gustin pleaded but he didn't pull away when Sophraea hugged him even harder.

"Do what you must," she said, "and I'll hang onto you. No matter what happens, we can all get out of here together."

She felt more than heard the big sigh that shook Gustin's chest. Once again, he muttered and waved his arms in complicated gestures. A pale lavender glow illuminated the very tips of his fingers and the end of his nose. A few more pink sparks shot off the top of his head.

In the light that Gustin cast from his own magic, Sophraea could see the dark outlines of Feeler and Fish barely a few steps away from her. Fish, who could see better in the low light than any of them, waved at her. Catching Feeler's hand, Fish started toward Gustin and her. With some relief, Sophraea grabbed Fish's scaly fingers in her own hand, squeezing them tightly. Even if Gustin's spell failed, they could still form a human chain and grope their way out of the tunnels if they had to.

But the light swelling outward from the wizard's hands and head warmed and darkened into a crimson aura, continuing to grow in strength. As the circle of illumination spread, the tunnel walls began to glow again and the flame in Feeler's lantern sprang to life.

A few moments later, the tunnels had been fully restored to the normal poorly lit conditions found in the sewers of Waterdeep.

"It worked!" Sophraea cried and gave Gustin one more one-armed hug around the waist before quickly releasing him and stepping away. Her cheeks were flushed and she felt a little warm, a condition that she decided was due to the excitement of being able to see again.

Gustin suffered no such shyness. He stuffed his wand and book back into his tunic, grabbed Sophraea, and pulled her into a strong embrace, lifting her off her feet and spinning her around. He only let go upon hearing a hollow cough from Feeler.

"Sometimes, even I think I'm a genius," Gustin exclaimed with a grin as the light in the tunnels grew ever brighter. "But, just in case this goes out again, let's leave now."

As she turned to lead them back to Dead End House, Sophraea tripped over the brocade shoe lying discarded upon the ground. She scooped it up and showed it to Gustin.

"What should we do with this?" she asked.

The wizard scratched his bearded chin and frowned. "I'm still certain that it is the key to reversing this curse," he said. "Maybe we need to destroy it. Burning? Burying? Immersion in running water?"

"Which one?" Sophraea asked.

Gustin gave one of his rippling shrugs. "It's hard to know," he admitted, "without the original spellbook."

"And that's with Lord Adarbrent."

"We think," the wizard pointed out.

She answered with a shrug of her own.

"So what do we do with this?" Sophraea asked, contemplating the tarnished shoe in her hand.

"Take it with us," Gustin decided, plucking it out of her hold and once again wedging it under his belt.

A movement at the entrance of a tunnel caught her eye. Something large and distinctly bony was emerging from one of the tunnels that led farther under the City of the Dead.

"Gustin," Sophraea exclaimed, "the curse is still working!"

"We can't be sure," he said.

"I am certain," replied Sophraea, seeing two more corpses line up behind the bony skeleton in velvet robes. The dead made their stately way through the tunnel toward them, marching stiffly, staring straight ahead. "Gustin, I think we should go now!"

The dead, unlike the ones encountered at dawn, seemed to be advancing with a steadier tread. One bore a rusted antique sword and made the occasional slow slashing motion with it. Another held aloft a tattered but obviously antique banner bearing the insignia of a long dead religion. Once again, the most noble of Waterdeep's corpses were on the march toward Dead End House. And this time, they were taking the lower route to the basement door.

Gustin finally spotted the increasing army of dead accumulating in the tunnels. He grabbed at Sophraea and began pulling her away from the corpses on parade.

Feeler gave a shout. Fish dropped back a step or two. More corpses appeared at other entrances to the tunnel. Many of these dead wore rusted armor and rotted leather, and carried shields or spears.

"They're taking portals now," exclaimed Feeler. "These must be from the heroes' graves."

"You mean all the dead are heading toward Waterdeep?" Sophraea was appalled. The ancient nobility roused out of the tombs within the walls of the City of the Dead were a fair number. What if all the corpses from the outlying graveyards started tele-porting through tunnels and into the City of the Dead above them!

Eventually the sheer numbers would overwhelm any defenses set into the walls or gates.

Gustin groaned. "I didn't end the curse! I think I strengthened it."

"Come on," Sophraea said to Gustin. "We have to get home and warn everyone."

It took her less than a moment to get her bearings. The tug of each monument in the City of the Dead felt stronger than ever before.

Sophraea pointed to a narrow feeder tunnel that they had passed once before. She ran to it and peered through the entrance. "I don't see any moving skeletons or other revenants. I think it would be safer to go this way to Dead End House."

"I don't think we can avoid this," Gustin muttered. The tunnels behind them echoed with the steady tramp of marching feet. Feeler and Fish dropped back, keeping a wary watch over their shoulders. So far, none of the dead had reacted to them. Instead, the corpses seemed to be hurrying to a predetermined destination.

With her sight of the City of the Dead above them filling her vision, Sophraea could barely see the tunnel walls around them. She could feel a tug in her breastbone pulling her toward her family home and the gate above, the only exit the dead could use to escape the graveyard.

"Perhaps we're going the wrong direction," said Gustin, when Sophraea led them through the corkscrew turns of the narrow tunnel. "This isn't like the way that we used the last time."

"No, this is the right way," said Sophraea, acutely aware of the dead filling the tunnels behind them and the graveyard above them. Like the tide moving water in Waterdeep's harbor, Gustin's amplification of the curse was drawing them nearer and nearer.

"I still think we are going to have problems when we get there," said Gustin, his shoulders twitching as if he too could feel the growing numbers of the dead walking above them as well as behind them.

Sophraea was right about the tunnel leading back to Dead End House. It joined the main tunnel just a short way before the basement door.

Gustin was right about their problems increasing.

An army of the dead stood facing the door, weapons raised as if poised to attack.

TWENTY-FOUR

Row upon row of skeleton soldiers stood at attention in front of the basement door of Dead End House. The skeletons faced the door as though waiting for it to open.

"How do we get past them?" said Sophraea.

She stared, appalled, at the rows of shining spines revealed by holes in their decrepit armor. Every skeleton was outfitted in a motley collection of rusting plate and rotting leather. Each carried a pitted sword or a bent spear.

"They look pretty brittle," whispered Gustin in her ear. "Maybe we could bowl them over."

"With what?" she snapped back a little louder than she meant to.

The noise didn't seem to matter to the skeletons. No heads turned under dented helmets to seek them out. Instead the entire bony squadron looked uncomfortably like they were waiting for someone to come along and command them. Perhaps an angry hero returning from the far fields, she thought.

"I may be able to raise up a little wind," Gustin said, "but that spell is better outside than inside."

"What will it do down here?" Sophraea whispered.

"Don't know," said Gustin. "Haven't ever tried it inside before. Should be interesting."

"We would do better to summon the door's watcher," suggested Feeler. His fellow gravedigger Fish hissed and shook his scaly head. Feeler frowned at him and shook his own head back, the tentacles writhing in agitation around his face.

"The watcher will let Sophraea pass," Feeler said to Fish's

unspoken objection. "And the rest of us who dwell at Dead End House. It knows its duty."

Fish pursed his lips and made a slight popping sound.

Feeler shrugged, "Sophraea can call it; she's a Carver."

"I've never even seen it," Sophraea objected.

Vaguely, she remembered the uncles talking once or twice about whistling for the door's watcher but she thought that was an adventure that belonged to their youth. Neither she nor any of the family in her generation had ever needed to invoke the guardian who watched over Dead End House's lowest entrance.

"Any Carver can command it," said Feeler. "But you need a whistle to wake it."

"Is there one on this side of the door?" Sophraea asked. As far as she knew, two whistles were in the house. Like all the children, she had been shown the one on the hook in Feeler's rooms and the other one hanging near Myemaw's kettle in the kitchen. As she recalled, they'd all been firmly told the silver whistles were not toys and must never be used except under the direst of circumstances.

Having a squadron of skeletons assembled for the invasion of Dead End House probably counted as dire enough, Sophraea decided.

"There's one whistle concealed in a hollow rock in this tunnel, for any Carver who might need it on this side of the door," revealed Feeler.

"Really? No one ever told me that!" she exclaimed. "You'd think they might have done."

"And where's the rock?" asked Gustin in a suspicious tone of voice.

Feeler pointed silently at the closest skeleton. One of the dead guard's booted feet rested on a smooth gray stone that stuck up a little from the floor.

"Of course that's where it is." Gustin sighed.

Sophraea hefted the basket full of bricks and shook them in front of his face.

"How good are you at throwing?" she asked Gustin.

With a grin, he reached into her basket and pulled out one of the half bricks.

"I used to knock nuts out of the trees by throwing stones at them," he said. "And I was pretty good at skipping stones too."

Sophraea pulled another half brick out of the basket and tossed it twice in her hand to get a feel for the weight.

"I used to be able to hit Leaplow at one hundred paces with his battered old ball," she recalled.

Gustin handed the remaining two chunks of brick to Feeler and Fish.

"Ladies first," he said gallantly.

"Shove them back as much you can," Sophraea said, "I'll go for the whistle."

"We will defend you while you summon the watcher," Feeler said. Fish nodded.

"Very well," said Sophraea, "on the count of three. One, two . . ."

"Three!" they all yelled.

Sophraea's brick scored a direct hit on the booted skeleton standing on the hollow rock. The brick struck the helmet with a clang. The skeleton's whole head flew off and rolled past the row of skeletons standing in front of it.

"Well done!" Gustin shouted.

The confused and now headless skeleton spun about, blindly waving its crooked sword, which nicely hooked into the spear of the skeleton standing next to it. Both creatures went tumbling in a tangled clatter of bones and plate armor.

But there were still three more standing between Sophraea and the stone.

Gustin's brick cracked the ribs of one skeleton, sending it reeling away. Feeler and Fish managed to jostle their skeleton targets with bricks to the shoulder blade and the hipbone respectively.

The skeleton soldiers spun as though trying to determine the origin of the attack. The empty eye holes in their skulls stared unseeing.

Sophraea darted forward, with Gustin and the rest just a pace behind her. Out of the corner of her eye, she saw the wizard scoop up the crooked sword dropped by the skeleton.

He swung the blade in a wide circle, its rusted edge clicking against bone as he forced dead warriors back.

Feeler and Fish grabbed the nearest skeleton, and, like her brothers with a wishbone, they snapped the creature in two. Feeler used the legs to beat back the others. Fish lobbed the head, the clavicle, and other parts at various attackers.

Sophraea kneeled and curled her fingers around the rock. The niche hadn't been opened in years. Passing feet had shoved it tightly into its hole.

Feeler shouted, "Hurry!"

The rest of the skeleton army was starting to stir, turning reluctantly away from the door to face the foes that had beaten down their fellows.

Sophraea scrambled at the rock, looking wildly around for something to lever it out of its niche. She spotted a rusted bit of armor within reach. She had no idea what it was. It was flat and had a sharp corner and that's what mattered. Scooting on hands and knees between falling skeletons, she touched its edge, lurched, and managed to grab it.

Bones dropped around her from disintegrating skeletons. A severed hand bounced off her shoulder. She saw it, bit back a shriek and scooted backward.

Holding the metal piece in both hands, she wedged it under

the rock's edge and dug between the paving stones. The gray rock tipped up.

Nestled into a carved crevice was the silver whistle. She quickly pried it loose and set it to her lips.

Sophraea blew with all her might, a blast of shrill sound.

In the shadows above the basement door, the watcher stirred. It stretched its wings slowly, scraping against the ceiling as it leaned forward out of its niche. It tilted its horned head and yawned, revealing its back molars as well as the curving tusks at the front. The flexible front paws clenched a little tighter on the stone ledge where it sat, crumbling the edge into gravel that showered down on the skeletons assembled below.

"Protect the door!" Sophraea yelled to it. "Keep out anything dead!"

The watcher gave a ponderous nod at her simple commands and launched itself from its niche with a powerful kick of the heavy back legs. It sailed a few feet on its basalt wings before landing with a thud in the center of the skeletons. The gem dust that coated its skin glittered in the pale light of the tunnel. The big wings snapped out, knocking four skeletons down.

The rest of the skeletons turned toward this new attacker, rushing forward to grapple with the guardgoyle.

"It's alive," Gustin breathed, "but it is stone too. And responding to commands. That's beautiful magic!"

The wizard seemed transfixed by the guardgoyle's sweeps of its horned head. Each jab drove back another skeleton.

Sophraea dropped the silver whistle into her apron pocket. She'd replace it in its hiding place another day. She grabbed her basket with one hand and Gustin's arm with the other because the wizard still stood motionless, watching the guardgoyle.

"Why didn't you tell me what it was?" Gustin complained as she dragged him away. "How old is it? Who cast the spell? Does

249

your family have a copy of the spell in their ledger? Or even a note about when it was done?"

"We can look later," Sophraea promised as she propelled him toward the door. "Gustin, come on!"

Two skeletons broke off from the fight with the guardgoyle to try to block their escape. Sophraea swung her basket and Gustin stuck out one long leg. The spear carrier ducked the basket only to be tripped up by Gustin and fall heavily against the sword bearer. Both went down in a clatter of bones. The rib cage of one became entangled in the leg bones of the other. They thrashed and rolled across the floor.

Hand-in-hand, Sophraea and Gustin hopped over the skeletons.

Feeler stepped in front, pulling out the iron key for the Dead End door. With a quick snap, he unlocked the door and shoved it open.

"We best go before the watcher starts screaming," Feeler said, pushing Gustin and Sophraea forward. Gustin stretched his neck, still trying to get the best possible view of the guardgoyle's movements.

Nipping in behind them, Fish nodded vigorously, already clapping his hands over his ear holes.

Still fighting in the middle of a knot of skeletons, the guardgoyle opened its big mouth in preparation for a scream.

Fish slammed the Dead End door shut as quickly as possible. Although the heavy wood door muffled the worst of the guardgoyle's shriek, everyone winced at the burst of sound.

"I wonder if skeletons can be deafened," Sophraea said, rubbing her smarting ears.

Feeler gave a sympathetic shrug. His tentacles were wrapped tightly around his head, effectively creating earplugs for both ears.

"I do not think the dead will be able to pass it," he said.

"There were so many following us in the tunnels," Sophraea worried. The dead that she'd seen in the tunnels seemed much more substantial and dangerous than the ones who had been dancing through the upper gate in the last few days. She had a feeling that these corpses wouldn't be content with just knocking at Rampage Stunk's windows.

"But the guardgoyle is very strong and all the corpses that we saw moving in the tunnels were very old and quite rotted. I do not think that they will be able to overcome it," Feeler stated. "But Fish and I will stay here. If the door is in danger of being breached, we will retreat to the higher levels, barring the gates and locking other doors behind us."

"Thank you," said Sophraea with a quick hug for both of her old friends. "But don't take any chances. Come up to the kitchen if there is any danger at all!"

"Is that where we are going?" asked Gustin, following her up the stairs past the lower defenses of Dead End House.

"Myemaw will know that I roused the watcher," Sophraea explained breathlessly over her shoulder. "And she'll call the family in. That's the drill in case of a serious attack."

"Your family has a drill for attacks?" Gustin leaped up the stairs behind her.

"All the old trade families in Waterdeep do." Sophraea twisted around a bend in the stairs and saw the welcome outline of the parlor door above her. "There're tales of the old battles in the streets. So we're always taught to be prepared. Bolt down and stay put, that's the safest way to avoid harm."

But even as they emerged into the front parlor, Sophraea could hear the sounds of fighting coming from the courtyard. She rushed to the window and saw Stunk's bullies trying to force their way into the yard from the public gate. Bentnor, Cadriffle, and their brothers were holding them off with hammers, tongs, and some long lengths of boards intended for coffins.

From the huge grin that split Bentnor's face below his bloody nose, Sophraea judged that he was having a wonderful time bashing the redheaded goon in front of him. Bentnor's wide shoulders, where his heavy leather work apron didn't protect him, dripped blood from a mass of scratches. Nothing serious yet, Sophraea decided, because the injuries weren't slowing him at all. One of Stunk's fatter guards screeched as Bentnor rammed a board into his midriff.

"That's not good," said Gustin, pointing over her shoulder in the other direction.

Sophraea spun to peer through the window toward the Carver's former gate into the City of the Dead. The newly mortared bricks were starting to bow forward. Sophraea's father and her uncles rushed to the bricked over gate with lumber to shore it up.

A brick plopped out of the wall and a ghastly hand reached through. It pulled at the next brick. Sophraea's father Astute crashed his mallet down on the grasping fingers. The corpse on the other side obviously felt no pain. It continued to worry at the bricks blocking its way.

Sophraea's mother swept into the courtyard, leading the Carver aunts and other wives. The women all carried pots, pans, brooms, and buckets of steaming hot water as well as some wicked carving knives. With a curt wave of her free hand to the left and right, Reye directed the women to split into two groups, one to reinforce the defenders of the street-side gate and the other to help the men trying to hold back the deceased nobility intent on breaking in from the graveyard.

Even Sophraea's old grandmother was in the yard. Myemaw threw her black ball of yarn toward Stunk's bullies. The yarn wound up the legs of the thin man who was always complaining, entangling him from ankles to hips. He tipped forward and crashed to the ground, yelping as he fell.

With a quick *click* of her knitting needles, Sophraea's grandmother summoned back the yarn and redirected it toward another thug.

"It will be night soon. Everything is getting worse," said Sophraea, spinning away from the window and heading toward the center staircase. "We need some real help."

"Where are you going?" said Gustin, pelting up the stairs after her.

"To Volponia!" Sophraea shouted back, praying as she went that the former pirate queen would know what to do!

TWENTY-FIVE

Realizing her family's tactics would only delay the invasion of Dead End House, Sophraea flew up the stairs to Volponia's room.

Gustin was hard on her heels.

When they reached the landing just outside Volponia's door, the wizard grabbed her hands. "Look," he said.

From the tower window, Sophraea clearly saw that Rampage Stunk's men were well into the courtyard. Behind them strode the fat man. From his gestures, it appeared that he was instructing his men to herd the Carvers into the center of the yard.

Bentnor, Cadriffle, and the rest of the younger Carver males were not giving up, despite equally urgent gestures from Reye and Myemaw, who were trying to pull the family back toward the house. From this angle, Sophraea could not see the City of the Dead or the graveyard gate. But the worried glances in that direction from all the women suggested that the graveyard gate was being breached by the dead.

"I'm going to die," said Gustin, peering down into the yard. "Look at the size of Stunk's men. Look at the size of your family. I'm going to go down there and try to stop them from killing each other and end up being crushed between them. Or be overrun by corpses bent on revenge against Stunk."

He gave a huge sigh, but there was that peculiar undercurrent of joy in his voice, that bubbling excitement he always exuded in the worst situations. Just being near him made the extremely worried Sophraea feel a little more confident.

"We don't have time to stand around talking," Sophraea said as she hurried up the stairs.

"When I was small," he responded with a laugh, "I dreamed about this. Fighting a great battle in Waterdeep. Just like my guidebook promised!"

"Nobody has to die," Sophraea retorted as she reached back to grab him and drag him after her. "We will stop this somehow."

Although, at that moment, she had absolutely no idea how she could save her family.

"No," said Gustin, shaking his head just as firmly as Sophraea so often shook her head at him. "I'm going to die this afternoon and there is nothing that your huge collection of male relatives can do to me after that."

"What were you nattering about? We don't have time for this!"

"Yes we do!" announced Gustin. He grasped Sophraea's shoulders and turned her to face him. His eyes were burning a brilliant green and the hum of a small spell slipped through his smiling lips.

Sophraea felt her feet leaving the floor. Gustin's smile broadened. She floated upward until her mouth was level with Gustin's smile.

"Gustin!"

He pulled her to him. She could see nothing but the emerald sparkle of his eyes gleaming under those absurdly long lashes.

"Gustin!" she squeaked again. "What were you doing?"

"This," he answered. And he kissed her.

TWENTY-SIX

Flustered and flushed from Gustin's kiss, Sophraea wriggled free of his grasp. The minute her hands left his shoulders, which felt harder and broader than she had expected, her feet thumped back onto the floor.

Although she would have given almost anything to have examined his face for a moment longer, she dashed toward Volponia's room.

Timing, Sophraea moaned to herself, timing is everything and she just didn't have any time left. Or she would have stayed still longer and maybe kissed him back.

She burst through the door into Volponia's room. Still, despite that recent distraction, she suddenly knew exactly what to do and who could help them. She rushed to Volponia's bed and bent over the old woman sleeping under her silken quilt.

"We need to fetch Lord Adarbrent here," Sophraea said, shaking awake her dozing great-aunt. "Immediately. He started this and he must stop it!"

"Don't ruffle my ruffles so," scolded Volponia as the former pirate queen pulled herself up higher on her feather-stuffed pillows. That day, the gilded headboard of her bed was carved in the shape of a rearing dragon.

"What is happening?" Volponia asked the agitated Sophraea dancing from foot to impatient foot at the end of her bed.

"We don't have any time left," panted Sophraea. "Stunk's bullies are in the yard, the dead are breaking through the wall. The family is all downstairs fighting but they can never stop them all. We need Lord Adarbrent and his spellbook."

Fully awake now, Volponia's eyes narrowed as she listened to Sophraea's tale. Spotting Gustin in the doorway, she pointed at the young man.

"Is that your wizard?" she asked.

"Yes . . . no," Sophraea stuttered to a halt and then started again. "We can never get to Manycats Alley in time, but you can fetch Lord Adarbrent here. The way that you bring everything to your room."

A faint frown drew down the corners of Volponia's lips.

"Fetching a cup of this or a bite of that is one thing," she said. "A living man is quite another."

"But you did it to Myemaw once," said Sophraea, "when you wanted her for something and she was too slow on the stairs. Rang your bell and fetched her up here."

"And she was cross about it for days." Volponia's expression lightened. "Lord Adarbrent may not want to be snatched from whatever he is doing either."

"I don't care!" declared Sophraea with a stamp of her foot that sent her straight back into childhood. In a slightly more reasonable tone, she added, "We never asked for him to send the dead through our gate. Now Stunk's here and he's going to punish the Carvers for something that Lord Adarbrent did. And that's not fair!"

"But will he care about fair?" asked Gustin. He moved forward into the room with the gingerly step of a tall man surrounded by a multitude of china ornaments and other gewgaws, all eminently breakable and all wobbling on the top of spindly little tables.

"Actually," responded Volponia. "He might care. For the one thing that I would be willing to swear about Dorgar Adarbrent is that he is an honorable man. Besides, if he allows the Carvers to be driven away, who will bury him in the manner that he expects?"

Patting the chiffon ruffles swathed around her throat into order,

Volponia reached for her crystal bell. She rang it once, a single high sweet note sounded through the room.

"I want to see Dorgar Adarbrent and I want to see him now!" Volponia stated in the same clear voice that once rallied frightened men to their posts on a storm-tossed ship.

A flash of light and Lord Adarbrent appeared between the slightly tippy three-legged table and a six-drawer trunk. As always, he was dressed from head to toe in rusty black, and had evidently been about to go outside, for his hat was in one hand and his sword cane was in the other.

The ancient noble of Waterdeep blinked to find himself in a room so fussy and filled with antique furniture swathed in billows of lace that it could only be the bedchamber of a lady of a certain age.

"Madam," he said, correctly identifying Volponia propped up on her feather pillows as the owner of the room and his probable summoner, "how dare you bring me here in such a fashion?"

"Don't complain. I saved your old legs a long climb up some very steep stairs," snapped Volponia.

"Impertinent woman, you have snatched me from important business."

"Grave mischief, you mean. It must stop, Dorgar."

The nobleman blinked at the familiar use of his name and then leaned closer to peer at the occupant of the bed.

"Captain Volponia," Lord Adarbrent said, and he gave a deep bow, the deepest that Sophraea had ever seen. "I should have remembered your family connections and your complete lack of respect for the nobility of Waterdeep."

"Yes, you should have remembered my family," snapped Volponia, but she returned his bow with a courteous nod. "And also what the nobility of Waterdeep, most especially your family, still owes me for the return of *Syllia's Star.*"

Gustin turned to Sophraea, a question framed on his lips, but she just shrugged. She'd never heard this story. The old lady rarely doled out complete tales of her long and apparently colorful past.

"As I recall," Lord Adarbrent said, "you were well paid for the ship's rescue and no questions were raised about your other, hmm, shall we say 'maritime activities' when you decided to retire. And forty years, Captain Volponia, is a very long time to wait to claim a favor. I doubt any that sailed on the *Star* are still alive today."

"But you and I are still here and we both remember the old codes," she said to Lord Adarbrent. "For a nobleman of your character and lineage, it is less than honorable to involve my family in your feud!"

Lord Adarbrent winced and waved his hand in a fencer's acknowledgment of a hit.

"And who do you think would maintain your tomb in the City of the Dead if the Carvers were destroyed?" Volponia continued to scold.

"It was never my intention to involve the Carvers," said Lord Adarbrent with a heavy sigh. "This was a matter of dispute between Rampage Stunk and myself."

"Look outside! No matter what you meant, there's a battle going on in our courtyard!" interjected Sophraea. "And it's our family in the middle, dealing with Stunk and the dead that you raised up."

"I rather underestimated Stunk's stubbornness," confessed the old nobleman as he shifted a little on his feet, rather like a guilty schoolboy faced with owing up to a prank. "I thought a night of ghostly visitors, maybe two nights, would discourage him from building in the City of the Dead. Then, with a few words in the right places, others could be frightened away from trying the same trick. Buying up the tombs of extinct families and tearing them down to build some modern monstrosity is despicable!"

A mottled flush spread across Lord Adarbrent's pale features as he explained. The old man's hand visibly clenched on his sword cane.

"So you endangered these children to save some moldering tombs?" asked Volponia with a tilt of her head toward Gustin and Sophraea.

"And what will these children inherit if we tear down the history of Waterdeep!" Lord Adarbrent roared.

"Very little, if you and Stunk destroy this house between you!" Volponia shouted back, striking one hand so hard against the head-board that the dragon's head nodded back and forth above her.

Lord Adarbrent coughed and modulated his tone, obviously reluctant to continue a shouting match with the bedridden Volponia.

"We have already lost so much," he continued in a quieter voice. "And greed has always been our greatest flaw—we allow men like Stunk far too much simply because they have heavy purses."

Sophraea placed one hand lightly on Lord Adarbrent's forearm. "I know how much you care for Waterdeep," she said. "But my family is part of its history too. And if we are lost, then what have you gained?"

Lord Adarbrent sighed and patted her hand. "You are a good girl," he stated, as he had throughout her childhood.

"No," Sophraea answered slowly, trying to put all her jumbled thoughts of the past few days into a declaration that the old man would understand. "I am a woman grown and I know that no monument is worth more than a single life, even the life of Rampage Stunk. We show great respect to the dead in this family, but we hold the living dearer still."

The expression on Lord Adarbrent's face was impossible to read. The angry flush along his cheekbones began to recede. He closed his eyes and heaved another deep sigh.

"I am sorry," Lord Adarbrent said finally. "I let my temper rule my judgment. You are right. It is time I ended this curse."

"Can you do that?" asked Gustin.

"I can try," Lord Adarbrent replied with a thin smile. "It's not simple. My cousin Algozata was an amazing woman in many ways. She wrote this ritual in her book so that it could be invoked at least once by anyone. It did not take a wizard to begin this curse. I think it will not take a wizard to end it. First, the object that you found, that shoe hanging off your belt, needs to be returned to the owner's tomb."

"But?" said Gustin, in the voice of a wizard who just knew a "but" was coming.

"If the tomb is not sealed, the ghosts will continue to try to cross at the Dead End House's gate. And sealing the tomb," admitted Lord Adarbrent, "will destroy anyone who tries it. It was this part of the curse that killed my cousin Algozata."

"Anything else?" asked Gustin. Two deep lines of worry in his forehead drew the wizard's dark eyebrows together.

"There's some doggerel in Algozata's spellbook that needs to be recited by someone watching," admitted Lord Adarbrent. "It's quite short and can, like the earlier portion of the ritual, be said by anyone holding the spellbook."

"So all you need is the shoe and the spellbook, and you can summon all the dead back to their graves?" asked Sophraea.

"Quite," said Lord Adarbrent. "It will mean the sacrifice of one life, as I have said, to close the tomb's door. But once it is done, the dead will lie as peacefully in their graves as they ever do in Waterdeep."

With some relief, Gustin observed they didn't have the spellbook.

"So nobody," he continued, staring hard at Sophraea, who was whispering another request into Volponia's ear, "need risk her neck by taking it into the City of the Dead. Which means"—he straightened

261

his chin and Sophraea noticed that he actually looked quite heroic—
"no wizard need die trying to close the tomb door for her."

"But I have a plan," said Sophraea, with a quick smile of
appreciation to Gustin for his oblique offer to help, "and getting
the spellbook will be the easy part."

It was the rest of her plan that she wasn't too sure about. But she
didn't say that out loud.

TWENTY-SEVEN

With a nod from Sophraea, Volponia rang her crystal bell.

"Algozata's spellbook," the old lady requested.

A dusty and distinctly rank-smelling spellbook appeared immediately in the middle of her pale pink down comforter.

"That's all I can do for you today," Volponia told her visitors. "Sophraea, I can't fetch anything more until after dawn tomorrow."

Sophraea kissed the former pirate queen's cheek in thanks. She stored the spellbook in her wicker basket, paying no real heed to Volponia's grumbles about the marks left behind on the comforter.

"I can't change the bed until tomorrow either," Volponia said.

"I'll bring you another cover from my room," Sophraea promised her.

"You had better," said the old lady and then added, "so don't do anything foolish and come safely home again."

Sophraea gave a brisk nod to the two astonished gentlemen staring at this domestic exchange and said, "Shall we go?"

"What are you going to do?" asked Gustin.

"I'm going back to the City of the Dead. You heard Lord Adarbrent. All we need to do is close the tomb door on this shoe. By the way, my lord, is it the Markarl tomb?"

"Yes," said the startled nobleman. "How did you know?"

"We found the shoe directly beneath that monument and Gustin thought that there had been odd magic in its vicinity," Sophraea explained.

"That's right. I did," said the wizard, a momentary flash of pleasure relaxing his worried expression. Then, more sternly, he told Sophraea, "But you can't go back into the City of the Dead. For one thing, the courtyard is a battlefield. For another, reversing the curse is going to kill someone!"

"If I don't, this battle will kill a good many more people," Sophraea began.

Lord Adarbrent cut off her next sentence.

"I will close the tomb door," the old nobleman said. "After all, as Captain Volponia so rightly stated, I began this spell. The only honorable action is to close the tomb door as my final act."

Sophraea nodded. "The door has to be closed but does it have to be someone living who does it?"

Lord Adarbrent frowned heavily. "I don't recall Algozata's ritual mentioning anything about that. In fact, the first two times that she invoked this particular curse, she used an animated corpse to end it. Both times the curse ended as she wished. I don't know what became of the corpses."

"I thought you said that the curse killed your cousin," Gustin observed.

The old man's expression grew even more sour. "The third time that Algozata used this particular ritual, the family discovered what she had done. And she was given no choice but to close the tomb door herself. I was a child then, but, as I recall, it was not a painless death," he declared.

This dry recital of Adarbrent family justice made Sophraea shiver. The stone face of Gustin's statue had more kindness in it than the old lord's features.

"What do you want to do? Recruit one of the corpses from the City of the Dead? I'm willing," Gustin asked her, "but I've never had much luck with necromancy."

"Would a statue work?" Sophraea asked. "Suppose you bring the stone man to life, the one my father carved for you. Animating stone is your best magic, or so you keep saying."

"My statue!" Gustin exclaimed. "He could really be a hero of Waterdeep!"

"Absolutely," said Sophraea, ready to lead everyone downstairs.

"My stone men can walk. I never asked one to close a door," he admitted.

"If he can't do it, we'll think of something else," Sophraea said. She tried to sound more confident than she felt.

As she passed near the bed, Volponia caught her hand.

"Don't forget that ring you're still wearing. Even a half wish is better than nothing. You might need it before the night is done," said Volponia. "There is so much that can go wrong."

Sophraea gave a curt nod. She rather wished that Gustin hadn't told her so very often that magical items could be undependable and dangerous.

TWENTY-EIGHT

The courtyard of Dead End House was awash in rain, fighting bodies, and general chaos. Rampage Stunk's guards were still trying to herd all the Carvers into the center of the courtyard as Sophraea slipped out the front door with Gustin and Lord Adarbrent.

Bentnor and the younger men led the charge against Stunk's men. With heavy mallets, they struck at the bullyblades. The younger Carvers used their hard heads and fists as much as their makeshift weapons. They butted and punched, jabbed and weaved, and even bit an ear or two.

They kicked with hobnailed boots, hooking knees or ankles to send their opponents flying.

If there hadn't been so much water and mud underfoot, the Stunk's bullies might have overcome the Carvers' tricks, certainly they were better armored than Sophraea's relatives. However, the sheer slickness of the cobblestones worked in the Carvers' favor. The young masons and coffinbuilders whipped their large leather-aproned bodies into the heavily armored men and sent them skidding backward to sprawl on the cobblestones. More lost their footing every time the full weight of the Carvers struck them.

Bentnor wrestled one bully into the mud. The iron kettles and brooms of his mother and his aunts kept the screaming man pinned down while Bentnor leaped up to hook another around the neck. Cadriffle followed his brother into the fray, swinging a heavy mallet to protect his twin's back.

"Go on! Fight!" Stunk yelled at his men, as they tried to retreat and regroup. "What do I pay you for?"

But it was Stunk's shouted orders, "Don't kill anyone yet! I want to question them!" that actually slowed the battle. His men didn't dare use their swords so were hobbled in their efforts.

By the time Sophraea reached the courtyard, the army of dead from the graves had nearly broken through the family's gate. She saw the hastily mortared bricks and reinforcing boards shatter. Debris was scattered at the base of the wall.

The family was pushing back Stunk's men but they were distracted by cries for help from their fathers, desperately seeking to shore up the defenses of the Dead End gate.

"We need to reach your statue!" Sophraea cried over the din of the fighting.

Gustin nodded, stretching his head this way and that, trying to spot a clear path to the door of Astute Carver's workshop.

The current melee effectively blocked their route.

"Stay here," Gustin said to Sophraea. "I will go around them."

"No," she replied, catching his hand in her own steady grip. "We'll go together!"

Lord Adarbrent gave a grim smile and unsheathed his sword cane.

"Allow me to clear the way for you," he said.

Like a black storm, the old man fell upon Stunk's bullies, striking them from behind, a slash high to the head, a cut low to the knee. Stunk's men howled as the old man's cane lashed across their faces and other vulnerable points.

The startled fighters fell back, only to be urged forward by Stunk's bellow of rage as he recognized the old nobleman swirling through his guards.

"Keep fighting, you stinking cowards!" Stunk roared. "Catch him! Kill him!"

The fat man rocked back and forth in his agitation, his meaty hands chopping at the air as if he could beat Lord Adarbrent down himself. At the same time, the greasy merchant stayed well behind his men and made no actual attempt to join the fight.

Lord Adarbrent moved too quickly for Stunk's fighters. He teased them with thrusts and backward steps, drawing the conflict ever farther away from the center of the courtyard and closer to the street-side gate.

The rest of the Carvers, recognizing their noble friend, rushed to his aid.

"Now," Sophraea said to Gustin.

They darted across the yard. Gustin flung open the door to Astute's workshop. A startled kitten gave a mew of protest and dashed under the workbench.

In the center of the room, the statue lay upon the table. Astute had done exactly as he had promised. The stone man looked real. Faint lines creased the corners of its eyes, the veins across the back of its hands showed clearly, even the skin of the face and neck that showed above the elaborate armor had the pores of a living man.

"It's wonderful," breathed Gustin. "Look at the grip that he's got on that sword. Just as if he was struck down in battle. Your father is a genius! It would have been my very best hoax ever!"

"Hurry!" Sophraea urged him. Peeping around the workshop door, she could see that Lord Adarbrent and the younger Carvers aiding him had managed to drive Stunk's men back against the street-side gate.

But none of Stunk's men pushed back. With Lord Adarbrent in the fight, his opponents drew knives and swords, ready to use the cutting edge against the old nobleman and any who defended him.

When one fighter thrust at Lord Adarbrent with a naked blade,

Cadriffle gave a great cry and smashed down his mallet, shattering the sword with a well-struck blow.

In numbers, Stunk's men and the Carvers were evenly matched, but Sophraea could see that the rich merchant's private soldiers held the advantage in armor and weapons. Luck, so far, had favored her brothers and her cousins, but not even men of their size could hope to prevail forever against so many.

"Hurry," she said again to Gustin.

Beside her, Gustin held open his guidebook, the illusion of a map slowly dissolving to reveal the spells and rituals hidden beneath. He began to chant, a deep sound like the boom of a bronze bell. His voice rolled through the workshop. The kittens yowled in their basket. Astute's chisels and mallets rattled on their hooks.

As before, a red glow infused the wizard's frame, illuminating the workshop. Ordinary things, iron nails and empty jars, shone in the shadowy corners of the room.

At the center of Gustin's spell, the stone statue glowed. Light poured from the wizard to the statue until the shimmering ball of magic completely cocooned it.

And then, between Sophraea's inhale and exhale of wonder, the light winked out.

The kittens still howled under the workshop bench. Gustin slumped, his lax hands nearly dropping his precious spellbook. The ordinary gloom of twilight once again filled the workshop.

"Did it work?" Sophraea whispered, unable to speak any louder, nearly strangled by excitement and worry. The statue lay inert upon the table. If the spell had failed, they would have no choice but to try to end the curse without its aid. And that, Lord Adarbrent had sworn, meant certain death for someone.

Gustin raised his head slowly, as if the weight was almost too much for his neck to bear. But the grin that he gave her was as cocky as ever.

"It really is my best magic," he declared in triumph.

With ponderous motion and a sound like the grinding of a millstone, the statue slowly rose from the table. Two stone feet landed with a thump upon the floor. With a solid tread, the statue marched toward the workshop door.

Gustin pulled the brocade shoe out of his belt and thrust it at the statue. "Take it," he commanded. "Return it to the Markarl tomb."

The statue gave no response. Gustin went closer, circled the stone man, and pushed the shoe between its hip and its hand. The beautifully carved fingers were slightly curled to look natural. The little shoe glittered in the stone grasp.

"Does it know what it carries? Will it know to put it inside the tomb?" Sophraea asked.

Gustin shrugged. "I have never asked one of them to do anything more than walk."

Sophraea bit back her doubts. They had no other choice.

She flung the door wide open. The stone warrior stomped past her into the courtyard.

"Go on!" Gustin shouted at his creation. "That way. To the City of the Dead!"

Outside, the fighting continued. Lord Adarbrent still held off Stunk's men, but the old nobleman had been forced back to the center of the courtyard.

Even as the statue stomped toward the gate into the City of the Dead, the denizens of the graveyard began to overrun the Carvers attempting to block the graveyard gate.

One particularly ambitious corpse knight rode his skeletal horse up the mossy stairs leading to Dead End House.

Halfway through the gate, the ghastly equine opened its mandible in a silent scream. The heavy hooves skidded on the steps leading out of the City of the Dead.

Slowly, surely, the creature slid backward to the confusion of its rider, which twisted its skull completely round on its shoulders to see what the problem was.

"Ho! Starting a fight without me! I don't think so!" yelled Leaplow from behind the horse's hindquarters.

Black-and-blue but grinning widely, Sophraea's enormous brother gathered up the heavy skirts of the skeleton horse's armor and dragged it out of the gate.

The knight fought to turn the horse, but Leaplow's grip was too strong. For the moment, the dead warrior, his horse, and Leaplow blocked the gate leading into the Dead End courtyard and kept the other dead from entering.

The booming tread of the statue crossing the courtyard startled all the combatants. Everyone turned to watch Gustin's stone fighter stride toward the graveyard gate.

Stunk's men broke off their attack of Lord Adarbrent and stood openmouthed.

"Stop him," the fat man screamed. "You'll all be street beggars if you don't stop him!"

His men hesitated and then raised their weapons and circled the stone man. One slashed at the statue with his short sword. The blade shattered on the granite head and the statue marched on.

"Clubs!" Stunk screamed. "Mallets! Don't use your blades, you idiots!"

"Wood," someone shouted and they all raced to pick up anything that could be used as a club.

"Rocks," yelled another.

The courtyard was littered with building materials. Armed with boards and stone urns, Stunk's men raced back toward the walking statue.

"Don't let them smash it!" screamed Sophraea.

"We're defending a statue?" yelled Bentnor.

"Yes," she yelled back.

"All right," he agreed. Then he shrugged and motioned to his twin. The two men picked up the nearest of Stunk's fighters trying to wrestle a half-carved tombstone into the statue's path. With a heave and a grunt, Bentnor and Cadriffle threw the armored man across the courtyard into a couple of others. The twins gave a ragged cheer, as if they had scored a goal in one of their endless ball games.

Stunk's men gave a unified growl. They dropped the junk they had picked up from the courtyard to draw their own weapons. Swords were fully out and they swung back toward the younger Carvers with blades upraised. Lord Adarbrent sped forward, obviously trying to place himself between the two lines of very angry men.

Gustin drew a deep breath and raised his own hands, only the faintest glow of magic quivering at his fingertips. His eyes were sparkling green as he advanced toward the two sides.

"I hope this spell works," he muttered. "Want to give me one more kiss for luck?"

"Somebody is going to get killed." Sophraea tried to keep one eye on her family and an equally desperate eye on Gustin.

"Probably me," Gustin agreed. But he winked at her as he moved cautiously forward. "Try not to worry too much!"

Sophraea wrung her hands, twisting round and round Volponia's ring.

"I wish that they would all freeze in place until we can get into the City of the Dead," she said. The ring flared hot upon her finger and then icy cold.

The usual Waterdeep drizzle dissolved into fat snowflakes. The snow began to fall faster and faster. Soon the swirling white storm obscured the crooked chimneys of Dead End House.

A cold wind swept through the courtyard, tumbling Stunk's fighters and Sophraea's family into the drifts of snow piling up.

Even the dead were blown away from the gate, pushed back into the City of the Dead. Sophraea heard Leaplow give a shout as the knight and his rotting horse slipped on the sudden ice that slicked every surface.

Only Gustin's statue seemed impervious to this strange winter storm. It strode on, snow settling on its shoulders so it appeared as if the statue wore a white mantle over its carved armor.

"What have you done, Sophraea Carver?" Gustin asked.

"I made a wish," replied the stunned Sophraea. "Volponia said something about the ring containing only half a wish. I was not expecting anything like this!"

"I think it was more like a wish-and-a-half," said Gustin.

The statue passed Sophraea's uncles and aunts and stomped down the little stairs leading into the City of the Dead.

"We better go," said Gustin. "We need to finish the spell at the tomb."

Sophraea checked her basket. Lord Adarbrent's spellbook was still safely stored there. She stepped cautiously on the cobblestones of the courtyard. The stones were slick under her feet, but not impossibly so. Everyone around her slipped and slid, knocked prone and unable to regain their feet, caught by her wish.

Gustin started to slide and snatched at her shoulder to steady himself. As soon as he touched her, he stopped falling.

"Interesting," the wizard noted. "Hang onto me, Sophraea, until we get into the City of the Dead."

She threaded her arm through his. They picked their way around the fallen fighters toward the gate.

Of the fighters in the center of the courtyard, only Lord Adarbrent managed to stay upright. He swayed from side to side, the snow-filled wind billowing out his coattails.

Sophraea grabbed his arm. At her touch, the old nobleman stopped swaying.

"Can you walk?" she asked.

He took one careful step and then another. He nodded at Sophraea.

Gustin and Lord Adarbrent, with Sophraea in the middle to steady them both by hanging onto their arms, followed after the marching statue.

The statue marched straight ahead, its eyes fastened on its goal. It seemed more than willing to follow that one instruction from Gustin, to walk to a named destination. But what if that was all it could do?

"Then one of us has to put the shoe inside," Sophraea muttered to herself as she pushed through the snow after it. "And one of us has to close that door."

The ghastly knight righted its skeletal horse as they passed. Over her shoulder, Sophraea saw the knight gather up the rotting reins of its steed but give the creature no signal to move.

Leaplow yelled and tried to get to his feet, only to slip and fall again.

"That haunt is still watching us," Gustin informed her.

Sophraea's own sense of movement within the City of the Dead informed her that all the dead were changing their course, turning back from the gates and other exits, and moving slowly toward the north of the graveyard, toward the Markarl tomb.

She didn't know if it was the token that the statue carried or Algozata's horrible spellbook that attracted the dead's attention. She tried to be glad that they were no longer trying to invade Dead End House or the rest of Waterdeep.

But she wondered if ending the curse would be enough. Ever since Gustin tried to reverse Lord Adarbrent's spell, she'd sensed a change in the atmosphere. The noble dead were no longer content with playing tricks on the living, such as rattling a few windows at Stunk's mansion or causing a few houseplants to wilt.

Something worse had woken; something that hungered for more than petty revenge.

Up in Volponia's room, her plan had seemed so simple and so clear. In Volponia's room, she'd thought she knew all the answers. In Volponia's room, she had not been afraid.

But as the snow blew bitter in her face and the noble dead began to move again within the City of the Dead, Sophraea wondered if she'd been right.

For the sun was setting, and the dead were always stronger at night.

She shivered. She had no more wishes in the magic ring. She had to rely on her own courage and the courage of her companions. Would that be enough?

TWENTY-NINE

Once the trio had passed through the gate into the City of the Dead, Sophraea's wish began to loosen its grip upon everyone in the courtyard. The snow continued to fall, but at a gentler rate.

First to struggle to their feet were Rampage Stunk and his fighters.

Stunk saw the flick of Sophraea's cloak disappear through the gateway.

"Follow them!" he bellowed at his bewildered men.

As Stunk and his men disappeared through the gate, the Carvers finally found themselves able to rise out of the snow.

"Sophraea!" cried Reye, starting after her daughter.

Astute followed hard on the heels of his wife and the rest of the Carvers followed him.

Everyone tumbled through the ravaged opening of the graveyard gate, following the clear tracks of the stone statue leading them north, deeper into the cemetery.

>===W===<

As always in the City of the Dead, Sophraea's vision shattered into pieces. She felt as if she looked through the eyes of a dozen Sophraeas, all showing her glimpses of this part of the graveyard or that part.

"Your eyes are burning blue," Gustin stated. "Your face is shining like a candle. Sophraea, what do you see?"

"Too much," she replied.

All around her, she could see the outlines of the dead, keeping pace with her as she followed Gustin's statue.

Every tomb's occupant, every grave's sleeper, was awake. And waiting to see what would happen next. Gustin's own attempt to reverse the curse earlier had roused them all.

Behind her, she could see just as clearly that Rampage Stunk was urging on his frightened men. He did not know the pathways, the twists and turns, as she did. But the marks of the statue's passage were clear in the snow and he would have no problem following them.

And behind Stunk came her family, Astute and Reye, Leaplow and Bentnor, all the uncles, aunts, cousins, and sisters-in-law. All following because they thought she needed help. And she was terrified for them all.

"Sunset," whispered Gustin, as if raising his voice could disturb that expectant hush that filled the City of the Dead.

At her other side, Lord Adarbrent walked without comment. But she knew the old nobleman also was aware of the dead keeping pace with them and the enemies following behind him. It was written in the straightness of his back and the keen glances he darted from side to side.

Snow continued to fall, muffling their footsteps upon the paths, granting an eerie quiet to the memorials they passed. The shadows seemed deeper, blacker, in contrast to the white piling up at the base of the tombs.

But when Sophraea concentrated her vision on what was actually before her, she could see to the west the faintest glimmer of red.

"Not sunset, not just yet," she answered Gustin.

Lord Adarbrent too glanced to the west.

"Not quite night," he agreed. "But almost. And not a night to be long within these walls."

"No, we'll do what needs to be done and leave," Sophraea said. Then her vision of what was behind her obscured her sight and made her stumble on the path. Gustin caught her and held her steady.

"Stunk's men," she informed him, "they saw my family and they've turned back. They'll be fighting again."

And blood spilled upon the snow, on that night and in that place, would bring disaster upon them. That thought sprang into her mind as easily as she knew the right turn to take or the name of the monument that they were passing.

"Too many of the dead are awake," she said, desperate to convey her insight to the men beside her. "We need to keep everyone moving, keep my family and Stunk's men from fighting! If they do fight, it will be like meat thrown before hungry dogs!"

"Can you make a light, wizard?" asked Lord Adarbrent, turning back the way that they had come.

Gustin nodded. A blazing ball of white light appeared in his cupped palm. He tossed it once or twice and then flung it upward. It whizzed into the sky, breaking apart in a shower of sparks.

Shouts came from behind them. Gustin's firework had been seen!

"That will bring them running," said Lord Adarbrent. The old man stood in the center of the path, an old-fashioned silhouette against the snow. Flakes settling on his black hat formed a pattern like a white plume. "It is me that Stunk wants. He will pursue me farther into the graveyard. Let the dead follow us if they wish."

"No," protested Sophraea. "You don't understand. It's not like it was before. Something is stirring. Something worse than before."

"But it started with the spell that I cast," said the old man. "So, let me help now, to make amends."

"If you leave us, you might not be able to find your way out," Sophraea said. Out of the corner of her eye, she could see paths shifting, bushes bending down to hide the way, and, everywhere, shadows weaving black webs of confusion. On this night, only a Carver could safely find her way out of the City of the Dead. Sophraea was sure of that!

"If I am lost," Lord Adarbrent said, "then it is a sacrifice I make for one of the great families of Waterdeep. Captain Volponia was right. Waterdeep needs Carvers, just as much as it needs nobles and wizards, merchants and adventurers, and all the rest. Your family is as much a part of Waterdeep's history and its future as all the rest. You keep the City of the Dead beautiful. And you keep it safe."

Sophraea chewed her lip. Letting the old nobleman sacrifice himself for her family seemed wrong. The snowflakes fell like cold tears on her upturned face.

Another shout, this one behind them, made her turn. The topiary dragon galloped toward them, half swimming through the snow. Briarsting rode high on his bushy steed's neck, waving wildly at them.

"It's all chaos and confusion, from one end of the City to the other," the thorn called to them. "The City Watch has shut all the gates. The Blackstaff and the Watchful Order are warding all the walls!"

"Are there any living in the City of the Dead?" Sophraea called.

"Just that crowd that's following you," said Briarsting. "We saw them pass and knew you had to be close. I've been searching for you all afternoon. Met your brother chasing the dead down the paths toward your house. Now there's a boy who likes a fight! And then, every light and flame went out. That's when the Watch started yelling for everyone to clear out and locked down the gates!"

"That was me!" said Gustin.

"Did you know dousing the light was like ringing an alarm in the ear of every corpse within these walls?" the thorn inquired.

"It wasn't intentional," Gustin said.

"And there's a great statue stumping its way toward the Markarl tomb," the little man added, standing high on his perch and squinting his eyes against the flurries.

"That's mine too," said Gustin.

"Well, you have had the busy afternoon," Briarsting concluded. "But now what?"

"We need your help," Sophraea said. "Yours and every guardian that you can rouse."

"Every ghost and spirit with a friendly feeling toward Waterdeep is striving to keep the gates closed tonight," Briarsting stated.

Sophraea closed her eyes for a moment and, in her Carver vision of the graveyard, she could see that Briarsting was right. Glimmers of silver and gold stood before the public gates and along the wall, working as hard as the City Watch and the wizards of the Watchful Order on the other side to keep Waterdeep protected from the dead in the coming night. Heroes and legends, even the bright flare of some long-forgotten dead god, ringed the outer perimeters to hold the living city safe.

Only the Carver's gate and Dead End House behind it was unprotected. Lord Adarbrent's curse was a black break in the shimmering circle of ghostly goodwill.

"We need to get to the Markarl tomb," Sophraea said, her eyes popping open to contemplate her companions. "But can you bring my family and Stunk and Stunk's men there too? Help Lord Adarbrent lead them that way, but keep them from fighting?"

The topiary dragon swept its tail from side to side, sending up a spray of snow.

"We can do it," Briarsting swore.

"Are you sure?" said Lord Adarbrent.

Sophraea nodded firmly. "Your noble dead will not sleep if they smell blood within these walls," she said with conviction. "Keep my family and Stunk's men apart but bring them to us. We need them all to be there when this is finished."

So we can get everyone safely out of the City of the Dead, she thought, but did not want to jinx her luck by speaking this out loud.

Catching Gustin's hand, Sophraea hurried toward the Markarl tomb.

They passed the reflecting pool. Out of the corner of her eye, Sophraea saw that the weeping warrior no longer covered her face. The stone woman stood very straight, stone sword and shield upraised, to protect whatever lay beneath her feet.

At the corners of other tombs, guardgoyles were stirring, beaks open and ready to scream, wings outstretched to beat off any intruders. Perpetual flames burned bright enough in the dishes outside tomb doors to reveal the elemental faces within the fire. Certain fountains shot higher into the night as the water spirits within roused themselves against the torpor caused by snow and ice.

Briarsting was right. All the guardians of the City of the Dead were awake.

Running through the snow, drifts as high as Sophraea's knees, they caught up to the stone statue as it entered the little circle of land that Stunk had claimed for himself. A few marker stakes crunched under the statue's feet as it continued toward the open door of the Markarl tomb.

A pale young lady in a gold brocade dress and shoes stood in the doorway. She smiled sadly at Sophraea and Gustin.

"I am so sorry," Sophraea said to the ghost, "but this must end."

She pulled the spellbook from her basket. "What must we say?" she said, flipping open the book.

Gustin raised his hand and cast a wizard light over her shoulder to illuminate Algozata's spellbook.

"A bit of doggerel," the wizard said. "That anyone could read. That's what Lord Adarbrent said."

"But what page?" In her distress, Sophraea almost tore the pages, flipping one after the other. Strange symbols, written in uneasy colors, flashed before her eyes.

The silence of the graveyard was once again shattered by shouts and muffled cries. One voice above the rest was clearly her brother Leaplow, yelling "Sophraea! Gustin! Are you all right? Where did this bush come from?"

A black shape slid next to Sophraea. Lord Adarbrent shook the snow from his wide coat cuffs with a practiced twist of the wrist.

"Almost amusing," he huffed. "That creature cut the crowd in two and ran them here like a well-trained sheep dog with two flocks."

The Carvers were pressed back against one tomb, held there by the sweeping tail of the topiary dragon. At the beast's other end, equally at bay from the snapping teeth and Briarsting's occasional flourish of his thorn blade, Stunk and his men huddled together.

The ghost lady stared at Lord Adarbrent. She lifted one glimmering hand toward him.

"Farewell, my dear," said the old man in the softest voice that Sophraea had ever heard from him.

Lord Adarbrent took the spellbook from Sophraea.

"I began this," he said. "Now, let me finish it."

The pale lady stepped aside, disappearing back into the shadows.

"It's stopped," moaned Gustin, staring at his creation.

The statue had marched to the first step leading into the Markarl tomb. There it stood, rocking back and forth slightly on its stone heels.

"It has to go inside, and come out again, and close the door," instructed Lord Adarbrent, nose almost resting upon the pages of Algozata's spellbook as he tried to read it in the dim light.

"Maybe if I move closer," said Gustin.

"Is it safe?" said Sophraea.

"Truly, I don't know," the wizard replied. He moved up to the statue and laid a hand on its stone shoulder. The faintest purple light sparked when he touched his creation.

"My spell is holding," he said.

"Go on, go inside," Gustin spoke directly into the statue's beautifully carved ear. Rather than commanding, his voice took on a coaxing tone.

For a breathless moment, the statue stayed still. Then, with a ponderous creak, it took one step forward into the tomb, and another, and another.

"Don't touch the tomb or the tomb's door," called Lord Adarbrent to him. "Stay back a little and you should be safe from Algozata's curse."

The statue stopped in the center of the tomb's floor.

"Now, put your burden down," Gustin instructed it.

Again, it stood for a long moment before bending down and placing the shoe in the center of the floor.

Then, the statue straightened and, with Gustin's repeated coaxing, retreated out the door.

Without hesitation, Lord Adarbrent turned the pages to Algozata's curse and began to recite the ending of the spell.

Undercutting his words were Gustin's continued instructions. "Grab the door, push it, push it."

Sophraea chewed her knuckles, darting glances over her shoulder at the crowd held at bay by the topiary dragon.

The statue pushed the bronze door of the Markarl tomb shut.

Lord Adarbrent ended the last verse with a sigh and nodded to Gustin.

"Lock!" Gustin commanded.

The statue turned the iron key in the lock with a hollow *clang*. Then it swiveled in place and leaned its back against the entrance of the Markarl monument. The statue froze into place, a heroic paladin surveying the City of the Dead, a permanent guardian for the tomb.

Sophraea felt a collective sigh heave out of the very earth of the graveyard. She closed her eyes and saw the noble dead fall back from the walkways and paths. The marchers ceased marching, and the dancers ended their spinning dances. The knight upon his skeleton horse reared once and galloped away.

All around the perimeter of the City of the Dead, its shining guardians strengthened their circle of protection. The black streak that formed a path for the dead to the Dead End gate disappeared.

Algozata's curse was finally broken.

"We did it!" Sophraea spun in her excitement to congratulate Gustin and Lord Adarbrent, only to halt in mid-spin. For now, with the other dead fading away to their tombs, she could see what flew down the path toward them.

Black robes swirled around gray skin shrunken upon the bones. Eyes burned with red fire. Gems, dulled under years of dust, studded the remnants of the broad seafarer's belt and heavy axe.

This was what she'd felt moving in the City of the Dead ever since Gustin had amplified Algozata's curse. This was the "something bigger" that had bothered her as they had fled the tunnels. This was the anger that she'd felt when they'd come back into the City of the Dead.

This corporeal ghost arrived with a roar even as Sophraea tried to cry out a warning.

"Dorgar Adarbrent!" bellowed the ghost. "How dare you wake me!"

Lord Adarbrent fell back before a fury even greater than one of his own rages.

"Grandfather!" he choked out.

"Spells! Foul magic!" The ghost cried unhooking his axe and swinging it so the wind whistled over the blade. The spectral breeze knocked everyone back a pace. "What have you done, Grandson?"

Gustin tried to counter with a spell, a fizz of sparkling light that streaked toward the ghost. Lord Adarbrent's aggrieved ancestor batted it aside with his axe.

An answering wave of cold rolled over Gustin, chilling even Sophraea standing several paces back. The wizard's teeth chattered in his head and he pitched to his knees in the snow.

Sophraea ran forward, flinging her arms around Gustin's shoulders. Tremors of chill shook the lanky wizard's frame. Sophraea rolled him over, lifting his head out of the snow and cradling it in her lap.

The ghost of Royus Adarbrent advanced on his grandson. Lord Adarbrent held his ground, chin up and staring straight ahead.

"What have you done, Dorgar?" bawled the ghost.

"Protected Waterdeep," answered the old man with dignity.

"By waking every ghost? By using dreadful spells? Algozata's book should have burned with her body. How dare you bring it here?" the ghost snarled. With every shout, the ghost swung his axe, each stroke coming closer and closer to Lord Adarbrent. The old man did not flinch.

Each slice of the axe through the air swept the area with a bitter wind. Frost formed on every leaf of the topiary dragon. Briarsting trembled on the creature's neck, turning from green to gray with the cold. The Carvers huddled together and even Rampage Stunk was struck silent with the chill.

Under each icy wave emanating from the axe ran a current of terror. Sophraea fought to stay still and not run screaming. She clutched Gustin's shoulders, anchoring herself to the wizard. Gustin groaned.

The Carvers held their ground. Sophraea could hear her father and her uncles talking in their rumbling voices to the rest, urging them to stay together and wait for this phantom to quit the place.

Stunk's men were not so calm. Most dropped their weapons and ran. Stunk stayed where he was, swaying back and forth as he always did, fingers clenched at his side. His hate-filled eyes remained fixed on Lord Adarbrent.

Sophraea bent over Gustin. His eyelids fluttered. "Wake up," she pleaded.

The wizard blinked up at her. "I'll be all . . . all . . . r-r-right," Gustin ground out between shudders. "J-j-just cold."

"We need help," she stated when the ghost of Royus Adarbrent was almost upon his grandson.

Gustin gritted his teeth and heaved himself out of Sophraea's lap. He planted both hands in the snow, shoving himself into a kneeling position. The faintest sound of a spell spilled from his lips. He raised one trembling hand and traced shapes in the air. The magic spilling from his hand etched a circle in the snow around Sophraea and himself.

Sophraea felt as if a candle had been lighted in her heart. Warmth spread through her. The terror rolling off the ghost receded.

"Can you extend the circle?" she whispered to Gustin.

"I'm trying," his voice was barely a breath and his shoulders shook under her hands as she tried to steady him. "That ghost is very strong."

Standing directly in front of Lord Adarbrent, the phantom Royus let his axe drop until the head rested on the snow. The burning eyes narrowed, scanning the face of his grandson.

"You have courage," the ghost stated in a calmer voice as Lord Adarbrent remained standing still before him.

The faintest smile twisted up the corners of the old man's lips.

"I am too old and too close to death to be afraid of it," the nobleman said.

The ghost rubbed his chin, the same contemplative gesture that Sophraea had often seen Lord Adarbrent use.

"Algozata was executed by the family for this spell," the ghost said finally.

"Yes," answered Lord Adarbrent immediately.

Still Royus Adarbrent hesitated.

The furious Rampage Stunk burst out, "Go on! Kill him! What are you waiting for!"

The angry fat man ducked around the frosted topiary dragon, striding forward with his odd rolling gait.

"Finish him!" Stunk yelled at the ghost.

The phantom swung around to stare at Stunk.

"Who are you," he said in exactly the same angry accents that his grandson always used, "to tell an Adarbrent what to do?"

He raised his axe high over his head and swung down.

"No!" screamed Sophraea.

With unbelievable quickness, Lord Adarbrent thrust his sword cane between the axe and Rampage Stunk. The axe struck the stick, shattering it, as Stunk scrambled backward to safety. The force of the blow made the old nobleman gasp and almost go down to one knee.

But when the phantom whirled around, Lord Adarbrent straightened his back and stood tall.

"Why did you save him?" he said, the flames of his eyes so bright that Lord Adarbrent's shadow streamed out black against the snow behind the old man.

"Because she is right," answered Lord Adarbrent, indicating Sophraea standing stock still, afraid to move and break this odd truce. "If we spill blood here tonight, the stain will spread to Waterdeep."

The phantom raised his head, looking over the City of the Dead. Then he contemplated Sophraea.

"A Carver, are you not?" he said with the calmest voice he had used all night.

"Yes, my lord," she answered with a steady voice although her hand trembled on Gustin's shoulder.

The phantom nodded slowly. "No blood?" he asked to make sure.

"The dead are returning to their graves," she said. "But if we create any more disturbance, we will never quiet them down."

A sour expression flitted across his ghastly features.

"Very well, Grandson, you live tonight," he said. "But this is the end of your tricks. I trust the Carvers will keep an eye on your activities from now on and keep you from any more foolish actions."

"I promise, my lord," said Sophraea quickly, before Lord Adarbrent could answer. "No more raising of the dead."

The phantom gave a curt nod and decreed, "But there must still be punishment. Grandson, I forbid you to rest with the family. When your death comes, let the Carvers find you a grave far from the Adarbrents. You are banished from burial near us."

Lord Adarbrent bowed his head in acquiesce.

With a swirl of its rotted black cape, the ghost of Royus Adarbrent faded away from view. Where he had stood, the snow was smooth and white and free of any marks.

"That's it? That's all?" Rampage Stunk bounded up to them. "You ruin my business with your tricks. You try to steal my tomb! And you just get banished from your family plot!"

"This tomb was never meant to be yours in the first place," returned Lord Adarbrent hotly.

"You miserable old man," screamed Stunk. "If that ghost won't kill you, I will!"

He charged at Lord Adarbrent, dragging a dagger out of his belt.

"Stop him!" Sophraea yelled at the topiary dragon.

Frost flew as the creature swept its tail in a wide arc. The prickly end crashed against Stunk's shins, tripping him into the snow.

The rest of the Carvers swept past the topiary dragon to encircle Lord Adarbrent, creating a wall of solid Carver flesh between him and the furious Stunk.

Sputtering, the fat man struggled to his feet.

"I will destroy you!" he screamed at Lord Adarbrent. "And your friends! I'll ruin you all."

As Rampage Stunk continued to rant, Sophraea helped Gustin to his feet.

"Do you have any spells left?" she asked him.

"A light to see us home," he answered with a quick hug. "And a whirlwind spell. Although, after all that knocking about, I might not be able to manage more than a small breeze. Maybe you should give me another kiss, just to warm me up."

"That's enough of your teasing," Sophraea answered him, although she almost kissed him despite the fact her entire family was watching this exchange closely. "It's time to go home. But I don't want Stunk following us."

"I can help with that," Gustin told her.

Rampage Stunk was still screaming at Lord Adarbrent. Leaplow growled and raised his big fists to bloody the nose of Rampage Stunk. Sophraea stepped in front of her brother to face down the furious merchant and his tide of threats.

"Get out of my way!" yelled the fat man, rocking back and forth in his wrath.

Sophraea stared him down. "Do you know where you are?"

Rampage blustered back, "What do you mean?"

"You are in the City of the Dead, it is night, and there is only one family in all of Waterdeep who can always find their way home from this place in the dark. And we are *not* going to help you!" Sophraea announced.

With that, Gustin loosed his whirlwind to make snow swirl even thicker around Rampage Stunk.

The Carvers disappeared from Stunk's view, hidden behind a curtain of snow.

Sophraea grabbed Gustin with one hand and Lord Adarbrent with the other. With the rest of the family following her, she turned toward Dead End House. The snow fell heavily all around them, muffling their footsteps as they swept around the corner of the Deepwinter tomb.

In the light kindled from Gustin's magic, Sophraea saw the shallow steps that led up from the path to the hole in the wall carved out long ago by her family. With a sigh of relief, she led her friends and family safely out of the City of the Dead.

The shouts and screams of Rampage Stunk escalated behind them, but none of the Carvers looked back. Crashing sounds drifted across the silent graveyard as the fat man blundered down one path and then another.

"Will the dead claim him?" Gustin asked.

"No," said Sophraea, seeing again all the ghosts of the City of the Dead. Some still drifted along the pathways. There was mischief in the darkness but no malice, no hatred, anymore. "They may tease and trick him, as they will any who wander unprotected, but they will not seek blood tonight. I am sure of it."

Briarsting and the topiary dragon escorted the Carvers as far as their gate.

"Try to keep him from falling into an open grave," Sophraea said to the thorn, as the sounds of Stunk's blundering grew fainter and farther away.

The little man shook his head at her. "You need a harder heart, girl," he said, "or all your enemies will outlive you."

"There's nothing finer than a tender heart," Gustin answered him.

Sophraea blushed as Briarsting responded, "Yes, but you think she's perfection already. Keep her safe, wizard!"

"I'll keep myself safe," Sophraea answered with her usual spirit.

"But let me help with that task, it's been so much fun these past few tendays," Gustin whispered in her ear, making her blush even harder.

"Hey," said Leaplow, "what are you saying to my sister? Do we need to have a talk?"

"No!" said Sophraea so emphatically that the rest of the family laughed. She shoved Leaplow up the stairs. "You leave Gustin alone! No fights! No bets! No wrestling matches! He's a friend!"

The rest of the family chuckled as Sophraea scolded her brother all the way into the center of the courtyard.

Once everyone was through the Dead End gate, Astute Carver dragged a few boards from the wreckage left from their battle and propped the lumber before the opening. The black-and-white Carver cat twined around his legs in greeting and then slipped past him to sniff at the temporary barrier.

"We'll need to reforge the gate," said Perspicacity.

"In the morning, Brother," answered Judicious with a pat on his shoulder.

"In the morning," agreed Astute in his usual calm voice.

"Sophraea Carver, your skirts are soaked through," said her mother. "Come inside, and tell us your adventures."

"Yes, Sophraea," said Bentnor. "Where have you been, little cousin?"

And suddenly she and Gustin were surrounded by her swarm of a family, big, warm, and loving. Exclaiming, arguing, hugging, as they recounted their battles with Stunk and the dead.

"Stunk thought he could steal our ledger!" yelled one cousin.

"He thought he could control the City of the Dead, buy and sell tombs in it like houses in Waterdeep!" shouted an aunt.

"Guess he knows different now," said several Carvers together.

"Come on," said Sophraea to Gustin, "let's find something to eat."

"Maybe your grandmother can make soup and toasted bread," Gustin responded.

"That's a wonderful idea!" Leaplow said, clapping the wizard on the back and making Gustin stagger. "I could eat a whole loaf! With cheese melted across the top! Fighting always makes me hungry."

THIRTY

The next morning, Sophraea stood in the snow, watching her uncles rehang the Dead End gate. Perspicacity had forged extra flourishes and twists to the iron bars and Judicious had supplied a beautifully polished brass knob and lock. Astute and Sagacious helped them hang it while Vigilant gave them plenty of advice.

"Well, doesn't that look fine," said Gustin, making his way carefully across the slippery cobblestones. Although the storm had passed, the air was still unusually cold and the snow was very heavy on the ground.

Sophraea nodded. "They thought they'd do it a little fancier, knowing it wouldn't be broken any time soon," she explained.

"No signs of haunts during the night?" he asked.

"None at all. Everything has been quiet."

"There you are! I thought you were going to sleep the day away!" A voice sounded high above their heads.

Sophraea looked up. Briarsting stood on the wall between the graveyard and Dead End House. A Carver cat walking along the wall hissed at him but turned tail with a mew when the little man poked his sword at it.

"What are you doing there?" Sophraea asked.

"Waiting for you two. You left some trash in the City of the Dead last night," the thorn replied. "We'd consider it a favor if you'd get it out."

"Stunk," said Sophraea.

"And others," answered Briarsting. "A few of his guards made it as far as a public gate last night, and the City Watch dragged them out this morning. But Stunk and a couple of others are still up in the north end."

"We'll help," said Sophraea, her always troublesome conscience pricking her to find the fat man and lead him out of the City of the Dead.

"Best we come with you," said Judicious, when she explained to her uncles why she needed them to open the gate just after they had gotten it hung to their satisfaction.

"I'll go with you too," said Gustin.

"Do you have any spells today?" she asked him.

"Lots," he said, sending a spark flying off his fingertips. "I had a wonderful supper last night, a good sleep in a soft bed, and a fine breakfast complete with your grandmother's rolls!"

"I noticed you managed one more than Leaplow," Sophraea teased as they went down the stairs into the City of the Dead.

"I felt I deserved it," answered Gustin without shame.

Great drifts of snow still decorated the tombs in the City of the Dead. The place was hushed and subdued after all the excitement of the night. The guardgoyles perched on the edges of mausoleums had tucked their heads beneath their wings. The weeping warrior once more covered her face with her hand. The perpetual flames burned low and steady while the fountains burbled softly under their crusting of ice.

Sophraea let her vision expand until she could see all the City of the Dead. Wherever she looked, she saw only peace and stillness. The noble dead were quiet and content at last.

"It's really a pretty place," observed Gustin as they crunched through the snow.

"It's beautiful in the spring," answered Sophraea. "When the trees bud out and the new leaves appear. And summer, well, in the summer, it's the coolest and most lovely place in all of Waterdeep. Families come in the summer, just to walk along the paths and admire the flowers."

"You know, I still haven't seen the monuments at the south end," Gustin said. "The famous ones that everyone is supposed to go look at."

"I'll take you," Sophraea promised.

"Good," said Gustin, tucking her hand through his arm.

The topiary dragon bounded up to the party, sending sprays of snow over all of them with enthusiastic sweeps of its tail.

"Call it off, call it off," sputtered Sophraea, wiping snow off her face for the second time.

"Sorry," said Briarsting. "The old boy had an exciting night and he hasn't quite calmed down yet."

Sophraea's uncles were inclined to pause and admire the shaping of the topiary dragon.

"Didn't Fidelity work on this one?" Judicious asked his brother.

"Think so. There're sure to be details in the ledger. I'd forgotten that there were any left in the graveyard. Thought that they'd all gone to seed long ago," answered Perspicacity. "Nice to see that this one survived."

Sophraea urged everyone on.

"We should find Stunk," she said.

"If you say so, pet," answered Perspicacity.

Following Briarsting's directions, they discovered Rampage Stunk at the far north end of the City of the Dead. He lay curled against a tombstone and whimpered when Sophraea placed a gentle hand upon his shoulder.

Although he had only been lost for one night, the fat man's ruined physique bore the marks of magical mischief.

"Not everyone was completely in their graves when he blundered past them," explained Briarsting. "Nothing deadly, but the ghosts never did like him trying to empty out those tombs."

Rampage Stunk's once black hair had been stripped of its glossy dye and was completely white. The merchant's face bore numerous small scratches, as if he'd been dragged through bushes. Most strange of all, he appeared to be half his original weight, and apparently he had aged by many years.

"Saer, saer, can you get up?" Sophraea tugged at the merchant's clothing, only to have the rich cloth tear away under her hands. Looking closer, Sophraea saw that all of Stunk's clothing was as rotted as if it had been buried for several years.

"I don't think he knows us," said Gustin, peering closely into Stunk's face. The merchant mewled under his examination, turning his head away and hiding it in his hands.

"Will he be all right?" Sophraea asked. She had not meant for so terrible a vengeance to fall upon Stunk.

"There's healing for such things," said Gustin, straightening up. "But it will take some time. He's still alive and that's a greater mercy than he was prepared to show Lord Adarbrent or your family."

"There're some others over here!" called Briarsting.

Poking under snowy bushes and peering around tombstones, Sophraea discovered the remainder of Rampage's thugs in various states of distress. Although not as bad as Rampage, they were all relieved to be found.

"Can you show us the way out of here?" asked one redheaded goon in a very small voice.

"Yes, yes, not to worry," answered Judicious. "Just help us carry this poor fellow away." He heaved Stunk up on his shoulders.

"We'll take him home," Judicious said to Sophraea. "And explain to his lady what has happened. I know her. We've built coffins for her family for years and done all their burials. She did not marry well, but she is a lady for all that."

"I'll go home," said Sophraea, "and let the others know."

"Do you want me to go with your uncles? I might be able to make some suggestions to the lady for her husband's care," said Gustin.

"We can go with them as far as the gate," Briarsting called from the back of the topiary dragon.

"That would be best," Sophraea said. "I can find my way home easily enough."

—W—

Sophraea retraced her steps toward Dead End House. A sudden impulse drove her to take the path leading to the Markarl monument. She was not surprised to find Lord Adarbrent sitting on the snowy step of the little brick-and-mortar tomb. Behind him, Gustin's stone statue stood firmly against the door, keeping watch across the other monuments.

Lord Adarbrent acknowledged Sophraea's approach with a formal nod of his head. The old man was dressed as always in black from head to toe. All that was missing was his sword cane, shattered in the previous night's fight.

"Who was she?" Sophraea asked Lord Adarbrent. "The lady in this tomb?"

"My first love, my dearest love," the old man whispered. "Vyvaine. She died so young. Her family has long since gone too. I'm the only one left in Waterdeep who even remembers her name."

"Was she beautiful?"

He shook his head. "I remember her on the way to her first ball. I was her escort for that evening, some family connection that made her father ask me to take her. Vyvaine came down the stairs to the carriage." He sighed and murmured, "A plain girl in a fine dress with little golden shoes on her feet. She wasn't beautiful at all. She was better than beautiful. She was unforgettable."

The old man stood up with a sad smile, absently brushing the snow from his coattails.

"What happened to her?"

"Summer fever. A bad year that year. They died by the hundreds in the South Ward. Many fled the city."

297

"But you stayed?"

He nodded. Sophraea saw, as she had seen the night before when he faced his ghostly grandfather, the fierce gleam of pride and strength in his steady stare. "Waterdeep needed me. There was work to be done."

Lord Adarbrent looked over his shoulder at the tomb as if he could see past the stone paladin standing guard against its door. "I should have sent her away. But she wouldn't go. She said the city needed her help too. And I did not want her gone. We were to have been married that fall."

"I am sorry."

"After she died, I could not bear for them to take her away. Not far away through the portals. The family still had this vault and I persuaded them to leave her here." Lord Adarbrent stood up. "I would never have touched Algozata's spellbooks except that evil Stunk bought my poor girl's tomb for himself. I knew when he started to empty the tomb beside this one that she would be next. They would move her some place far from me." And then abruptly, he said, "Do you know where I am going to be buried?"

"Not in the Adarbrent mausoleum?" she asked thinking of the ghost's proclamation of the previous night.

"It was a very mild punishment," replied the nobleman with his wheezing chuckle. "I have had far different plans for years."

Lord Adarbrent pointed at a small marble casket, standing on four lion's paws and almost touching the Markarl tomb on the south side. "There. It took some years searching through your family's ledger but I found one small bit of land left unclaimed in the City of the Dead, right next to the Markarl tomb. Your father carved that casket for me many years ago."

Sophraea looked at the stone casket. It was quite small, only built for one corpse to occupy.

"So you were always planning to be buried here?" she asked.

Lord Adarbrent smiled.

"I never thought that it would stay empty for so long. In some ways, I suppose I'm no better than Stunk, rearranging this graveyard for my own selfish desires." The old man shrugged.

"Ah," she murmured. She simply didn't know what else to say.

"After all, I am the last of my family. Who will care where I am buried? When Waterdeep no longer needs me, I will rest near my dear unforgettable girl. In my own place at last, where I want to be."

"We will care," Sophraea answered him, her voice a little hoarse but her words as fiercely stated as ever. "And we will remember you. Always. You have been a good friend to us. To me." She sniffed and straightened her shoulders, adding briskly, "Most of the time. Just, no more rituals cast in the City of the Dead."

"I promise." Lord Adarbrent bowed deeply to her, as deep as he had bowed to Volponia. "You always were a good girl, Sophraea Carver, and I think you will be an amazing woman in the years to come. As long as there are those like you in Waterdeep, my burdens are much lighter."

Blushing at his praise, Sophraea left Lord Adarbrent to his memories. She crossed the path and circled past the Deepwinter monument. She slipped through the Dead End gate.

"It's a funny name," said a voice above her head.

Sophraea latched the gate and looked up. Briarsting was sitting cross-legged on the snow-covered wall. The topiary dragon peered over the thorn's shoulder at the girl. One brown leaf fluttered down over a bright berry eye in a friendly wink. The big leafy ears waggled back and forth in a topiary greeting.

"What's wrong now?" Sophraea asked the pair.

"Nothing, nothing at all. Your uncles carried Rampage Stunk out with no problem. We just wanted to make certain that you reached home safely. But I was thinking Dead End House was a peculiar name for your house," Briarsting replied.

"Dead End House? It's always been called that. It seems very appropriate to me."

Briarsting glanced at the courtyard filled with Carvers. The younger boys had swept the remaining snow into large piles. Someone had fetched the battered leather ball from the barn and so most of Sophraea's brothers, cousins, and nephews were knocking it back and forth according to their own loudly shouted rules.

Leaplow kicked the ball straight through a pile of snow, incurring either a penalty or a goal, and certainly earning a pile-up of bodies all flung on top of him.

Her uncles Vigilant and Sagacious were lined up watching, their arms resting on each other's shoulders. Sophraea's father shouted nonsensical instructions to his buried son while the beards of his brothers quivered with laughter. Out of the windows, screaming just as many instructions and laughing even harder, all the aunts shook their heads over the boys' game.

"See," said Briarsting, standing up and brushing the snow off his seat in an unconscious imitation of Lord Adarbrent, "there's nothing dead to be found on that side of the wall. Not an end that I can see. It's too full of life, too fond of beginnings, that house of yours."

He swung up to the neck of the topiary dragon. The pair turned and headed back into the snowy quiet of the graveyard.

"I'll visit you soon," Sophraea called through the gate. Briarsting gave a wave over his shoulder. "I promise!"

Then she turned and plunged into the game occupying the yard, kicking the ball right out from under the nose of a startled brother and sending it sailing over a pile of snow with a whooping cry of triumph.

THIRTY-ONE

Gustin sat on a block of marble in the courtyard. It was a clear, cold day, the sun sparkling on the icicles dripping off the edge of the roof. Two Carver cats basked in the warmth on the top of a newly polished coffin.

After three days of freezing cold, Sophraea's half wish was melting away. Waterdeep was sliding back to its usual warmer wet winter weather. The stone man was permanently stuck in front of the tomb. Gustin's repeated attempts to reanimate it had failed, Algozata's old curse being far stronger than any ritual that he knew.

Sophraea's father joined Gustin in the yard.

"I'm sorry," said Gustin. "I just don't have enough coin to pay the remainder of what was owed on the statue. And I haven't quite come up with a scheme to make any more. Give me a day or two, though, and I'll think of something. I usually do."

Astute shrugged. "I'm not worried," he said. "You can pay me back with magic."

"Magic?"

"Rituals. Whatever you want to call it. That trick that you do with stone, making the statue walk. That would save us a lot of hauling."

"That one works best for me," agreed Gustin, rubbing the back of his neck. "Besides working off a debt, any chance for a little more?" Gustin just had to ask.

Astute crossed his arms and appeared to ponder the question for a long moment. "You keep your room, you continue to eat free meals, and I don't ask you about sneaking off with my only daughter into the tunnels beneath the graveyard and who knows where else."

"Ah," he mumbled. After once again assessing the truly amazing breadth of shoulders possessed by Sophraea's father, Gustin indicated that this was a fair deal indeed.

The bell on the public gate jangled and Lord Adarbrent appeared in the entry.

"My friends." He bowed slightly in the direction of Astute and Gustin.

"It is good to see you as always, my lord," Astute answered. "What news?"

"The rumors appear to be quite true," Lord Adarbrent said. "Lady Ruellyn will take over her husband's business while he recuperates."

"How is he?" asked Sophraea, running down the house steps to greet Lord Adarbrent.

"No great change," Lord Adarbrent replied. "She has called in healers to make him comfortable. I hear Rampage Stunk now spends most of his days dozing in front of the fire."

"The lady may find a docile husband much to her liking," Gustin observed.

"Quite," said Lord Ardabrent with a quelling look. "Such speculation would be rude, however."

"And the others? Those guards that we found in the City of the Dead?" Sophraea asked.

"Well enough, as far as I know. And a certain hairy individual has been persuaded by the City Watch that Waterdeep is not the best city for his residence," the old nobleman told her.

"Oh," said Sophraea.

"Your father mentioned that the doorjack had caused you some distress. I thought you would not mind a very small intervention on my part," said Lord Adarbrent.

"Leaplow said something about looking for him and walking

him through the City of the Dead," Sophraea revealed.

"Your brother's most recent black eye is still quite evident. This seemed a simpler solution."

Sophraea exchanged a quick glance with Gustin. The wizard realized that she'd acquired yet another protector or, given the family's long history with Lord Adarbrent, the old man had always been one of Sophraea Carver's champions. It truly was incredible that he'd survived that first kiss, he decided. Still, life was dull without challenges, Gustin thought to himself, and one of these days he would talk her into a second kiss. Then he could worry about how to avoid being crushed by Leaplow or her other enormous male relatives. That would be an exciting challenge and, looking at his own personal dark dearling of Waterdeep, one quite worth it.

"But what about the old ladies?" Sophraea asked Lord Adarbrent. "The ones that Stunk cheated out of their homes?"

"For those still living, Lady Ruellyn is making reparations," said Lord Adarbrent. "After all, she is a lady and not a merchant."

"I'm still surprised that we didn't have the City Watch or the Blackstaff here, asking questions," Sophraea said.

"My influence is not inconsiderable," returned Lord Adarbrent. "And I was able to persuade certain people that the fewer questions asked the better. After all, the Carvers are known to be a reputable family who provide an invaluable service to Waterdeep."

In short, thought Gustin, the Carvers actually do know where the bodies are buried and, more importantly, will make sure in the future that the finest of Waterdeep will continue to be buried exactly as they wish.

Lord Adarbrent pulled a stiff piece of parchment out of his pocket.

"I believe that you wanted this," he said, presenting it to Sophraea.

With wide eyes, she unfolded the letter of recommendation.

"Oh," she said. "How did you know? I never remembered to ask you for this."

"Captain Volponia mentioned your ambitions to join the sartorial trade. I must say," he continued, "I agree with her that it seems a rather tame outlet for your talents."

"Volponia told you!" Sophraea exclaimed. "When?"

"I called on her last night," said Lord Adarbrent. "In a more conventional manner than my previous visit."

"Really?"

A look of amusement softened the old man's face. "Although she claims a few more years than myself," he said, "we remember the same Waterdeep. I enjoyed our conversation very much and will call again."

With a bow to Astute and a promise to return in a few days, Lord Adarbrent took his leave.

>——W——<

Sophraea turned the letter over in her hand.

"So you'll leave here for that fine dressmaker's in the Castle Ward?" said Gustin. "All billowing lace, pretty silks, and nothing but the chatter of ladies from morn until night."

"It sounds a little dull, doesn't it?" said Sophraea. "Sewing seams all day, I mean. And I would miss my family."

"So what are you going to do?" asked Gustin with some trepidation and a little anticipation in his voice.

"Do you have your guidebook with you?" she countered.

He patted his pocket. "Always," he said. "I might go for a walk later. There's still so much I haven't seen in Waterdeep: the Blackstaff's Tower, Cymbril's Walk, and, really, most of the famous monuments inside the City of the Dead. We never did go look at those!"

Sophraea held up her wicker basket. She had packed it with a lunch for two.

"Let's take a look at the monuments today," she suggested. He hadn't asked her for a second kiss, not for a whole day, but with more than a little anticipation and no trepidation at all, Sophraea thought he might that afternoon.

Deciding one's whole life in a moment was not necessary, she realized as she crumpled up Lord Adarbrent's letter of recommendation and stuffed it in the bottom of her basket. There was time enough for dozens of adventures, just as Volponia always said, and a girl didn't have to live in a dress shop or go outside the walls of Waterdeep to find them.

But, because she was always ruthlessly honest with herself or tried to be, Sophraea did admit to herself that adventures in the company of a certain brown-haired, green-eyed, lanky wizard might be more exciting than anything Volponia ever encountered on her old pirate ship. She'd simply have to let the future happen to find out.

Just then, she continued out loud, "Fish is worried that something odd happened in the portal that they use on the south end. He thinks somebody has been sneaking into that tomb. Maybe a graverobber. I said we could go and take a look."

Gustin was still protesting that he wanted to see the sights, not more corpses and ghosts, as he followed her to the Dead End gate. But he did follow her and Sophraea noticed that the emerald gleam of his eyes was noticeably brighter under those lashes that were ridiculously long for a man.

"Stop complaining," said Sophraea, unlatching the wrought iron gate. It swung open with a friendly creak, her uncles having decided to forge the squeak back into the gate hinges. She started down the moss-covered steps into the City of the Dead. "You know that as long as you are with me, you won't get lost. Besides, Volponia gave me another ring from her jewel box. She's almost certain that the spell in this one will work."

ONE DROW • TWO SWORDS • TWENTY YEARS

A READER'S GUIDE TO

R.A.SALVATORE'S

THE LEGEND OF DRIZZT®

"There's a good reason this saga is one of the most popular—and beloved—fantasy series of all time: breakneck pacing, deeply complex characters and nonstop action. If you read just one adventure fantasy saga in your lifetime, let it be this one."

—Paul Goat Allen, B&N Explorations on *Streams of Silver*.

Full color illustrations and maps in a handsome keepsake edition.

Richard Lee Byers

The Haunted Lands

Epic magic • Unholy alliances • Armies of undead
The battle for Thay has begun.

Book I	Book II	Book III
Unclean	**Undead**	**Unholy**
		February 2009

Anthology
Realms of the Dead

Edited by Susan J. Morris
January 2010

"This is Thay as it's never been shown before . . . Dark,
sinister, foreboding and downright disturbing!"
—Alaundo, Candlekeep.com on *Unclean*

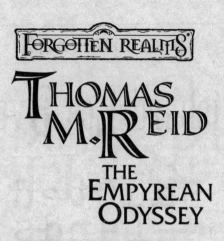

FORGOTTEN REALMS

THOMAS M. REID

THE EMPYREAN ODYSSEY

What could bring a demon to the gates of heaven?

Book I
The Gossamer Plain

Book II
The Fractured Sky

Book III
The Crystal Mountain
July 2009

What could bring heaven to the depths of hell?

"Reid is proving himself to be one of the best up and coming authors in the FORGOTTEN REALMS universe."
—fantasy-fan.org

FORGOTTEN REALMS

The New York Times BEST-SELLING AUTHOR

RICHARD BAKER

BLADES OF THE MOONSEA

". . . it was so good that the bar has been raised.
Few other fantasy novels will hold up to it, I fear."
—Kevin Mathis, d20zines.com on *Forsaken House*

Book I	Book II	Book III
Swordmage	**Corsair**	**Avenger**
		March 2010

Enter the Year of the Ageless One!

TRACY HICKMAN
Presents

The Anvil of Time

The Sellsword
Cam Banks

The Survivors
Dan Willis

Renegade Wizards
Lucien Soulban

The Forest King
Paul B. Thompson
June 2009

The lost stories of Krynn's history are coming to light.

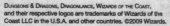

DRACONIC PROPHECIES

JAMES WYATT

From acclaimed author
and award-winning game
designer James Wyatt, an
adventure that will shake
the world of EBERRON®.

STORM DRAGON
AVAILABLE NOW IN PAPERBACK

DRAGON FORGE
AVAILABLE NOW IN PAPERBACK

DRAGON WAR
IN HARDCOVER AUGUST 2009

The Gathering®

Everything you thought you knew
about MAGIC™ novels is changing…

From the mind of

ARI MARMELL

comes a tour de force of imagination.

AGENTS OF ARTIFICE

The ascendance of a new age in the planeswalker
mythology: be a part of the book that takes fans
deeper than ever into the lives of the Multiverse's most
powerful beings:

Jace Beleren
A powerful mind-mage whose choices now will forever
determine his path as a planeswalker.

Liliana Vess
A dangerous necromancer whose beauty belies a dark
secret and even darker associations.

Tezzeret
Leader of an inter-planar consortium whose quest for
knowledge may be undone by his lust for power.